Murder Takes Patience

GIACOMO GIAMMATTEO

Also by Giacomo Giammatteo:

Fiction:
Friendship & Honor Series:
MURDER TAKES TIME: Friendship & Honor: Book I
MURDER HAS CONSEQUENCES: Friendship & Honor: Book II

Blood Flows South Series:
A BULLET FOR CARLOS: Blood Flows South: Book I
FINDING FAMILY: Blood Flows South: the Beginning (A Novella)
A BULLET FROM DOMINIC: Blood Flows South: Book II

Redemption Series:
Necessary Decisions
OLD WOUNDS (Coming late 2014)

Non-Fiction:
No Mistakes Careers
NO MISTAKES RESUMES: Book One of No Mistakes Careers
NO MISTAKES INTERVIEWS: Book Two of No Mistakes Careers

Sanctuary Tales (True Stories From An Animal Sanctuary)
WHISKERS & BEAR (Coming soon)

Murder Takes Patience

FRIENDSHIP & HONOR, BOOK III

GIACOMO GIAMMATTEO

INFERNO PUBLISHING COMPANY

Warning: Spoilers for the first two books of this
series are on the next page.

If you want a refresher of who some of the characters are from the first two books, read the pages that follow. If you haven't read the first two books, you might want to.

Police:

Frankie "Bugs" Donovan — Nicky Fusco's best friend from childhood. Now a Detective in Brooklyn.

Lou Mazzetti — Frankie's partner.

Sherri Miller — Frankie and Lou's partner from book 2.

Lieutenant Morreau — Frankie's boss.

Carol — Admin in Homicide Department.

Kate Burns — Medical Examiner, and Frankie's girlfriend.

Alex — Young boy who Frankie took in after his mother abandoned him.

Keisha — Alex's friend in the apartment building.

New York Mobsters:

Dominic Mangini — Head of one of the Five Families (Also appears in Blood Flows South series)

Manny Rosso — Head of one of the Five Families. Was underboss to Tito Martelli in book one.

Tito Martelli — Was head of one of the Five Families.

Fabrizio — hit man for Dominic Mangini.

Giorgio — Works for Manny Rosso.

Wilmington, DE. Characters:

Nicky "the Rat" Fusco — former hit man trying to go straight.

Doggs Caputo — local mob boss in Wilmington, DE.

Monroe — leader of a black gang in Wilmington. Served time with Nicky in prison.

Angela Fusco — Nicky's wife.

Rosa Fusco — Daughter of Angela and Nicky.

Sister Mary Thomas — Nun who taught Nicky and Frankie.

Paulie "the Suit" Perlano — childhood friend of Nicky and Frankie

RULES OF MURDER

A reader emailed me and asked if there would be any more books with Nicky and Frankie. I thought I had mentioned this before, but for those of you who don't know.

There will be at least six books in the Friendship & Honor series—one for each of the "rules of murder," as outlined by Gianni "Johnny Muck" Mucchiato in Murder Takes Time. Each book's title is one of the rules.

1. **Murder takes time**—Never rush. Know what you are going to do before, during, and after the job. Know your victim. Their face. Routines. Neighborhood. Family.

2. **Murder has consequences**—When doing a job you must never, ever, let it get personal. Each assignment is just a job. If it gets personal, it will have consequences.

3. **Murder takes patience**—If someone has a routine, trust it. Wait them out, and it will pay off. As for yourself, never be predictable. Don't shop at the same place. Don't eat at the same place. Don't do anything at the same place or at the same time or on the same days.

4. **Murder is invisible**—To be good at this, you must be invisible. And since you can't really be invisible, you have to practice not being noticed. There is a difference between being seen and being noticed. If you have to break rule number three, make sure you adhere to rule number four.

5. **Murder is a promise**—If you enter into a deal to murder someone, that is a promise, a secret pact. Once you take the assignment, you need to finish the job, or it could come back to haunt you.

6. **Murder is immaculate**—Don't leave any clues, and make sure you clean up loose ends.

The darkest places in hell are reserved for those who maintain their neutrality in times of moral crisis.

~ Dante Alighieri

Thoughts

Even good people are haunted by nightmares. Some people are kept awake by things they did in the past: Lies they told, people they cheated, laws they broke.

The worst people are haunted by more than lies or broken laws. Their sleep is stolen by the people they killed.

I'm not like any of them. I'm not bothered by lies, or broken laws. Not even by the people I've killed.

What keeps me awake is thinking of the people I haven't killed *yet*.

~ Nicky Fusco

CHAPTER 1

A STRANGE GOODBYE

Debbie Parnell's alarm blared, and then a second alarm went off, insurance against her falling asleep and missing the meeting. The combo pried her out of bed. She stumbled to the bathroom, brushed her teeth, dressed in a dark-blue business suit, then glanced at her watch. *Plenty of time for coffee.*

While waiting, she dialed Chad.

"Why are you calling me at this time of morning?"

"I knew you'd be up; rising stars don't sleep in."

"Neither do falling stars," Chad said. "What do you need?"

"Nothing really, I was just calling to give you the privilege of driving me to the airport."

"I thought you had an early appointment in Brooklyn."

"I do, but I was hoping you could drive me to the airport after I finished. We could use the time to catch up on work."

She heard him sigh and knew what was coming. "As much as I'd love to, I can't. I have to interview someone this morning, and it's in the opposite direction. And I have no idea how long I'll be."

"In that case, I better get ready. See you when I get back."

"Have a safe trip," Chad said.

Debbie finished her coffee, stuffed a few more items into her suitcase, double-checked which outfits she packed, and then set everything by the door. Within twenty minutes the driver arrived and she was in the car on her way to the meeting. Traffic was horrendous.

"What's holding us up?" she asked.

"An accident near the bridge," the driver said.

"You need to find a way around this. I'm cutting it close."

At the next traffic signal, he turned and detoured through Brooklyn Heights. As he passed a brownstone, Debbie caught a glimpse of someone out of the corner of her eye.

Chad?

She was tempted to roll down the window and holler to him. The man stood on the steps of a house, and it looked as if he was using a key to open the door. *What's he doing? He doesn't live here.* Her curiosity was piqued. She typed a message on her phone and emailed it to herself.

What is he doing in BH?

It took 25 more minutes to get to her meeting, and the whole way she wondered if that was Chad she saw, and what he was doing in Brooklyn Heights, at that house. *He said he had an interview.*

Debbie finished her meeting on time, and arranged for a car to drive her to the airport. After going through security and settling in to a comfortable chair at the lounge for frequent flyers, she dialed Bruce.

"What's up?" he asked. "Anything wrong?"

"No. Nothing's wrong. But something strange happened on the way in."

"Tell me."

"We hit traffic, and the driver detoured through Brooklyn Heights. I could have sworn I saw one of my coworkers entering a house there."

A slight pause followed, and then Bruce said. "Maybe they forgot something. Or—"

Debbie's voice raised. "No. You don't understand. The person doesn't live there."

Bruce laughed. "Deb, I know you're under a lot of stress, but I wouldn't worry about it. Get on your flight, relax, and focus on a successful trip."

"Jesus Christ! You don't take anything seriously. We're in the middle of a huge deal. We can't risk exposure of any kind."

"I *do* take things seriously—important things. The rest I leave for you to worry about."

"Screw you. This *is* important. Suppose this hints at insider trading."

"Okay, you're right. I'm sorry I trivialized it."

"What should I do? Should I tell Bob?"

"I wouldn't. It could be something as innocent as an affair, if you want to think of that as innocent. And if it is something fishy, you don't want to be involved. You could end up getting hurt."

Debbie switched the phone to her other ear and leaned back in the chair. "Maybe you're right," she said.

"I know I'm right, but I'm amazed you're admitting it."

Debbie laughed. "Okay, you convinced me. I won't say anything. At least until I get back."

"How long will you be gone?"

"I already told you. Two weeks."

"I forgot. So relax and have a great trip. I miss you already."

"Miss you too," Debbie said.

CHAPTER 2

ALARMS AND EARLY MORNINGS

One week later—Brooklyn, New York

Shortly before 6:00 AM he poured a cup of coffee and enjoyed the first taste of sunlight as it squeezed through the slats of the wood blinds. He read the paper, finished dressing, then made his way down the stairs to the street. He liked to take a second cup of coffee with pastry at a café a few blocks away. It was a good place to sit and watch. The waitress led him to an outside table.

He smiled. "Nice morning, isn't it?"

Her return smile was instantaneous, but forced. "Very nice. It's about time we had sun."

"Yes, it is," he said. "I'll have—"

"Coffee and a scone, right?"

His smile vanished. She'd picked up on his patterns. *How did she know I wanted a scone today?* "You read my mind."

"Be right back," she said and scurried away.

He watched her go, checking to see if she talked to anyone.

A couple at the table to his left chatted in low voices. From the tone, and the aggressive posturing, he could tell they were arguing.

The couple to the right were laughing. They seemed happy.

He turned his attention to the pedestrian traffic, but kept his eye on the time. Fifteen minutes had disappeared, along with his scone and coffee. The waitress hurried by, barely slowing down as she dropped his check on the table. His cursory "thanks" trailed in the air behind her. He wondered if today would be a wasted day.

As the thought ruminated, the unmistakable sound of high heels clicking on the old brick walkway caught his attention. There was a rhythm to the sound, as if the owner of those heels was avoiding the cracks in the herringbone pattern. He tried not to look but curiosity yanked his head around. She was still forty or fifty feet away, heading in his direction. The sight of her stirred another thought.

What eles is it about the sound of those heels?

There was noise on the street—cars driving by, other people walking, horns blaring. Why did those heels intrigue him?

A peculiar beep drew his focus down the street. He didn't know why; lots of horns were beeping. This one sounded…different. He had listened to enough of them over the years. Each had a unique sound—impatience, anger, graciousness, aggression. This one was…a polite beep. A draw-your-attention type beep. The high-heeled woman turned toward the sound of the beep then walked to the car. She leaned in and kissed the man driving. A goodbye kiss. A peck on the cheek.

Had she forgotten to kiss him? Did she not love him anymore?

As he wondered about the dynamics of that relationship, the car pulled away and merged with traffic. The clicking sound of her heels resumed, consuming him.

Of all the noise on the street why had her heels drawn his attention? They shouldn't have, and yet…they did.

Karma, he thought.

She walked toward him, her long tanned legs, cute-as-a-button ass, and confident strut building an image of the perfect woman. Blonde hair danced on her shoulders with each step. Even from forty feet away he could sense the vibrancy, see the smile, feel the warmth.

As she drew closer, the outline of her body under that too-tight skirt screamed—look at me. It did the job. He was looking, along with everyone else.

A small piece of paper blew across the walk, in front, and then behind her. When she stooped to pick it up he got a glimpse of perfection. He imagined she wasn't wearing panties. That's when he decided she would be the one. If everything else fit, she would be the perfect candidate.

He made a note of the time as she continued down the street, swinging her hips with a subtle invitation. He wanted to follow her. Get right up behind her and crawl up her skirt. Not today though. He had rules. Besides, he'd memorized the car's plate. Even if she didn't come this way again, he'd find her.

Patience, he reminded himself. *I must practice patience.*

CHAPTER 3

BACON AND EGGS

Brooklyn, New York

Frankie Donovan's eyes popped open, but not from the sun bursting through the crooked blind. The unmistakable aroma of fresh-brewed coffee woke him, and that brought a smile. He got out of bed, put pants on, and made his way to the kitchen. Coffee brewed in the French press, eggs were being fried on the front burner, and bacon sizzled on the back. And Alex, Frankie's semi-adopted son, was singing. At 7:00 in the morning.

Frankie rubbed the last bit of sleep from his eyes. "What the hell, Ace? Keep this up and I might decide to let you hang around a while."

"Don't even joke about that shit, FD. I'm here to stay, unless you're ready to throw Kate out. She loves me."

"In case you haven't figured it out, the only reason you're here is because you help me attract the ladies."

"Take a lot more than a cute kid to help you in that department." Alex flipped the eggs and splashed some grease from the bacon over the top. "You want it medium?"

"Nothing's changed."

"Anyway, I was 'bout to say, I ain't seen no ladies beatin' on this door, 'cept Kate, and she only comes around because of me."

Frankie did up the last few buttons on his shirt. "While you're cooking you should have a dictionary open. In case you haven't noticed, *'bout and 'cept* aren't acceptable words."

Alex flipped the spatula in the air, caught it, then scooped the eggs onto a plate, which he handed to Frankie. "That's why I stay here, FD. You make me laugh every morning."

"You mean that, *and* the fact that CPS is after your ass. And your mom abandoned you."

Alex shrugged. "Might be some of that, too."

Frankie took his plate to the table and poured orange juice in two glasses. "You want coffee?"

"I didn't make it just for you."

Frankie poured the coffee and brought the cups to the table, sitting across from Alex.

"A kid your age shouldn't have coffee."

"Bull—"

"Hey, watch the mouth."

"I didn't say it."

"You were going to. You know the rules."

"Yeah, I know. No cursing in the house or smoking in the house, and clean up your own mess."

"Be thankful for the leniency. You *definitely* shouldn't be smoking."

"You neither."

"That's beside the point," Frankie said.

"I'll tell you what's beside the point, you smoking in the house when I'm not here."

"Who told you that?"

Alex cocked his head, closed one eye, and stared at Frankie. "You think I can't smell it?"

He looked at Alex and smiled. "All right. I won't smoke in the house anymore."

"I was hoping you'd say we could both smoke in here."

"Not gonna happen."

"Figured," Alex said. "What you got goin' on? Any big cases?"

"Nah. Hasn't been a good killing in a long time. I'm getting bored."

"Me, too. Guess I'm gonna have to get a job after school or something."

"Like hell. Get your grades up to par and maybe I'll let you, but not till then."

"What kind of grades did you get?"

"Not relevant."

"Not relevant? You become the DA now?"

Frankie gobbled his breakfast, dumped the last sip of coffee into the sink, then leaned over and rubbed the top of Alex's head. "See you later, Ace. Be good. And make sure to watch for CPS."

"See you tonight, FD. I love you."

Frankie was reaching for the doorknob, and stopped cold. He wasn't used to someone telling him they loved him. It both embarrassed him and made him want to cry. He walked back to Alex and kissed the top of his head. "I love you too, you little shit."

The ride to work was different, as it had been ever since Frankie took Alex in. Before Alex, all Frankie thought about was the current case. Now he thought about Kate more often, and about how to keep CPS from finding Alex. *CPS. What a joke that is. Should be Child Persecution Services, not Child Protective Services.*

Funny how one little thing can change a life. Some kid's mother takes off and all of a sudden, I've got a family.

***

Lou Mazzetti trudged up the stairs, forcing himself past the halfway mark, where he usually stopped to catch his breath. He turned in his notice yesterday, and this morning's exhaustive climb confirmed that his decision to retire was the right one. All he had to do was convince Lieutenant Morreau to let him finish out the next two months in an office on the first floor.

"Good morning, Carol. How is the sweetest receptionist in Brooklyn?"

Carol's head darted side to side. "That *sounds* like Mazzetti's voice, but those weren't his words. Is there a ventriloquist around here? Am I on a reality show with hidden cameras?"

"I thought I'd be nice to you in my last days," Lou said. "My wife insisted on it."

"Did you tell her that it won't make up for twelve years of harassment?"

"She'd laugh at twelve years. We've been married for thirty."

Carol blessed herself. "Poor soul."

"You want coffee?" Lou asked.

"No, but you better get some. The lieutenant is waiting."

Lou started toward the coffee room.

"And get some for Donovan. I hear his loud mouth coming in the door."

***

Frankie Donovan chatted with half a dozen people before he reached the stairs, and then he took them two at a time. Mazzetti waited with a coffee in hand.

"Showing off, Donovan?"

"Keeping in shape." He took the coffee from Lou. "I don't want to end up retiring before my time."

Lou looked at Carol, then back to Donovan. "How does everybody know I'm retiring. I just decided yesterday."

"You know what they say about good news," Carol said.

Lou and Frankie started toward Morreau's office. "I'll tell you what I won't miss," Mazzetti said. "That magpie sitting behind the desk."

"Pay him no mind, Carol. He still loves you."

Sherri Miller was sitting in a chair across from Morreau. When Lou entered, she got up to hug him. "Good to see you again, Mazzetti."

"No hug for me?" Frankie said.

"I didn't think you were the hugging type."

"I make exceptions," Frankie said, and hugged her. "Good to have you back. You look great."

"I'm putting Miller back with you two," Morreau said.

Frankie looked to Morreau, then Miller. "That's great, but we've got nothing to work on."

"Have some of your dago friends kill somebody," Mazzetti said. "We haven't had any mob killings in a while."

Frankie looked at Miller. "Are you ready to come back? I thought you wanted out of homicide."

Sherri lowered her head. "I thought so at first, but when Lieutenant Morreau asked me, I realized I missed it."

They made small talk for a few minutes and then Lou patted her back. "Great to have you with us. Come on, let's get coffee."

Frankie waited until Lou and Sherri left. He closed the door and pulled his chair up to Morreau's desk. "She's not ready. Did you see how nervous she was? Besides, if she really wanted back she'd have come begging you. She sure as hell wouldn't have waited for you to ask her."

"Mazzetti's retiring in two months," Morreau said.

"I know all about it."

"I want Sherri to take his place."

"As my partner?" Frankie said. "No way."

"I thought you liked her."

"I like her, Lieu. I really do. She's funny, she's a dedicated cop, she's sexy as hell."

"Whoa, Donovan. Don't even say things like that."

"Bullshit. I can't speak the truth? Sherri *is* sexy. No denying it."

Morreau stared at Frankie. "Is *that* why you don't want her?"

Frankie leaned back in the chair. "I just got into a relationship that actually might work. I don't need temptation, and I don't want to go home dreaming about Miller's ass."

"What about Mazzetti?"

"I don't dream about his ass. If I ever do, I'll swallow my gun."

"Put a rubber band around your dick, or find something else that works. Miller is in. Done deal."

Frankie got up and shoved the chair against the wall. "Thanks for the support."

"Fuck you too, Donovan."

Frankie slammed the door on his way out.

CHAPTER 4

A SPECIAL FAVOR

Wilmington, Delaware

I made coffee while Angie cooked breakfast.

Rosa sat at the table, reading the New York Times on an old iPad. "Uncle Mario was mentioned again. Page five."

"If Frankie hears you call him Mario *you'll* end up on page five."

"You do."

"Only when I want to piss him off."

"He found that killer who got the stockbroker."

"Are you reading on that tablet thing?" Angie asked.

"It's an iPad, Mom. And yes, I'm reading on it. I do my crosswords on it too."

"Frankie's a good detective," I said.

"And hot."

Angie set the plates on the table. "Hot? He's your father's age."

"All my friends think he's hot."

Angie blessed herself. "If only I'd known about kids, I'd have re-thought abortion."

"Mom, you're so full of it. You're half a nun already. If I didn't hear you and Dad fool around at night, I'd—"

Angie flushed. "Rosa! My God, watch your mouth."

I covered up my laugh before Angie saw it. Rosa had guts; I'd give her that.

A baby's cry came from the living room. "Dante's hungry," Angie said.

"I've got him. He must have smelled the coffee."

"Nicky Fusco, if you try giving that baby coffee before he's ten, I'll shoot you."

"Ten? We were drinking it from the time we could hold a cup."

"And look how you turned out," Angie said.

"Nothing wrong with Uncle Mario."

"Of course," Angie said. "There's *never* anything wrong with Uncle Mario."

I picked up Dante and walked back to the table, patting his back as I winked at Rosa. "You should be a detective. You're good."

"Like hell she will," Angie said. "She's going to college and—"

Our laughter cut her short.

"Okay, smart asses." She plopped the last of the food on the table and pulled up a chair. "I'll take him, Nicky. You eat."

I sat next to her. "I got him," I said, and kissed the side of his head. "Babies smell so sweet."

"Not all the time," Rosa said, her head still buried in the iPad. "Dad, I need the name of a Titan that starts with C. Six letters."

I used my free hand to scoop some eggs onto a piece of toast. I ate the eggs then sipped my coffee. "I'm not good on mythology. The nuns didn't drill that in our heads."

"How about the pope who started the first crusade."

"Urban."

Rosa typed her answer in. "Leave it to Dad to know the Roman answers. Bet you wouldn't fare so well on American history."

Angie reached for the iPad. "Put that thing away. All you ever do is crosswords."

"Nothing wrong with crosswords," I said.

I knew she only harped on Rosa because Tony had always done crosswords. I'm sure she was afraid it would upset me. It did, some, but as I told Angie before, I had to get used to it. Some day we were going to have to tell Rosa who her real father was. If it was up to me, I'd have told her, but Angie wasn't ready.

Dante burped some foreign material on my shirt, which forced a laugh out of Angie. "I'll take the devil while you change."

"You should do like Mom does. Put a towel over your shirt when you're holding him."

I unbuttoned my shirt as I walked up the steps. "Remind me before he spits up on me."

"Hey, Dad, are we calling Uncle Mario?"

"I've got to get to work."

"C'mon, Dad."

"All right. When I get down."

It only took me a few minutes to change shirts. When I hit the bottom step, I saw Angie shaking her head as she walked with Dante and fed him a bottle.

"My God, you're a sucker."

Rosa got up to do dishes. "*Somebody* in this house loves me."

"Are you going to the dance?" Angie asked.

"If anybody ever asks me." Rosa gathered the rest of the dishes from the table. "I can't believe no one asked me. Do you think I'm ugly?"

"Ugly? You're gorgeous."

"No. For real. Look at me as a person, not your daughter."

Angie kissed her on the cheek. "Rosa, you're gorgeous. I'm telling you. Someone will ask."

"Ask what?"

"Don't act like you didn't hear, Dad."

"Just go with your friends. You'll find people to dance with."

"It's not the same," Rosa said.

I looked at the clock. "Time to call Bugs."

"How come he doesn't get mad when you call him Bugs?"

"Because that's his name."

As I dialed Frankie's number, I almost laughed remembering how he got that name.

He picked up on the second ring. "Don't tell me it's you, Rat."

"Hey, Bugs. Where are you?"

"At work. Why?"

Rosa hollered from the kitchen. "Ciao, Zio Mario."

"Did you tell her to call me Uncle Mario? You son of a bitch."

"I might have mentioned that it pisses you off."

"So tell me why I'm getting a call this early in the morning."

"Because Angie and I talked about it, and we want you to be Dante's godfather."

"What? You're shitting me."

"Not a bit."

A pause, then, "Nicky, you know I'd love to. I'm honored. Make sure you tell Angie I said so."

"She's right here. Tell her yourself." I handed the phone to Angie.

"Hi, Frankie. I told him to call you last week, but he wanted to wait until we got home and situated. You know Nicky."

"I couldn't be happier for you," Frankie said. "And thanks for asking me."

"Who else would we ask?" Angie said. "You and Nicky have been friends since birth, or close to it."

"It had been a long time," Frankie said. "I can't wait to see you guys."

"Me too. I'm giving you back to Nicky now."

I took the phone from Angie and plopped into my reading chair, kicking my feet up. "Hey, Bugs."

"So you named him Dante. I should have figured. Your dad was a great guy."

"I had to go the traditional route. Not many of us stick to the old ways anymore."

"Not many left that even remember the old ways," Frankie said.

"Ain't that the truth."

"Speaking of the old ways, don't let Sister Thomas hear you say *ain't*. She probably still carries that yardstick with her."

"I think she does, and my ass almost stings thinking about it. I'll have to make sure Dante doesn't get whacked with it."

"Speaking of Dante, I was afraid you'd do something stupid with the name."

"Like naming him Mario?"

"Exactly."

Rosa leaned in next to the phone. "Ciao again, Zio Mario. I saw your name in the paper."

"Hi, Rosa. How's my most beautiful niece doing?"

"Good. I can't wait to see you."

"I can't wait to eat some of your meatballs," Frankie said.

"I'll make them special for you. Gotta go now or I'll be late."

The front door slammed behind Rosa, but it was a *happy* slam, a trick only teenagers seemed to be able to do.

"Great kid you got."

"Thanks, Bugs. I lucked out." I stepped outside to finish the conversation. "You ever hear from Suit? I was gonna call and tell him the news."

"He's in Texas."

"What the hell is he doing there?"

"You know that's between us," Bugs said. "Things are getting better for Suit, but there might still be people looking for him because of how things went down with Tito Martelli."

Bad memories flooded my brain. Vivid images of Tito and all of his men. "You mean when I killed him?"

"You know what I mean," Bugs said.

"Is Manny one of the people not happy?"

"No, not Manny. He made out great. I'm talking about some of the others."

"Dominic Mangini?"

"Mangini would be a good bet, and he's the most dangerous one of the bunch, but no, he's fine with Suit."

"How does Mangini feel about me? I'm thinking of taking the family to New York this summer. It would be nice to know I don't have to worry."

"Take them somewhere else. I've heard Dominic has no quarrels with you—as long as you stay out of New York."

"Maybe I should call him."

"I wouldn't."

"Yeah. Guess I'll see as it gets closer."

Frankie paused then said, "Let me know a date on the christening."

"I will. And thanks again, Bugs. This means a lot to me."

"Hey, Nicky?"

"What?"

"Never mind."

I laughed. "Never mind my ass. What is it?"

I waited through a long silence before Bugs spit it out.

"I told you about Alex."

"Yeah. What's up? Something wrong?"

"I love this kid, Nicky. But CPS wants to put him in a foster home. No way they'd let him stay with me."

Knowing Bugs like I did, there was only one way to advise him. "You love the kid, right?"

"You know I do. I don't know how or why, but this kid's got me. And he's a damn good kid. All he needs is a break."

"You always were a sucker for a kid needing a break, Bugs." I thought about what I was going to say, but only for a second. "Alex likes it there, right?"

"Hell yeah. You should have seen him when I first told him he could stay. It was like I'd given him a present."

"Okay, here's my advice—fuck the law."

A second or two of silence was followed by Frankie's laughter. "That's it? *Fuck the law.* That's your advice?"

"You heard me. Fuck the law. Sometimes you have to decide yourself what's right and wrong. Or are you gonna let some asshole who never met Alex decide what happens to him for the rest of his life?"

"I'm a cop," Frankie said.

I did my best to rein in the sarcasm, but I probably didn't succeed. "Oh yeah, I forgot. That changes everything. Cops don't break the law."

"Point taken. I'll think about what to do. In the meantime, you take care. And say bye to Angie."

"Yeah, see ya', Bugs."

I went back in the house for a refill on coffee. Angie was sitting at the table, shoveling breakfast into Dante's mouth. That boy loved to eat.

"How was Frankie?" she asked.

"He sounded good. He was glad we asked him."

Angie smiled. "He'll make a good godfather."

I looked around. "Is Rosa gone?"

"She left while you were talking."

I hugged Angie. "Guess we'll have to be quieter at night."

"Or stop."

"I'll go with quieter."

Angie rolled her eyes and blushed as she swatted my arm.

"Did you tell Frankie we're coming for a visit?"

"What?" I grabbed my briefcase and headed for the door.

"I asked if you told Frankie we were coming up."

A lump built in my throat. I hated lying to Angie, but making her worry made me feel worse. "I told him," I said. "See ya' tonight."

Now all I have to do is find a way to tell Dominic Mangini.

CHAPTER 5

FOLLOWING

Brooklyn, New York

Three days after he'd seen High Heels, the killer returned to the café. Good fortune provided the same table he had last time, and a glance at his watch confirmed it was the same time. He ordered tea instead of coffee. That waitress had gotten his order right one too many times for his liking.

"No scone this morning?" Her smile disturbed him. He didn't have time for that nonsense.

"Just the tea."

She returned quickly with his order. "Thanks," he said.

He sipped tea, his gaze roaming left to right, stopping now and then to eavesdrop on a conversation. Every few seconds he glanced toward the street. He was halfway through his tea when his diligence paid off.

The car stopped. She got out, but not before kissing the man goodbye. Then came the show as she paraded down the street, hips moving in tune to the song in his head, *"Take Me Home Tonight."* He felt certain that every man who saw her would love to take her home on any night.

He gulped down his tea, left a tip on the table and moved out among the crowd. He fell in behind High Heels at a safe distance, walking at a steady pace, moving with the crowd. Sometimes he raced past her, glancing her way. She wore a wedding band. Did she keep her vows? Soon enough he'd find out.

The crowd thinned then, at the corner, bunched together as they waited for the light to change. He let her go in front of him, taking the opportunity to watch her from behind. Her pert little ass blessed the pinstripes on her skirt with a sexy kiss on every bounce. He reached down to straighten himself.

He followed High Heels for three more blocks, until she disappeared into a large office building. Fortunately, it was the *perfect* office building. He didn't bother following her inside. No sense in risking exposure to surveillance cameras. Besides, he had plenty of ways to gather the necessary information. All he needed was time. *And patience.* He had to keep reminding himself of that. Acting on impulse got you caught.

He went to work, took an early lunch, and got back to her building in time to follow her. Another woman accompanied her to a café across the street. Both of them wore skirts that were too short for decency. When High Heels sat, hers bunched up on her thighs. He wanted to crawl up there and take a peek. He'd like to see what she was so proud of.

He felt confident he could take her now. Dispense with all this trailing nonsense. But everything had to be confirmed. Even an infidelity as sure as hers. No doubt she was unfaithful. But then he reminded himself; observation was required. *And patience.*

For almost a week more, he followed her. It took a while to gather the information he needed, but now he knew a lot about little High Heels. *About Sandy.* Where she worked, where she lived, and most importantly, who she slept with when her husband was out of town. That last bit was what he'd been waiting to find. Turned out Sandy had quite the appetite.

For three more days he watched her, waiting for the right time. On day four, the stars aligned. Her husband didn't drop her off; another man did. And she seemed to have an extra bounce to her step, perhaps in anticipation of a rendezvous. As High Heels sashayed past him, a shiver ran up his spine. He felt it in his bones. *Today* was the day. He picked up the phone and made a call.

Alibis had to be established. Things were now in motion. Tonight the killer would strike.

***

Sandy finished the report she'd been working on, then shut down Excel and the computer. She put a few folders in her briefcase, then took them out again, laying them on her desk. No way she'd be doing work tonight. She picked up the phone and dialed. Justin answered promptly.

"I was hoping you'd call."

"I'm up for dinner," she said.

"And…"

Sandy took a quick glance around. "And anything else your devious mind can cook up."

"That's what I wanted to hear. Meet me at Ming's. We'll grab dinner and get a room."

"How about you pick me up?" she asked.

A pause, then, "Six o'clock?"

"Works for me."

"Wait for me outside," Justin said.

Sandy agreed, hung up, and dialed her husband's cell.

He answered with his usual cheerful greeting. It had gotten to the point where the sound of his voice sickened her.

"What did I do to deserve a call from the busy one?"

"Sorry if I bothered you," she said. "I just wanted to let you know that I won't be available on the cell until late. I got called to a last minute dinner deal with our client from Tokyo. They're in town."

"And they didn't give you any warning?"

"No, and that worries Ed. He thinks they may be shopping the deal with a competitor."

"Some final negotiations, huh?"

"I hope not, but you never can tell. Anyway, I wanted to let you know. When do you get home?"

"Two days."

"See you when you get here."

"Love you, honey. Good luck."

"Thanks. I might need it," Sandy said, then grabbed her phone and purse.

***

The killer waited in his car across the street. He hoped she wouldn't be long.

Sandy came out just before six, getting into a car with a man the killer didn't recognize. That didn't matter. He wasn't her husband; that's all he cared about.

The killer followed them to the restaurant. They used valet parking. He parked a few blocks away and walked back, finding a small café with a clear view of the restaurant. As soon as he spotted them exiting the restaurant, he would leave. He figured he'd still have time to get to his car and back before the valet returned with theirs.

He didn't have to wait as long as he thought. She must have been eager.

When they exited the restaurant, the killer paid his bill and walked briskly down the street to his car. He had to circle the block in his car twice before they got theirs. The man opened the door for Sandy and she got in. The killer smiled. Now it was a simple matter of following them. They opted for the Marriott Hotel in Brooklyn Heights, an ideal spot for the killer. It provided ample opportunity to slip in, park, and get back out again unnoticed. Then he could mingle with the crowds at the Fulton Street Mall.

They used valet parking again at the hotel. The killer waited at Tony's Pizza across the street. He set a fast pace to the back of the hotel, going in through the employee entrance. When he reached the lobby, they were still checking in. He waited until the clerk handed them their room cards, then went to the elevators and pushed the button. They arrived momentarily. When the doors opened he stepped inside and moved to the back. They got in and pushed the button for the sixth floor.

"What number for you?" the man asked.

"Six," the killer said.

The elevator stopped twice on the way up. When it opened at six, they got out, and the killer followed, making sure to keep a good distance behind. They entered room 632. He walked past, gave them time to enter their room, then turned around and went back to the elevator and down to the lobby.

CHAPTER 6

JUDGMENT

The killer waited. He figured there would be little foreplay. Perhaps a shower, not much else. After fifteen minutes had passed he walked to an isolated phone in the lobby and dialed room 632. It rang several times before the man answered. He sounded agitated.

"Hello!"

"Sir, I am sorry to bother you, but there seems to be a problem with your credit card."

"What do you mean?"

"It did not go through, sir. They declined it."

"That's impossible. Run it again."

"We have. Twice."

"Do it again. There is *no* problem."

"Yes, sir," he said, and hung up the phone.

The killer waited less than a minute then called back.

"What!" The agitation level had risen considerably.

"Sir, I am truly sorry, but it was declined. I'm sure it's an error, but...do you have another card we can use?"

"What? Yes, of course. I still don't know what the problem is. There's nothing wrong with that card." His tone had changed. Still agitated but mixed with embarrassment.

"I understand. It happens a lot. Perhaps we can run another card."

"Yes, do that."

"Will you be coming down, sir?"

"Coming down for what?"

"We will need to run another card."

"Can't it wait? I—"

"If you prefer we can send someone to your room. It will be less of an inconvenience."

"All right, but hurry up."

"He'll be right up. Again, my apologies."

Back in the elevator, the killer pushed the button for floor six. He put on his gloves, checked his gun, then put his hands in the coat pocket. When he got off the elevator, no one was in the hall. He knocked gently on the door. The lock turned and the man yanked the door open. He held a credit card in his hand.

"I *know* one—"

He must have seen the gun, even before he recognized the killer as the man who rode up the elevator with them.

"What the hell is going on?"

"Step to the bed, please. And be quiet."

The man, dressed only in a pair of boxers, backed up, hands in the air. The killer scanned the room. The shower was running. "Tell Sandy to come out of the shower. Do it in a calm voice."

"How do you know her name? Who are you?"

"All in good time. Call her."

"What should I say?"

"Just ask if she's done yet."

He seemed to gather himself. "Sandy, are you done yet?"

The water turned off. "What?"

"I said, are you done yet?"

"Getting impatient, are we?"

The killer whispered, "Say, 'I can't wait for dessert.'"

"I'm hungry. I can't wait for dessert," the man said.

"This is your lucky night. The wait is over."

The killer whispered again. "Tell her you're on the bed."

"I'm under the covers. Hurry up."

She opened the door, stepped into the room and toward the bed, towel wrapped around her wet body. A smaller towel around her head.

The killer grabbed her from behind, his hand covering her mouth. He pressed the gun into her back. "Don't say anything. And don't turn around. Follow instructions so I don't have to hurt you."

Her voice had panic in it, almost tears. "Justin, what's going on?"

"Kneel on the floor," the killer said. He turned to Justin, "Put a sock in her mouth."

"A sock?"

The killer's voice reflected his frustration. "Put your sock in her mouth or I'll stuff her with something else."

"I'll do anything you want," Sandy said. "Just don't hurt us."

"I'm sure you will, but that's not what I'm here for." He glared at Justin. "The sock. Now!"

Justin grabbed one of his socks and shoved it into Sandy's mouth.

The killer had Sandy do the same to Justin, and then he instructed them to lie on the bed in a "sixty-nine" position. Several times Justin tried speaking, but the killer stopped him with a threatening gesture. Sandy kept her eyes closed most of the time.

"Keep your eyes closed. It won't take long."

He walked to the man's side of the bed, grabbed a pillow and set it over Sandy's face, which was buried in Justin's genitals. The killer shoved the gun up Justin's ass and fired twice. Justin spasmed a few times. One shot to his head took care of that.

The bullet hit the side of Sandy's face as it exited. She rolled off the bed, bouncing up when she hit the floor. The killer grabbed her, shoved the gun against her head. "Lie down. Be calm."

She cried, but did as he instructed. The killer then put a shot into Sandy's head, and two more into her vagina, each one muffled by the silencer and the pillow over the gun.

Cleaning up the place didn't take long. They hadn't been there long enough to mess it up. He did, however, fold their clothes and put them in drawers. He hung the towels over the bar, and rinsed the tub. Afterward, he emptied Sandy's purse and took Justin's wallet. He put the contents into a small shopping bag he brought for the occasion.

As he left the room he flipped the Do-Not-Disturb sign to the proper side, then rode the elevator to the lobby. The killer made a quick stop at the dumpster, walked down the street and circled around to the restaurant where he parked. Hungry now, he opted for a meal before going home.

CHAPTER 7

LOOKING FOR ALEX GREENE

Alex left school and started down Church Street on his walk home. He passed the crack dealer on the corner by the Indian restaurant, turned down offers to run drugs for the gangs on Rogers Avenue, and ignored the line of hookers offering services to every man who passed, afraid one of them might be his mom. A few blocks later he turned the corner toward home. Keisha was out front by the stoop talking to a woman who looked like she didn't belong. He couldn't put his finger on why he thought that, but it was the same feeling he got when he saw a cop in the neighborhood. Except FD.

Keisha gave him the tug-on-her-braids signal, that told Alex to keep walking. He slowed and listened as the woman asked Keisha questions.

"I'm looking for Alex Greene. Do you know where he lives?"

Keisha shook her head. "Can't help you."

"You don't know where he is?"

"Like I said. I don't know."

"When did you see him last?"

"Last time I saw Alex was when his mom left. Six months ago. Maybe more."

"I have a report saying he still lives here with a man in this apartment building."

"Lady, I don't know who told you dat shit, but Alex ain't been here since his mom left."

"Young lady, you have a mouth on you."

Keisha cocked her head and planted her hands on her hips. "Yes, I do. And you got an ass on you. 'Bout twice as big as it should be."

The lady puffed herself up. "What is your name young lady?"

"It ain't Alex. That's all you need to know."

Alex felt as if his heart would pop out of his throat. He did his best not to stare but it seemed as if the woman could see right through him, as if he wore a name tag that read, "I'm Alex Greene. Come get me." He swallowed hard, forced his legs to slow down, and kept his pace slow. He nodded to his friend as he passed. "Keisha."

"What you doin' walkin' on my block, little man? Better get your ass home fast."

Alex picked up his pace, concealing the smile that popped on his face once he passed them. Now all he had to do was find a place to hide.

***

Keisha waited until the woman from CPS turned the corner, then she ran the other way, searching for Alex. She circled the block twice, asked every kid she knew, but after half an hour there was still no sign of him. Panicked, she ran for home. She bounded up the concrete steps of the stoop, up two flights of stairs, down the hall, and flung open the door. "Mom! Call FD. Something's wrong."

Keisha's mom came out of the kitchen, apron stained with chili sauce. "What's wrong, girl? Something happen to Alex?"

"CPS was looking for him, and now he's gone. You've *got* to call FD."

"Keep your pants on. I'm calling. And his name is Detective Donovan, or Mr. Donovan, not FD."

Keisha rolled her eyes. "Just call."

***

The call came in while Frankie was sharing coffee with Lou and Sherri.

"Donovan."

"Detective, this is Linda Johnson, Keisha's mom."

Frankie sat up straight. "What's going on? Is everything all right?"

"I don't know. Keisha said a woman from CPS was here asking questions about Alex. Now he's missing."

Son of a bitch. "I'll be right there."

Frankie ran two red lights before deciding to put the siren on. Even with that he had to lean on the horn several times to get people to move. *Assholes have no respect anymore.* He didn't know what he would do if CPS got Alex. That boy deserved a lot more than some fucked up foster home. Frankie slammed the brakes, swerved to miss a delivery truck, then hit the gas to scream through an intersection. A near miss with a motorcycle scared him. He eased off the gas. Even with the reduced speed he made it home in record time, screeching around the corner and coming to a stop in the middle of the street. Linda rushed to greet him.

"Anything?" he asked.

She shook her head. "Keisha is out looking with some friends, but so far, nothing."

"Son of a bitch." Frankie looked up and down the street. "Anybody check the bodega?"

"I did. He hasn't seen Alex."

"How about the one a couple of blocks over? Alex knows him. He might have gone there."

"I didn't go there, and I don't think Keisha did, either."

Frankie jumped in his car and drove over. He left it in the street in front of the other store. "Kim, you seen Alex around? I can't find him."

Before Kim could answer Alex raced out from the back room and threw his arms around Frankie.

"I ain't goin' with them, FD. No way." He cried and wrapped his arms tighter. "What are we gonna do?"

"For now, we're going home to eat. We'll figure out the rest later."

Frankie handed Kim his card on the way out. "You ever need anything, call me. I owe you."

Keisha and her mom were waiting outside. Frankie parked and walked to the apartment with Alex still hanging on him. He stayed that way until Keisha grabbed him. "Boy, where'd you go? I was lookin' everywhere."

"I hid out at Kim's. I figured they wouldn't look there."

Linda hugged Alex and kissed his head. "Why don't you two come up for dinner? I'll throw some hotdogs on."

"I'd love to, but Kate is bringing stuff over to cook." Frankie paused. "You and Keisha are welcome to join us."

She waved him off. "No, I'll—"

"Come on, Mom." Keisha tugged on her arm. "Kate cooks almost as good as you."

Linda shook her head, laughing. "This girl is too smart already. You hear that, Detective? *Almost* as good." She laughed more. "All right, if you're sure you don't mind."

"I don't. We'd love to have you up. Give me half an hour to get cleaned up."

"I'm going with Alex," Keisha said.

"Girl—"

"It's all right," Frankie said. "They won't bother me."

"We'll see you in half an hour then."

When Linda arrived, Frankie handed her his card. "I've got my private cell phone on here in case you ever need me."

She reached for her purse, sitting on a small table by the door, and slipped the card inside. "Good. I didn't know where to call today."

"I don't mean to put you on the spot, Ms. Johnson, but can I count on you as an emergency contact at his school?"

She smiled. "First off, it's Linda. I got enough people calling me Ms. Johnson."

"All right, Linda. Like I said…"

She stared at Frankie for a second, then grabbed his hand and squeezed it. "Detective, there was a time when I didn't trust white people. Didn't even like them. But I see the way you treat my girl, and I know what you've done for that boy…" Her eyes teared up and she leaned over and kissed Frankie on the cheek. "I'll do anything I need to help Alex. He's a good kid."

A warm feeling rushed through Frankie when she said that. "Thanks," he said.

"Used to break my heart to see him being raised by that no-good woman. I never told him this, but I'm *glad* she left."

Frankie didn't say anything, but he'd often thought the same thing. "Come for dinner," he said. "I'll introduce you to Kate."

Half an hour later, Linda arrived. Alex and Keisha set the table while Frankie introduced her to Kate.

"What's for dinner?" Alex asked.

Kate tapped him on the shoulder, and said, "Breaded chicken, mushroom risotto, and pencil-thin asparagus cooked in garlic and olive oil."

"Hot damn."

Frankie booted him in the butt. "Alex!"

"Sorry, FD. But you *know* that's my favorite meal."

Frankie poured wine and, throughout dinner, Alex and Keisha filled the gaps in conversation with laughter, mostly about silly things at school. Frankie cleared the table while Kate and Linda got dessert. Kate was pouring coffee when Frankie's phone rang.

"Hello."

"Frankie, it's Sherri."

"What's up?" Frankie said.

"I was just checking to see if everything was all right with Alex."

"He's good. Thanks for asking."

"Okay, see you tomorrow."

Frankie thought it odd that she called just to ask about Alex. "That's it?"

"That's it," Miller said. "Sounds like you have company. I'll see you tomorrow."

Frankie hung up and slipped the phone in his pocket.

Kate took a sip of coffee, watching Frankie out of the corner of her eye. "I thought she was sidelined."

"She was pulling desk duty while she recovered," Frankie said. "Morreau wanted her back with us since Lou is retiring. I can't believe she's back so soon after being shot. Girl's got guts. I'll give her that."

Kate flipped a quick smile. "And she's going to take his place? Be your partner?"

"That's the plan for now," Frankie said.

After finishing her coffee, and more chatting, Linda stood and stretched. "I really have to be going," she said, and took her coffee cup to the sink. "Kate, thank you so much for dinner. And for a lovely evening."

"It was nothing. We'll have to do it again."

"I'd like that," Linda said. "I see nothing but kids all day. It's nice to talk to an adult now and then."

Linda picked up her purse and called to Keisha. "Time to go."

"I'm staying," Keisha yelled from the other room.

"Young lady…"

"She can stay," Frankie said. "We might watch a movie."

"Not for me," Kate said. "I'm following Linda out the door."

"Guess it's just me and the kids then." He leaned over and kissed Kate goodnight, then said goodbye to Linda. "Thanks again for your help."

"Anytime. See you tomorrow."

After they left, Frankie grabbed the remote. "Okay, what do you guys want to watch?"

"Why did Kate go?" Alex asked.

"I don't know," Frankie said. "Guess she was tired."

"She was pissed," Keisha said.

"No way," Frankie said.

"Oh yeah, trust me, she's pissed. She don't trust that bitch."

"Whoa. Watch the language," Frankie said. "Are you talking about Sherri?"

"What's the matter with you?" Keisha said. "Don't you see nothing?"

Frankie sighed. He didn't want to stop and correct the grammar, but… "You mean, don't I see anything and, yeah, I think I do. I am a detective."

"And people wonder why the criminals get away." Keisha laughed. "You missed Kate rolling her eyes when you talked about that girl. And she cringed when you bragged on her, and worst of all, she damn near puked when Sherri talked in that sickening sweet voice."

"You heard *all* that?"

"Heard it? Girl's got a megaphone for a voice."

Frankie rolled his own eyes. "How old are you?"

"Old enough to know shit like that don't fly," Keisha said. "But don't be telling my mom I said nothin' like that."

"Whoa," Frankie said.

"Sorry," Keisha said. "I know you don't like me cursing."

He shook his head. "I'll say whoa again. I was correcting your grammar not your cursing."

Alex wagged his finger at Keisha. "And you know dat ain't allowed in dis damn house, girl."

Then he laughed so hard he fell to the floor.

Keisha kept her seat but barely. Frankie tried to keep it in, but he couldn't and soon joined them. "All right. I guess I deserved that."

He grabbed his coffee cup and started for the sink, but Alex took it from him.

"We'll get this, FD. You got enough to worry over."

Keisha helped Alex with the rest of the dishes. "Don't worry," she said. "Listen to me, and I'll have you square with Kate in no time."

Alex reached out his hand to bump fists. "And you thought busting criminals was tough."

Frankie didn't sleep well that night. Between nightmares about CPS getting Alex and worrying over Kate, he barely slept an hour. Sometime around six he thought he heard the phone ringing. A few seconds later Alex barged in.

"Hey FD. Better get your ass up. Looks like you got a body."

CHAPTER 8

STRANGE POSITIONS

Frankie pulled up to the hotel and flashed his badge. Mazzetti and Sherri were waiting in the lobby, Lou sucking on a cup of coffee and holding an unlit cigarette.

"You can't smoke in here," Frankie said.

Sherri sighed. "Three hotel employees have already told him. I think he does it to piss people off."

"You're finally learning, Miller. Everything he does is calculated to piss people off."

Lou put the unlit smoke in his mouth and headed toward the elevators. "If you two want to get to work today, we've got a couple of bodies on the sixth floor."

"A couple?" Frankie said.

"Where's Kate?" Lou asked.

"On her way. Should be here in a few minutes."

Lou led the way to room 632. The cop who arrived first on the scene was waiting at the door, with an assistant hotel manager at his side.

The cop reached out his hand. "Duncan," he said to them, and then, "You're gonna love this."

"Bad?" Frankie asked.

"Strange," Duncan said.

An overwhelming smell of cleanser hit Frankie as soon as he entered.

"Somebody do this?"

Duncan shook his head. "It was like this when I got here. It's mild now."

"Jesus Christ!" Frankie hated smells, especially chemical smells. "Open some goddamn windows."

"Would you look at this," Lou said.

The bodies were on the bed in a sixty-nine position, socks stuffed in their mouths. Both of them had gunshot wounds to the genitals and head. There was a note attached to the woman's head with a pin.

Sandy, Sandy
Tastes like candy.
To catch the dude who did her in
Look for someone tall and thin.

Frankie leaned closer. "What do you make of this, Lou?"

"Sexual pervert?"

"We know that. I mean, do you think the guy really is tall and thin, or is he the opposite?"

"We don't know enough yet."

"Notice how the note only refers to her. Doesn't mention her partner. This was all about the woman. The guy just happened to be here."

"Happened to be here screwing her," Lou said.

"Where's her purse?" Miller asked.

Frankie turned to Duncan. "Find a purse?"

"Room is just like we found it." He leaned in and whispered, "Unless the maids took it. Wouldn't be the first time."

"What about clothes?" Frankie asked.

"We found them folded and stacked on the nightstand and in drawers. No wallet."

Frankie glanced around the room. "Check out the maids, Duncan. See if they have a locker, and ask them to look in their cars."

"We've got no—"

"They might be illegal. If they are, they won't mind. *Unless* they took the purse."

"I'll get on it."

"Got a twenty on the nightstand," Lou said. "I can't see the maids taking the purse and not the twenty."

"Twenty dollars is a lot to leave the maids for one night."

"And I bet the last hair on my head the bill is clean. No prints. No DNA."

Frankie looked at Lou and then Miller. "Do you leave the tip money the night before, or do you wait until you're ready to go?"

"I wait," Lou said.

"Me, too," Miller said.

Lou shook his head. "So this sick son of a bitch pops this couple then leaves a tip for the maids. Talk about screwballs."

Frankie nodded. "Have a few uniforms question all the employees. And get someone digging through dumpsters."

"At the hotel?" Duncan asked.

"Further. Take it four or five blocks in each direction. I want every dumpster checked."

Duncan started to leave. Frankie hollered to him. "Get help. It needs to be done before the pick up."

Frankie called the assistant manager, who had been standing to the side. "How did you find the bodies?"

"The maids found it when they cleaned."

"This early?"

"The maids said the door had a 'Please Clean Room' sign turned out."

"Anybody touch it?" Frankie asked.

"I don't know. I—"

"It won't matter." Kate Burns walked in with a smile on her face. Two assistants followed her in. When Kate turned and saw Miller, her smile disappeared. She nodded to Mazzetti and Frankie, then said, "Miller, I didn't know you were back on duty." Her voice had an edge.

"This is my first assignment. The lieutenant wanted me out with the best."

"Good morning, Kate." Frankie was all smiles.

"What do you have so far?"

"Maids said they opened the door, saw the bodies, and scurried back out."

"They used that word—scurried?"

"I doubt it."

Kate stood beside the bed, staring at the bodies. "How many perverts do you think we have in our fine city?"

"One too many for this couple," Lou said.

Kate knelt to examine the wound on the male. "You think they were a couple, Mazzetti? I mean husband-and-wife type of couple?"

"I'm guessing they were married but not to each other," Miller said.

Kate looked up at Frankie. "What about you?"

"Don't know yet," Frankie said. Then to Lou. "Make sure the unis talk to all of the maids who work this floor. Miller, get the hotel video from last night."

Frankie moved closer to Kate. "How was Alex?"

"Scared. Which is what took me so long to get here. He stayed with Keisha's mom, but he seemed okay when I left."

Frankie breathed deeply. "I have to do something about this."

Kate was examining the female's vaginal wounds. "This son of a bitch was really sick."

"What am I gonna do about Alex? He's scared to death of CPS."

"How about you let us process the scene. We'll talk about the other tonight."

Frankie got up. "You're right. Let me know what you get from here."

"It won't be much," one of her assistants said. "This place is *clean*. No prints, no hair, nothing."

Frankie stared at him. "No prints at all?"

"Not just no prints. Like I said, no hair in the tub or sink or toilet. Nothing that I can see anywhere. Whoever did this did a damn good job."

Kate was done before long, leaving Frankie to go over the scene with Lou and Sherri, and to try and piece together how it went down.

Lou returned to the room and joined the conversation. "How did he get them on the bed?"

"We know he had a gun," Sherri said.

Frankie nodded. "Yeah, but how did he get inside the room? Did they open the door for him? Didn't they look to see who it was first?"

"Maybe they knew him," Sherri said.

Frankie looked at Mazzetti. "You get anything from the maids?"

"They're scared shitless. Seemed clean to me."

"How about surveillance, Miller?"

"They're getting us video now. We'll have it before we leave."

Lou tapped Miller on the arm. "Why don't you rush them?"

She shot Lou a look but headed out the door. Lou turned to Frankie. "Kate okay?"

"How the hell do I know. The day I figure women out I'll probably die."

"Or wake up and find out you're as old as me."

"Like I said…"

Ten minutes later, Miller returned. "He's on it. I made sure."

Half an hour later, Duncan returned from dumpster-diving. "Got a purse. Wallet too."

Frankie jumped up. "Where?"

"Dumpster down the street, just like you figured. Only had to go elbow deep to get it."

"Come on, Lou," Frankie said. "Let's get this processed so we can see what we've got. Miller, wait for them to process everything and meet us back at the station." Frankie looked through the purse. "No phone?"

Duncan peered in the purse. "Guess not. I didn't look."

"And you didn't find the guy's phone?"

"You've got everything we found."

Frankie closed his eyes and shook his head. "The guy had to have a phone. Her too. Find them. And hurry up."

"The phones weren't in the dumpster."

"You said you only had to go elbow deep to get the purse. Find the phones or you'll be spending the weekend at Staten Island going through the dumps."

"Fuck this," he said, and stormed off.

Frankie turned to Sherri. "Monitor that situation, Miller. You can't leave here without phones. Between the two of them, there has *got* to be at least one cell."

"We'll find them," she said, and followed Duncan out the door.

Lou and Frankie were right behind them. Lou lit a smoke as soon as they got in Frankie's car. "Everything okay at home?"

"Yeah, why?"

"You seem tense. Kate did too."

"Nah. Nothing."

"Spit it out, Donovan. We're partners."

Frankie cursed a slow driver, switched lanes. "CPS came looking for Alex yesterday."

"Ah fuck!"

"Yeah, scared the shit out of me. Scared him even more. He could hardly sleep last night."

"What are you gonna do?"

"I don't know. I've got to worry about this case right now."

"All right. Let's worry about the case," Lou said, and he flipped open a notepad.

"First question—why did the guy leave the 'Please Clean Room' sign out? Did he *want* us to find the bodies?"

"You think he did it on purpose?" Frankie said. "Maybe it was a mistake."

"From the looks of the scene, he didn't make many mistakes."

Frankie nodded. "Yeah. So if we assume he did it on purpose—why?"

"You've gotta figure that if he puts the 'Do Not Disturb' sign out, the maids wouldn't have found the bodies for another five or six hours, minimum."

"Which means the dumpsters would have probably been emptied, so we don't get the purse and wallet."

Lou lit another cigarette. "Right. So why go to the trouble of dumping them if he wanted us to find them?"

"Something doesn't fit, Lou."

"I hate smart criminals. They make me feel inadequate."

"Maybe he just made a mistake."

Lou laughed, which turned into a cough. "Yeah."

CHAPTER 9

NOT MANY CLUES

Frankie and Sherri mulled over the evidence while Lou made more coffee. Carol was putting up a chart. "If you dagos are going to spend more time in here, tell the lieutenant to up the coffee budget."

Lou walked in, hands full. "That would be one dago and two half breeds."

"I forgot you were a thoroughbred, Mazzetti." Carol's laugh sounded more like a snort. "Imagine that, using thoroughbred and Mazzetti in the same sentence."

"You see what happens, Miller? I told you they were prejudiced against Italians."

"What's the scoop?" Carol said. "I saw the photos. Pretty gruesome stuff."

"You're a morbid sort," Mazzetti said.

"Only reason I'm here."

Frankie studied the victims' report. "The woman was married, but not to the guy she shared her fate with."

"What about him?" Lou asked.

"Single. Engineer. No record. That sounds like a scene you need to check, Mazzetti. Take a uniform and check his apartment."

"You think it was the husband?" Sherri asked.

A young officer walked into the room holding a bag. "Officer Richards just delivered the phones."

Frankie looked up. "Where'd he find them?"

"In another dumpster about a block from the first. He said you owe him big time for this."

Frankie looked at the bag, then at Lou and Sherri. "Three phones? We'll get them processed and get the records dumped, then see what we've got."

"Why three phones?" Sherri said.

"My guess is one of them had a burner to cover the affair," Frankie said.

"If he was single, the extra one must have been hers."

"You think the husband knew about the affair?" Sherri asked.

"Guess we're going to find out." Frankie got up from the table. "Let's go, Miller."

"Where?"

"To get these phones dusted, see what we've got on voicemail and calls, then off to Long Island. Somebody's gotta tell the husband she's dead. I want to see how he takes it."

As Frankie drove through Brooklyn, he worried about Alex…and Kate. She was pissed at him, but he'd done nothing wrong. That didn't seem to matter, and he couldn't stand the feeling in his gut. If this was what love was about, he didn't know if he wanted it.

"What do you think?" Sherri asked.

"About what?"

"The husband."

Frankie's phone rang. He reached for it, saw it was Kate and decided to let voicemail pick it up. Last thing he needed was Kate to hear Miller's voice.

"Aren't you going to answer that?"

Frankie chose not to answer Miller either. "Why don't you think it's the husband?"

"Can't see it," Miller said. "Did you hear his voice on those calls? That was the voice of someone worried. He didn't know where she was. And he called *thirteen* times."

"What about the other voice mail, the one from the unknown caller?"

"He sounded pissed at someone."

"Yeah. I'll be eager to talk with him—if we find him," Frankie said.

"We better find him, because I'm sure the husband didn't have anything to do with it."

"I know, but we still need to see what his alibi is."

"I guess you want me to tell him?"

"I think it would be better that way."

A few minutes later Frankie parked outside a small ranch house. The lawn needed cutting, and it could have used some paint, but overall it was nice.

"What was her name again?" Sherri asked.

"Sandy Krenshaw."

The door opened before Frankie could knock. A tall blond-headed guy greeted them with a voice to match the panic on his face. He sounded worse now than he had on the messages.

"Is this about Sandy? Are you the police?"

Sherri held out her badge and stepped forward. "I'm Detective Sherri Miller, and this is my partner, Detective Frankie Donovan. May we come inside, Mr. Krenshaw?"

"Is everything all right? Is Sandy okay?"

Frankie thought the guy looked ready to crumble. "Sir, why don't we go inside."

"Is something wrong? Is she hurt?"

Once inside, Sherri took his hand and led him to a chair. A framed picture of Krenshaw and his wife sat on the table next to him. Sherri picked it up.

"Is this your wife, sir?"

"Yes." He seemed to compose himself a little. "Please tell me what's going on."

Sherri sat next to him. "Sir, I'm afraid there is bad news. Your wife was found dead this morning."

"Dead! Oh, God. It can't be." He stood and walked around. "Where? What happened?"

"Perhaps you should sit," Frankie said. He wanted to see the man's reactions as Sherri talked.

He sat next to Sherri, and she took his hand again. "She was murdered."

"Murdered! How? Who… Where was she murdered?"

"In a hotel room, sir. I'm sorry."

"A hotel?" He got a strange look on his face. He grabbed the picture from the table and shoved it in Sherri's hand. "You must be mistaken. Look at that picture. Whoever you found, it's not her. It *can't* be her."

Frankie stood and came beside Sherri. "I'm afraid it is your wife, Mr. Krenshaw. We found her license and purse not far away."

Krenshaw lowered his head, shaking it. "A hotel? What was she doing in a hotel?"

Sherri looked to Frankie, then back to Krenshaw. "Sir, another man was killed with her."

"What! Who?"

"Is there someone we can call, Mr. Krenshaw? Anyone who can come sit with you?"

"Was it another man?" He stared at the wall, a blank look on his face. "I just spoke with her last night. She told me she loved me."

"May I get a glass of water, Mr. Krenshaw?"

He started to get up, but she stopped him. "I can get it."

He pointed to the kitchen. "The refrigerator has ice water."

Sherri took her time getting water so he could shed a few tears. Frankie joined her.

"Let's wrap this up," Frankie said. "No way this guy did it."

Frankie gave it a minute or so, then they went back in. "You said you spoke to her last night. What time was that?"

"Around five, I think. She said she had a dinner meeting with a client."

"And where were you?"

"I was in Dallas. I wasn't supposed to be home until tomorrow, but I finished up early." He wiped tears. "I tried calling her all night. I—"

"Is there anyone you can think of who—"

"Might do this?" He shook his head. "I don't know *what* to think right now."

"Do you want us to call someone?"

"No. I'll call my sister."

Frankie handed him a card. "You'll have to come down to identify your wife, sir. And to get her things. Call me, and I'll arrange it."

Krenshaw was in zombie land now. He could barely talk. "Okay. I'll call."

He was crying again as he showed Frankie and Sherri to the door.

"We could have asked a lot more," Sherri said. "We didn't—"

"The guy is a basket case. Forget that he lost his wife; he lost his image of her too. Did you see him? He had no idea she was messing around. We'll talk again when he picks up her stuff. By then we'll have more to ask, and he'll be in better shape. And to be safe, have Carol check on his flight from Dallas. Make sure he was on it."

"Anything else?"

"We got what we came for, Miller. Now we know to keep looking. I have a sick feeling we haven't seen the last of this killer."

CHAPTER 10

ANALYZING THE EVIDENCE

Lou was at the station when Frankie and Sherri returned. "Anything from the husband?"

Frankie shook his head. "He was worse in person than on the voicemails. If this guy had anything to do with it, he deserves an Oscar."

From the other room, Carol's voice intruded. "I already checked. He *was* on the flight from Dallas."

"Thanks for the update. You can climb back on your perch now."

"Screw you, Mazzetti."

Lou walked with Sherri and Frankie to the coffee room. "Women keep saying that to me but I don't think they mean it."

"Did we get an ID on the unknown caller yet?" Frankie asked.

"Guy named Chad Benning. In the last week, eleven calls were made to his phone from the disposable cell. He called back four times. Most of the calls didn't last long, but in the last one he left a message, which you heard."

"Let's hear it again," Frankie said.

Lou located the recording on the computer and pressed play.

"I'm telling you for the last time. Stop fucking calling me. You got that? Don't ever call me again."

"That guy sounds pissed," Frankie said.

"Pissed enough to kill," Lou added.

Frankie nodded. "I assume you're getting what we need on him."

"We'll have it tomorrow."

Sherri poured a cup of coffee. "Where do we go with this? Why aren't we questioning him right now? You guys are supposed to be teaching this rookie something."

Lou propped his feet on the table. "You've learned how to cuss and drink coffee. What the hell did you expect?"

"Don't forget Donovan got me shot."

"I forgot about that," Lou said. "That means you're not a rookie anymore."

"We'll question Benning tomorrow, *after* we get background on him," Frankie said, then turned to Lou. "What did you find out about the dead guy?"

"Not much. He was an engineer for a telecom company. They're running his financials as we speak. We'll go see his boss tomorrow, but I don't think we'll get much. Like you said this morning, it's about the girl."

"So if it's not the husband, then who?" Sherri got up and paced. "You think the guy had a girlfriend who got jealous?"

"No way a woman did this," Lou said.

"We get anything on the note?" Frankie asked.

Lou opened the folder. "It was written on the hotel's stationery, using the hotel pen. No prints. Nothing special about the pin in her head. Could have come from anywhere."

"What about the handwriting?" Sherri asked.

"The killer printed. Our guy said it looks as if he went out of his way to make it different from typical handwriting. We might still get something out of it, but I wouldn't count on much."

"We need to check with coworkers. Mazzetti, you and Sherri do that in the morning. Sandy's friends might open up to another woman. I'll take the hotel surveillance."

"What about the phone dump?" Miller asked.

"We didn't get it yet, but considering there was a burner and a regular cell, I think we'll get *something*."

Shit! I forgot to call Kate. "I'll be right back." Frankie stepped down the hall, dialing Kate's number. "Hey lady, how's it going?"

"Busy."

"Too busy to talk?"

A long silence. "About last night…"

"Don't worry, Kate."

"No. I got jealous. I shouldn't have. I've got no right."

"Stop right there. You *do* have the right. But there's nothing to be jealous about. I work with her. That's it. Final. This is the new Frankie Donovan."

Silence again.

"I love you, Kate."

"You took me by surprise, Mr. Donovan."

"I figured it's about time I express my softer side."

Kate laughed. "I'll see you tonight. Be on time. I'll cook."

"Sounds good. See you then."

"I'll be there around seven. And Frankie…thanks. That means a lot to me."

"See you at seven."

Frankie leaned against the wall and smiled. That was the first time he'd said those words since marrying his first wife, and he hadn't *really* loved her. This time he meant it. It made him feel warm inside.

He went back to the coffee room.

Sherri said, "Okay, what do you think? Do we have another maniac on our hands?"

"No doubt about it," Lou said. "Nobody leaves clues to crimes unless he is planning on doing more."

"How do you know it's a 'he'? It could be a woman."

"We've been through that," Frankie said. "This is a guy without doubt. Forget the fact that he talked about her pussy—women are too smart to leave clues. Guys just think they're too smart."

Sherri sipped her coffee. "Now you hit on a point I can't argue."

"Now we have to figure out how to catch this asshole before he hits again, because he *will* hit again."

Lou looked at the note on the pad. "What can we tell from this? I've never been good at puzzles."

Sherri moved closer to Lou, sharing the page with him. "I can't say it's a puzzle. It's a few lines. 'Sandy, Sandy. Tastes like candy. To catch the dude who did her in. Look for someone tall and thin.'"

"Guess we check the surveillance tapes for someone tall and thin," Frankie said.

"And short and fat, and short and thin, and everything in between," Lou said. "Just in case our killer's lying."

Frankie sighed. "I'm catching a smoke before we start."

"Go home, Donovan. Miller and I will get this."

"I said I'd get it."

"Yeah, well, we figure you should go home. Get in a better mood for tomorrow, 'cause you know it's going to be a long day."

Frankie stared. "All right, Lou. Thanks. You too, Miller. See you guys in the morning."

Kate had dinner cooked by the time Frankie got home. Alex and Keisha were in the bedroom playing videogames. Kate poked her head in. "Time to eat."

Alex and Keisha raced to the table, laughing as they fought over the most comfortable chair. Keisha won. "Hey, FD. How's it going?"

"Not so good. You're in my chair."

"Should've grabbed it first," Keisha said.

Alex placed the dishes on the table. "You know the rules."

Frankie poured wine for Kate and himself. "How's it goin', Ace? You doin' all right?"

"I'd be better if we could get outta here and move somewhere else."

"Maybe when they make me captain."

"Why don't you and Kate get a house?" Keisha said.

Frankie looked at Kate. They both laughed. "Maybe we will," he said. "Who knows?"

"How's your case going?" Alex asked.

"Not much to go on yet. We're waiting on the phone dump from one of the victim's cell phones."

Alex got apple juice for Keisha and water for himself. "You mean the luds?"

"Luds?" Keisha asked. "What are luds?"

"Local usage details," Alex said. "Anybody who watches Law and Order knows that."

Kate laughed. "We're getting old, Frankie. Kids nowadays are too smart for us."

Smalltalk occupied the rest of dinner. Then, after clearing the table, Alex and Keisha returned to their videogames.

Frankie made sure they were out of earshot then whispered to Kate. "I want you to know. There's really nothing to worry about with Miller. First, she's my partner and I would never do anything with a partner. Second—"

Kate shook her head. "Miller is stone-cold gorgeous, as you men say. And her body…I can't even *dream* of having a body that good. What am I supposed to think?"

"I wouldn't do it," Frankie said.

Kate reached out and grabbed his hand. "When I lie on my bed at night and reason it out, I know you're telling the truth. But in the everyday world my emotions get carried away. I finally let myself…love you…There, I said it. I let myself love you, and I don't want to lose that."

Frankie moved closer. He brushed her hair with his fingertips, and kissed her. "You'll never lose me. I promise."

"Take an oath?"

"I swear."

"Okay. I'm good with that. I know how you people are on oaths."

"You people? Are you getting prejudiced?"

She kissed him. "Go to hell, dago."

"I love you too, Irish."

CHAPTER 11

WELCOME HOME

Bruce Stewart got in his car and headed toward the airport. There were few things he despised more than driving in New York, especially if it involved picking people up at the airport. The phone rang. It was Debbie. He looked at his watch.

Late. She'll be pissed. Again.

"Hello."

"Where are you?"

"Stuck in traffic. I'm about fifteen minutes away."

"Damn it, Bruce. I'm supposed to be at a meeting in one hour."

"You better call and tell them you'll be late."

"You knew you had to pick me up. Couldn't you have left earlier?"

Like it matters now. "Sorry. I got tied up this morning. I thought I had enough time."

"This is a *big* meeting. I can't—"

"You're the star of the show, Deb. They wouldn't dare start without you."

That finally earned him a laugh. A small one, but it broke the mood. "I'm such a bitch."

"I hadn't noticed."

Another laugh. "Point made. I'm outside of baggage."

"See you soon," he said.

Bruce pulled up twenty minutes later, got out, tossed her bags in the trunk, then gave her a quick kiss. "Get in, the meter's running."

"Take me straight to the hotel. That's where the meeting is."

"I missed you, too."

Debbie leaned over and kissed his cheek. "I *did* miss you. It's been a tough two weeks. After this launch I'll be able to relax."

"Maybe we can even have some fun."

Debbie dug through her purse. What began as a controlled search turned quickly to panic. "I can't find my keys."

"Did you take them with you?"

"I thought I did." She pulled things out that shouldn't have been able to fit in a purse, setting them on the seat beside her. "I can't believe I don't have my keys. I must have left them at home."

"At home? How did you do that?"

"Remember? I had a driver take me to the meeting and then straight to the airport."

"I've got an extra set of keys. How about I meet you after work? We can—"

Debbie shook her head as she dialed a number on her cell. "Not tonight. I'll be swamped, and I've got another presentation tomorrow. Besides, I have spare keys at work." She leaned over and kissed him again. "I'll make it up to you when this is over. I promise."

"A promise? Now that sounds dangerous coming from you," Bruce said.

"Speaking of dangerous," Debbie said, "did you give any more thought to what I told you about?"

"You mean seeing your coworker at that guy's house?"

"Exactly."

"I wouldn't worry about it," Bruce said. "It's probably nothing."

"This person had no reason to be there, and besides, the man who owns that house has a long history of big investments. If the SEC gets the faintest whiff of something wrong—"

"We've been through this already," Bruce said. "They might have been visiting a friend. A cousin. Who knows? If you ask me, I wouldn't say anything. Let the deal go through, and if you still think something's wrong after that, report the person using internal channels."

Debbie bit her bottom lip and stared out the window. "Maybe you're right. I'll think about it."

Traffic slowed to a crawl as they entered the city, and the worse it got the more she panicked. Eight blocks from the hotel, she unhooked her seatbelt. "Let me out here. It'll be faster if I walk."

"Are you sure?"

"Positive. Wish me luck," she said as she swung her legs out the door.

"Good luck," he said, and watched her walk down the street.

Bruce waited at his house for Debbie to call. At five o'clock he decided to call her; she should have been done hours ago.

"Debbie Parnell." Her tone was rushed. She might as well have said, *I'm busy. Speak.*

"I thought you would have called," Bruce said. "How'd the presentation go?"

"Great! I smoked them." There was a moment of silence. "Sorry, I had to get somewhere I can talk."

"Smoked them, huh? I'm not surprised."

"I even amazed myself," Debbie whispered.

"I knew you would. Oh, I meant to ask, did you find your keys?"

"What?"

"Your keys? Did you find them?"

"No, but I'm sure they're at the house."

Bruce took a sip of water before continuing. "How are you going to get in?"

A pause, then. "What?"

She was obviously preoccupied. "I said, how will you get in the house without your keys?"

"I already told you—I have a spare."

"I could come over and—"

"Bruce! I said not tonight."

"You can't blame a guy for trying. I watched porn the whole time you were gone."

"How romantic."

"You better change *everything* starting with the locks. What else was on your key ring?"

"We're back to the keys again?"

"I'm serious."

"I'm sure they'll turn up." Debbie hesitated. "Although it is strange."

"What?"

"Last week when I was out of town, something else happened. I found spyware on my computer."

"Doesn't your work give you protection against that?"

"On my work unit, yes, but not my personal computer. I noticed it slowing down so I had it checked." Debbie stopped again. "Do you think someone is *spying* on me?"

"Maybe you should call the police."

"Don't be ridiculous."

"I'm serious."

"I don't have time to deal with the police."

"I don't know who would spy on you, but listen, you can't fool around with stuff like this. Get your locks changed. Clean out your system. Check your credit cards for unusual activity."

"You really think I should?"

"Absolutely. And get on the locks first. Call somebody tonight."

"Who should I call?"

"Ask your super. Or better yet, the doorman. He'll take care of it."

"All right. Thanks."

"I've got to go, but I'm serious. Get that stuff done. Whoever did this is likely after those hot videos we took of our lovemaking."

She laughed. "Maybe we should leak those videos ourselves and get rich and famous."

"Do you think it could be that guy you work with? The one you said was strange."

"No way. He wouldn't do something like this."

"Didn't you say he always tries to hit on you?"

"In case you haven't noticed, you happen to have a *very* hot fiancée. All the guys hit on me."

Bruce said nothing.

"You know I'm teasing. Come over tomorrow night, and I'll show you how much I missed you."

"What time?"

"Make it eight. We'll grab dinner across the street then make a night of it."

"Okay, see you at eight tomorrow. Love you."

"Love you, too. Bye."

***

The door to Debbie's office opened. Chad walked in. "Who was so important you had to leave?"

"It was Bruce," she said, and typed a reminder on her calendar to meet him the next night.

"You haven't told him?"

"I will. It's just…"

"Just what?"

Debbie stopped and looked up at Chad. "I never asked—how did your interview go?"

"Which one?"

"The early-morning meeting you had before I left town. Remember? You were supposed to meet me."

Chad smiled. "Right. I forgot. It went well. We might make her an offer."

"You didn't tell me it was a *her*."

"Does it matter?" Chad asked. "You're still seeing Bruce. Even worse, he thinks you're in love with him. When are you going to get the guts to tell the man you don't want him in your bed anymore?"

"He's a nice guy. I hate to hurt his feelings."

"But you don't mind screwing me on the side."

Debbie's eyes narrowed. Lips pursed. "Don't talk to me that way."

"Or what?" Chad's laugh was taunting. "You know what kind of woman you are."

"Screw you, Chad."

"Yes, you will. See you tonight."

CHAPTER 12

BACK IN TRAINING

Wilmington, Delaware

I woke at five-thirty, like I used to in prison. Going back to the old ways was hard at my age, but I knew if I slacked up now, it would be harder come forty. I downed a glass of orange juice, grabbed a bottle of water, and headed for the woods. A few blocks later I raced up the first hill, avoiding the paths and keeping to uneven ground.

Some people think that running is running, that it doesn't matter where you do it. For cardio training they may be right, but for practical purposes—something different altogether. Running on a treadmill got my heart rate up, but it did nothing for stabilizing my ankle muscles. Running on rocks adapted them to the twists and turns I'd encounter if I chased someone through alleys and over rooftops—running in the real world. If I stuck to treadmills, I'd end up with twisted or broken ankles.

In my old line of work, that meant I'd end up dead.

I jumped over a tree that fell a few months ago, damn near slipped on the leaves, but recovered balance and continued toward the railroad tracks. They were ideal for this kind of training—the slopes were lined with rocks which made running on them treacherous.

I had a routine. I'd run all the way to Elsemere on the rocks, then turn around under the bridge and run back on the rails. That was the most difficult part—running on a rail not quite three inches wide and slippery, especially when it was wet. I'd been doing this since I was a kid, though, so I guess I had gotten used to it.

That thought made me remember jumping trains as a kid. We'd wait at the curve where they slowed down and jump on the ladder at the back of one of the cars. After a while we got enough courage to climb on top of the cars and run up and down—until Jimmy Borelli's cousin fell off and got caught under the train. It cut him in half. I cried all the way home that day. Cried most of the night, too, not able to get the image of his body cut in two out of my head.

As I navigated a curve, I slipped off the track, twisting my ankle. I caught myself before it got bad. *Focus, Nicky.* I picked up the pace the rest of the way home, completing what I had calculated to be a five-mile run. A *hard* five-mile run.

At home I went to the basement for the rest of my workout. I put a bag of cement on each shoulder—96 pounds each—then went up and down the steps with them until I couldn't do it anymore. Then I grabbed two twelve-inch cement blocks in each hand and walked around the basement. I couldn't go far with them, but I kept it up until my hands either bled or my arm muscles spasmed and just wouldn't work. Extreme stretching finished off the program. I showered after that and got ready for breakfast.

Angie should be up by now.

"Coffee's on the table, Nicky."

Angie was unloading the dishwasher. I kissed her on the cheek. "Thanks, babe."

"I see you've been working out again." Her voice had a suspicious edge to it.

"Figured I better get in shape before I lose it all."

"That's the only reason?"

"What else could there be?"

She handed me a few dishes to put away. "I don't know. Just asking."

"I talked to Frankie last night. They have another nutcase running wild in New York."

"What else is new?"

Rosa came bounding down the steps. "What did you say about Uncle Mario?"

"Some nutbag in New York killed a couple in a hotel room. Bugs doesn't think the guy's done either."

"Is he still coming down for the christening?"

"Depends on how this case goes. If he can, he will."

"I may have to help him solve it," Rosa said.

Angie got up to get more coffee. "Neither one of you is a detective—and don't forget it."

Rosa poured her coffee and took a seat next to Angie. "How did he kill them?"

"Pretty gruesome. I'm not saying how at breakfast."

"Where's the respect?" Angie said. "Doesn't anyone have respect anymore?"

"I'm going to check the news," Rosa said.

"It won't be in the paper down here," I said. "Not unless he kills a few more people."

Rosa sighed. "Dad, I don't read the 'paper' paper."

"I forgot."

"Get with it. Don't get old on me."

"Too late," Angie said.

"Did you work out again, Dad? I heard you up early."

"You don't want your father getting fat," Angie said, and walked to the bottom of the step. "I think Dante's up."

I shook my head. "I didn't hear him."

"You think we should get a set of those intercoms?" Angie asked.

"No need. When that kid wakes, you can hear him a block away."

"But suppose I'm out hanging clothes, or I'm in the basement doing laundry?"

"Then he'll cry a little. Exercise his lungs. In case you forgot, that's what we did."

"Nicky, I'm serious."

"Do what you want, but I need to go. I've got a lot of work to do."

Angie grabbed my arm. "Nicky."

"What?"

"Nothing is going on is it? I mean, with you working out so much, I…"

I held her face and kissed her. "I swear, nothing is going on. I'm clean, and I intend to stay that way."

That brought a smile. "Okay, see you tonight."

***

Rosa slumped into a chair at the cafeteria.

Sally put her tray on the table and sat next to her. "What's wrong? You've been acting strange all day."

Rosa opened her milk and took a sip. "Nothing."

"Nothing, my ass. Tell me."

She shoved a forkful of corn in her mouth and stared straight ahead. "Nobody asked me to the dance yet. When Rudy came by this morning I thought for sure he would." She sighed. "It's getting too late now. I'll probably be the only girl without a date."

Sally shrugged. "It's no big deal."

"Not for you. You have a date."

Jennifer walked by with a tray and took a seat across from Rosa. "What's up, guys?" Then to Rosa. "Why so glum?"

"She doesn't have a date to the dance," Sally said. "I told her somebody would ask."

"Bullshit," Jennifer said.

"What?" Rosa asked.

"Nothing," Sally said, and kicked under the table at Jennifer.

"Cut the shit, Sally." Jenn turned to Rosa. "Nobody will tell you this because they think it'll hurt your feelings, but you need to know."

Rosa straightened in her chair. "Tell me *what?*"

"Nobody's going to ask you because of your father."

Rosa threw her fork down. "What's my father got to do with anything?"

Jenn rolled her eyes. "Come on. What boy in his right mind is going to ask Nicky Fusco's daughter out? Mike Riley was the only one stupid enough to do that. Now that he's gone, there's nobody else."

"Why, because he was in prison? I can't believe it."

Jenn reached for her but Rosa pulled away. "Screw you, Jenn. You're just jealous."

Jenn waited for her to settle down. "Think about it, Rosa. You're beautiful. You have a great body. You're funny. Why wouldn't a boy ask you? Why wouldn't *all* the boys ask you? For shit's sake, even *I* got asked. Probably because they think they'll get laid, but at least they asked."

Rosa lost some of her edge. "Don't say that. You're pretty."

"That's bullshit, and I know it. Even my father knows it. He always talks about how pretty so-and-so is, or what a fox some girl on TV is. Never once does he say, 'Jenn, you're pretty.' I can't blame him. Just saying." She got close to Rosa and tapped her arm. "Listen, I'm not shitting you. This has nothing to do with your dad having been in prison." She looked away for a second then back at Rosa. "People say your dad is a killer."

"I know about that. But he served his time." Rosa started to say something else but Jenn interrupted.

"I'm not talking about that gang fight when he was a kid. I'm talking about your father being a friggin' hit man."

Rosa darted her eyes from Jenn to Sally, looking for a denial, but instead she saw Sally's agreement.

Dad? A hit man? What a damn fool I've been.

CHAPTER 13

A LITTLE BIT OF PLANNING

Brooklyn, New York

The killer followed Debbie to the restaurant. She was easy to spot with her long legs, dressed to show them off. He, on the other hand, was just another face in the lunchtime crowd, another suit rushing to shove calories down his throat so he could finish the day and do it all over again. Not her, though. She used lunch for other purposes—like stalking unsuspecting men and finding new lovers. She smiled as a man hugged her, then gave her a kiss. This was not the man she had been with a week ago.

Naughty bitch.

The killer went back to work, but by the time Debbie got home, he was stationed at a spot across the street from her apartment. She stopped to talk to the doorman before going inside. The doorman presented a problem.

The killer waited until it got dark then went to the back of the building. The older couple on the bottom floor were out of town. He broke one of their windows with a rock, went inside and made his way to the back bedroom. He slid the latch on the window so he could open it from outside, and then he went back out, careful not to leave any clues that he'd been inside. He smiled. He was done for the night and happy with his plan.

In the morning, the killer dressed in a light hoodie and shades. He hadn't shaved since yesterday. Not much of a disguise, but it should suffice. He rented a car, drove to the Bronx, and cruised Washington Heights until he saw a kid who fit what he needed. About twelve-years old, black, street smart or he wouldn't be hanging out in this area. The killer pulled to the curb and rolled down the window. The kid approached, eyes darting left and right, assessing the situation. He leaned on the car door, head poked barely inside.

"S'up, dude?"

"Looking for someone to do a job."

"I ain't no fag, if that's what you're lookin' for."

"Nothing like that. I need someone to deliver a message."

"A message? Don't try yankin' my dick."

The killer laid four, hundred-dollar bills on the seat. "Two of these are for you. Here's what I want you to do…"

Thirty minutes later, he dropped the kid off a block from Debbie's building.

The kid waited until no one was around then approached the doorman. "Hey, mister."

"What?"

"Dude, I'm in trouble. I broke a window."

"What window?"

"Out back. It was an accident. I didn't mean it."

"Shit! What's your name?"

"I can't be gettin' the cops involved or nothin'. My mom will kill me."

"You shouldn't have broken the window. What's your name?"

The kid reached into his pocket and pulled out two crumpled hundred-dollar bills. "I got two bills that say I never broke that window. Know what I mean? Just get it fixed. You can do it, right?"

"Two hundred? They won't even look at it for that."

"Don't yank my dick. You think I'm stupid? You can call insurance and put those bills in your fuckin' pocket." The kid turned his pants pockets inside out. "That's all I got."

The doorman looked at him.

"Look," the kid said, "you don't tell nobody I broke the window, and I don't tell nobody you got two bills. Deal?"

"Where'd you get the money?"

"Don't see how that matters."

"Get the hell out of here," the doorman said.

"Yeah, that's what I'm talkin' about," the kid said, and headed down the street.

The killer waited for the kid to get out of sight, and picked him up on the next block. They drove back to the Bronx in silence. When it was time to leave he handed the kid the other two hundred. "Keep your mouth shut about this."

"Ain't got nothin' to worry about with me, dude. You break any more windows, you know where to find me."

The killer drove away with a smile on his face. The doorman would pocket the money, fix the window and no one would ever know about it. And the bedroom window would stay unlocked until he needed it.

Can't wait to see you, Ms. Parnell.

CHAPTER 14

A FEW QUESTIONS

Frankie drove into work happy. He'd had a good night with Kate, and he felt good about the case. He didn't know why, but he felt good.

He took the steps to his office two at a time. "Hey, Mazzetti."

Lou was smoking. "Coffee's on."

"Don't let Morreau catch you smoking in here."

"What's he gonna do, force me to retire?"

"You going with Miller today?"

Lou looked at Frankie, squinting through tired eyes. "I thought *you* were hanging with Miller."

"I've got to take Alex to register at a new school; besides, you'll do better teaching her."

Lou dropped his cigarette butt on the floor and crushed it out. "Does that mean Kate doesn't want you working with Miller?"

"Shut up, Mazzetti."

"I figured you'd get the hots for her."

"Yeah, well it's not going to happen."

Sherri came into the office. "What's not going to happen?"

"You getting shot," Lou said. "Frankie swore he'd step in front of you next time and take the bullet himself."

"I hear that." Sherri poured coffee and sat next to Lou. "Are we going to Sandy's workplace?"

"You and Lou are," Frankie said. "I have things to do."

"Are you ready?" Lou asked.

"As soon as I finish this coffee," Miller said. "And by the way, Mazzetti, I'm driving."

***

As Lou and Sherri entered the building, he checked his notes. "Fifth floor. Perkins and Mischa."

"Lawyers?"

"Insurance."

Lou flashed his badge to the receptionist. "Detective Mazzetti. This is Detective Miller. We're here to talk to Mr. Ramos."

The receptionist lost her smile and nodded. "He's expecting you. I'll let him know you're here. Do you want some coffee or tea?"

"Not now," Lou said.

A few minutes later a man walked toward Lou, his hand extended and a somber look on his face. "John Ramos."

"I'm Detective Mazzetti, and this is Detective Miller."

"I have a conference room we can use."

"That will be fine," Sherri said, and followed Ramos down the hall.

"What can you tell us about Ms. Krenshaw?"

Ramos grabbed a bottle of water, offered some to the detectives, then sat. "She has worked for me about four years. In fact she's one…she *was* one of my best employees. She was never late, seldom missed work, and always got projects done on time."

"Did you know she was having an affair?" Sherri asked.

The question seemed to catch Ramos off guard. "An affair? I…no, I didn't. But I knew very little about her personal life."

Sherri leaned forward and smiled. "So you and she…you didn't…"

Ramos blushed. "Me? No. I'm happily married."

"Was she seeing anyone from work?"

Ramos seemed to give it thought. "I really can't say. You should talk to Izzy Warner. She and Sandy were close."

"Anything you can think of, anyone who…"

Ramos shook his head. "I wish I could help, but other than her work, I knew nothing about her. Izzy might. Ask her."

"Okay, Mr. Ramos. If you don't mind, could you ask Ms. Warner to come see us? If we have more questions for you, we'll call." Sherri handed him a card. "And if you think of anything, here's my number."

Izzy walked in ten minutes later, introduced herself and sat next to Sherri. "I can't believe what happened to Sandy. None of us can."

"How well did you know her?" Lou asked.

"We were good friends. We ate lunch together almost every day, told each other our problems. We shared dreams. That kind of thing."

"What kind of problems did she have?"

Izzy shrugged. "You know, the usual."

"Why don't you tell me," Sherri said.

"You know…self-esteem problems. Money problems."

"Husband problems?" Lou asked.

Izzy squinted her eyes. "Those, too. So what? Lots of people have trouble with their marriages."

"Not all of them have affairs to solve them," Lou said.

Izzy turned on Lou. "You say that like she was a whore. She had a damn affair. Big deal."

"This one got her killed," Sherri said. "It *was* a big deal."

Izzy stood. "Are we done?"

Lou stared, making sure she knew he was serious. "Ms. Warner, I know you think we're tainting your friend's name, but we're not. She was found dead with a man who wasn't her husband. People will know. We're trying to find out who killed them. I would think you'd want the same thing."

Izzy glanced around, as if to make sure no one was nearby. Then she focused her attention back on Lou before sitting. "Sandy had been seeing this guy for a while. Maybe three or four months."

Lou wrote down what she said. "Why did she get a disposable phone last week?"

"She didn't."

"We found one with her purse. And there were several calls to another man. Was she seeing someone besides Justin?"

"No. She wasn't like that."

"So you don't know anyone named Chad?"

She shook her head. "I've never heard of him. And Sandy would have told me."

"Maybe she—"

"She'd have told me."

Sherri handed her a card. "If you think of anything…"

Izzy nodded. "I'll call if I do."

Lou lit a cigarette as he got into Sherri's car. "That was a waste of time."

"Toss the butt, Mazzetti."

He flipped it out the window. "It's getting to be where you can have sex more places than you can have a smoke."

"Don't you wish you could still do it?" Sherri waited a second, then said. "I mean the sex part."

"Go to hell, Miller." Lou pulled another cigarette from the pack and put it in his mouth without lighting it. "I don't think Izzy was lying. What about you?"

"I'm with you, but a lot of people *think* their friends would tell them everything, right up until the time they find out they didn't."

"I hear that," Lou said.

"So what made Sandy get the throwaway last week? What changed?"

"Let's talk it over at the station. The reports should be in."

Frankie was back at the station when Lou and Sherri arrived.

"Did you get Alex taken care of?" Sherri asked him.

"Not yet, but pretty soon, he'll be safely tucked into a new school."

"Which one?"

"St. Edwards."

Lou whistled. "Did you start taking money from your dago friends again?"

Sherri laughed, but she stared hard at Frankie, waiting for an answer.

"I told them I needed tuition money," Frankie said. "It won't cost much more than a few favors."

The look on Miller's face made Frankie speak up. "We're not serious, Miller. Now let's get to work."

Sherri shook her head. "If CPS wants to find him all they have to do is search the schools for his name."

"He's registered under my name."

"Oh shit," Lou said.

Change was jiggling in Frankie's pocket. He did that when he got excited. Or nervous. "He'll be fine."

Carol walked in with a folder. "I updated the file with the new reports. You should have enough to stay busy."

"Thanks, Carol." Frankie opened the folder. "We have Justin's prints on his phone and Sandy's prints on both of the others."

"Who did she call?" Lou asked.

"On her main phone, she called her husband, work..." Frankie popped his head out the door. "Hey, Carol who does this Jersey number belong to on Krenshaw's phone?"

"Her sister. I thought I put it on there."

"That's all right. Thanks."

Frankie got back to the report. "Her husband, work, sister, pizza delivery, dry cleaners, gynecologist...that's about it."

"What about the burner?" Sherri asked.

"Strange. Just one number—that Chad guy. And it has calls from him, but that's it. No one else."

"So where did she call Justin from?" Lou asked. "And why call Chad from a separate phone?"

"Good question," Frankie said, making a note in the file.

Sherri said. "And she lived on Long Island and Justin was in the Bronx. How did they meet? They didn't work together."

"Get with that friend at work. See if she knows," Frankie said. He continued going through the file. "No semen. So the son of a bitch got to them before the act."

Sherri leaned over Frankie's shoulder, looking at the file. "Let's listen to Chad's voicemails again. He seems to be the key."

"Most of them were hang-ups," Frankie said. "Number four is where it gets interesting."

'You better stop calling me. Do you hear? Stop calling.'

"Sounds like he was getting pissed," Lou said.

"But that's nothing like the last one. Listen."

'I'm telling you for the last time. Stop fucking calling me. You got that? Don't ever call me again.'

Lou whistled. "I'd say we better pay Chad a visit."

"Carol, can you find out where Chad Benning works? Please?"

Carol came in a few minutes later wearing a big smile.

Lou glanced at her. "You look like you just saw that rookie patrolman naked. What's up?"

"Guess where Mr. Benning works."

"I give up," Lou said.

"Anderson, Bergen and Silverstein."

"Is that supposed to mean something?"

"Not the name, Mazzetti, but that firm is in the same building where Sandy Krenshaw worked."

"Son of a bitch!"

"Ain't that right," Carol said.

Frankie got up from the table. "Let's go. You're driving, Miller."

"Seventeenth floor," Carol said as they started down the steps. "And if that rookie is naked, Mazzetti, send him up."

Lou laughed the rest of the way down the steps. "Crazy bitch."

The receptionist at Anderson, Bergen and Silverstein was as stiff as the name implied. "May I help you?" she said, with a tone that implied she didn't want to.

Frankie showed his badge. "Detective Donovan. I'm here to see Mr. Benning."

"Is he expecting you?"

"No."

"I'm afraid—"

"He'll want to see us," Frankie said.

Chad Benning came out within five minutes. He was six feet two inches of charm, and had a smile that stretched across the room. As he approached, his hand shot out like the arm of a slot machine.

"Chad Benning. What can I do for you?"

"Perhaps we should go somewhere private," Sherri said.

He led them to a small conference room off the lobby. "What is this about?"

Frankie handed him a card. "Detective Frankie Donovan. These are Detectives Miller and Mazzetti. We're here about Sandy Krenshaw."

Chad got a strange look on his face. "Who?"

"Sandy Krenshaw."

He cocked his head to one side, then back. "I don't know any Sandy Krenshaw."

Lou pulled out a picture of her, the one from the crime scene, and shoved it in Chad's hand.

"Oh God!" He quickly handed the picture back to Lou. "She's dead."

"You want to tell us about it, Mr. Benning?" Frankie asked.

"Tell you about what? I've never seen that woman before."

Frankie got up and walked behind Chad, then back in front again. "If you didn't know her, why were you calling her?"

"Calling her? I never called her."

"Where were you the night before last?"

"Home."

"All night?"

"Yes. I brought work home, then read a book."

"What book?"

"Does it matter, Detective? A book. A mystery. What difference does it make?"

"Just curious. I'm a reader too."

"If you must know, it was a John Sandford book. One of his *Prey* novels."

"Good books," Frankie said, then nodded to Sherri, who placed a digital recorder on the table and pressed play.

'You better stop calling me. Do you hear? Stop calling.'

"Is that your voice?" Frankie asked.

Benning looked puzzled. "I don't know…it sounds like me, but…"

"But what?"

"I didn't leave that message."

Sherri pressed play again.

'I'm telling you for the last time. Stop fucking calling me. You got that. Don't ever call me again.'

"How about this one? Did you leave *that* message?"

Lou leaned in close to Benning. "How do you explain your voice being on her cell phone if you don't know her? That *is* you telling her not to call anymore."

Frankie moved in closer, until his face was inches from Chad's. "What happened? Was she wanting something more than a quick screw? Was she blackmailing you? Do you make good money, Mr. Benning?"

Benning stood. "I think it's time for you to leave."

"We're not done asking questions," Frankie said.

"Then wait until I call my lawyer."

Sherri started to say something but Frankie grabbed her arm. "That's all right. We're leaving. But you may want to call that lawyer. We'll be back."

"We screwed that up," Frankie said as he got in Sherri's car. "My fault. I pushed too hard."

Lou shrugged. "Sometimes it works. Other times…"

"Yeah, other times they cry 'lawyer' and shut their mouths."

"He's our guy. We'll get him."

Sherri hit the horn, cursed at a driver, and made a left turn. "We'll need a lot more than what we have now. Especially once he lawyers up."

Frankie punched the dash. "I want everything we can get on this guy. Lou, have Carol dig up financials. Have somebody interview coworkers. His neighbors, too. And take Sandy's picture with you. I want to know if she's ever been at his home or if anyone from work ever saw them together."

Frankie looked at Sherri. "Go back and talk to Sandy's friend at work. See if you can jog her memory about Mr. Benning."

"I have his picture."

"What?"

"I snapped one on my cell. I'll show it to Izzy."

Frankie smiled. "Put in in an array of pics from the station. We don't want anything to go wrong if she IDs him."

***

Chad went to the elevators, got off on fifteen, and went straight to Debbie's office. He was pissed but he put a smile on his face.

"What are you doing here?" Debbie said.

"I came to see if you wanted to do something tonight."

"I'd love to, but I'm tired. Thanks for asking, though."

"How about dinner?"

She hesitated, then shook her head. "Really, I'm tired. Another time, okay?" She said the 'okay' in her sweet sexy voice, the kind she used only when she wanted something.

"Sure. Fine." Chad maintained his smile until he got back into the elevator. He punched the button for seventeen, then squeezed his fists as the elevator rose.

Bitch!

CHAPTER 15

ALL THE PRESIDENT'S MEN

Wilmington, Delaware

I fed Dante while Rosa cleaned the table.

"I'll do the dishes, Mom."

Angela stretched and yawned. "What did I do to deserve this treatment? You're doing the dishes and your father has Dante."

"Guess you're free for the night," I said.

Angie grabbed a book and went to sit on the stoop. She loved reading there, especially with the warm spell we'd been having. I waited until the door closed then joined Rosa in the kitchen. "Anything wrong?"

"No. Why?"

"You haven't been yourself the past few days."

"Nothing's wrong." She continued washing dishes, never turned to look at me. That was his first sign that something was wrong.

"All right, just checking. If you need to talk…"

"I'll let you know."

"Anybody ask you to the dance yet?"

A huge sigh followed. "Not yet. And I doubt if anyone will. Getting late for that."

"Not even Mike Riley?"

"Not even him." She mumbled something.

"What?"

"Nothing."

"I didn't hear you."

"I said it was nothing. Okay?" She finished drying the last few dishes and hung the towel on the rack. "I'm going out."

"Where?"

"I don't know. Probably to get Sally and go to Jenn's house."

I didn't like her evasive answers, but I let it go. *Something* was bothering her, and she obviously didn't want to talk about it with me. "Okay, don't be late. And be careful."

"Yeah. I know."

***

Rosa and Sally picked up Jenn and the three of them headed up to St. Anthony's. They hung around the church, met some boys, drank a few beers, talked some more. The guys soon left and before long it was dark.

"We better be getting home," Sally said. "I don't like being here at night."

"Nobody's going to bother us," Jenn said.

"We should go visit Abby's mom," Rosa said. "Come on, it won't take long. She's at St. Francis."

They walked the few blocks to St. Francis Hospital, where they stayed a while visiting Mrs. Perlante, then left.

As soon as they got outside, Jenn lit a smoke. "Couldn't wait to get out of there. I hate visiting sick people."

Sally hit Jenn on the arm. "That's a disgusting thing to say."

"You want me to lie? Are you telling me you like it?"

"No, but it's the right thing to do."

"Maybe, but that doesn't mean I have to like it. I hate visiting sick people."

They walked about two blocks down DuPont Street. Rosa reached for Jenn's cigarette. "Give me a hit."

"You don't smoke."

"Sometimes I do. I feel like it tonight."

"What else you girls feel like?" A voice from the side startled them. Rosa jumped. Jenn and Sally screamed.

Two black guys stepped in front of them, one behind. The one who'd spoken was rough-looking, scary. He sported a big thick necklace and a gold tooth, and the grip of a gun showed in his waistband. "No need to get all worked up. We ain't chasin' no white meat. Just want your purses."

"Bullshit," Rosa said. "Earn your own money."

The leader pulled out a switchblade, brought it close to Rosa. "Like I said, no need to get worked up. But I *do* need those purses. Give 'em up and nobody gets hurt."

Sally started crying. She handed him her purse. "I don't have one," Jenn said, squeezing Sally's hand. Rosa held her purse tightly.

The leader nodded to the guy next to him. He snatched Rosa's purse and rifled through it.

"Shit, DuPree. She's got a coin," he said, pulling it out.

DuPree took it from him and looked at the coin, the face of President Monroe staring at him as if he'd done something wrong. The coin was a safe-passage token given out by his boss—and only to a select few. "Where'd you get this?"

Rosa put a little defiance in her tone. "My father gave it to me."

"Who's your father, bitch? Don't play games with me."

"His name's Nicky Fusco and if—"

"Shit!" the other guy said. "Nicky the Rat?"

"That's him," DuPree said. He flashed a big smile, then returned the coin and everything else to Rosa and her friends. "Tell your father that DuPree says we're even now."

"What do you mean?" Rosa asked. She straightened herself, and tried to hide the fact that she was trembling.

"You just tell him that DuPree said we're even." He turned to the guys with him. "You and Ten Spot make sure they get home safe."

As DuPree walked away he hollered back. "Make sure you tell Nicky what I said."

DuPree's men walked Rosa and her friends to Front Street. Jenn and Sally thanked them. When they were out of earshot, the girls turned to Rosa.

"I can't believe what just happened," Sally said. "I thought we were dead."

"I thought we were raped," Jenn said. "But we were saved by Nicky Fusco."

Sally lit a smoke, fumbling with her lighter. She looked at Rosa. "And you still don't believe what we said about why nobody asked you to the dance?"

"Maybe you believe us now?" Jenn said.

"There's a reason," Rosa said. "But it's not what you think."

"*Sure* there is. Come on. *Get real.* That was DuPree, one of Monroe's top dogs. He was scared shitless when he heard who you were."

Jenn grabbed Sally's smoke to light hers. "I'm gonna have a T-shirt printed that says 'I know Nicky Fusco.'"

"You mean Nicky the Rat," Sally said, and laughed.

Rosa didn't. "It's not funny, goddamnit." She ran down the block, crying.

Jenn and Sally caught up to her on the next block. "I'm sorry. We didn't mean anything. I mean, to us, it's cool. I wish my dad—"

"No, you don't. Trust me. You *don't.*"

***

At breakfast the next morning, Rosa looked upset. I waited until we both had coffee. "What's the matter?"

"Nothing."

"'Nothing' won't cut it this morning. I let that go last night."

"You want to know what's bothering me? Okay. *I* want to know what the hell is going on. Boys are afraid to ask me out. Parents won't let their kids hang out with me. Who *are* you?"

"You'll find people like that all the time. It's—"

"I'm not buying any cheap excuses this time, Dad. Tell me."

Angie hollered from the kitchen. "Keep the argument civil."

"Not this time," Rosa said. "I want the truth and I want it from Dad."

Angie stepped into the room. "Rosa!"

Rosa turned to her. "What? You and Dad preach all the time about me being honest with you. Shouldn't it work both ways?"

I grabbed Angie by the arm before she lost control. "She's right. We can't ask for anything different."

Rosa stood, right leg cocked to the side, hands on her hips. "So?" Her voice carried a lot of attitude.

I thought quickly, and decided to spit it out. "When I was young, I spent time in prison."

This was more difficult than I thought. I hated telling her, even though it felt good to get the truth out. I was afraid of what she'd think of me. "Those were ten years I could have spent with you and your mother."

Rosa scoffed. "I already knew that. Why were you in there?"

"I killed a boy in a gang fight."

"It was an accident," Angie said quickly.

I held Angie back, shaking my head. "What I did was wrong, Rosa. I deserved the time."

"What else?" Rosa demanded.

"What do you mean?"

"I told you about the rumors at school. I know how kids can be. I figured a lot of it was exaggeration, so I never asked. But last night..."

Something in her tone alerted me. This was more than kids talking at school. "What happened last night?"

Rosa had a glare in her eyes. She slammed something onto the table. The Monroe coin. "You want to tell me what this is about?"

The look in her eyes and the tone of her voice pissed me off. I held my temper, though. "Maybe I will. *If* you sit down and calmly explain what you're talking about."

She yanked the chair out and plopped in it. "I got mugged last night."

My heart raced. "What?" Before I could say anything else Angie rushed to her side.

"Mugged? What happened? Are you all right?"

"*Of course* I'm all right." Her voice had sarcasm added to the attitude now. "I'm Nicky 'the Rat' Fusco's daughter. Who's going to hurt me?"

Angie's lips twisted into a frown. "Knock off the attitude."

I gave Rosa a minute. "How about you tell us what happened."

"I'll tell you what happened. Me, Jenn and Sally were walking home—"

"Sally, Jenn and I," Angie said.

"It's not time to correct grammar, Mom." Rosa huffed. "We were walking home and three black guys stopped us. One of them had a knife. I saw a gun in another guy's waistband. They took our purses, which had our lives in them: cell phones, money, credit cards. Then one of them pulls this coin out of my purse and shows it to the leader guy—Dupree. Then he asks who my father is. I say Nicky Fusco." Rosa wiped a tear away. "Then the guy *freaked* out. All of them did. One of them says, 'Nicky the Rat' and Dupree says, 'That's him.'"

I sat there but said nothing.

She stared at me, demanding an answer. "So you want to tell me why the leader of one of Monroe's gangs, the toughest in town, is afraid of *you?*"

Angie sat at the table next to Rosa. "I want to know too. You haven't done anything, Nicky, have you?"

I put on a smile. "I did time with Monroe. Helped him out in prison. I guess he feels he owes me. That's why he gave me that coin."

"Bullshit, Dad."

Angie slapped at her but missed. "Don't talk to your father like that."

Rosa glanced to Angie then back to me. "Bull. When DuPree heard your name, he freaked out. It was like in the movies. And the other one said 'The Rat?'"

"They were just showing respect."

"Respect? Gangs from the toughest part of town, the President's District? That's bull. Those guys were scared shitless."

"Rosa!"

"Cut the crap, Mom. I need to know."

"Your father's a different man now. That's all in the past."

"It might be in the past for him, but it's not for me. I have to live with his reputation every day. I can't get a date. Friends can't come to my house. Jesus Christ, I can't even get mugged."

Angie reached to slap her again, but I held up my hand to block her. "She has a right to know."

"We'll talk in here," I said, and headed to the living room. I sat on the sofa and motioned for Rosa to sit next to me. "If I tell you it may make things worse. It will burden you with secrets that must be kept."

"What do you mean?" Rosa asked.

"I mean that what I tell you cannot be repeated to anyone. Ever."

She nodded. "I know."

"No, you don't know. There will be times when you want to tell someone. When you're angry with someone and want to frighten them with what I'm about to tell you. Or impress them. Or simply share your burden with someone you love." I waited until I knew I had her full attention. "But you won't be able to. And this not only means now, but it means the future. With a husband. Or with kids. *Ever.*"

The tension in her face went from *attitude* to worry. She was scared. *Good.* "It's not an easy thing to keep secrets, especially terrible ones. And mine are terrible ones."

"What did you do?"

"Before I tell you, I want you to think hard about it. And listen to what I have to say. I've already told you about the secrets. The other thing is that what I tell you may change the way you feel about me. You'll say it won't. But it might. So take the night. Think it over. If you still want to know in the morning, I'll tell you everything."

CHAPTER 16

A CALL TO UNCLE MARIO

Wilmington, Delaware

Rosa struggled to get through the day. She had a fight with Jenn and Sally; they wouldn't quit talking about the mugging. Finally Rosa made them promise they wouldn't say anything about it to anyone. She didn't know how long they'd keep that promise, but it should be good for a while.

By the time she got home she still hadn't figured out what to do about her dad and his secrets. He'd scared her, the way he talked about keeping them secret forever. It was one thing for teenage girls to say that to each other, but something in his eyes when he said it…She just didn't know. Nobody mentioned it at dinner, or afterward. It was like it never happened. Maybe they were hoping it would go away. Or pretending that it never happened in the first place.

The problem was, it had.

That night, Rosa went to bed worried. And curious. She couldn't sleep. Around midnight she called Uncle Mario. *He'll know what to do.*

After three rings she almost hung up. After five she reached for the end button.

"Hello."

"Uncle Mario?" she whispered. It seemed like the thing to do that time of night. Besides, she didn't want her parents hearing. "Uncle Mario, it's Rosa."

"Is something wrong?" His voice had a nervous edge to it.

"No. It's just…"

"Is Nicky okay?"

"Dad's fine. I just need someone to talk to. I hope you don't mind."

"I don't mind."

"How are you feeling, Uncle Mario?"

Frankie laughed. "I'm great. But sometimes it's easier if you just say what's on your mind."

"You sound like my father."

"We *did* grow up together. So tell me what's wrong."

"I don't know, it's just…"

"Just what?"

"People at school, they…say things about Dad."

"Like what?"

Rosa twisted her hair, worried about what to say. "I don't know how much you know about dad. I mean, you're a cop, and…"

Frankie laughed. "I know *everything* there is to know about your father. Just tell me what's troubling you."

"They call him a killer. Some kids even said he was a hit man." Rosa felt good to have it out. It made the rest come easier. "Some gangs are even afraid of him. And—"

"Slow down, Rosa. Take it easy."

"Sorry."

"Tell me what you mean by gangs being afraid of him."

Rosa repeated the story from last night, including the part about DuPree saying to tell Nicky that they were even. She told him how they were afraid of Nicky and even walked them halfway home.

"That all can be explained. I know the guy you're talking about. Not DuPree, but his boss, Monroe. He did time with your dad."

"Dad told me that."

"What he probably didn't tell you was that Monroe helped me too. Remember last year when your dad helped me out on the jam when my sister's husband got killed?"

"I remember."

"Monroe helped me. Actually, he helped your dad get information for me."

"Wait, you worked with a gangbanger?"

"I didn't work with him, but sometimes things aren't as neat and pretty as people think, especially under the surface."

Rosa tried digesting what Frankie was telling her. "Monroe was only part of the problem. What can you tell me about Dad before that? When he was in New York?"

"I won't tell you anything about your father. I don't think you *want* to know. What I will tell you is this: Nicky Fusco saved my life three times. And he saved my ass countless times. We took an oath as eight-year-olds and to this day he has never broken it." Frankie took a deep breath. It sounded as if he lit a cigarette. "Your father would cut off his hand before breaking his word. *That's* the kind of man Nicky Fusco is."

"But do you know what he's done?"

"I told you I know everything. What you have to remember is that sometimes things that seem horrible have a reason."

"Some people say he killed a bunch of people in New York. That he was a hit man."

"I was assigned the investigation to find out who was killing all of those people. Some thought it was Nicky and that he was a hit man. I can tell you this: I spent almost a year investigating those crimes, looking at everyone, and in the end, I cleared your father."

"So he didn't do it? He's not a killer?"

"I didn't get to be Detective First Class by putting the wrong people in jail. And if you want to know about the gang fight that sent him to prison, that was my fault."

"How?"

"Your dad was supposed to go out with your mom that night. He only came to the fight to save us because he heard they had guns. A guy from the other gang shot and killed a friend of ours and then tried to kill me. That's when Nicky shot him. And that's why they sent him to prison."

"Is that the truth, Uncle Mario? Really?"

"I'd never lie to you, Rosa."

"Okay, thanks. I really appreciate it."

"If you ever need to talk, call me. No matter what time it is."

"Okay. Thanks again."

***

I was up early, reading the paper when Rosa came down the stairs. She was whistling. She put coffee on and started cooking eggs. "You want toast, Dad?"

"What did you decide?"

"About what?"

"About what? You busted my ass about wanting to know my past, and I told you to think about it."

"I decided I don't want to know." Rosa leaned over and kissed me on the cheek. "Love you, Dad."

"What about the kids at school? And the things they say?"

"I can handle them. I'm a Fusco."

I could have died right then. That's how proud she made me. I held back tears that wanted to come, and then got up and hugged her. "Yes, you *are* a Fusco. And I'm proud of you."

Rosa left for school. The door hadn't even closed yet when Angie came over. "That might have satisfied Rosa, but not me. I need to know what's going on."

"Nothing. I swear."

"Nothing? Like when all of those people got killed last year when you happened to be 'working' Frankie's case. Or *nothing* like when all those people in New York got killed?"

I breathed slowly, making sure my voice was steady. I could lie to the cops. Hell, I could lie to the pope, but I hated lying to Angie. "Nothing— plain and simple. *Nothing.*"

She stared at me for what must have been ten seconds. "All right. But I won't go through this again. I won't lose you now that we have a family."

I hugged her. "You'll never lose me, Angie. I promise."

CHAPTER 17

MEMORIES

Brooklyn, New York

The killer waited outside Debbie's building. He knew what time she got off and he knew her routine. He followed her to the cleaners, watched her pick up her clothes. Then he followed her to the grocery store, keeping out of sight while she filled her cart with fruits and a few veggies. She went home afterward.

He stopped a block from her house. Sipping coffee, he walked down the street, careful to stay out of sight. Debbie waited for her lover, and when he arrived, they went up to her apartment. The doorman saw them. Maybe some neighbors, assuming they were attentive. The killer went to a diner and took his time eating, watching. When the lights went off in her apartment, he paid his tab and left the diner.

He circled the block, headed north and circled the next block, ending up on the back side of her building. The window on the bottom floor was still unlocked. He slid it open, climbed onto the sill, used a cloth to wipe his shoes, then slipped inside, careful not to disturb anything. Once inside, he made his way to the front door. He listened carefully, heard nothing, and let the door creak open. Then he moved quickly down the hall and into the stairwell. The elevator would be too risky.

The killer exited the stairwell on Debbie's floor, moved quietly to her door, and listened. After thirty seconds of no sound he opened the door. As suspected, they were in the bedroom. A nylon stocking covered his head and face. Latex gloves on his hands. He tiptoed down the hall, stopped five feet short of the room, and listened to them make love.

Debbie moaned. The killer risked a peek. The guy's head was between her legs. She was holding him there, her legs spread. Feelings stirred in his pants, a desire to join them, partake of the forbidden fruit…but he'd leave that for another time. Tonight was for a different purpose. He rubbed himself through his pants, not wanting to risk leaving evidence. He didn't have long to wait. Soon she was moaning again.

Now.

The killer stepped quietly into the room. Mr. Lover was buried in her cunt. She was writhing. A shot to the back of the head took care of Mr. Lover. She opened her eyes and screamed. A shot to the head took care of her too. The killer wasted no time. He shot her once in the vagina, positioned Lover's head back where it had been, shot him in the ass, then looked around.

After a moment of reflection, he began the tedious process of cleaning up, paying special attention to the bedroom. As messy as her apartment was, it took a long time. The bathroom was worse than filthy, and her toothbrush looked as if she scrubbed the toilet with it. When the killer finished, he checked the hallway, left the apartment, and exited the same way he entered. The police would have a lot to think about with this one.

CHAPTER 18

NO ANSWER

Bruce called Debbie's cell phone three times but got no answer. He called work and her assistant picked up. "Cindy, is Debbie in? This is Bruce."

"I was getting ready to call you. She never showed. I'm concerned because she had a meeting, and she never misses meetings."

"I already tried her cell."

"I did too. And her home phone. No answer."

"I'm going over there now," Bruce said. "I'll let you know."

"All right. Be sure to call me."

Bruce arrived at her apartment in twenty minutes. The doorman was outside, a smile on his round face.

"Jack, have you seen Debbie this morning?"

Jack seemed to give the question thought then shook his head. "Not this morning, Mr. Stewart. Have you called her?"

"Three times. Something must be wrong." Bruce looked at his watch, then a few seconds later he looked again. "I'm going up," he said. "She never misses work."

Jack looked around, nervous. "I'm supposed to stay here. I…"

"No need for you to come up. I've got keys."

Jack asked one of the tenants exiting the building. "Can you watch the door for a few minutes? I have to check on something."

After the man agreed, Jack grabbed Bruce's arm. "All right, let's go."

They exited the elevator and walked quickly to her apartment. Bruce knocked hard on Debbie's door. Several times. "I'm opening it," he said, and took out his key. He turned the bottom lock, twisted the handle, and went in. "Odd. She didn't have the deadbolt on."

As soon as he stepped inside he stopped. "Something's wrong." He headed toward the bedroom. "Debbie, are you here?"

Jack followed.

When Bruce reached the bedroom he pushed the door open and froze. "Jesus Christ! Oh my God." He started for the bed, but Jack shouted.

"Don't, Mr. Stewart! Wait for the police."

Bruce stopped, staring at the two bodies. He put his hands to his face and cried.

Jack took him by the arm and led him out. Bruce plopped on the floor, leaning against the wall. "Call the police. I'll wait here for them."

"Don't go back in there, Mr. Stewart. I'll get a relief and come back."

***

Frankie grabbed his favorite pair of Moreschi shoes, his favorite Zegna pants and a shirt to match. He wanted to look good for Alex; besides, he figured he better enjoy the nice clothes while it lasted. With Alex around, he wouldn't be able to afford the good stuff much longer. Damn shame about that. Of course he could always start taking bribes.

"Hey, Ace, you almost ready?"

"Been ready, FD. Just waitin' on you."

Frankie came out a minute later. "Let's go."

"You look like you're going on a date."

"I'm taking my best buddy to school. What's more important?"

"This the school we looked at the other day?"

Frankie heard the hesitation in his voice. "St. Edwards, yeah. You okay with that?"

Alex shrugged. "Sure. Guess so."

Frankie knelt next to him. "How about telling me what 'guess so' is all about. What's bothering you?"

Alex looked at Frankie as if he were from Mars. "New school, FD. That's what's bothering me. The new kid gets his ass kicked, gets made fun of, everything."

"I know it's tough. I can't even imagine how tough it is nowadays, but you're tough too. You can make it. And you've always got me to call."

"You gonna come arrest them when they mess with me?"

"Damn straight. Cuff 'em too. Right in the hall."

Alex laughed. "Okay, let's go. I'm all right."

Frankie tousled his hair. "You're better than all right. And don't forget about your name."

"I know—it's Alex Donovan."

"Just like we practiced. You hear somebody say 'Hey, Greene' ignore them. Hard as it might be, you have to forget. Your name is Donovan now."

"So when somebody asks me what nationality I am, I can say Irish?"

Frankie laughed. "Damn straight. Irish it is. Black Irish."

It took almost half an hour to get to school. Frankie would have to do something about the transportation if it took this long every day. Fifteen minutes after they got there, he had introduced Alex to Father Murphy. As they talked, Frankie's phone rang.

"Donovan."

"We've got more bodies."

"Same guy?"

"Same guy," Lou said.

"Where?"

Lou gave him the address.

"I'll meet you there. I'm over at St. Edwards."

Father Murphy was still talking with Alex.

"I know new schools are tough, but don't worry. I won't let anything happen to a fellow Irishman."

"You got a body, FD?"

"Two of them."

"Better go catch them bad guys," Alex said, then gave Frankie a big hug. "Thanks. And don't worry. I'll be okay."

"I know you will. See you tonight."

***

Frankie jumped in the car and headed toward the scene. Lou and Sherri were already there when he entered the apartment. The first thing that struck him was the cleanliness. And the smell of bleach. Frankie hated chemical smells.

Lou walked over. "Yeah, I see the look on your face. Clean, right? A little too clean. I'd say the killer spent hours in here."

Frankie noticed a guy sitting on the sofa, staring at the wall. He cocked his head in that direction.

Lou pulled Frankie aside. "Debbie Parnell and a Mr. Robert Elliott are dead in the bedroom. This is her place." Lou gestured to the guy on the couch. "Bruce Stewart is her fiancé. He found the bodies."

"He do it?"

"I don't think so. The doorman was with him when he found the bodies, but we haven't asked much of either of them."

"Where's the doorman?"

"Went to the can. He'll be right back."

"Let's get the fiancé over with. I don't want him here when Kate comes. Besides, I want to experience it just like he did."

Frankie walked over to the couch, pulled a chair from the kitchen table and sat. He handed the man a card. "Mr. Stewart, I'm Detective Frankie Donovan. I understand you've met Detectives Mazzetti and Miller."

He nodded.

"I know this is a difficult time, Mr. Stewart, but if you could walk us through what happened, it might help."

"I called her this morning but didn't get an answer. I called several more times and then I called Cindy. Cindy is her assistant at work. When she told me that Debbie hadn't called in and had missed a meeting I knew something was wrong. That's when I came here."

"Why were you calling her?"

"I call her *every* morning. To say hello, see if she needs a ride to work, that kind of thing."

"Where do you work, Mr. Stewart?"

"Fortunately, Detective, I don't have to work. When I do, it's usually from home. Sometimes I volunteer helping young companies get going, or with charitable organizations."

"I see. And so you came here after calling her work…"

"Yes. Jack…" Bruce gestured toward the doorman who had returned, "Jack was outside, and I asked him to come up with me. When Debbie didn't answer, we went in."

Frankie was writing. "Hold on. You said you went in…"

"I have a key."

Bruce started to go on, but stopped. "It was odd, Detective, but the deadbolt wasn't locked. I remember thinking that strange at the time."

"Debbie was a cautious person?"

Bruce shook his head. "On the contrary, she was neglectful about most things, but she *did* lock her door. She got into a habit of that after an incident a few years ago when she was mugged."

He stood. "I need some water."

"I'll get it," Sherri said.

"Was Debbie always this meticulous about her apartment?"

"Good Lord, no. Far from it. She liked things clean but she never kept them this clean. I mean, when she came to my house she would complain if it was dirty, but her place was no prize. Nothing like what you see here."

"How clean *did* she keep it?"

"Like I said, clean enough. But Debbie wasn't averse to sweeping a little dirt under the carpet if you know what I mean."

Frankie watched Bruce's expressions, looking for any sign of something out of place. "I don't. Explain."

Bruce raised his head staring at the ceiling fan. "One time a friend was coming for a visit. Debbie asked me to help her get the apartment ready. She did dishes while I vacuumed. She told me not to move the furniture, just go around it. And she didn't dust inside the lampshades, or do the blades on the ceiling fan. She *never* cleaned the tile in the shower. A good spray was all it ever got." Bruce sipped on a bottled water. "Not that I'm one to talk. She accused me of being a neat freak, and I'll admit, I'm a little compulsive about things being in order, but nothing like what you have here."

Bruce leaned forward, hands on his knees. "You know, there was something else. Her keys were missing. She came back from a business trip last week and said she couldn't find her keys. I told her to ask Jack to have the locks changed."

Frankie looked to the doorman.

Jack lowered his head. "I called, but…they haven't done it yet."

Lou walked over to Jack. "So she told you about the missing keys and you didn't get the locks changed?"

"I'm sorry." He looked to Bruce. "Mr. Stewart, I am *really* sorry. I called them but didn't think it was an emergency." When no one said anything, Jack continued. "People lose their keys all the time."

"You couldn't have known," Bruce said, then looked at Frankie. "Another thing. She said there was spyware on her computer."

"Spyware?"

"Yes. She discovered it while she was out of town. But it was her personal computer. If someone got in, they could have gotten her passwords, anything.

"And she said someone from work was bothering her."

"Bothering her how?"

"Some guy was always trying to hit on her. When I suggested she report him she laughed. She said *everyone* tried hitting on her." Bruce buried his head in his hands and cried. "I can't believe she's gone."

Frankie waited a while before going on. "Mr. Stewart, did you know she was seeing another man?"

Bruce closed his eyes and shook his head. "No, Detective. I didn't. But even if I had, I wouldn't have killed her, if that's what you're thinking. I loved Debbie."

"Were you two having troubles?"

"Apparently we were, but I didn't know it. She was the kind of woman who loved attention from men. She enjoyed flirting." He stopped for a moment. "I guess part of me liked that. Another part of me was jealous. Most of the girls I went out with before Debbie had to be plied with martinis before you could kiss them. Debbie...she was different. *Quite different.*"

Frankie leaned back, gave him space. "I'm sorry, Mr. Stewart, but I have to ask this. Where were you last night?"

"Home. By myself. I wanted to come over, but she...she said she was tired, and that she had to prepare for a meeting." A few more tears came. "I didn't even call because I didn't want to disturb her."

"Mr. Stewart, would you mind giving us a DNA sample?"

"On principle I object, but if you're telling me it will help catch the guy who did this, I'll do it."

"I don't know yet," Frankie said. "Tell you what. Let's wait. If we need it, I'll let you know."

"You've got my number. Just call."

Frankie heard Dave Shu's voice in the hall. Dave worked for Kate at the ME's office. *Good. Maybe she's not coming. I don't need her and Sherri here together.*

"Okay, Mr. Stewart, I think we have all we need for now. We may have more questions for you later. And you have my card. If you think of anything, call me."

Bruce got up. "I will. Thank you."

After Bruce left, Frankie turned to the doorman. "Jack, right?"

"Jack Corrigan."

"Jack, tell me about this morning, and last night."

"Mr. Stewart told it straight, sir. As far as last night, Ms. Parnell came home with a...different gentleman than Mr. Stewart. I think it's the guy in the bedroom, but I didn't stay to get a good look."

"And you came into the room with Mr. Stewart? He was her fiancé?"

Jack looked to the side then down. "*He* thought so."

"What's that supposed to mean?"

"I don't know."

"You said it for a reason. This is a *murder* investigation, remember."

"I just mean that she often came home with other men."

"And Bruce didn't know about it?"

The doorman shook his head again. "As I said, he was a nice guy. I never told him. I doubt he knew."

"Anything else unusual?"

Jack shook his head. "Not that I can say, except…"

"Except?"

"Last night I thought I saw one of Ms. Parnell's other…friends driving by."

"What time?"

"After dark. I don't remember exactly."

"Do you know him?"

"Not by name, but he's been here with her before."

"And it wasn't Mr. Stewart?"

He shook his head vigorously. "No, I'd recognize him. This guy had blond hair and he—"

Sherri stepped forward. "Take a look at this picture, Mr. Corrigan."

He pointed at the phone. "That's him. That's the guy. No doubt about it."

"But he didn't come inside?" Sherri asked.

"Definitely not. I'd have seen him."

"Okay," Frankie said. "You can go, but call us if you think of anything."

Lou grabbed Sherri's phone and stared at the picture. "Looks like our boy Chad better have a *damn good* alibi this time."

Frankie waited for Corrigan to get out of earshot. He turned to Miller, anger in his voice. "Didn't I tell you earlier about that shit? You can't ask for an ID based on one picture. Get a photo spread and do it right next time."

CHAPTER 19

SCENE OF THE CRIME

Frankie headed toward the bedroom. "Let's take a look at the bodies before it gets too close to lunch."

"You might skip lunch today," Miller said. "It's not pretty."

"None of them are pretty."

"It's awfully damn clean in this apartment," Sherri said. "My place hasn't been this clean since I moved in, and maybe not then."

"My place has never been this clean," Lou said. "And never will, unless my wife dies before I do."

"Are you trying to tell me that you keep a cleaner house than she does?" Sherri asked.

"I didn't say that. But if she wasn't there, I'd eat out and hire a maid. There'd be nobody to mess it up."

Frankie walked into the bedroom, shaking his head. "No doubt it's the same guy. Look at that position."

Debbie was lying flat on her back, legs spread wide. Elliott's head was buried in her crotch.

"I think our guy is obsessed with cunnilingus," Lou said, then he looked at Frankie. "Where were *you* last night?"

Sherri rubbed Frankie's back and cooed, "Oh, Frankie, I didn't know."

Dave Shu came into the room with Kate. She pushed by them, shooting daggers at Frankie. "Donovan," she said.

Frankie damn near swallowed his tongue. She *would* have to come in just then. Goddamnit.

"Hey, Kate. How's it going? Hey, Dave."

Dave placed his bag on the floor. "I'll get the bathroom."

Kate knelt next to the guy, examining the head wound. "One shot to the back of the head. Small caliber. I doubt he saw it coming." She slid his head to the side. "One shot to her vagina. Same as last time." She went back to inspecting the dead guy. "One to his rectum. Say what you want about our killer, he's consistent."

"Why shoot them there?" Sherri asked.

"I'd say he's pissed," Lou said. "This has sexual pervert all over it."

Kate stood. "I don't think so. I won't know until we get them back to my place, but I don't think there was any penetration. No semen. Unless he's ejaculating and then cleaning it up, there's no indication it's sexual."

"Jealousy," Frankie said. "Or revenge."

Kate looked at him. "I'd say that's more like it." She moved up to the wound on Debbie, leaned down to examine it. "Did you get Alex settled in?"

Frankie smiled. "Father Murphy took care of him. I'm sure he'll introduce him to some of the kids and make him feel comfortable."

"He all set with the Donovan name?"

"I think so."

"Good." Kate looked at the wound on Debbie again. "Same thing—one shot, small caliber. I'd say he stood at the bottom of the bed, shot the guy, then her. Probably only took a few seconds."

"So she might have had time to get off a scream," Lou said.

"Possibly," Kate said. "It's another thing entirely if someone admits to having heard it."

Dave came back to the room. "That bathroom is clean enough to eat from. The drains have no hair. The hairbrush has no hair. I doubt the toothbrush has DNA on it."

"She couldn't have kept it that clean," Sherri said.

"It wasn't her. This place has no prints anywhere. Not the vanity, the mirror, the toilet, shower, bathroom sink, nothing. Whoever did this knew how to clean and he must have spent a hell of a lot of time here."

Lou put an unlit smoke in his mouth and pretended to puff on it. "So other than being useless, how's it going, Dave?"

Dave stared at him. "No Asian jokes today?"

"Christ's sake, I'm not like that. Give me a break."

He lowered his head. "Sorry, Lou."

Frankie sighed, as if impatient. His stance and the tone in his voice showed it as well. "You're sure it wasn't her?"

"Come here, Donovan. Look at this." Dave Shu led Frankie to the bathroom and lifted the drain stopper in the sink. "Check this out. No hair, no dirt, no grime. *Nobody,* and I mean *nobody* cleans like this. The killer did this as sure as I'm from China."

"What province are you from?" Lou asked.

"How do I know?"

"Just thought you might be up on your ancestry, that's all."

"So if I told you I was from the Hubei province, would you know where that was?"

"Hell no. They all sound the same to me." Lou and Sherri laughed like hell and wouldn't quit until Dave joined in.

"All right, Lou, you got me good on that one. But watch out; I'll be after you."

"Frankie," Kate called.

Frankie went to the bedroom. "What's up?"

She picked up a piece of paper with tweezers. "This was under the woman's ass." She placed it in an evidence bag and set it on the bed.

Debbie, Debbie, what a girl.
Her pussy tasted like cinnamon swirl.
Don't take my word; she's on the bed.
If you don't mind eating the dead.
Want to know what happened?
Ask her man.
First he killed her
Then he ran.
Catch him.
Catch him.
If you can.

"So the guy *is* obsessed with cunnilingus," Lou said.

Frankie almost choked. If Miller said anything…He turned to her. "Canvas the floor above us. Make note of each apartment, who you talked to, and who you didn't."

"Okay," she said, but she glared at him as she left.

Lou picked at Frankie's shirt. "I meant to say it earlier, but don't you look dapper today."

"Dapper?" Frankie said. "Did you say dapper, Mazzetti?"

"I think I did."

"Nobody says dapper anymore."

Kate was back on the floor, kneeling beside the man's body. "I like the word; in fact, I may start using it myself."

Dave Shu came into room. "This guy didn't miss a thing."

"Actually he did," Kate said. She was on her knees using tweezers to pluck something off the floor. She held it up for them to see. "This was under Mr. Elliott's knee."

"A hair?" Frankie asked.

Lou leaned forward to get a closer look. "Please tell me it's blonde."

"Just like Goldilocks," Kate said and dropped it into the evidence bag.

Dave Shu rubbed the top of Mazzetti's head. "I know it's not from you. I would have noticed it missing."

"A Chinese comedian. That's all we need."

Kate moved Elliott's other leg, looked under it. "Keep at him, Dave. Mazzetti deserves everything he gets."

One of the other techs came in from the kitchen. "You won't believe this. The guy wiped down every piece of silverware and all of the glasses. I'm not through with the dishes, but I'm guessing we'll find the same."

"Son of a bitch," Frankie said. "He must have spent the night here."

"Wouldn't take as long as you think," Kate said. "He could run through silverware in a few minutes. Dishes and glasses a little longer, but not much. If he's worried about pots and pans, it's basically handles." Kate stood and let the tech take more photos. "The question, Donovan, is why he did it."

"Guess we've still got a lot to figure out."

Kate moved to the other side of the bed and examined Debbie's wound again. "You notice the difference here? He rushed this."

"How so?"

She looked at Mazzetti and Frankie. "At the first one, he stuffed socks in their mouths and then posed them. He took time shooting each one exactly where he wanted to. This is different. No socks. No posing. He came in here and shot them in the act. From the looks of the angle, he didn't even wait until he got behind Elliott. It looks as if he shot him while still walking in. And he shot Parnell from the foot of the bed, where he stood. At the first scene, both shots were pointblank range."

"More rage on this one?"

Kate shook her head. "I don't know. Rage. Jealousy. Something. It's like he couldn't wait to shoot these two. My guess is that the shots to the rectum and vagina were afterthoughts. I'll let you know when I'm done."

Kate and Dave packed their equipment and left the room.

Lou scratched his head and sucked on a dry cigarette. "Guess we've got work to do, Donovan."

"Frankie, can I see you a minute?" Kate asked.

"Be right back, Lou."

Frankie walked down the hallway. Kate stood at the front door.

"What's up?"

She reached up and kissed him on the lips, then whispered, "When you're dressed up like this you make me want to go home early."

Frankie kissed her back. "Those bodies aren't going anywhere."

"Like you'd do that." She slapped his butt. "See you tonight. We're good."

Frankie grabbed her and kissed her softly. "You know I love you, right?"

"Quit saying that. You're scaring me," she said, but she smiled. "I'll pick Alex up. Don't be too late."

"See you," Frankie said. "Thanks."

Lou had the cigarette lit by the time Frankie got back to the room. "Fuck, Mazzetti, you can't smoke in here."

"Who's gonna complain? Not her."

"All right. Fuck." Frankie took out a smoke and lit it. "We both might as well poison the place."

"CSU is gone. Who's gonna complain?" Lou grabbed a teacup from the kitchen and used it for an ashtray. "Kate bust your balls about Miller?"

Frankie raised his eyebrows. "I figured she would, but no, she was great. Even hinted at a romantic evening."

"Be careful. She may have a pair of scissors in the bed."

"What?"

"You know, like Sharon Stone in that movie. I saw it the other night."

"That movie is ancient. You just saw it?"

"Kind of. It might have been the twentieth time, but yeah, I just saw it."

"You know she's damn near as old as you."

"Yeah, but she looks better," Lou said. "And besides, I don't dream of her as she looks now, only what she looked like back then."

Miller came back in the room. "Stop dreaming, boys. Focus on the case."

"What did you learn from upstairs?" Frankie asked.

"Anybody see anything? Hear anything? Smell anything?" Lou asked.

"Nobody ever hears anything," Sherri said.

"Don't forget where we are," Lou said. "Folks don't talk. They don't see things, or hear things, or even think things. It's not good business."

"And you agree with that?"

"I didn't say I agree, just that I understand."

Sherri frowned and shook her head. "I don't."

Mazzetti put his cigarette out in the teacup. "Doesn't matter if you agree. It's the way things work. We've got to live with that and find ways around it."

"So did you learn *anything*?" Frankie asked.

Sherri flipped open her notepad. "Four people either weren't home or didn't answer. Six heard nothing. One thought she heard a scream."

"Did she call it in?"

"No way. She thought it was the TV."

Frankie paced, jiggling his change. "This guy cleaned every fucking thing in the house. Even the goddamn silverware and glasses. Kate had the right question—why?" He pointed to Sherri and Lou. "Think about what Kate said. Why would the killer clean everything. He couldn't have been in all those places. Possibly the bathroom if you want to stretch things, but no way the kitchen, and certainly not the silverware drawer or the glass cabinet. So why clean them?"

"Because he's been here before," Sherri said. Her voice rose, and she smiled for the first time since Kate left. "He's been in this apartment before and he doesn't want us to know it."

"Like Chad Benning," Lou said.

Frankie nodded. "All right, let's finish canvasing. How about you and Miller take the floor below. I'll get the first floor."

Frankie took the elevator to the ground floor. The first two apartments yielded nothing, the third worse than nothing—an old guy who had conspiracy theories in abundance—and at doors four and five no one answered. Frankie made note to check back with them. He knocked on the door of the next apartment. A middle-aged woman dressed in jeans and a white blouse opened the door.

"My name is Detective Donovan. I'm investigating an incident upstairs."

"I don't know anything," she said, and started to shut the door.

Frankie moved closer and used his foot to stop the door from closing. "If you could just take a minute."

She looked up at him through a pair of glasses that looked as if they'd been purchased in the 80s. "I already told you. I don't know anything." Then she shoved hard on the door until the lock clicked.

Frankie heard a dead bolt slide into place. He shook his head and moved on. She might have held the secrets to the universe, but he wasn't staying around to pry them out of her.

Lou and Sherri were waiting for him outside. "We locked up," he said.

"Get anything?"

"Nothing," Sherri said. "You?"

"The same kind of nothing as you," Frankie said.

"What now?" Sherri asked.

Frankie pulled out his phone. "Hang on. I'm calling Stewart." He dialed a number on his cell, waiting while it rang.

Bruce Stewart answered after four or five rings. "Hello."

It sounded as if he'd been crying. "Sorry to bother you, Mr. Stewart. This is Detective Donovan."

"Did you find something?"

"Not yet. We're still questioning people, but I need to know where Debbie worked."

"Anderson, Bergen and Silverstein."

"Okay, thank you. And again, I am so sorry for your loss. We'll be in touch if anything develops."

Frankie hung up and turned to Lou and Sherri.

"Judging from that smile, you got something," Lou said.

"Guess where Ms. Parnell worked."

"Don't tell me it's the same building," Sherri said.

"Not just the same building, the same company as Mr. Chad Benning."

"Son of a bitch!" Lou high-fived Sherri.

Frankie shook his head. "That's not how you do it anymore, Lou. You've got to bump fists, like this."

"I'll tell you what I'm gonna bump—that fuckin' pervert Chad Benning. Bump him to hell and back."

"Let's go get him," Sherri said.

CHAPTER 20

YOU CAN'T HIDE A SECRET

Sherri said, "Frankie, how about if I take Krenshaw and show Izzy the picture of Chad, while you guys handle Parnell?"

"Make sure you have an array of photos," Frankie said. "Or do a sequential. That's even better." He turned to Lou. "You handle Parnell, I'm going to pester Benning."

"He lawyered up. Remember?"

"His coworkers didn't. I can ask them all the questions I want."

"Ooh, that'll piss him off," Sherri said, and then she reached over and snatched the cigarette from Lou's mouth. She stepped into the elevator, exited on the fifth floor and made her way to Perkins and Mischa. She showed the receptionist her badge. "I'm here to see Izzy."

The young girl smiled. "She just walked in a few minutes ago. I'll call her."

Izzy made her appearance with coffee in hand. She was shorter than Sherri remembered, but she owned a big voice. "Detective, I didn't expect to see you again."

Sherri opened the folder. "I have a few pictures. I want you to see if you recognize any of them."

Izzy went through them one at a time, shaking her head as she passed each one. When she hit the sixth one, she stared for a long time. "I've never seen any of them."

"You're sure?" Sherri wanted so badly for Izzy to finger Benning.

"As sure as I can be. I might have passed them on the street or in the building, but I don't know them. Why, do you think one of them did it?"

"We're not certain of anything yet. It's early in the investigation."

"How did her husband take it?"

Sherri lowered her voice. "We're not allowed to comment on the case while it's still active."

Izzy flushed. "I'm sorry. I should have known."

"Is there anyone else we can talk to that might have known Ms. Krenshaw?"

"Besides me, she didn't have many friends. If I think of anything I'll call. I still have your card."

Sherri got up to leave. "Great. And thanks again for the help."

***

Lou got off at fifteen and went to the receptionist where Parnell worked. "I'm Detective Mazzetti. I need to speak with Ms. Parnell's assistant."

The girl at the desk was barely more than a teenager, but she handled herself well. "That would be Cindy. I'll have her come right down."

Cindy showed up in less than five minutes, surprising Lou. "I'm Detective Lou Mazzetti, I'm here—"

Cindy nodded. "You must be here about Debbie. Come with me." She turned and started down a long hallway, her heels clicking loudly on the tile floor.

Lou wasn't surprised that she knew about the murder. News travels like wildfire in an office building. "Who told you about it?"

"Bruce Stewart, her fiancé."

"He called?"

"No, I called him to see if he knew where Debbie was. She was supposed to be at a meeting this morning and it was unlike her to miss. Especially without calling." Cindy opened the door to a small conference room and sat in the first chair, hands on lap. "I still can't believe she's gone."

Lou noticed she didn't seem to be that upset. "You didn't like her much, did you?"

Cindy scrunched up her face and stared. "I might not have been invited to her cocktail parties, but I respected her work." She looked at the door, then back to Lou. "The thing is, around here they frown on mourning. On anything that makes a person miss work. We don't even get off for deaths of in-laws except under special circumstances."

Cindy had a mature voice. It matched her age and looks, and the way she wore her hair, as if she just walked off a movie set from a 1970s TV show.

"Sorry," Lou said. "I get cynical sometimes. And grumpy. Even my wife tells me that." That brought a smile to Cindy's face.

"We all get that way at times," she said.

"What can you tell me about Ms. Parnell? What was she like?"

Cindy reached behind her and grabbed a bottle from a tray. "Water?"

"No thanks." *What happened to offering people coffee? And an ashtray.*

"Debbie was into two things—work and men."

"That sounds a little odd considering she had a fiancé."

"Fiancé my ass. Bruce was too good for her. She was a…well, in my day we would have called her a loose woman."

"That's polite," Lou said.

"She led that poor man around on a leash. He treated her like gold and she…well, I think you know what I mean."

"So you really *didn't* like her."

"I know it sounds like that," Cindy said, "but I did like her. She had a great sense of humor, was intelligent, and, for all of her faults, she treated me like gold. She even shared her bonuses with me." Cindy focused on Lou's eyes. She seemed more intense. "Let me tell you, *that* is a rare thing, especially around here."

"Strange woman," Lou said.

"Yes, she was."

"Did Bruce Stewart know about her flings?"

"Not as far as I know. I think it would have killed him. He doted on her."

"I have to agree with you on that. He seems like a nice guy." Lou wrote a few things in his notepad. "How about Robert Elliott. Did you know him?"

"Is that who was with her?"

Lou looked around. "I shouldn't have said. Keep this quiet, will you?"

"No worry, Detective. I knew Robert by name only. He used to work here but left before I arrived. About five years ago."

As Lou wrote more notes, Cindy continued.

"I'll tell you who's no good—Chad Benning."

Lou perked up. "Chad Benning?"

"He works upstairs in marketing."

"Why do you say he's no good?"

"He treats women like dirt. And Debbie was no different. I think she was getting away from him, though."

"She used to see him?"

"For about a year."

"And what makes you think she was breaking it off?"

Cindy leaned close and whispered. "Last night, as I was leaving, Chad stormed into her office. I heard them arguing, and her telling him she was tired. I left after that but when I was waiting for the elevator, Chad rushed past me and got into a car going up. I saw him punch the buttons and holler 'bitch' before the doors closed."

"This was last night?"

"Definitely."

"Okay, Cindy. Thanks. You've been *very* helpful. Don't tell anyone we talked and remember, don't mention the other guy's name."

"I won't."

"One last thing. Did Debbie keep things neat and clean?"

"That depends on who you ask."

"What do you mean?"

"She kept her desk and work area immaculate, and she insisted I do the same. I'll show you if you want."

Lou brushed it off. "You said it depends…"

"Yes. I'd been to her apartment a few times to pick things up. It was *not* the same. It wasn't filthy, mind you, but it was far from clean."

"How?"

"Dishes in the sink, floors needing vacuuming, the place hadn't been dusted in weeks, clothes on the floor, maybe a glass or two on the tables."

Lou nodded, taking notes.

"But she liked her men to be clean," Cindy said.

"Tell me about it," Lou said.

"Everybody she dated was a 'neat freak' as Debbie called them. I think she liked that, as a balance to herself."

"Stewart, too?"

"I can't say for sure, but she always called him a neat freak. Chad Benning, too. And one other guy she dated."

"Thanks," Lou said, then handed her a card before leaving to meet Frankie.

"Detective?"

"Yes?"

Cindy whispered, "If you want to know more about Chad, you should talk to Lisa Oberson." She pointed to a corner office. "She's in today. You might find it helpful."

Lou smiled. "I will. Thanks."

He waited for Sherri; having Sherri in the room with Lisa might help. Five minutes into the conversation he knew he'd been right and let Sherri do the talking.

She scooted her chair close to Lisa's, crossed her legs, put her notepad away, and looked at Lisa with a big smile. "What can you tell me about Chad Benning?"

Lisa looked away. "Nothing, really. We only went out a few times."

Sherri didn't say anything for a moment. "I heard you dated for a few *months,* not a few times."

Lisa shrugged. She tried to laugh it off. "It seemed like years."

"Good years or bad ones?"

"I don't know. Some of both."

Sherri sat back in the chair. "I always find that I tend to look at past relationships as one way or the other—either it was good and I'm glad it was part of my life, or it wasn't good, and I wish I had been smart enough to never start it."

Lisa stayed quiet for a moment, then, "I guess if you put it that way, Chad would fall into the latter category. I *definitely* wish I'd never gone out with him."

"Why?"

Lisa leaned forward. "Is this confidential? Because I have to work here. I can't…"

"It's absolutely confidential."

Lisa still seemed hesitant, but Sherri waited her out. Eventually, Lisa continued.

"Let me put it this way, he almost raped two women in marketing. I guess technically it was sexual assault. One of them was going to file charges, but he talked her out of it."

"Don't you women talk to each other?" Sherri asked. "You work together. How does this information not get shared?"

Lisa lowered her head. "Part jealousy. Part embarrassment. Every woman thinks she's the one who can tame him." A fake smile popped onto her face. "I thought the same thing. 'I'll be the one. I'm different.'"

"But you weren't," Sherri said.

Lisa raised her eyebrows and shook her head. "Not even close."

"Tell me about it."

"Chad gets real offended if you break it off with him."

"'Real offended.' How?"

"I don't know…"

Sherri leaned closer and whispered. "I think you do know. Tell me. It will stay between us."

Lisa looked at Lou, then leaned toward Sherri. "When I told him I didn't want to see him anymore…he started stalking me. I got phone calls in the middle of the night from unknown numbers, and anonymous notes left on my car, suggesting I leave town. Things like that."

Sherri let her have a few seconds. "He never did anything to you, though? Physically, I mean."

Lisa shook her head. "Nothing like that. But he scared me. I thought about quitting. I even called a headhunter to see if they could find me a new job."

"What made you stay?"

"I asked for a transfer within the building. Now I'm in a different department, on a different floor, and I have no dealings with him. It was enough to put a stop to it."

"Okay, thanks," Sherri said. "This helps a lot. And don't worry; I won't tell anyone."

***

Frankie rode the elevator to seventeen, walked through the double-doors—wondering how much the etched glass had cost—then flashed his badge to the receptionist, Rhonda, according to her nameplate. "I need to speak to Ms. Parnell's boss."

Rhonda looked at his name again, "That would be Danette Barrows. I'll call her."

Frankie paced while he waited.

"Would you like coffee, Detective?"

He looked up at the young woman behind the desk, cute as a button and a warm smile to boot. "No thanks. Had plenty today."

Barrows came out a few minutes later. Well-dressed, trim, short hair. The whole package spelled business, as did her demeanor.

"I was told you wanted to see me, Detective."

Frankie would have shook her hand, but it wasn't offered. "Is there someplace private we can talk?"

"What is this concerning?"

Frankie leaned close. "We're investigating a homicide. Debbie Parnell was murdered last night."

Her eyes went wide, but other than that, her face didn't register much emotion. "I heard about that. I can't believe it." She looked around, almost as if she wanted to ensure that no one heard. "There's a room down the hall we can use." She turned to Rhonda. "I'll be in conference room A if you need me."

Frankie followed her. He waited until she was seated before speaking. "I'm going to need to speak to some of the employees. In particular, anyone who might have been close to her."

Danette nodded. "Of course. Where did this happen?"

"At her apartment. Another gentleman was also killed."

Her eyebrows raised. "Bruce?"

"No. Mr. Stewart wasn't there. Do you know him?"

A shake of the head. "I've met him once or twice. That's the extent of it. He seemed nice." She seemed to be giving thought to something. "Was anything stolen? Her computer? Her phone?"

Jesus Christ, she's worried about company information. "Her work computer and phone were found at the apartment, but her personal laptop was missing. Our forensic people are going over the other items now."

"Detective, there is sensitive information on them."

"Trust me, none of us have the money to buy stock even if we had the tips."

She laughed.

"Tell me what you can about Chad Benning," Frankie said.

"You think Chad had something to do with this?"

"We don't know what to think yet. Can you tell me about Ms. Parnell and Mr. Benning? Anything might help."

"You mean, were they seeing each other?"

"That would be a start."

"I'm not sure, but it wouldn't surprise me. Debbie wasn't the kind of woman to stick to one man, and I think every man in the building was chasing her."

"She *was* pretty."

"Pretty is only half of it. You'd have to have known her. She was sexy as hell." Barrows stopped and looked at Frankie. "Don't get any wild ideas about relations between Debbie and me. I'm not a lesbian, but I'm confident enough in my sexuality to say she was a *very* sexy woman. Debbie had the whole package—if you know what I mean—looks, attitude, dress…" Barrows glanced at Frankie, her eyes running up and down his body. "You look as if you know about that." She smiled, then added, "And no, I'm not making a play for you."

"Damn."

She laughed again.

"Ms. Barrows, did you know Robert Elliott?"

"Is that who she was with? I'm surprised."

"Why is that?"

"Robert used to work here. They had a thing for a while but it ended quickly." She looked up at Frankie. "And no, I don't know why."

"Is there anyone else in the office she was close to, besides Mr. Benning?"

Another shake of the head. "Not that I can think of. Her assistant might know more."

Frankie stood. "I appreciate your time. And just so you know, I intend to mess with Chad's head. Don't be surprised if he gets upset."

"Nothing would please me more, Detective. I keep Chad around because he is brilliant and one of the best at what he does, but that doesn't mean it wouldn't thrill me to see him fall."

Frankie laughed this time. "Thanks again for your time," he said, and handed her a card.

***

After Frankie found out where Chad worked, he headed for the coffee room closest to him. As luck would have it Chad was there talking to a young woman, a smile on his face and bullshit rolling off his tongue. Chad had an attitude that went with his good looks. If he ever gave up marketing he could be a pimp. Frankie moved between them and faced the woman.

"Excuse me, I'm Detective Frankie Donovan, from Homicide."

The woman's eyes went wide. She stared at Frankie, then shot a look to Benning. "Homicide?"

"Yes, we're here about the Parnell murder."

Her hands flew to her face. "Debbie was murdered?"

Frankie had been watching Chad when he spoke. "It happened last night. I'm sorry. I thought the office knew already." Chad did a good job of seeming shocked—a fake gasp, his hand shot to cover his mouth. But it was fake. Frankie had done this enough to know. "You hadn't heard either, Mr. Benning?"

"How did it happen?" Chad asked.

"Same way as those other murders. Remember the ones we asked you about?"

The woman looked up. "Chad, what is he talking about? What other murders? Why is he talking to you?"

Frankie turned back to her. "We are investigating a series of sex-related murders and had questions about Mr. Benning. That's what I needed to see you about."

Chad laughed. "Joanne, he's kidding. He—"

Frankie squinted and put on his meanest look. "I'm not kidding, Joanne. I don't joke about four murders."

"I have to go to work," Joanne said, and lowered her gaze.

Frankie handed her a card. "I'll need to speak with you later."

She nodded but got away as fast as she could.

"What the hell are you trying to do?" Chad said.

"I'm sorry, Mr. Benning, I can't talk to you."

"What the hell do you mean you can't talk? You're talking to everybody else about me."

"I understand, sir, but the last time we spoke you told us you wanted a lawyer."

"You can't just go around talking to people about me."

"Actually, I can. We have to gather information, and this is one of the best ways for us to do our jobs."

"Fine. I'll talk to you."

"Are you waiving the right to an attorney?"

"Yes, I am."

Frankie pulled out his iPhone, and turned on the voice recorder. "I am recording this, Mr. Benning. Are you waiving your right to an attorney?"

He leaned in close, spoke a little louder. "This is Chad Benning, and yes, I am waiving my right to an attorney."

"Where were you last night?"

Chad looked around. "How about if we take this to my office?"

Frankie followed him in. Chad closed the door and sat behind a big—make that huge—cherry desk. "As to last night, I left work around 7:00 and went to a bar. Actually, I went to a couple of bars."

"Which bar?"

"It's down on…I don't remember, but it's not far from Debbie's place."

"Did you go to Ms. Parnell's last night?"

"No, but…"

"But what?"

"I was going to but she brushed me off."

Frankie narrowed his eyes and leaned forward. "Explain what you mean by 'she brushed you off.'"

"I don't know," Benning said. "I asked if we could get together and she said she was busy."

"Were you having an affair with Debbie Parnell?"

"No. Not really."

"Were you ever in her apartment?"

"No."

"So you didn't have a key?"

Chad balled his right hand into a fist. "No, Detective. I had no key."

"Her neighbors said they heard an argument, and they heard a woman scream." Frankie stared at Chad. "Why don't you tell me about the argument."

"What the hell are you talking about? I already told you I wasn't there."

"Did you fight about the other guy?"

Chad's jaw tightened and the vein in his forehead bulged. He was getting pissed. "I *wasn't* there."

"That's not what the doorman said." Frankie leaned across the desk, getting real close. "He *saw* you."

Chad swallowed hard. Looked away. "He must have been mistaken."

Frankie stood. "We can do this one of two ways. You can come to the station with me and answer a few questions. Or, I can arrest you and cuff you and drag you out of here like the scum you are."

"You can't arrest me." Chad wore a smirk that pissed Frankie off.

He pulled out his cuffs, walked around to where Chad sat and grabbed his left wrist. Frankie yanked it behind Chad's back, tugging a little harder than he should have. "You have the right to remain silent. You—"

A few of Chad's coworkers gathered outside his office, staring through the window.

"We don't have to do this," Chad said, his voice shaking. "I'll go with you, just take these cuffs off."

Frankie smiled as he put the cuffs away. "Let's go, Mr. Benning. We shouldn't be long."

CHAPTER 21

A FEW MORE QUESTIONS

Frankie put Chad in an interrogation room, asked if he wanted coffee, and then stepped outside. He rushed to Carol's desk. "Sweet, beautiful Carol. I need a favor."

"I keep telling you to stop being redundant. Whenever you're nice to me, it goes without saying that you need a favor. What is it this time?"

Frankie handed her Chad's cell number. "I need everything you can tell me on calls or texts he got last night—who, what, when, where…all of it. And fast."

Carol brushed her hands in the air. "Of course."

Frankie went back and stood beside Lou and Sherri, watching Chad through the glass.

"How long are you going to let him sit there?" Lou asked.

Frankie sipped on his coffee and smiled. "Until his coffee's cold."

"If I ever have to interrogate you, that's what I'm gonna do," Sherri said. "Serve you cold coffee and spray the room with cleaning chemicals before you go in."

"Might as well kill me."

"You think he'll lawyer up?" Sherri asked.

"Not a question of will he, just *when* will he."

"It's really a question of how soon you piss him off," Sherri said. "You have a way of doing that to people."

"Don't knock it," Lou said. "It takes a lot of practice, and Frankie's good at it."

"He has it perfected, I'd say."

"Yeah. Yeah. Enough bullshit from you two. I got him here, didn't I?"

"Are we going in there today?" Lou said.

Frankie stared through the window. "Waiting on the coffee."

Lou took the lid off his bottled water and poured some in Chad's coffee, then he dipped his finger in. "It's cold. Let's go in."

Sherri scrunched her face into a frown. "You dipped your *finger* in his coffee."

"Damn, and I forgot to wash my hands."

"That's cold, Mazzetti."

"It is now."

Frankie opened the door, walked over and handed Chad his coffee.

He sipped it. "That's terrible."

"Sorry," Frankie said. "We don't have the best here, but after a while, it's just caffeine."

Chad moved the cup to the side. "Let's get this over with."

Lou sat across from Chad and to his left. Frankie across to his right, with Sherri closer to the end of the table. Frankie took out his notepad, flipped a few pages while Chad watched him.

"Tell me about your relationship with Debbie Parnell."

Chad leaned forward and looked up at Frankie, attentive. "We went out a few times. Dinner, a show…"

"Then back to her place?"

He hesitated. "Maybe once…no…twice. I was there twice."

"So earlier, when you said you'd never been in her apartment…that was a lie?"

Chad sighed and looked toward the ceiling. "Yes, Detective. I lied. I didn't want you to think I had anything to do with this, and I thought it would confuse the issue."

"And the issue is…what?"

"That I didn't do it."

Frankie flipped his chair around, leaned the back against the table toward Chad, and rested his arms on the table. "I want to believe you, Chad. I honestly don't think you did this. The problem I have is that you're a goddamn liar. You've been lying to us since we met you. And when people lie to me, I presume they're guilty."

"Look—"

"No, you hear me out. This is how it works. You tell me the truth. If I think you're innocent, we cut you loose. Simple as that."

Chad nodded, but he waited a few seconds before responding. "All right. Debbie and I had a thing going for a few months, but we called it off about a month ago."

"How many times were you in her apartment?"

"I don't know. Half a dozen times. Maybe more."

"Spend the night?"

"Never. She wouldn't let me. She…"

"What?"

"She had a fiancé."

Sherri got up and walked around to face him. "While she was sleeping with you?"

He nodded. "I wasn't the one engaged."

"That makes me sick," Frankie said. "I'm going to take a piss."

He walked out and joined Morreau, watching through the glass.

"What's your take so far, Donovan?"

"Too early to tell. I like him for it, but we need more. I came out here to watch for a while. Better perspective."

"Good idea," Morreau said. "Let Mazzetti drive him crazy for a while."

Lou had a notepad in front of him. He kept silent a moment, then, without looking at Chad, said, "So you had a key."

"No, I…" Chad closed his eyes, shook his head. "Yes, I did have a key. But I wasn't there that night."

"Who else had a key?"

"I don't know. I assume her fiancé did."

"Why did you go there last night?"

Chad pursed his lips. "I explained this already. I had asked her if I could come over. She brushed me off, said she was tired."

Lou waited. He was good at letting people stew. "So why did you go over?"

"I knew she wasn't tired. Debbie had more energy than one of those damn rabbits on the battery commercials."

"Energy as in *bedroom* energy?"

Chad smiled. "That too, but no—just energy. All kinds of energy. She always wanted to be doing something. I'm telling you, she *needed* two men, maybe more. She wore me out."

Lou made a few notes. Never looked up. "So why was it you went there?"

"I've told you three times."

"Actually you haven't."

"To see if she was meeting someone else. I thought her fiancé might be coming over."

"How did you get in the building?" Lou still hadn't looked at Chad.

Chad's face reddened. He clenched his fists. "I *told* you. I did *not* go into her building. Not that night."

"He's starting to get frustrated," Morreau said.

"Lou hasn't even gotten started."

Chad fidgeted, moving his hands around, scratching his arm, rubbing his neck. "Detective, your partner asked me about the phone messages I left on that other lady's phone…I can explain that."

"I'm listening."

"I didn't leave them for her."

"So you said."

"No, I mean, that wasn't a lady's phone I called. Some guy had been calling me all week, asking about investments. He kept bugging me. I finally lost patience."

"A guy? An investor?"

"Yes."

Lou whistled. "Good story."

He let Chad sit for a moment more, then, "Did you know Debbie was seeing Robert Elliott? Did you know Robert?"

Chad looked down at his hands. "No. And no."

"You're sure you don't want a lawyer?"

"I already told you. I want to get this over with. I've got work to do, and I don't want you pestering my colleagues."

Lou looked at Frankie's notes. "Okay, so tell me why you lied at the office. You said you weren't having an affair with Debbie. That you had never been in her apartment. And that you didn't have a key to her place."

"Don't you people listen? The other detective already asked all that." He grinded his teeth, closed his eyes and opened them, then glared at Lou. "I'll say it one more time. I didn't see how it mattered. I didn't kill her, so it didn't make a difference."

"Lying to the police during an investigation can get you in a lot of trouble."

"It was harmless."

Morreau watched through the glass with Donovan. "Now he's pissing Benning off."

Carol came up behind them. "Since Donovan is out here, you must be talking about Mazzetti."

"I'm guessing that's Carol behind me," Frankie said.

"How did you know? Getting psychic on me?"

"The sunshine precedes you, eternal optimist."

"Screw you, Donovan. Goddamn half-breed dago/mick prick."

Morreau laughed. "That's what you get, Frankie. Don't mess with Carol."

"That's right," Carol said, and handed Frankie a paper. "Here's the report on Benning's phone." She started back to her desk. "And don't bother saying 'I owe you one, Carol.' You owe me too many as it is."

Frankie tapped on the door and handed the information to Mazzetti. Lou sat back down, and flipped through his notepad. "Let's see. You had a key. The doorman saw you the night of the murder. You don't remember the bars you visited." He slammed the notepad on the table, and, for the first time, looked at Chad. "Why don't you just tell me what happened? And don't forget that we already know, so no more lies."

Chad sat with his hands folded in front of him. He was silent.

"Did you fight about the other guy?"

"There was no other guy."

Lou got up and walked behind him, and set the photo from the crime scene on the table in front of Chad. "Then whose head is buried in your girlfriend's crotch?"

Chad barely reacted. "That must have been a client she brought home for dinner."

"Some dinner," Lou said.

Chad clenched his fists. "Screw you."

Lou walked some more then came up behind him again, leaned close, and whispered. "Tell me again which bars you went to the night of the murder."

"I've already told you that I don't remember, Detective. I'm sure you didn't forget."

"We're going to check all of the bars in that area." When that comment drew no reaction from Chad, Lou went back to his notebook. After a few seconds, he said, "The way I figure it, is you're using the bars to provide an alibi. When we check, we'll probably find a few drunks who remember seeing you, but they won't be able to point to a time." Lou got up and paced, then he walked over and got in Benning's face. "I'll tell you what I think, Chad. I think you went to Debbie's place, saw her with another man, and got pissed. You stopped in a few bars to establish an alibi, then went up and killed them."

Chad did an admirable job of controlling himself but the strain of the interview was evident. His face reddened, and he clenched both fists. "Ask the doorman. I never stepped foot inside that building. Not that night."

"We know how you got around that," Sherri said, and then she moved real close and let her breath run up the back of his neck. "What *really* happened? Did she like threesomes? Did you get tired of watching?"

Lou stepped in, just as close. "Was he better than you? Is that what went wrong?"

Chad jumped up and tried flipping the table. "Fuck you. I want my lawyer. Now!"

In the hall, Frankie smiled at Morreau. "It was inevitable."

Lou looked at Sherri. "I'm betting Robert was better than Chad."

"Probably bigger, too," Sherri said.

"I want a lawyer," Chad said. "Give me a polygraph. I'll prove I didn't do it."

"A polygraph? You're a marketing guy for an investment firm. Beating a poly is probably a requirement to get hired."

Frankie walked in. "What the hell happened in here?"

"Mr. Benning got upset when Sherri suggested he didn't like sharing."

Frankie walked over and stood beside him. "Mr. Benning, you have the right to remain silent. Anything you say can, and will, be used against you in a court of law."

"What are you doing? You can't arrest me."

"Don't interrupt, Mr. Benning. Let me finish. You have the right to speak to an attorney, and to have an attorney present during any questioning. If you cannot afford a lawyer, one will be provided for you at government expense. Do you understand your rights as I have read them to you?"

"Yes, of course I do."

"I want you to sign this card stating that you have been read your rights and that you understand them."

"What for? You're taping this, aren't you?"

"Sign the card, Mr. Benning."

Chad signed it. Frankie spun him around. "Hands behind your back, Mr. Benning. I'm placing you under arrest for the murders of Debbie Parnell and Robert Elliott."

"You don't need those cuffs."

"You will be transported for processing and arraignment. Your lawyer can meet you there."

"I'll get you for this."

Frankie got within inches of his face. "Is that a threat?"

Benning stared.

"Make sure he gets his call," Frankie said, and slammed the door when he left.

CHAPTER 22

NARROW THE LIST

Lou brought coffee for Sherri and Frankie. "I guess we got *that* piece of shit out of the way."

"Not for long," Frankie said. "He'll be out on bail in a couple of hours."

"We've got enough to put him away," Sherri said.

"Not even close," Frankie said. "Maybe if that hair from Parnell's apartment matches, but without that, it's weak and circumstantial. Even with that, it's weak."

"We got some pretty strong stuff in there," Lou said. "Besides, when the judge okays the search warrant, I guarantee we'll find something at his place."

"Maybe," Frankie said, and sat up straight. "Okay let's go over what we have. Miller, you've got the files. Spit it out."

Sherri opened the folder.

Lou started a list on a legal pad.

"Sandy Krenshaw called him from her cell numerous times the week before she died. He called back three times and left messages. The last voicemail is one a jury should find damaging."

"Let's hear it again," Lou said.

Sherri punched the play button on the recorder in the file.

I'm telling you for the last time. Stop fucking calling me. You got that? Don't ever call me again.

"You're right," Lou said. "That's a good piece of circumstantial."

"But we can't even prove it was her phone," Frankie said. "A good lawyer—"

"We've got her prints on it and it was found in the dumpster with her purse and the other phone. What else do you want?"

"Just saying, a good lawyer will raise reasonable doubt. He'll suggest the killer could have put her prints on the phone after she was dead. And he'll question why she only had the phone for a week." Frankie stopped, looked at Lou and Sherri. "Why *did* she only have it for a week? Did we miss something that made her get the disposable?"

"Maybe she wanted to get away from Chad," Sherri said.

Lou shook his head. "She called him from that phone. A bunch. If she were trying to get away from him, why call him on the new phone?"

Frankie was getting excited. "This is the kind of stuff that will get us answers. Let's see if we can tie her definitively to the phone."

Lou made a note. "What else have we got?"

"The doorman saw Benning at the apartment the night of the murder," Miller said. "He has no real alibi. He has access and motive."

"A weak motive," Lou said.

Frankie chewed on the end of a pen. "The way I see it, we have at least two big problems. The phone question and how the killer got into Parnell's apartment."

"And into the hotel room," Sherri said.

"Right. How did he get in the room? Most people lock the doors. Even the ones who don't lock doors at home lock hotel rooms. And besides, they lock automatically. Even the deadbolts are easy enough to break, but it wasn't broken. So we have to assume they let him in. Why?"

Sherri tapped on the table. "Which brings up the bigger question—why did Parnell let the killer into her apartment?"

"She knew Chad," Lou said.

Sherri shook her head. "Unless they were into the threesome thing, there is no way she's letting another guy in her apartment while one is already there." Sherri shook her head. "Two guys in an apartment with a woman? They'd be marking territory all over the place."

"I'm with Miller," Frankie said. "He had to use a key. But that still leaves us with how he got into the building. The doorman swears he didn't come in."

"Yeah, well…"

"How about you two check it out. Look that building over good. See if there is any other way in. And we should take another look at the hotel video now that we know what Chad looks like."

Carol popped her head in.

"Hate to disturb this brilliant strategy session but Central Booking called. Seems they had a problem with Mr. Benning."

Frankie jumped up. "What happened? Did he get away?"

"Somebody attacked him."

Lou smiled. "And justice for all."

"Morreau is pissed. Benning's lawyer is telling everyone you set it up."

"Me?" Frankie asked.

Carol nodded. "The guy who attacked him is Bruce Stewart, the fiancé."

"Ah shit," Frankie said.

"How the hell did he find out?" Sherri asked.

"Benning's lawyer is swearing Frankie told him so he could get Benning."

"Son of a bitch."

"Guess you're going down there, Donovan. Sherri and I have work to do."

***

Frankie went to see the desk sergeant at Central Booking. He thought he recognized the guy but the name wouldn't come to him, but then it did just as he was showing his badge. "Hey, Bob. Don't know if you remember me, but we worked together at the 15th."

"How the hell could I forget, you crazy fuckin' Irishman. What brings you to the slums?"

"Here about the guy who was attacked—Benning."

"He yours?"

"Yeah, we like him for the Couples Murders as the press is tagging them."

"No shit? Sick fucker." Bob looked at his sheet. "I'll send somebody to get him."

"Actually, Bob, I'm looking for the one who attacked him. I don't give a shit about Benning."

"So you *did* tell the guy where to find Benning."

Frankie held up his hands. "No way. Don't go spreading that around. Benning's lawyer is already stirring up trouble."

Bob thumbed through the sheet again. "Stewart. Let's see…" He craned his neck, searching the room. "Hey, Monson. Take Donovan to see the nut who attacked Benning."

Monson was four inches short of six feet, but he had to weigh in at about 220. He walked up and punched Frankie on the arm, like he always did. "Donovan, where you been? I thought you died."

"I did," Frankie said. "Just came back today."

"Now I remember why I was happy you left."

Frankie caught up on old times as they walked. Nothing had changed. "What are you holding Stewart on?"

"Nothing right now. The other guy didn't press charges, at least not yet. He didn't hit any of us. Ran into the cops holding Benning but didn't hit them. We can keep him if you want."

"Were you there?" Frankie asked.

"I was outside catching a smoke."

"What happened?"

"Guy comes out of nowhere and slams into the guys holding Benning. Then he starts mauling the guy, scratching his face, yanking out his hair, kicking him, even tried biting him. And the whole time he's screaming, 'You killed her, you bitch. You killed her.'"

"That it?"

"Yeah. Nothing serious. It only lasted about ten seconds."

"He resist when you guys stopped him?"

Monson shook his head. "Never."

Frankie nodded. "See if I can take him with me. The guy lost his fiancée yesterday, and as far as we know, Benning is the one who did it. On top of that, Stewart found out she was with another guy."

"I'm surprised he didn't have a gun."

"Yeah. I think I would, but Stewart's not like that. Seems pretty straight."

"I'll clear it with the sarge while you chat."

Frankie found a quiet spot and sat to talk with Bruce. "What the hell were you thinking?"

"I don't know. I just...I wanted to kill him." He said it with teeth and fists clenched. "I've never felt like that before, but when I saw him...if I had a gun..."

"Good thing you didn't."

Bruce lowered his head. "What will happen to me?"

"For right now, I'm getting you out of here."

"You can do that? For real?"

"Don't get too excited. I can get you out now, but if Benning presses charges, you'll have to answer for them."

"He wouldn't dare."

"Don't put it past him. He *would,* and his lawyer may encourage it. If he thinks it will make Benning look more sympathetic, he definitely will."

Bruce nodded.

"How did you find out he was going to be here?"

"Cindy told me you took him away from the office. So I found out where he would be brought for processing and came here to wait."

Frankie let him sit for a moment. "Why did you do it?"

"I can't stop thinking about Debbie. It's been haunting me. I can't sleep. Can't eat." Bruce held out his hands. "Look at me, Detective. I can't hold still. I couldn't even drive down here. I had to take the subway."

Monson walked by and gave Frankie a thumbs-up.

"I'll tell you what, Stewart, how about I take you home and we talk?"

"I can go now?"

"Yeah, you can go."

"Thanks. But don't bother driving me. I can take the subway."

"I don't mind. Besides, I have some questions for you anyway."

And I want to see that apartment of yours.

***

After Lou and Sherri reviewed the hotel security tape they headed down to Parnell's apartment building.

"How do you want to do this, Mazzetti?"

"Let's check everything."

They walked the outside of the building but saw nothing unusual. Miller checked a few windows until Lou told her to stop. "That's all I need, somebody shooting your ass because they think you're a burglar."

"Because I'm black?"

"Because you're trying to open their windows. I'd shoot you."

"You probably never shot anyone in your life."

"Not for lack of trying."

"Let's go talk to the doorman. Maybe he remembers something."

When they rounded the corner, Jack was talking to a woman on the sidewalk. He was ten feet from the building and faced in the other direction. Lou grabbed Sherri's arm. "Hang on. Let's see how attentive old Jack is."

After a couple of minutes of talking a car pulled up. Jack opened the back door, took out a few shopping bags, and leaned his head inside, talking to the driver.

Lou nudged Sherri. "See that other woman walk in the building? *That's* how the killer got in. Jack was probably chatting it up with some sweet thing and Benning walked right by. He could have waited right here, knowing it would happen sooner or later, or, he could have sent a sweet young thing by in a car to distract him."

Sherri looked at him with her eyebrows raised. "Is that all it takes to distract you guys—a pretty young thing?"

Lou seemed to give it thought, then nodded. "Yeah, that's about it. And the closer to naked she is the less pretty she needs to be."

Sherri rolled her eyes. "Let's go see the apartment again. And try to keep your mind on the investigation."

"You mean, and not your butt."

"Stop it, Mazzetti. I'm gonna choke."

They walked in and made their way to Debbie's apartment without running into anyone.

Sherri said, "If the guy had a key, all he'd need to do is wait until he knew they were in bed and let himself in."

Lou lifted the crime scene tape and let them in. The place still smelled of cleanser. "When we convict this guy I want him to clean my house before sentencing. In fact, maybe the judge can order it as part of community service. He has to clean my house every week."

"I hear you. Let's walk this through."

"The killer comes in while they're in the bedroom. He steps quietly down the hall." Lou and Sherri went through the motions, walking the hall.

"His gun is drawn," Sherri said.

"He goes into the room, sees them in 'position' and…"

Sherri stepped quickly from the door to the foot of the bed. "Fires," she said. "One to the back of Elliott's head. Parnell screams, and then he pops her."

"And what time did she scream?" Lou asked.

"I think it was about 9:30. We'll check when we get back."

They stared at the bed, looked around the room.

"Didn't waste any time," Lou said. "Kate didn't think the bodies were moved, which means he caught them in the act. The odd thing is how cold this guy is. If this was jealousy, you'd think more passion. More mistakes."

"We have a smart one on our hands, Lou. He plans it out."

"The real puzzler is that he stayed to clean the place."

"Not just clean it, he sanitized it."

Lou's phone rang. "Mazzetti."

"You now have a warrant."

"Goddamn. That's what I want to hear."

Lou looked at Sherri. "Got the warrant. Let's get Donovan and find some evidence."

CHAPTER 23

A FRIENDLY VISIT

Frankie drove slowly as he made his way to Bruce's house, slower than traffic demanded. He wanted to get more information about Debbie and Chad, but didn't want to set Bruce off any more than he already was. Infidelity was a touchy subject. No one knew better than Frankie.

"I can imagine how you feel, Mr. Stewart."

"I doubt that, Detective. I planned on marrying Debbie. At night, I went to sleep dreaming of the life we'd share." He turned his head and looked out the window. "I thought she felt the same way." Bruce looked at Frankie. "We talked about kids. She wanted four. Can you believe that? Most women, especially career women, wouldn't dream of that many, but she knew it was important to me."

Frankie hated talking about personal issues, but he needed to get Bruce's trust. "On a different level, I understand. My father treated me like shit, and I never knew why. I figured he just didn't like me. Later, I learned it was because my mother was running around on him." It was Frankie's turn to swallow some emotion. "Last year he died. At the funeral, I found out that I'm probably not his son." Frankie choked back a tear.

Shouldn't have started down this road.

"No wonder he hated me. If I had known…"

"It wouldn't have done any good," Bruce said.

"Why do you say that?"

"Trust me. It wouldn't."

"I guess I believe you. I haven't been able to keep a relationship. I got divorced early. Had a lot of girlfriends since. Nothing worked."

"And now?"

"I finally have a relationship that I think could work. But I'm afraid of it."

Frankie drove in silence for a moment. "I hate to ask this, but did you ever suspect anything?"

"No."

"I'm sorry, Mr. Stewart. I truly am."

They went about half a mile before Bruce spoke again. "The crazy thing is…that morning, when I found her…the first thought I had when I saw them was that she'd been raped. Then I thought…if this guy raped her, then who killed them? It wasn't until Jack said something that it hit me. I barely remember anything after that, not until you came."

"For what it's worth, I don't blame you for doing what you did." Frankie paused and glanced at Bruce. "To Benning, I mean."

"If I had a gun, I think I'd have shot him," Bruce said.

"Mr. Stewart, I said I don't blame you, but I *am* a detective. You shouldn't say things like that in front of me."

He lowered his head. "Sorry. I know it's just talk, but right now it's how I feel. I want him to suffer like Debbie did."

"I understand, on a different level. My best friend's wife was killed. Gunned down in front of a church."

"How did he deal with it?"

Stupid shit. What do I tell him…that my friend mutilated five mobsters to get even?

"He's still dealing with it, but he's getting better."

A few blocks later, Bruce said, "Turn left at the next block. It's not far."

"I didn't picture you as a Red Hook guy."

"I used to live in Brooklyn Heights."

"Ouch."

"It's not what you think. I'm an artist. I like it here."

After three more blocks Bruce pointed to the left and said, "I'm on the corner. You can let me off here, unless you want to come in."

Frankie almost said no, but remembered what Stewart had said back at the apartment, how he insisted that *someone* had cleaned Debbie's place. He even invited Frankie to come see his "dirty" apartment. Frankie thought it odd at the time, as if he were saying, "Look, it's not me." Sort of like the kid who empties his pockets when he knows the stolen candy isn't in there.

"I could stand to use the restroom," Frankie said. "If you don't mind."

"Of course not. Park where you can. Spaces are difficult to come by, even here."

Stewart lived in a renovated warehouse, though the renovated part was arguable. Paint was peeling; the door was almost off its hinges. General disrepair described it best. The inside was under construction—at least the front room was. Drop cloths covered the furniture—what there was of it—and half of one wall was painted.

"Excuse the mess, Detective. I'm remodeling. It takes a while when you do it yourself."

Frankie looked around. "When we talked earlier you said you didn't have to work."

Bruce laughed for the first time since Frankie had picked him up. "If you're wondering why I live here if I can afford better—you have a right to. I sometimes wonder myself. And I'm doing the remodeling because it gives me a sense of accomplishment. I enjoy the work. And the solitude."

They walked into the kitchen. The glass table was a mess, tools all over one end, and a paint tray next to them. A cereal bowl leftover from breakfast—complete with a few drops of spilled milk—sat across from the paint.

Bruce went to the fridge, grabbed a bottle of water. "Do you want water?"

"No thanks, but—"

"I forgot. Bathroom. It's down the hall on the left. Second door."

Frankie closed the door then reached for the toilet paper, but the holder was empty. A roll sat on the back of the toilet. He tore off a piece, used it to lift the seat, then took a leak. When he was done he flushed and tossed the tissue in with it. The sink had toothpaste globs in it, and the trashcan was overflowing. He opted to *not* wash his hands.

Frankie's cell rang. It was Mazzetti but he let it go to voicemail.

Bruce was sitting at the kitchen table when Frankie returned. He had moved the cereal bowl aside. "You doing okay, Mr. Stewart?" Frankie asked. "You seem pretty calm for what you've been through today."

"Thank you for asking. I'm fine now. I had time to reflect while I sat at the station. I decided I *did not* want to be in jail. I will have to rely on you to bring justice."

"That's what we're here for." Frankie fidgeted a moment. "Mr. Stewart, I hate to bring up a sensitive subject, but did you know the man Debbie was with?"

"I didn't look at him closely, but…" He turned his head, then got up and walked across the room. "If you don't mind, I'd rather not talk about it. Perhaps tomorrow or the next day would be better."

"Of course," Frankie said. "I need to get back anyway." He set a card on the table. "In case you lost the other one, here's my card. Call me if you get the urge to kill Mr. Benning."

Stewart gave a fake chuckle. "I will. Thank you."

As he walked toward the door, Frankie glanced to the back yard. Several sculptures adorned a stone patio. "It looks nice out there. I wish I had a back yard."

Bruce waved him off. "I might trade you. Tending to it is a lot of work."

"Where did you get the sculptures?"

Stewart beamed. "They're mine. Thank you for asking."

"Impressive," Frankie said, and then walked toward the front door. As he reached for the doorknob, he turned to Bruce.

"I shouldn't tell you this, but we *will* get him."

"I assume you mean Benning."

"Yeah. We've got evidence that I'm convinced will be enough to nail him. Just relax and give us time."

Bruce nodded. "I will. Thanks for letting me know."

Frankie got in the car, dialed Mazzetti, and headed toward the station.

"Where are you, Donovan?"

"On my way back from Red Hook. Why?"

"Red Hook? What the hell. Anyway, meet us at Benning's place. We have a warrant."

"Miller with you?"

"Sitting on my lap."

"I'm twenty minutes away. See you there."

***

Chad Benning lived in a nice building off Eighth Avenue in Chelsea. Lou and Sherri were waiting for Frankie.

"We going to find a gun?" Frankie asked.

"I hope so," Miller said. "Be nice to close this up."

"Be nice to keep the body count at four," Lou said.

Sherri showed the warrant to the doorman, and then to the building manager, who hesitated about letting them in the apartment, even with the paper. Sherri stopped short of saying "It's either let us in, or we break it down," but from the looks Donovan gave the guy, he understood.

"Should I call Mr. Benning?" the manager asked. "It seems like I should."

"Do what you want," Lou said. "Won't ruin my day."

A few seconds later, the manager opened the door. Lou stepped in first. "Clean. Very clean." He wiped his finger across an end table. "No dust. What kind of single guy has no dust on his end table?"

"Remind me—"

"I know, never to come to my place. I have news for you, Miller: you aren't invited."

"Let's each take a room," Frankie said. "Be gentle. I don't want his lawyer complaining."

"I'll take the kitchen," Lou said.

"Just search, Mazzetti. Don't eat."

"I'll take his bedroom," Sherri said.

A few minutes later Lou walked into the bedroom where Sherri was. "I found a key ring with Debbie's name on it."

"Bag it," Frankie said. "And hope we get as lucky with the gun."

Half an hour later, Sherri came out of the bedroom. "Not a damn thing."

"Place is clean," Mazzetti said. "But it's not like Parnell's place. That apartment was spotless."

Frankie came out of the other bedroom to join them. "Nothing in there either."

"So where did he stash the gun?" Sherri asked.

"He could have dumped it by now. He's had plenty of time."

"Might have a storage place," Mazzetti said. "Or a safe deposit. Could be anywhere."

"Let's go through everything one more time," Frankie said.

The front door opened. Chad Benning walked in. "What the hell is going on?"

"I can't believe it took your high-priced attorney this long to spring you," Lou said, and then he showed Benning the search warrant. "We are executing a search warrant. You're welcome to stay, but keep out of our way and don't touch anything."

"What are you looking for? I can't believe this shit. It's embarrassing."

"It'll be a lot more embarrassing when we find the gun," Lou said.

"And when we match that hair we found in Debbie's apartment to you."

"How long will you be here?" Chad asked.

"We're getting ready to leave," Frankie said. "Do you have a safe deposit box?"

"No."

"How about a storage facility? Rent space anywhere?"

"No. And I don't even know if I should be talking to you."

"That's fine. We're done."

"Have a good day," Lou said.

As they were leaving, Benning whispered to Frankie. "You'll regret this. Trust me."

CHAPTER 24

FAMILY DINNER

"You two going back to the station?" Frankie asked.

"I have to get my car," Lou said. "Why, you need something?"

"I don't like where this is going," Frankie said. "We've got no gun, no real motive—other than possible jealousy—and no witnesses."

"We've got a ton of circumstantial," Sherri said.

"With the lawyer Benning's got, that will get us nowhere. We need more."

"What do you want to do?" Sherri asked.

"I still like Benning, but I want to cover all the bases."

"The only bases we have are Benning or Stewart," Lou said. "Krenshaw's husband has an alibi. As for Stewart, he told us up front he was by himself; he didn't even try to provide an alibi. Surfing the web is no alibi."

"Can we check on that?" Frankie asked. "Is there any way we can get his service provider to tell us if his computer was active on the Internet that night, and at what times?"

Sherri made an unlady-like, maybe even inhuman-like noise. "They can tell you anything nowadays. I'll ask Carol to check on it."

"Are you second-guessing on Benning?" Lou asked. "If it's between Benning and Stewart, I know which one I'm voting for."

"Covering all bases, Lou. Just because we only see two suspects doesn't mean there aren't more. The killer might be somebody we don't even know about."

"It's a little late to be thinking that," Sherri said.

"Better than after putting Benning behind bars." Frankie said. "See you guys in the morning."

***

On the drive home Frankie tried to relax, but all he could think about was Benning, and he didn't like it. If Chad killed Debbie Parnell, wouldn't he hide the key ring? Wouldn't he have gotten rid of Krenshaw's cell phone? Then again, all the circumstantial was obvious—too obvious.

Maybe that's his game. Maybe he's making it so obvious that it's not believable.

Frankie's cell rang. It was Kate. "What's up, Irish?"

"Back at you, half-breed. Are you on your way home?"

"Be there in fifteen minutes. You want to catch a bite to eat?"

"Cops with kids can't afford to eat out; besides, I've got dinner started."

"Okay. See you soon."

Please don't let it be pot roast.

Alex ran to greet Frankie at the door. Frankie scooped him up and spun him around. "How'd it go at school today?"

"Good. I didn't have to worry about CPS. Not at school anyway."

"What's that supposed to mean?" Frankie looked at Alex, then Kate. She gestured toward the kitchen. A business card lay on the table.

"That was on the door when Alex got home," Kate said. "It's from CPS. It scared the hell out of him."

Frankie knelt beside Alex. "Why didn't you call me?"

"I called Kate. I can't go messin' with murder investigations over something like this."

"But you can go messin' with my autopsies?" Kate said. "So that's how it goes?"

"You know what I mean, Kate."

She laughed. "I know. You can call me anytime. Don't even think about it."

Frankie lost his smile. "Did you see the CPS card on any other doors, or just ours?"

"I didn't look. I saw it and came inside."

Frankie patted his back. "It's okay."

"It's not okay. Nothing's ever okay."

"Don't worry," Frankie said. "We'll take care of you."

"We'll take care of you," Kate said, "but you need to help on that front—like keeping the door locked. I'm surprised CPS didn't just walk on in."

"Shit," Alex said. "Sorry, FD. I forgot to lock the door again."

Kate took the meat out of the oven. "Frankie, how about you slice the roast while Alex sets the table."

"Smells good," Alex said. "I love pot roast."

"Me, too," Frankie said. *Once a year.*

"Any breaks on the case?" Kate asked.

Frankie set the meat plate on the table and sat between Kate and Alex. "We got a warrant for our prime suspect's apartment, where we found one of the victim's keys, but nothing else."

"That's good, isn't it?"

"Not good enough. We need to have some concrete evidence."

"These deaths were gruesome," Kate said. "Especially the—"

"Whoa," Alex said. "Can we cut the body talk while we're eating."

"I didn't even think," Kate said. "I'm sorry."

"That's all right."

Frankie sliced the meat and put some on Alex' plate. "How was school? Make any new friends?"

"Not really."

Kate looked over at Alex. "Not really. Is that yes, or no?"

"I guess it's no, since I didn't bring anyone home for dinner."

Frankie set his fork down and stared. "I know you're upset about the CPS thing, but it's no reason to be an ass."

"Whatever."

"*Whatever.* That's how you treat Kate after she cooks a good meal for you?"

"Sorry." A minute later, Alex cleaned his plate, washed it, and put it in the dishwasher. "I'm going to do my homework."

When the bedroom door closed, Frankie looked at Kate. "What the hell is wrong with him? Is he that upset by CPS?"

Kate lowered her voice. "I tried telling you earlier, but Alex was always around. Father Murphy called. Alex got into a fight at school."

"What?" Frankie checked the recent calls list on his phone. "Why didn't he call me?"

"Alex told him to call me."

"What the hell? Am I that much of an ass?" Frankie got up and headed toward Alex's room.

"He doesn't need to be yelled at."

Frankie stopped, turned and pecked Kate on the cheek. "You're right. That's why I need you here."

He knocked on the door.

"What?"

"Can I come in?"

"Up to you."

Alex sat at a makeshift desk, but he wasn't doing homework. Frankie sat on the bed. "You want to talk?"

"That priest rat me out?"

"That's his job."

"I thought priests could keep their mouth shut about anything. Even a murder."

"Only if it involves confession. A priest running a school is no different than a principal in your old school."

Alex doodled.

"What happened?"

"Nothing."

"So you were just walking down the hall and a fight spontaneously combusted?"

Alex held back a laugh. "You're an ass, FD."

"I know. Why don't you tell me what happened? Then two asses can know."

Alex *did* laugh this time, but it quickly disappeared. "Some kid called me a nigger."

Frankie jumped off the bed. "What? Who the hell…" He grabbed his cell.

"Who you calling?"

"Father Murphy."

Alex reached for the phone. "No way. You can't do that to me."

"I'm not doing anything to *you*, I'm gonna get this other kid's ass kicked out."

"That's what I'm talking about. You do that, and I'm dead. I'll have to fight every day."

Frankie put the phone away, but he paced. "I'll be damned if you'll have to go through this."

"I been going through that all my life. It's no big deal."

"Well it is now. I'll be *goddamned* if I'll have somebody treat you like that."

Alex looked up at him and laughed. "Wasn't it you who taught me that nobody can make a fool of you but yourself?"

Frankie looked down at him and smiled as he tousled Alex's hair. "I guess you're right. My bad."

"Since I'm staying with you now, I think we'll have to make a recording of that."

Frankie sat on the bed again, silent for a moment. "So what are you gonna do when it happens again? You know it will."

"I'll hit whoever says it. If I do that enough, it'll stop."

"And you'll get expelled."

Alex shrugged.

"Did you tell Father Murphy what happened?"

"I ain't no rat."

Frankie nodded. "I'll tell you what. How about I call Father Murphy, and—"

"No way. I already said."

"Hear me out. I'll call Father Murphy and let him in on what happened, but I'll make him promise not to mention it to anyone. At least that way, he'll know what's causing the fights and won't blame you."

"He'd do that?"

"He would. We can trust him."

Alex held out his hand to bump fists. "Ring him up, dude."

"I'll *dude* your ass."

Alex laughed. "Thanks, FD. You're the best."

Frankie kissed him on the forehead. "I'll call Father Murphy in the morning. In the meantime, let's say we tackle this homework you seem to be having a tough time getting to."

"I can do this shit, it's just—"

"Alex, I know it's tough to change things, but we both need to work on our language. It's one thing when you're out with friends, but let's make a deal where we can curse around each other, to an extent, but you can't when you're around other adults or women."

"Not even around Keisha?"

"She's a woman isn't she?"

"Yeah, but she doesn't care."

"No exceptions. I've got a secret for you. No matter what a woman tells you, they like it when you respect them. Someday that will pay off."

"So how come you curse around Kate?"

Frankie raised his eyebrows and sighed. "Caught my ass there, didn't you?"

"Uh huh."

"Okay, starting tomorrow, I'm gonna work on no cursing around Kate."

"So who taught you all this shit—stuff? Your mom?"

Frankie laughed. "No way. It was actually a friend of mine, a guy named Nicky."

"That Rat guy you talk about?"

Frankie looked down at Alex and rubbed his head. "Yeah, that's him. The Rat."

"I thought he was some bad dude."

Frankie hesitated. "I guess you could say that, but you know what, Ace? I've found out that you can learn something good from *anybody* in life. All you have to do is look."

"Wasn't nothing to learn from that bitch mom I had."

"Don't call her that."

"Why not?"

"She was your mom. That's reason enough."

Alex opened the lid on a cigar box that Frankie had given him and slipped something inside. It was where he kept his special things.

"What have you got?"

"Nothing."

"Looks like a piece of paper to me."

"Bitch can't even spell. I'm glad she's gone."

Frankie sat next to him, his arm coming to rest gently on Alex's shoulder. "I think you already know that it makes no difference if a person can spell, or write, or read. It's what's inside that counts."

"Wasn't nothing inside that bitch." He grabbed the paper and handed it to Frankie. "Take a look at this."

The paper had been torn in half, but the bottom was still there.

No mater wat you think, Alex, I love you. I just cant be a mom. I do love you tho.

Mom.

Frankie let Alex seethe for a moment. "I know it might seem like she didn't care, but somewhere deep inside, your mom loved you."

"Bullshit."

"Her problem was that she didn't love herself."

"That doesn't make sense." Alex turned to him. "Why you trying to cover up for her? I *know* you didn't like her."

"Because for whatever else she is, she's still your mother. That means something."

"Not to me."

"It might not mean anything now. Hell, it might not later. And I'm not telling you to love her. All I'm saying is that for the time being…don't *hate* her. If you hate somebody long enough, you'll end up hating yourself."

"I know I ain't never gonna be like her."

Frankie thought for a moment. Giving advice to kids was not something he was used to. "Try to remember those days when your mom was feeling good. When she was off the junk, and she was happy."

"I remember them."

"I know you do. And I could always tell because you were so happy those days."

Alex smiled.

Frankie squeezed his shoulder. "That's what I'm talking about. When you think of your mom, think of those times. Remember her for the days she was good."

Alex nodded his head. "Guess so, FD. Anyway, don't worry about this homework. I'll get it done."

"Okay. And whenever you want to talk, let me know." As he left, he turned back to Alex. "Don't forget to lock the damn doors from now on."

CHAPTER 25

THE FRUIT STAND

Jan Morris got out of bed then threw on a pair of jeans and her favorite top, the one with the glittery butterfly. Today *was* going to be a good day even if she had to force it. She put water on for tea, decided to trade in her sneakers for sandals, then shuffled around the kitchen humming an old Louis Prima song. Her father used to listen to him all the time. She stirred an Equal into her tea and drifted to what she had to do today. She thought of calling her dad—he'd waited so long for grandkids—but it was still too early to call. He'd gotten to be a late sleeper in his old age. She'd wait a few hours and then call and tell him the wait was over.

I hope it's a girl.

She told Jeff last night at dinner and then they celebrated before he caught a late-night flight. Jan patted her stomach, smiling. It was still taut, but not for long. After a little cleaning, she made a list of what had to be done. A visit to the fruit stand was high on the list. She had to start eating right.

***

The killer took his time at the fruit stand, waiting for the crowd to leave. He hated touching people, getting their germs on him. He once read about a decontamination gun in a science fiction novel. Ever since, he'd wanted one for himself. It would have saved a lot of showers.

When the last person left, he stepped up and selected a few Jersey tomatoes, instantly dreaming of a tomato sandwich with garlic and basil.

A woman brushed against him, said, "Excuse me," and went about rummaging through the zucchini, selecting a long, fat one. He wondered what she planned for it.

Perhaps her husband is away, he thought, and that brought images of Susan. *I know what Susan would have done with it—shove it between her legs.*

Whenever he thought of Susan, he pictured a man's head buried between her legs. He tried shaking the memory, but it was always there. Haunting him. Burned in his mind.

The killer shot the woman a parting glance, thought about doing her, then dismissed it. He shook his head. The killing was over. He was done. The cops were too close.

He picked two apples, praying they'd be crisp. Selected a few spears of pencil-thin asparagus, then moved to the peaches. The woman bumped into him again, the chocolate-brown one. Her eyes sparkled, her voice—so velvety smooth—enchanted him. He glanced down to unpainted toes. *Good.* He hated painted toenails. Best of all, there was no chance that this one was blonde. He *despised* blondes.

"I'm so sorry. I've been a klutz all day." She flashed a smile that seemed practiced.

He smiled back, but thought, *What decent woman would flirt with a man like that?* Still, she was attractive. He moved away, resisting temptation, but he kept his eyes on her. That much, he couldn't resist. She picked out a cantaloupe, held it in her hands, caressed it, sniffed it. Smiled at it.

Before he knew it, he was next to her. "I hate to bother you, but I never can tell when one is ripe." He flashed a smile the warm, friendly kind that women liked. The kind that said I'm harmless, take me home with you. Let's snuggle under the covers.

"It's easy," she said. "If you press on the end, right here, it should give a little, but not too much. If it's too soft, that means it's overripe; too firm, and it won't have any taste."

"Oh, is that all?" *No need to worry about firmness, dear.*

She blushed. "Actually, I prefer the smell test." She brought the fruit close to her face, closed her eyes and breathed deeply. "Ah…smell that," she said, and handed him the cantaloupe. "Now *that* is a ripe melon."

The killer held the cantaloupe an inch or so from his face, closed his eyes, and breathed in. "You're right. I can smell it. Thanks, this will save me a lot of time and money."

"Not a problem," she said, and put the one she'd selected into her basket.

He watched her walk away, her tight little ass dancing in her jeans. He debated whether her ass cheeks were doing the rumba or the samba. Either way, she was cute, and *very damn sexy.* She oozed sex. The killer wondered if she tasted as good as she looked. *Like a Hershey's bar.* He restrained an urge to lick his lips, but he vowed that when he got her alone he'd sniff her to see if she was ripe. She'd appreciate that.

Maybe I'm not *done. One more would put the icing on the cake, so to speak.* Her last smile made up his mind. He'd soon find out if she tasted as sweet as chocolate.

CHAPTER 26

CHASING LEADS

Frankie finished breakfast then went to Alex's room. He was fixing his hair, but taking his time about it. He looked worried.

"Better hurry up," Frankie said. "Don't want to be late for school. You might miss a fight."

Alex smiled. "You know what you are?"

"Yeah, I know. But you can't say it because we have a new agreement about cursing in the house."

"All I heard you say about cussing was I couldn't do it around girls. You ain't no *girl,* are you?"

"You want me to drop you off at school?"

"Nah. Just call Father Murphy so he doesn't think I'm a gangsta' or something."

Frankie looked at his watch. "I'll call him on my way in. And let me know if anything happens. *Me,* not Kate."

"They don't let us use phones in the school."

"If something happens, call me. I don't care if it's against the rules."

"I got it covered," Alex said. "You worry about catching the bad guys."

Frankie kissed Kate goodbye and headed out the door. "You gonna be here tonight?"

"Can't," she said. "I have bodies lined up for autopsies like they're waiting for concert tickets."

"Okay, have fun," Frankie said. "And tell Alex to call Linda if he needs anything."

Frankie called Father Murphy on the way in. The priest wasn't too happy when he heard what the other kids called Alex, and he promised to keep an eye out. "Don't forget, Father. He doesn't want you to do anything."

"I haven't been a priest all my life. I know how this works."

"Thanks."

The next call was to Nicky. Frankie left him a voicemail. "Nicky, I'm hoping to wrap up this case soon. After that I should be free. We can get together then."

Lou and Sherri were already hard at it when he got to the station. "Anything new?"

"Trying to put it all down so it makes sense," Lou said. "I went by Parnell's place on my way home. The key from Chad's house fits."

"But he'd already told us he had a key," Frankie said.

"I know. This confirms it."

Sherri opened a folder. "We have ballistics showing all of them killed with the same gun. We have Parnell's computer being infected with spyware, and then being stolen. And her keys being stolen." Sherri looked up at Frankie. "That's one we haven't talked about. It seems awful coincidental that her keys were stolen a week before she was murdered."

Lou nodded. "You're right. Chad didn't need them, and Stewart had keys. So who took them? And why take her personal computer but not the other?"

Frankie nudged a chair aside with his foot and set three cups of coffee on the table. "Mark it down as one more goddamn thing we don't know about this case."

Carol followed him into the room. "I have that report on Stewart."

"About what?" Frankie asked.

"About whether he was on the Internet that night."

"They gave it to you?"

Carol shrugged. "Kind of. A friend of mine works at his service provider. And don't worry; she checked without leaving a trace."

"What's the verdict?" Lou asked.

"According to her, Stewart was at home most of the night and active on the computer. There was a forty-five minute lull around 8:00 and again a little after 11:00, but other than that, he was very active. He downloaded a lot, visited a lot of sites. She said there was no discernible pattern to indicate that it was a bot."

"What the hell is a bot?" Lou asked.

"Dinosaur," Carol muttered. "A *bot*, Mazzetti, is an automated program. He could have had something like that set up to go to websites on its own. My friend said it's not too difficult to do."

Frankie shook his head. "For what it's worth, I don't see this guy being able to do that."

"I also checked with the IT department where Debbie worked. The spyware on her computer was nothing special—run of the mill, not malicious. They cleaned it up and sent her home, so to speak."

"Thanks," Frankie said.

"That doesn't tell us much about Mr. Clean," Lou said.

Sherri stared. "Who?"

"Mr. Clean," Lou said. "That's what I named this guy."

Frankie shook his head, but Sherri laughed. "You have to admit, 'Mr. Clean' fits."

"Now that Miller recognizes my brilliance, I'll finish my coffee."

Frankie spread the files across the desk. "Okay, let's start over and go through everything we have. We're missing something."

"What do you think we're missing?" Sherri said.

"I don't know yet. But you don't kill four people and not leave a clue. We just have to find it. It's something at the scenes or it's in our notes, but it's there."

"I hear what you're saying, Donovan, but you better hurry up and solve this. You only have me for the next two months."

"Shut up and help us find a killer," Frankie said.

Two hours later Lou pushed his chair back and kicked off his shoes. "That does it for me. If you guys don't find something, the killer's getting away."

Sherri looked at him with narrowed eyes. "That's it? You're giving up?"

"I'm not giving up; I'm retiring early."

"He's full of shit," Frankie said as he sorted through papers in Krenshaw's folder. "At the first hint of a clue, he'll get off his fat ass and run for the door."

Lou popped a cigarette into his mouth. "That was the old Lou Mazzetti. This is the new me. A life of luxury and no responsibility."

"Don't get too comfortable," Sherri said. "I might have something."

Frankie stopped searching and looked up. "What've you got?"

"I've been going through her phone. There's an email from a couple of weeks ago that says, 'What was he doing in BH?'"

Lou didn't move. "What was *who* doing in BH?"

"I don't know, Mazzetti. I just found it."

"'BH' could be Brooklyn Heights," Frankie said. "But Lou's got a good question. Who's *he*?"

"It's an email from Parnell to herself." Sherri said.

Lou sat up in the chair. "When did she send it?"

Sherri looked at the date and cross-checked it with the timeline on the file. "Day she left town—8:12 AM."

"Any other emails that morning?" Lou asked.

"A lot. This was a busy lady." Sherri took time reading. When she finished, she said, "She had a lot of business emails, but none of them look strange. And this was the only personal email."

"And she sent it to herself?" Mazzetti leaned forward and slipped his shoes on.

"Not only did she send it to herself, it's the only email she sent for the next three hours."

Frankie stood and walked around the table. He pulled a toothpick from his jacket pocket and chewed on it. "You have her phone records there?"

Sherri looked through the file. "Right here."

"Who did she call that morning?" Frankie asked.

Miller traced her finger down the list. Carol had documented who owned the numbers on all the phone records. "Guess who's first at bat?"

Lou slapped his hand on the desk. "I *knew* it. Benning, isn't it?"

"Chad Benning," Sherri said.

Frankie didn't join the celebration. "Who else?"

Sherri looked again. "A car service and Bruce Stewart. That's it until that night."

The toothpick in Frankie's mouth snapped. He took it out and tossed it in the trash. "Give me Benning's number. In fact, give me Stewart's number, too."

Frankie took a seat and dialed.

"Mr. Benning, this is Detective Donovan."

"Donovan? Was that your doing, siccing that maniac on me?"

"Believe me I had nothing to do with it. But I do have a question. What did you and Ms. Parnell discuss on the phone the morning she went out of town?"

"What? How the hell do I know? She went out of town a lot."

"This was two weeks ago, and it was the last trip she made before she was murdered."

A short pause followed, then, "I don't know. I can't remember."

"Perhaps if you come to the station it will jog your memory."

Benning stepped back a bit. "It was nothing. If I recall, she wanted me to drive her to the airport."

"And that's all? She called just to ask you to drive her? That's what you're sticking with?"

"That's it. Why? What's the problem?"

"Nothing, Mr. Benning, it's just…"

"What?"

Frankie let him stew a moment. "We found a note in her phone that said, "What was Chad doing in Brooklyn Heights?"

"What?"

"Do I need to repeat it?"

"No, but that doesn't make sense. I wasn't in Brooklyn Heights."

"Not ever?" Frankie said, and waited while he let the question sink in.

"Are you saying you've *never* been in Brooklyn Heights?"

"No. Of course not. It's…I'll tell you what. Fuck this. Call my lawyer," he said, and the line went dead.

Frankie smiled at Lou and Sherri. "I think the man is agitated."

Next Frankie called Stewart. "Did Ms. Parnell call you the morning she was going out of town?"

"She did. It was while she was waiting to board the plane."

"What did you talk about?"

"Nothing, really. Debbie liked to talk about herself so that's what we usually talked about."

"We found a note in her email that said, 'What was Bruce doing in Brooklyn Heights', and it was dated that morning. What *were* you doing there, Mr. Stewart?"

He laughed. "Detective, I don't know what game you're playing, but I was *not* in Brooklyn Heights that morning, and I can't imagine why Debbie would say I was."

"We'll get back to you on it," Frankie said, and hung up.

Lou had his hand raised when Frankie looked at him.

"What's that about, Mazzetti?"

"I'm casting my vote for Benning," he said.

Sherri raised hers. "Me, too."

Frankie nodded. "I'm with you, but I'll reserve judgment. Let's turn over a few more rocks."

CHAPTER 27

AN UNWELCOME GUEST

The killer woke in the middle of another dream. It must have been the fourth time, and every one had been about the girl from the fruit stand. *Cantaloupe Girl.*

He looked at the clock—5:30. Only half an hour before his alarm would go off. After drinking coffee and dressing, he walked to the café down the street. Sometime between his last dream and getting seated, he decided not to kill the girl. She had earned a reprieve. As he sipped his espresso he thought about Susan. She had been his first. They say you never forget your *first* of anything. It was certainly true about first kills. He remembered this as if it were yesterday. The fear still gripped his chest and made his heart race. And the joy of seeing the look on her face when she realized what he planned to do.

But he hadn't been very good at killing back then. He would have been caught if Leo hadn't discovered his crime first. And that meant he had to take care of Leo—an inevitable event. The killer learned a valuable lesson from those kills. They taught him to clean up after himself.

The waitress came by. "More espresso?"

The killer thought about it. "I think I will, thanks." Now he had time to mull things over. Regardless of whether he killed Cantaloupe Girl, one thing was certain—Donovan had to go.

He paid the tab, went to the building where Parnell had worked, checked on a few things, and made a call. He would go home now. That would be his alibi: being home.

The killer threw on a jogging hoodie, a big pair of shades—the kind they wore in the 70s—and then he stuffed latex gloves and lock picks in his pocket. He left the house wearing jogging pants and carrying a gym bag. Inside the bag was a knife—a plain kitchen knife, the kind you can get from almost any store. If the police stopped him, he'd say he was carrying it for protection—it's a dangerous world out there. He had been mulling over where to kill Donovan and decided his apartment would be best. He would be relaxed there, not as tense or alert, and Donovan needed to be caught off guard. His reputation for being trigger happy preceded him. The killer did not want to catch Detective Donovan prepared. That would buy nothing but a ticket to the grave.

He started out the door, then reevaluated his decision on the knife. If he was going to kill Donovan in his own apartment…wouldn't it be proper to use one of his own knives? *Yes, I think so. Good idea.* He put the knife back in the drawer then left, locking the door behind him. The apartment was a good idea. He liked that. Killing Donovan in his apartment presented DNA problems, but the killer had some ideas about that, too.

He parked his car about half a mile away on a street where it wouldn't get noticed. Maybe stolen, but not noticed. Then he jogged toward Donovan's building. He turned the corner. No one was there. As he approached the front door, he did a quick look to see if anyone was watching then went inside and climbed the steps to Donovan's apartment. The hall was clear. The killer knocked gently, then a little harder. He pressed his head to the door. Thought he heard a noise, but then…nothing. Another check in the hall before he got out his picks. He opened the door in less than a minute, though it seemed like five.

"Hello, anyone here?"

Once inside, he adjusted his hoodie. He put a nylon stocking on his head, settling the edge of it on his forehead, ready to be pulled down at a moment's notice.

***

Alex scrambled under the bed, like he used to do when he was real little and his mom would have her *guests* over. He lay under the bed, trembling. Afraid to make a noise. Someone was in the apartment, and he didn't recognize the voice.

He scrunched up real small and slid toward the wall, deep into the shadows. The gap between the floor and the bed was maybe eight inches. Big enough for whoever was out there to spot him. He squeezed deeper into the dark, his heart racing. A wool blanket lay folded under the bed. Alex pulled it over, in front of him.

Footsteps sounded on the kitchen floor.

Don't come in here.

Someone was talking in the other room but Alex couldn't make out what was said. Then he heard singing. The floorboards creaked. Alex curled up tighter, afraid he'd make a noise. The blanket made him itch. He tried not thinking about it. He had to get FD. He'd know what to do. Alex thought about getting his phone off the nightstand, then worried it might ring. If it rang…

He stretched his legs out a little, positioning himself so he could crawl to the other side without hitting anything. He had stuff stored under the bed and didn't want to make noise. He moved an empty shoebox—*very slowly*—toward the bottom of the bed, hoping it would block the view from the living room. One of his sweatshirts was under there too. He pushed it with his leg, stretching it out as far as it would go, until it was next to the shoebox. Now if he could just get to the phone. Only a couple of people had his number, but Keisha was one of them. And she was famous for calling at the wrong time.

Alex crept toward the far side of the bed, poked his head out, then, when he got far enough, he turned on his side and stretched to reach the phone.

Then the front door opened.

CHAPTER 28

ROUGHING IT

After Frankie downed his fifth cup of coffee, he prepared to go home. Kate wouldn't be over tonight, which meant he and Alex would be roughing it. That normally meant frozen pizza and old movies.

Carol was at her desk when Frankie passed. "What are you still doing here?"

"I thought I'd wait for the crowd to clear out downstairs," she said. "You know how I excite those young studs."

"Can't keep their hands off you, huh?"

"Been a problem all my life."

Frankie laughed. "Any word on when we get the DNA back on that hair Kate found at the scene?"

"Why don't you ask her?"

"I haven't talked to her since this morning and she won't be by tonight."

Carol shook her head. "Nothing yet. I'll let you know."

"Goodnight, hot stuff."

"See you tomorrow, Donovan. Let me know if the coast is clear."

Frankie headed home through ridiculously bad traffic, his mind wandering from one problem to another. Even problems were better than traffic. He thought of calling Alex to see how his day had gone, but figured he'd wait until he got home to talk to him. A flash of anger raced through him as he thought about those kids who called Alex nigger. *Little pricks.*

He made a mental note to see Linda, and make sure she'd be okay watching Alex if an emergency ever came up. He never knew when he or Kate wouldn't be available. *Better stop and get Keisha something special.* He hadn't done that in a while. She and Alex liked it when he brought them treats.

He stopped at a bodega to buy cigarettes and something for the kids. Damn cigarettes were a fortune now, tempting him to make a trip to Delaware to buy some cheap ones.

Frankie picked up a bag of Cheetos for Alex and a couple of packs of Keisha's favorite gum—watermelon—and a large bag of Ruffles. She loved Ruffles. He laughed as he thought of Keisha—always happy and always with dirt on her face from playing.

A little dirt can't hide a pretty face. That's what Mamma Rosa used to say. She was right. Then again, the longer Frankie lived, the more he realized that Mamma Rosa was right about everything.

"That will be $14.55," the guy at the counter said.

Frankie paid, got in his car and started for home. Mamma Rosa's saying jarred something in his head, but he couldn't think of what. He grabbed his phone to call Lou, but when he went to dial, the phone rang instead. "Hello?"

"Bugs?"

"Nicky, is that you?"

"I got your message. When do you want to get together? We can plan this around the christening if you think you can get down here then."

"If you can wait till I finish this case. It shouldn't be long. How are Angie and Rosa? And Dante? Damn, I almost forgot my soon-to-be godson."

"Everybody's doing great. How about you guys? What's it like going from bachelor to full-blown dad?"

"A lot tougher than solving homicides. Kids nowadays…"

"Stop sounding old, Bugs."

"I *am* old, for God's sake. Anyway, we need to get together. And you need to meet Ace. He's a great kid."

"I hope he's not like we were."

"No way. This kid's good."

"All right, we'll plan on it. Let me know your timing."

"Hey, I gotta go. I'm pulling up to my place and might have to fight for a parking spot."

"I don't miss that part of New York. See you later."

Before he knew it, Frankie was pulling into a parking spot just outside his door. *And people say miracles don't happen anymore.*

He grabbed the stuff from the bodega and climbed the stairs to Keisha's place. Linda answered.

"Hi, Linda. Keisha here?"

She looked down at the treats in the bag, shaking her head. "She's playing with a friend, but I see you're spoiling her again."

"It's been a while. I thought I'd bring her and Alex something." He handed Linda the gum and chips. "By the way, did anyone from CPS stop here in the past few days?"

"Had a lady by looking for Alex."

Frankie tensed.

"Don't worry. I didn't tell her anything. Said I hadn't seen that boy since his mother left with her drug-addict boyfriend."

"I'm sorry you had to lie."

"Don't you worry about me lying for you. I'll lie till I die if it means keeping that boy away from those folks. That's something you can count on."

Frankie leaned over and kissed her. "You're the best. That's why Keisha is such a good girl."

Linda's eyebrows raised. "Huh! I don't know about the *good* part."

"She's good, all right. I didn't know how tough raising kids was until I took Alex in. I just hope I'm doing the right thing."

Linda took his hand and patted it. "I've known Alex since he was born, and I haven't *ever* seen that boy so happy. You're a good man, Frankie Donovan."

"Not everyone thinks so."

"Shame on them. Alex does, and Keisha does. I trust the judgment of kids against adults any day."

"Thanks again, Linda. It means a lot to me."

Frankie had one more flight of stairs to get to his apartment. When he reached the top, he shifted the bag from his right to left hand, then opened the door.

CHAPTER 29

HELP

"Hey, Ace, you here?"

The killer waited for Donovan to step inside the apartment. He kicked the door shut, then swung the knife toward Frankie's kidney. At the last second, Frankie must have sensed something. He turned. The blade dug into his back.

"Nobody here but us," the killer said.

"Goddamn!" Frankie dropped the bag and stumbled forward.

The killer stabbed again. This one hit Frankie in the gut. It went deep. Frankie doubled over, and reached for his stomach. He tried getting away. The blade caught him again. Another gut shot. Blood poured out. Frankie fell over the back of the sofa and tried to get his gun drawn.

***

Alex heard Frankie call him, then he heard him curse. Then the sounds of fighting. The guy was hurting FD. Alex's stomach ached and he felt on fire, but he had to risk going for the phone. He crawled out from under the bed, grabbed the phone and dialed 9-1-1. At the last minute he remembered to put the volume low so the guy wouldn't hear. He got back under the bed and stayed in the dark.

A lady answered right away. "9-1-1. What is your emergency?"

Alex whispered, "We need help."

"9-1-1. Are you there? What is your emergency?"

Alex was shaking. His throat felt as if it had closed up. Frankie moaned. He was hurting. Alex had to risk it. He got as close as he could to the mouthpiece and spoke louder, but still in a whisper. "Somebody's killing my dad. Help us."

"What did you say? Someone is doing what?"

Alex moved as far away as he could. He spoke louder still. "Someone is in our apartment. He's killing my dad."

"Where are you? Are you safe?"

"Under the bed. I can't talk no more."

"Stay right where you are. Do not move. We have your address. The police and an ambulance are on the way."

"Tell them to hurry. Please."

"They won't be long. Now keep the phone on so I can hear. You don't have to talk."

Alex crawled to the other side of the bed again. He pushed the phone to the edge and left it there, then crawled back into the shadows.

***

Frankie rolled off the sofa to the floor, landing on his back. He moaned. The bleeding was bad. He managed to draw his gun and get a grip on it with both hands. Whoever had stabbed him was coming at him again. The shape was blurry, and he wore a mask.

Please don't let him get Alex.

The man was coming around the side of the couch, coming with the knife. Frankie aimed, fired once. It didn't stop him. Frankie fired again.

Then he felt the knife go in his chest.

***

The killer stabbed Frankie in the chest. How had he let him get to his gun? Now the cops would come. He raised the knife to strike again, but stopped at a sound.

Sirens! Have to get out.

He looked down. Donovan wasn't moving.

He stabbed him one more time, then rushed out the door, grabbing his gym bag on the way. He took the stairs to the second floor, looked down the hall, and saw a window at the end. He ran to it, tried to open it but it was stiff. When he got it open, he hang-dropped to the ground. Looked around. Saw no one. Removed the mask and the hoodie. Put both of them in the gym bag, put on his shades, then jogged away. It was only half a mile to his car. Assuming it was still there, he'd be gone before the cops knew where to look.

***

Alex heard the gunshot. He cringed, drew back and bundled himself into a ball. He prayed it had been FD's gun. *Maybe he got him.* When the second shot rang out, Alex got worried. He didn't hear FD. If he shot the guy, wouldn't he be saying something? Next he heard the door slam. *The guy left.*

Alex crawled out from under the bed. He peeked out and saw Frankie lying on the floor, a knife in his chest. He ran to him.

Frankie bled from several wounds. Alex put his hand on one to stop the blood. Tears were flowing. "Don't die, FD. Please don't die." He ran to the kitchen, where he grabbed some paper towels. He used them to try to stop the bleeding. He tried to remember anything he'd seen in movies, or on TV, anything to do with stopping bleeding. All he could come up with was applying pressure. He used both hands and pressed the towels into Frankie's cuts. Frankie didn't move.

"Don't die. Please don't die."

The door burst open, scaring Alex. Three cops rushed in, guns drawn. One was pointed at him.

"Don't move," one cop yelled.

"Did you call 9-1-1?" another said.

"Is there anyone else in the house?" the third guy asked. He was a sergeant. Alex could tell by the uniform.

"He's gone," Alex said. "I think he killed my dad. Help him. Do something."

EMS came through the door. "Step aside. Let us get to him."

They had to pry Alex off Frankie. Two EMS guys knelt next to him.

"We got a pulse!" the first one yelled.

They put something on FD's face, then gave him a shot. Before Alex knew what happened, they'd transferred Frankie to a gurney and carried him out. Four more cops came in the door.

"Did you see anything?" the sergeant asked Alex.

"I was under the bed." Alex cried hard. "I was scared. And now my dad is dead."

The sergeant sat next to Alex, patting his back. "Your dad's not dead, and it's not your fault. Frankie would be the first to tell you that."

"You know him?"

He nodded. "I've worked with him a few times. He's a damn good cop." The sergeant looked to the others. "Whoever did this has to be covered in blood. Get out there and find him. I want this fucker even if we have to tear this neighborhood apart."

The sergeant and one other cop stayed with Alex; the others went after the intruder.

"I've got to go to the hospital," Alex said.

"Where's your mother?" the sergeant asked.

"I got no mom. Just take me to the hospital. I need to be with my dad."

"You okay walking down the stairs by yourself?"

"Yeah."

The sergeant looked at him, with blood all over his shirt and pants. "How about changing clothes first."

"No. I need to get there."

"They'll have him in surgery for a while. We have plenty of time." *If he's not dead.*

"Okay. Be right back."

The second cop tapped the sergeant on the shoulder. "Didn't look good," he whispered.

"I know." He looked at the floor. "Lot of blood here."

Alex came out of the bedroom in new clothes, though he still had some blood on his face and hands. "I heard two gunshots. I think Dad fired at him."

The sergeant looked around. "Don't see a gun. The guy might have taken it with him." He turned to the other cop. "Tell them he may be armed. And have them check hospitals for possible gunshot victims, in case Donovan got him."

Alex cried all the way to the hospital, and the more he cried, the faster Sergeant Tucker drove. "We'll be there soon." He parked by the emergency entrance and took Alex inside. Lou Mazzetti was waiting. Alex ran to him.

"Have you seen FD? Is he okay?"

Lou hugged Alex. "The doctors have him in surgery."

"Is he gonna be okay?"

Mazzetti leaned down, looked Alex in the eyes. "I know how much Frankie means to you. He means almost as much to those doctors. They're going to do everything they can to get him well." He stood, took Alex by the hand. "How about we go grab some espresso, or a Coke if you want it, and we'll find a good place to wait."

"Has anybody called Kate? I need to tell her."

"Shit!" Mazzetti said. "I'll call her now."

"I'll do it," Sherri said. "Give me her number."

Lou gave it to her, then turned to Sergeant Tucker. "I want *everybody* you can get on this."

"You know it, Lou. We're gonna get this motherfucker if we have to turn the whole city over."

"First thing you do is look up a guy named Chad Benning. See if he has an alibi. Get his information from Carol."

"You got a reason to suspect him?"

"He's our number one suspect on a quadruple murder."

"The Couples Murders?"

"That's the one," Lou said. "Go find him."

Lou and Alex found a waiting room and sat in the chairs closest to the operating room door. Alex was nervous, his legs jiggling, hands shaking. Every five minutes or so he got up and paced.

"When are we gonna know something?"

"When they finish," Lou said. "You want something else to drink?"

"I'm okay. When will Kate be here?"

"She won't be long."

For half an hour Alex paced, and worried, and asked about Frankie. As he downed his third Coke, Kate came through the door. He threw his arms around her.

She hugged him, tears coming down her face. "It'll be okay, Alex."

"Did you talk to the doctor? Is he gonna make it?"

"I don't know. I wanted to see you first. I'll try to find the doctors now. You stay with Lou, okay?"

Lou put his arm around her. "I'm sorry, Kate. I know how you must feel."

"Any word?"

He shook his head. "Nothing since we got here."

"All right. Can you stay with Alex for a few minutes? I'm going to see if I can get some information."

Alex grabbed hold of her. "I want to come with you."

"You can't. I've got to talk to the doctors, but I'll be right back."

"Promise?"

She hugged him. "I promise."

Kate set a blazing pace down the hall to the nurses' station. She flashed her badge to the head nurse. "Dr. Kate Burns, Medical Examiner. I wondered if you could tell me what you've got on Frank Donovan."

"Hold on, Doctor. We're not ready to give him up to you just yet."

Kate cracked a small smile. "That's good to know. Is there anything you can tell me?"

"Are you a relative? Friend?"

"We're engaged." *Not quite, but close.*

The nurse looked around, whispered, "You didn't hear this from me. Got that?"

"I know the drill."

The nurse nodded. "One of the docs poked his head out a little while ago. He said your man had five stab wounds, three of them bad. One punctured a lung."

Kate slammed her hand on the counter. "Shit!"

"If he's got relatives, you might want to call them. The doc said it didn't look good."

CHAPTER 30

THE HOSPITAL

Lieutenant Morreau brought all of the detectives together for a briefing. "I know most of you have heard by now, but this is the update. Somebody stabbed Detective Donovan at his apartment today." He stopped to stare at them. "At his *goddamn* home. With his son there."

"How's he doing?" The question came from Rodriguez.

"Last word I got wasn't good," Morreau said. "Kate Burns called and said one of the stab wounds punctured a lung. He's still in surgery."

"What do you want us to do, Lieu? We have anything to go on?" Bacchus, an old timer, asked that one.

"All we have is a report of a jogger leaving the scene of Frankie's building. He was wearing gray sweatpants, a light blue top, and a pair of sunglasses. Big sunglasses. He was heading north around the time we showed up."

"Not much," Rodriguez said. "How about Donovan's cases? Anything to follow up on?"

"I'm heading to the hospital as soon as I finish. I'll get Mazzetti to write up a report and fill everyone in. They've been working the Couples Murders so there could be a connection. Until then, I want that neighborhood canvassed. Every household accounted for. If someone isn't home, leave a card. If they don't call, go back. If they still ignore you, sit on the house. We need a witness. Got it?"

"We're on it," someone yelled from the back. "Whoever did it ain't coming in alive."

"I didn't hear that," Morreau said. "Anyway, I gotta go. I'll have Mazzetti send his report as soon as I get there."

When Morreau arrived at the hospital, he found Mazzetti in the waiting room. "Any news?"

Lou shook his head. "Still in surgery. How about from the teams?"

"Nothing. I just sent everybody out canvassing. I hope we turn up something."

***

Alex was sitting in a chair, his head leaning against Sherri.

FD's boss, Lieutenant Morreau looked over. "Is that Frankie's boy?"

"Come on, I'll introduce you."

"Alex, this is Frankie's boss, Lieutenant Morreau."

They shook hands. "Alex, I'm very sorry about Frankie. We all are."

"Is he gonna be okay?"

Morreau looked as if he didn't know how to answer. "I'm sure he will. God wouldn't let a good guy like Frankie die."

"Somebody ought to call Father Murphy," Alex said. "I think FD would want him here."

Morreau looked to Mazzetti. "'FD'?"

"That's what Alex calls him—FD—for Frankie Donovan."

"I like it," Morreau said. "And that's a good idea about Father Murphy. Do you know his number?"

Alex pulled out Frankie's phone. "This is FD's cell. It'll be on here." He flipped through the contacts list until he found the number, and read it to Morreau.

"Maybe you should give the phone to me," Lou said.

Alex shook his head. "Not yet."

Lou whispered to Morreau, "I'll get it later. I'm sure there's nothing on there anyway."

Alex watched as cops came in and out of the waiting room. Some were beat cops in uniform, some were detectives. Other people came by too, a nice lady named Carol, a reporter named Shawna. Alex had seen her on the news before. He remembered because Kate didn't like her. It was that same kind of feeling he got when Kate talked about Sherri. Good thing Kate was still with the doctors. She wouldn't like Shawna being here.

Alex listened to all of them. Most talked to Detective Mazzetti, hoping to get updates on FD, and Mazzetti asked the cops if anything was new. Nothing was. It seemed as if *nothing* was the secret word today. Nothing was new on FD and nothing was being done on finding the guy who hurt him.

The reporter finished talking with Mazzetti, then handed him a business card and left. Said something about having to get the story out on time…Alex didn't hear it all. As he sat there, a big barrel-chested guy walked in with an armful of flowers. He looked around, spotted Mazzetti, and handed the flowers to him.

Mazzetti stared back.

"How's Donovan?" the guy asked. His voice was deep.

"What the hell are you doing here, Giorgio?"

"Manny wanted to send flowers. He said to tell you he doesn't like this kind of thing and if there is anything he can do, you let him know."

"Tell him that Donovan's not doing too great, and the last thing he needs is a couple of wise guys coming to visit him." Lou looked to the side, then whispered, "But tell Manny I said thanks. And I wouldn't be opposed to any leads that he might hear about."

Giorgio shook hands with Mazzetti, then left.

Lieutenant Morreau was staring at Mazzetti. "Is that the Manny I think it is?"

"There's nothing to it, Lieutenant. The guy respects Frankie, and he's just letting him know."

"What was the business about leads?"

"Lieutenant, that man and his crew hear of things we can only dream of. If he gets a lead, I'll take it."

"All I need is a reporter getting wind of this."

"Don't worry," Mazzetti said.

"All right, I gotta go. Remember to write that report."

"I'll drop it off, or send it back with Carol."

Kate came back a few minutes later. She looked sick, and she looked as if she'd been crying. Alex had seen those red, puffy eyes before.

Lou jumped up and rushed over. He held up his hand for Alex to stay put, but he got up and followed anyway.

"What's new?" Mazzetti asked.

"Nothing. He's still in surgery. It shouldn't be taking this long. It must be real bad."

Nothing again. Alex held back tears, but at least now he knew what to do. He slipped away, out the door and down the hall to the outside entrance. He found a quiet spot, pulled out FD's cell, and looked up the number. It rang six times before someone answered.

"What's up, Bugs? How are things in New York?"

"Is this Mr. Fusco?"

"Who's this?"

"My name is Alex."

"Alex…You live with Frankie, right?"

"Now I do. FD told me that if anything ever happened I was supposed to call you."

"Is something wrong with Bugs?"

Alex tried stopping his tears, but couldn't. He cried. Hard. "He got stabbed. Some dude stabbed him and…I don't know if he's gonna make it."

"Where is he?" There was panic in Nicky's voice.

"They took him to the hospital."

"Where are you?"

"I'm at the hospital now. I came outside to call you." He started sobbing again. "He's still in surgery. He's been in there for hours. Kate said it isn't good."

"Can you tell me which hospital?"

"I don't know the name, but it's close to our house."

"Okay, Ace, I know which one."

"You know my name?"

"Bugs always talks about you."

"Yeah, he talks a lot about you, too. Calls you 'The Rat.'"

Nicky laughed. "That's me, 'The Rat.'" There was a pause, then Nicky said, "Did they catch the guy who did it?"

"They didn't catch anybody. They don't have a clue who did it or even why."

"How do you know this?"

"I hear the cops talking. They all keep coming to the hospital and talking to FD's partner. And all they keep saying is that they ain't got nothing."

"When did this happen?"

"A couple of hours ago."

"I was talking to him as he was getting home. This happen at home?"

"I don't want that guy coming back, Rat."

"What guy?"

"The one who stabbed FD."

"You saw him?"

"I was in the apartment when it happened, but he didn't see me. I was under the bed."

"Okay, listen up. You'll probably be at the hospital for a while yet. And don't worry, the bad guy won't come there. Besides, Kate will keep you safe."

"Reason I called you was because FD always said you got things done, and nobody up here seems to be gettin' anything done."

"I try."

"So you comin' up, Rat?"

"I'm comin' up. Won't take me long."

"You gonna get the guy who did this?"

"Ace, you are going to have to worry about a lot of things in life. Catching the guy who did this to Bugs is not one of them. Whoever did this will pay."

"Thanks, Rat. I knew I could count on you."

"You hang in there. I'll see you soon."

"Okay."

"Alex?"

"Yeah."

"One more thing. Don't tell *anyone* I'm coming."

"I know how to keep my mouth shut. Don't worry about that."

CHAPTER 31

BAD NEWS

I grabbed my gym bag and went to the basement, to the back, behind the oil tank. There was a small block wall around the tank to hide it, and help with the noise. The blocks were twelve inches wide, and hollow. One of them wasn't cemented in. I moved the one aside, reached down the hole and got my gun—a Beretta, 9mm—and put it in the bag along with a few extra clips. I didn't know what I'd find in New York, but I didn't like being unprepared.

As I crossed the dining room on my way upstairs, Angie came in the front door carrying Dante. She had been visiting neighbors.

"What's the gym bag for?"

"Bad news, babe. Bugs is in the hospital, in bad shape. Somebody stabbed him."

"Are you going up there?"

Her voice had a worried sound to it, the kind of sound a mother makes when she knows her kid is about to do something wrong.

I set the bag down and hugged her, though it was tough while she was holding Dante. "I have to. For God's sake, he might die."

"It's that bad?" Concern replaced the worry in her voice.

"Alex said he's been in surgery for hours."

"Alex is the one who called?"

"Yeah, he had Bugs' phone. Christ, Angie, he was *in* the apartment when it happened."

"The guy stabbed Frankie in his own apartment?"

"That's what Alex said." I grabbed my bag. "Hey, babe, I have *got* to get going," I said, and headed upstairs.

I grabbed some pants from the closet, a belt, pair of shoes, and tossed them all on the bed. I shoved a disposable razor and some Q-Tips into the toiletries bag, along with toothpaste and floss. It landed next to the shoes. Next I climbed up, reached through the door to the attic and pulled down a bag. I kept my "special" hat in there, the one rigged to hold a derringer. I put that at the bottom of the gym bag. As I washed my hair, Angie came in.

"What are these binoculars for? Are you going bird watching?"

"Nothing, Angie."

"And what's *this* for?"

I heard her, but I couldn't see what she was talking about. "What?"

She tossed a towel to me. "I said, what is this for?"

Her tone had grown demanding. I dried my hair and looked. She was holding my gun.

"Nothing."

"Nothing? You're going to New York to visit a friend in the hospital and you need a gun?"

I walked past her to the dresser, pulled three pairs of underwear out of the drawer, grabbed a few pairs of socks and a few shirts. "Don't worry."

"'Don't worry.' That's all you can say?" She grabbed my arm and pulled me to face her. "For thirteen years I waited for you. I didn't mind the ten years in prison. It was the three years after you got out that bothered me. And you tell me not to worry…" She started to turn away, then, "It's not just Rosa who hears the tales about you, Nicky. Why do you think my friends don't come by? I pray every day that people will forget it all by the time Dante is old enough for friends. But now…" Tears formed.

I hugged her. "Angie, I'm serious. Don't worry. I'm not going to do anything."

"You can show me that by leaving the gun here."

I tried to come up with something to say, but nothing sensible came to mind. "I have to take it."

"I don't understand. If you're not going to use it, and I have nothing to worry about, then why do you need it?"

"I just do."

"*I just do* isn't an answer. Would you take that answer from Rosa?"

She was trying to drag me into a fight I couldn't win, and she was doing a damn good job of it. "This has nothing to do with Rosa."

"You're going to hunt this guy down, aren't you? Why don't you let the police do their job? Frankie's a cop. They'll put all of their resources into finding the man who did this." She let loose the tears and grabbed hold of me. "Nicky, I *cannot* lose you again."

I squeezed her. "That's not going to happen. I promise."

"What if you get killed? What will Rosa and I do? Who's going to raise her, walk her down the aisle?"

"Angie…"

"What if the cops find that gun on you? I know it's not licensed."

"Listen, I—"

"And what about your job? You can't just leave without notice. What's Joe going to say? Who will do the estimating while you're gone?"

"The same people who would do it if I got sick. Things like this happen. People get sick. People have emergencies."

"I *know* what you're going to do. You'll go to New York and hunt this man down. And then you'll kill him."

I pushed her away from me. "There is *no way* I'm going to kill *anyone*. I'm going to visit Bugs. I'll probably be sitting with him in the hospital room most of the day. What I'm *not* going to do is kill anybody."

"Then leave the gun. Or don't go." She had her this is final voice going strong.

I grabbed her by the shoulders. "Angie, I love you more than anything in the world, but Bugs is in trouble. I have to go."

"If you go to New York with that gun, then pack a big bag. And don't come back."

CHAPTER 32

CANTALOUPE GIRL

The killer took great pains to calm himself. He thought about the day and what had happened. It had not been a particularly busy day, though he *had* plotted, arranged, and put everything in motion to do away with a cop. The killer corrected himself—to do away with a detective first grade. A significant difference, though to the cops who worked at police headquarters there wasn't. They all bled blue.

The killer thought about what the cops would be doing: Combing every square inch of Donovan's apartment, searching for clues; tracking down leads from junkies and whores; and following up on every clue from *anyone* who would talk to them and whisper a possible lead in their ears. The killer had nothing to worry about. Even if they did find his DNA, he was safe. Now he was free, though he had thought of doing something to attract their attention. Maybe he should do Cantaloupe Girl tonight. *Hmm. Must give that some thought.*

As he ate a piece of fruit, he decided. *Yes, now is the time to do it.*

After dinner he put on his blue jogging suit, and tucked the gun into his pocket. He hadn't yet decided on how to do Cantaloupe Girl, but he'd certainly be taking his time with her. No rush job.

The killer jogged most of the way to her apartment, casting a sideways glance toward her window as he passed. The shades were open and the lights were on. She was home. Maybe she'd forget to close them and give him a peek of something sweet. And sour. Twice more he went around the block, each time checking to see if she made an appearance. On his third pass he saw her on the street, walking toward the café with another woman.

She smiled at two guys walking down the street. They looked gay. Still…she had no business smiling at them.

It made him want to take her now, do things to her that would make the Marquis de Sade blush. The killer breathed deeply, held it for thirty seconds, then exhaled in a slow, controlled fashion. Then he opened his eyes, quickly searching for her. Where…ah, there she was. At the first break in traffic he crossed the street, coming up behind her. Catching up required a slight increase to his leisurely pace, but nothing to worry about. He had plenty left. Enough to satisfy her, that was for sure. His thoughts again turned to what he would do to her when he got her alone. He decided he might take a ride on the Hershey Highway. She would probably like that.

Cantaloupe Girl and her friend sat outside near the sidewalk, close enough so the killer could smell her perfume as he passed by. He made sure the hoodie covered his head so she didn't recognize him. He breathed the scent in—peach blossoms. It suited her well. He liked peaches and chocolate.

A grocery mart across the street provided a good place to watch from. He parked himself outside the door and waited. They were preparing to close, but she shouldn't be long. A TV was playing inside. He heard something about Donovan. He grabbed a bottled water and set it on the counter.

"Was that about a cop?" he asked.

"Some friggin' lunatic stabbed a cop today. The guy who's been working those murders. What the fuck is wrong with people?"

The killer shook his head. "It's not safe out there; I know that much."

"Tell me about it. Last summer my niece got raped on her way home from school. Fifteen years old!"

She was probably begging for it. "Fifteen?"

The guy nodded. "Never caught him either."

The killer couldn't wait any longer. "The cop that was stabbed, did he die?"

"Not yet. They said he's in critical condition."

A lump built in the killer's throat. He had to wait a moment for it to clear before he could speak. "I hope he's all right. We can't afford to lose a good cop nowadays."

"I'm with you, buddy." He looked at the water bottle. "That it?"

"Yes."

"$3.82."

The killer handed him a five and waited on the change. "I imagine they'll be searching everywhere for the guy who did this."

"Bet your ass on that."

"See you around," the killer said, and walked out.

Cantaloupe Girl was gone. But that was all right. He had other things on his mind now. What was he going to do about Donovan? He looked at his watch. It was getting late. Cantaloupe Girl could wait till another night.

CHAPTER 33

BACK TO NEW YORK

I hated leaving this way. I couldn't take it when Angie was upset. Made my stomach churn and my head hurt. I felt tense all over and I lost all my patience—what little I had. But in this case I had no choice. As much as I loved Angie, I had to be there for Bugs. We had been friends since we were little kids, before school. Even before cigarettes, and that was a *long* time ago.

I hopped on I-95 and headed south toward the Delaware Memorial Bridge, opting to take that route through Jersey; it would have less traffic. The bridge had a lot of history to it, but the only thing I remembered was that it opened up a quick route to Wildwood, the best beach and boardwalk in all of Jersey. Hell, all the world for a teenager. Summer nights on the boardwalk were like heaven. *If only we could go back.*

I shook the daydreams off and focused on what I had to do. New York wasn't far and the Jersey Turnpike made it an easy drive, but I couldn't afford to speed. If I got caught and some wise-ass cop decided he needed to check my car, my ass would be back in prison. No way was that happening.

After crossing the bridge I headed north. Two hours and I'd be there, barring traffic. It would have been nice to detour through the backwoods of the Pine Barrens, but I had no time for that. Besides, they held memories for the old days, and the old days were gone. The Pine Barrens was where you buried people, where you disposed of guns and anything else that needed to disappear. And it was a popular spot, open to any of the guys from Philly, Jersey, or New York. Between the three it amounted to a lot of bodies.

As I thought about the Pine Barrens, I thought of my first gang fight, the one in the woods. Our woods weren't all pines, but for a city kid it was all the same. Only when we got older did we notice the differences in the oaks, maples, hickories, sycamores… When we were kids they were just trees with leaves. During the fall we could identify the oaks because they dropped acorns and we used those for acorn fights. Their sharp points on the end hurt like hell when pelted on bare skin.

I thought of all the fun we had as kids. Bugs, Tony, Mick…all of us. If I was going to be honest, it hadn't been all fun; in fact, it hadn't been much fun. Mostly trouble, fear, and hard times, but we made the most of it. *The most of it! What a joke. Mick and Tony dead, and Chinski. And Paulie off in hiding. Now Bugs stabbed.*

"Fuck me twice."

Stabbed. I thought about knives and the kind of people who used them. It brought back memories of the old days, back when we thought gang fights were *cool.* Of course that was before we'd actually been *in* a gang fight and before any of us had gotten hurt. Before Mick was killed.

I still remember the first one. We were fighting Hedgeville, a bunch of Polacks who'd done something to piss us off. I don't even remember what. Back then it didn't have to be much, anything could spark a fight, and once a fight got going, it usually escalated into a gang fight even if it started with only two kids.

As we headed toward the fight that night my gut began to ache. My stomach churned as if something alive was inside it clawing to get out. The closer we got the worse it got. I swung my chain, picked up my step.

"Gonna kick some ass tonight," I yelled, afraid my fear was showing.

A chorus joined me, to a man, but I knew they were as scared as I was. Maybe more. I never liked knives. I preferred the butt end of a cue stick or a chain. Give me either one against a guy with a knife any day. The truth was, knives weren't all they were cracked up to be in gang fights. They looked scary and could be intimidating, but if someone had a knife and was up against a chain or a club of any kind, they were in trouble—unless they were an expert at throwing knives and making them stick. But most people took a 50/50 shot if they threw a blade, probably less. And if that knife didn't stick in just the right place they were in deep shit. Even in close situations, a coat or shirt wrapped around the left arm served as good protection against a knife. They were mostly for robbing people who weren't armed. Worst of all, carrying the wrong kind, which was the only good kind to use in a fight, could get you arrested. That's why we always carried chains and cue sticks—neither one was illegal.

My phone rang. "Hello."

"Nicky, it's Joe."

"Hey, boss. I tried getting you earlier."

"What's up? You need something?"

"I've got an emergency. I have to go to New York, but I shouldn't be long. Maybe two days. Three tops."

The pause felt strained. "Have we got anything urgent that needs attention?"

"Nothing that can't wait till I get back. And I'll catch up on the hours. You know you don't need to worry about that."

He laughed, some of the tension gone. "I know that, Nicky. I hope things are okay. Call me if I can do anything."

"Will do, Joe. Thanks."

The call reminded me that I had to get a burner. It would definitely be needed in New York. Didn't want any calls traced to my phone. I got off the interstate a few miles up the road and went to a small town where I knew of a store with no video. I bought a disposable phone without ID— and without being captured on video—and grabbed a bite to eat, a bottled water, then got back on the turnpike.

I couldn't get the thoughts of Bugs out of my mind.

Please let him be all right, God. He doesn't deserve this.

Especially not after all Bugs had been through. Not now, when his life seemed to be going so great, settled down with Kate and Alex. Bugs talked about Alex as if he were his own kid. *Good for him.* But I knew how easy that was to happen. Everybody thought Rosa was my daughter. She wasn't, but I loved her as much as I could love anyone. Almost as much as Angie.

I had to shake my head to clear it. Angie being pissed at me didn't sit well. Made me nervous. Before I knew it I was doing ninety. *Whoa, I need to slow this pony down.*

I thought about what Bugs could teach Alex. It brought back memories of the things we learned from our parents, or in my case, from Mamma Rosa. But we learned from other neighbors and from our friends' parents. All of them preached about staying away from gangsters. They were a bad influence. But what they didn't think of was that gangsters were a good influence too.

They taught us other things—a different kind of honor, how to not rat out a friend, how to stick up for yourself, how to handle a situation you didn't expect, and most importantly, how to stand by your friends and watch out for them. They didn't have a lot of patience, and the whacks they gave us hurt more than the ones the nuns dished out, but there was a little bit of love in each lesson. And those lessons stuck with us. Maybe more than the others.

There were things our parents taught us that were good, qualities they had that we admired and respected, but there were things we didn't like about them too, and we swore we'd never be like that. The same went for the guys we loved growing up, the ones our parents called gangsters. They had bad habits and did a lot wrong, but they had admirable qualities too.

The one thing that had the greatest impact on us was that they never judged us. They saw a different talent in each of us; we didn't have to be the same.

Doggs Caputo ran the mob operations in Wilmington. He always said that Tony was the smartest son of a bitch he'd ever seen for a kid. Tony had a mind like a steel trap and could remember almost anything without writing it down. Doggs used to give Tony assignments that played to that skill. And Frankie would do anything for money, no matter how tough it was. He never quit until the job was done. Doggs liked that, and he bragged about Frankie.

Me, I was the one Doggs went to for the secret stuff. If he needed a numbers bag dropped somewhere, or a special delivery of sensitive materials, he'd send me. Doggs knew I'd never surrender that bag, and if I got caught by the cops, they'd never find out who gave me the bag. That's why they called me 'The Rat,' because I wouldn't talk no matter what. I guess the bottom line is that a person can learn good things from everyone, and anyone.

A beeping horn brought me alert. I had drifted into the left lane. *Wake up, Fusco.*

I got back to Frankie and his attack. The guy had used a knife. Why a knife? If a guy is targeting a cop, he could get a silencer. So why use a knife? Most people used knives on spur of the moment decisions, or to keep the noise down, or when they really don't want to hurt someone, just frighten them. And it was Frankie's own knife he used.

What the hell? Did he come there to talk and something went wrong? Or did he plan *on using Bugs' knife?*

I was coming up on the Verrazano-Narrows Bridge when my home phone rang. I glanced at the caller ID. It was Angie. I grabbed it before the second ring. "Hey, babe. Sorry about earlier."

"Dad, it's me."

"Is everything all right?"

"I'm fine, but what's wrong? Mom is all upset and crying. I've never seen her like this. Did you guys fight or something?"

Shit! "It'll be okay, Rosa. Try to calm her down. Talk to her. Do…I don't know…something."

"What happened?"

"Bugs got stabbed. He's in really bad shape. Last I heard he's still in surgery. I'm on my way to see him."

"Oh my God! Why didn't somebody tell me? Why didn't you take me?"

"It's a long story. If you can do me a gigantic favor…please help your mom feel better. I need that."

"Okay, Dad. But call and let us know as soon as you get there."

"I will. Love you."

"I love you too, and tell Uncle Mario I love him."

"Count on it. Ciao."

"Ciao."

It broke my heart to hear that Angie was still so upset. I knew she would be, but I guess I hoped, somehow, that she wouldn't be. I thought about everything she said—me missing work, risking prison again, the danger to myself—not to mention breaking my vow to her, and I knew she was right about all of it. But she never asked the most important question of all: *What will happen if Dominic Mangini finds out I'm in town?*

I didn't know the answer, but I knew I'd better figure it out. I was halfway across the bridge. I could see Brooklyn waiting for me.

CHAPTER 34

A LATE-NIGHT VISIT

I got off the bridge and headed toward the hospital. There were a lot of things I had to do, and at the top of the list was smoothing things over with Dominic, but for now I'd have to risk his wrath. I needed to see Bugs. Alex hadn't called, so I assumed Bugs was no worse…still, I needed to get there. I didn't know what the visiting hours policy was, but one way or another I planned on getting in. I parked in a dark spot, checked to make sure no one was around, then strapped my gun to a special holder I had installed inside the wheel well. After that, I locked the car and went inside.

"What room is Frankie Donovan in?"

She didn't even need to check. "He's in ICU."

Before I could ask she pointed to the right. "Take that elevator and follow the cops. You'll find him."

"Thanks."

I followed a couple of uniforms off the elevator. A few more were hanging around drinking coffee and looking nervous. "You know where Frankie Donovan is?"

The one closest to me gestured with a nod of his head to the left. "Down there. They're about to shut down visiting."

As I passed the waiting room I noticed half a dozen cops. Two more sat in the hall on chairs. Why were they in here instead of out looking for the guy who did this to Bugs? At the nurses' station, a young woman filled out forms.

"Frankie Donovan?" I asked.

She looked at her watch, then back to me. "Room six, but you only have a few minutes."

"Thanks."

My pace slowed. I felt anxious about seeing him. Maybe I was *afraid* to see him. I never did like hospitals. I hesitated, finally got the nerve, and went in. Bugs was lying in a bed, tubes down his throat, oxygen mask on, IV in his arm. He had more monitors hooked up to him than NASA.

Christ, he looks dead.

A chair sat beside the bed, next to the nightstand. On the other side was a hospital tray for serving food. Bugs wouldn't be needing that anytime soon. A plain-clothes cop lounged in a chair on the other side of the room. He was an older guy, and looked half asleep, but when I came in, but he perked up. I could always tell a cop, no matter what they wore.

"Can I help you?" he asked.

"Here to visit my friend." I took the seat next to the bed. I lowered the rail so it wouldn't be in the way, then for a minute or two I stared at Bugs. Just stared. My emotions were difficult to choke down. This was my best friend in life. If there was anybody I loved as much as Angie and Rosa, it was Bugs.

I was afraid to talk, not wanting tears to come out in front of strangers. I figured the cop couldn't hear me, so I risked whispering. "Can you hear me, Bugs? If you can hear me you better say something, 'cause I'm not saying this to your face."

I grabbed hold of his hand, leaned in and whispered, "I love you, Mario Francis Donovan."

I figured if anything would jar him awake it was calling him Mario Francis. He never moved. Didn't smile, or squeeze my hand, or open his eyes. Slobber dripped from his mouth. I got a napkin from the nightstand and wiped it. He'd be pissed if he knew how they had him dressed. Ever since he was a kid, Bugs dressed to the nines. Always the nicest clothes, clean and pressed, and never out of style. Bugs had worn silk boxers when the rest of us had Fruit of the Loom. Pale-green hospital gowns wouldn't cut it. I looked over and saw his Morseschi shoes, blood all over them. There would be hell to pay when he woke.

I looked to my right, and the cop tensed, his hand inching toward his gun. He stopped when I shot him a glare. I shifted the chair, giving the cop more of my back, then I moved the water cup on the table next to the bed. Water pitcher was more like it, one of those giant plastic cups with a straw permanently attached. The ones everybody took home from the hospitals and, for some reason, kept. Maybe it was a reminder of a near-death experience. I leaned in close.

"You're a mess. You look worse than when we fought Browntown and got our asses kicked. Remember that?"

I looked up at the monitors. His blood pressure was low—70 over 50. I patted his hand. "Did I ever tell you how much it meant that you stayed out with me the night my dad died? It meant a lot."

The nurse popped in. "It's time. You can come back tomorrow."

"Okay," I said, then turned to Bugs. "I'll be back tomorrow. You hang in there." I started to go then whispered in his ear. "And don't worry, I *will* get the fucker who did this to you."

When I left, the cop from the room was already waiting in the hall. He held out his hand. "Lou's my name."

I looked him over. He wore a suit, slightly crumpled. His shoes were worn and scuffed, and his hat looked as if it came from a movie set from the 1940s. I shook his hand. "Nice to meet you." I started to leave, but he stopped me.

Two more cops were stationed down the hall, a woman and a guy. They weren't in uniform but I knew they were cops. I could tell as sure as if they were elephants. The female stood, stared at me for a moment, then moved toward me. Lou waved her off. I noticed her attitude, though. Noticed the other cop, too. Tense. Nervous. She unsnapped the latch holding her gun.

Trigger happy, are you?

"Got a name?" Lou asked.

"Why? Is it a crime to visit a friend?"

"Who said anything about crimes? I asked if you had a name."

Once again, I turned to leave. This time he grabbed my sleeve.

"Going to have to ask you to show me some ID."

I thought about what to do. I had several IDs on me. If I gave him a false one and he took my prints later, he'd see the difference. Now that he had me placed in Bugs' room, there could be trouble for Bugs if anything happened. Bugs seemed to have good things to say about this guy—if he was who I thought he was.

"Your name Mazzetti?"

He looked surprised, but he nodded. "That's me. How'd you know?"

I decided to trust my gut, and held out my hand. "Nicky Fusco."

As we shook hands he stared. Recognition came almost immediately. "The Rat."

I didn't smile. "Some people used to call me that."

"You gave us a good chase a while back."

"That was a long time ago. In a different life."

Lou smiled. "Yeah, I know. Anyway, nice of you to come all this way to see Frankie."

"I was going to be in the area."

"All the way from Philadelphia? Gonna be here long?"

"I hope not."

"Here for anything in particular?"

"Just to see Bugs."

"And that's it? See Frankie?"

"He's my friend."

He patted my back. "Hope you have a good visit, Mr. Fusco. Have a good trip back."

"You're not getting rid of me yet, Mazzetti." I wrote my phone number on a piece of paper and handed it to him. "Call me if anything happens. Please?"

Mazzetti stared, then nodded. "I will. But don't call *me*. I don't need your number showing up on my phone."

"Right now, I need to find a place to stay. I'll be back tomorrow."

I walked down the hall, past the young black cop and the one pretending to be an intern. At the nurses' station, I turned and pushed the button for the elevator. It was going to be a busy night.

***

Sherri headed down the hall toward Frankie's room, her head turning to check on the stranger's departure. Lou was in the chair reading.

"What was that about, Mazzetti? Why'd you stop me?"

"He's a friend of Frankie's."

"He didn't look like a cop. Do I know him?"

Lou shook his head. "You don't want to."

"What do you mean by that?"

Lou put down his book. "You know how when you're a kid in school there is always somebody who you think, 'He's going to be in jail someday' or, 'He'll probably be a serial killer.' Something like that?"

"Sure, yearbooks are full of them."

"Well, this guy's all of them rolled into one. Good thing is, if we take our time on this case, we might get it solved for us."

Sherri took one of her famous stances, hand on hip, lips pursed, eyes flaring. "There you go again with that *shit* talk of yours. You letting me in on this?"

Lou looked at her for a long time. "I'll tell you as a partner who loves you. But if you ever bring it up to anyone else, I'll swear you are a raving lunatic who went off your meds."

"I get the picture. Go on."

"Remember those murders a few years back, the ones that put Bugs on top?"

It didn't take her long to recall. "Sure, the gruesome ones. Made both of you heroes."

Lou nodded toward the hall. "Far as I'm concerned, that's the guy who did them. I'm only telling you because I have a feeling we might run into him as we continue this investigation, and the last thing I want is you going up against that guy."

She looked out the door, back down the hallway. "No shit?"

"No shit."

"So you think he's here…"

"I think he's the kind of guy who pays back favors."

"Meaning?"

"I'm done talking about it, Sherri. All I know is that maybe we should find some deskwork to do for a few days. We may get lucky."

"And you're okay with this…this…killer—chasing down our leads?"

"Fine by me," Lou said.

"How is that fine? The guy is a killer. A goddamn—"

He grabbed her arm. "How about you and me go outside for a minute?"

Lou stood and yelled down the hall. "Bobby, watch Frankie. We'll be right back."

Once outside he talked quietly and calmly. "Let's get one thing straight. This guy has no charges against him and was never even questioned about those murders. Furthermore, he is not the kind of guy you want to accuse of being a murderer. And lastly, if this guy, no matter his talents, can help us catch the one who stabbed Donovan, I don't give a shit if he killed Jesus Christ. I *want* that guy." He glared at Sherri. "You've got to make up your mind if you can live with this, because I'm going with it."

CHAPTER 35

CALLING IN A FAVOR

I woke up early, showered, did some pushups on the floor, knocked out a few hundred sit-ups, then put water on for coffee. While it dripped I checked my phone for messages. Nothing. Not from the hospital and not from Angie.

Goddamn. Is she still pissed?

I don't know why that surprised me. It took a lot to set her off but once she got going, it took even more to bring her back. I looked at the clock—7:30. Angie would be up. I called her, let it ring five times. No answer. My gut twisted. I hated tension like this.

I read the paper while sipping coffee—the real paper, not the digital news that Rosa read. Bugs was all over the headlines.

Detective Stabbed. Police Have No Clues.

Somebody was gonna catch a lot of shit about that one. Whether they had clues or not they didn't want it spilled by the media. I scanned down the column. I didn't know how current this was but the article said Bugs was still critical. I thought of calling Mazzetti but figured I'd stop by later. He seemed nervous when I gave him my number. He'd probably shit if I actually called him.

The hospital would have to wait. I had urgent business to take care of and there was no sense in delaying; in fact, it was imperative that I *not* delay. The last time I was in New York I caused a lot of grief for the Five Families. It had been touch-and-go back then as to whether they'd come after me or not. Since then there had been an unwritten rule—if I stayed out of New York, they'd leave me alone. The reverse went without saying.

After finishing the coffee I got my car and headed for Bensonhurst, about six miles away. Driving there brought back a lot of memories—good and bad. The bad mostly revolved around Tony and how I left him lying in blood.

Mi dispiace, Mamma Rosa. I am so *sorry.*

***

Manny lived in a modest house in Bensonhurst, a section of Brooklyn still heavily populated by Italians and peppered with Italian restaurants, shops, and cafés. I drove past his house, didn't see anything out of place, then circled the block and parked at the next corner. I looked up his number and called from the burner as I walked down the brick sidewalk, past the breezeway, and up the three steps onto his porch.

"Hello."

"Manny, it's Nicky. We okay to talk?"

"Jesus Christ, ghosts of Christmas past and all that shit. Yeah, we're okay; I get the place swept all the time. How's it going?"

"Good. I need a favor, though, and I figured—"

"Yeah, I know. I owe you. What do you need?"

"I'd rather talk about it in person."

A long pause followed. Too long.

"I'm not going to do anything," I said. "If I wanted to, there would have been no phone call."

"Yeah, all right. So where are you? I'll meet you somewhere."

"I'm outside your door. Why don't I come inside."

The blinds cracked, then the door popped open. Manny damn near filled the opening. "How the fuck do you know where I live?"

I smiled. "I know where everybody lives. You should know that."

He stepped aside, letting me in, then poked his head out and looked down the street.

"I'm alone."

"So what's going on? What the hell you doin' back in the city?"

"Guess you didn't hear. Bugs got stabbed."

His hands flew in the air. "Hold on, Nicky. I had nothin' to do with it."

"Relax. I know it wasn't you. He's after some nutcase serial killer. Mazzetti figures him for doing Bugs."

Manny's eyes shifted to a spot behind me. The floor creaked at the same time. I dropped to the floor, pivoted and swept the legs out from under a guy a couple of feet from me. I had my gun pointed at Manny before I got back to my feet.

Manny had his hands raised in the air. "Hold up, Nicky. Goddamn, it's just Giorgio."

I looked down to see Manny's right-hand man, Giorgio, getting to his feet.

"Damn near killed me you stupid fuck."

"Sorry, Giorgio. I'm a little nervous."

"Put that gun away. You make me fuckin' nervous." Manny lowered his hands, and shrugged. "You want espresso?"

I grabbed a chair and pulled it to where I had a good view of both doors. "I could use some."

"Bugs all right?"

"Don't know yet. He's pretty bad."

Manny spooned the espresso into a pot on the stove. I was glad to see he still made it the old way. Weren't many people left who kept to tradition. I had always been fond of espresso. Of course, that might have had something to do with Mamma Rosa giving Tony and me coffee in our bottles at two-years old.

"What the fuck is wrong with people nowadays, Nicky? Nobody's got respect."

I nodded, knowing Manny would continue.

"I mean, you don't pop a good cop like Bugs no matter what he did. He's got a job to do, just like you and me. If he beats you at it, you tip your hat and do the time. You don't pop him."

"That's the way I see it."

"I hear you settled down. Got a family and a good job."

"You hear a lot way up here in Brooklyn."

"Yeah, well you know…some people make it their business to know where you are and what you're doing." He set the espresso cups on the table and poured one for me and Giorgio, then brought his from the stove. "Sugar?"

"This is fine," I said, and took a sip. "Are you one of those curious people?"

"Not me."

"Dominic?"

"You know Dominic. He's old school. He was the one vote against you when that shit happened with Tito."

"Just one?"

"You know I was with you. You did me a favor."

"I guess Dominic hasn't forgotten."

"A hundred-year-old revenge still has its baby teeth." Manny let his words sink in, then, "That's an old Italian proverb. Some people still believe in it. Dominic Mangini lives by it."

I had figured as much. "Remember that favor you said you owed me? I'm here to call it in."

The chair groaned as Manny shifted in his seat. "I thought you were just here to see Bugs."

"Somebody damn near killed Bugs. He might die." I slugged down the last gulp of espresso, and stared at Manny. "He's gonna have to pay for that."

"You should let the cops handle this," Manny said.

"We'll see."

"If this guy turns up dead, the press is gonna think the cops killed him for what he did to Bugs. And then they're gonna look real hard to find out who killed the guy. See what I mean?"

"Let's get back to Dominic," I said. "Anything you can do to smooth things over for me?"

Manny shrugged. "Maybe. I don't know. I'll put in a word for you. I owe that much, but I can't guarantee anything."

"That's all right. I'll take care of it myself."

"What, you going to see him? I think you're better off leaving it be. Get your business done and be gone before he knows you're here."

I laughed. "He probably knows I'm here already." I dropped my smile and looked at Manny. "And you know that."

He shrugged his big shoulders again. "Yeah, guess so."

I took the espresso cup to the sink and rinsed it. "Gotta go. Thanks for the espresso."

"Just so you'll know, Dominic has this guy named Fabrizio…"

"Yeah?"

"If Dominic decides to come after you, he'll use Fabrizio. He's good, Nicky. *Real* good."

If Manny was warning me about Fabrizio that meant he thought Fabrizio was better than me. I didn't like that.

"Thanks, Manny. I appreciate it." I turned to Giorgio. "Sorry about the leg."

"Nothin' to it, Nicky. Be good, huh."

***

Manny parted the blinds and watched Nicky walk down the sidewalk.

"Why did you tell him about Fabrizio?" Giorgio asked.

"Because I don't like Fabrizio," Manny said.

"But he works for Dominic."

"You gotta learn, Giorgio. Things are good with Dominic, but you never know in this business, and Fabrizio is too dangerous to have looming as an enemy."

Giorgio shook his head. "I don't know, Boss. Nicky's good, but I've seen Fabrizio work. Never seen nothing like him."

Manny shrugged, picked up his phone and called Dominic. He answered right away. "Hey, Dom, it's Manny. Yeah, thought you'd want to know…Nicky Fusco's in town."

"To see his friend?"

"So he says."

"Grazie, Manny."

"Prego."

Manny turned to Giorgio, wearing a smile. "Nicky…Fabrizio…either way I'm happy."

CHAPTER 36

A VISIT WITH KATE

I stopped at the hospital on the way back, figuring I'd give Manny a chance to get hold of Dominic. Maybe if Dominic thought enough about it, he'd soften up. From what I'd heard of him I doubted it, but…maybe.

I parked and walked into the hospital alongside two uniforms. So many cops were coming in and out of here, it looked like a station house. They should have been out finding the guy who did it instead of visiting Bugs. I walked into the waiting room. Lou nodded to let me know he'd seen me, but I had to wait fifteen minutes for him to break free. When he finished with the last cop he stepped into the hall and started walking. I followed.

"Any news?" I asked.

"Nothing much. He's still sedated with all that shit shoved down his throat."

"No word on who did it?"

"Nothing."

"Mazzetti, you have *anything* on the guy who did this?"

"No clue. I'm convinced it's connected to the case we're on, but…"

"But what?"

"I'm convinced it's connected, but it doesn't *feel* like the same killer. Why didn't he use the same gun? Why use a knife, and one of Frankie's knives to boot?"

"Other than speculation what do you have?"

"What the hell? You expect me to give you what I got? You think I'm gonna just give you my case file? Asshole. Besides, even if I wanted to, it's locked up in my car, the pretty little silver Taurus parked across the street."

"Thanks, Mazzetti. You're okay."

Lou grabbed my arm. "You didn't let me finish."

"Sorry, go on."

"The pretty little silver Taurus…with the *back door open* so people don't have to break into it."

"I'd kiss you if I weren't married."

Lou grabbed my arm again. "If you get caught, I'll say those files were stolen. It will be my word against yours."

"No need to lie. If I get caught, I'll say I stole them."

Lou stared at me. "Maybe you *are* okay."

"Do you have Kate's number?"

He gave me her cell but said he thought she took the day off to be with Alex and that she'd be here soon.

"Maybe I'll wait outside for her."

"I don't mind if you're in the waiting room. Just don't act like we're buddies."

"I'd be more comfortable outside. I'll wait in the car."

"The silver one?"

"Yeah, that one. No need to have those files go missing."

"Lot of notes in there," Lou said.

"I have a good memory."

"So I heard. See you around."

I walked out of the hospital, found Lou's car and climbed in. The case files were on the floor. I told Lou I had a good memory, but he was right— there were a *lot* of notes in here. Rather than risk missing details, I took the folder to a copy shop and got what I needed. I didn't need all the crap forms, just the meat. Afterward I replaced the folder in his car, and then I called Kate.

"Hello."

"Kate Burns, please."

"This is she. Who is this?"

"My name is Nicky Fusco, I'm—"

"I know who you are. I'm at the hospital. Can you call later?"

Judging from her tone, Kate didn't much like me. "Sure," I said and hung up. No sense in arguing on the phone.

I walked back to the hospital. Kate had gone in to see Bugs. A kid sat in the corner looking sad. I walked over, knelt beside him. "Are you Ace?"

He perked up. "You Mr. Rat?"

I tried not to laugh but couldn't help it. *Mr. Rat.* "That's me." I held out my hand. "Nicky Fusco."

He shook. "Alex Donovan. FD gave me his name."

I liked the boy already. He was proud of getting Bugs' name. "You want to go outside and talk for a minute?"

He followed me out. We found a bench to sit on under an old oak tree. There was even a breeze to keep us cool. I didn't say anything for a minute, waiting to let Alex get comfortable. "You see your dad today?"

"Just for a minute." He stared at the ground. "He can't even talk."

"He'll get better," I said, though I don't know why I said it. It always seemed like the thing to do in hospitals, keep saying the person will get better. Say it enough and maybe it will come true. Like wishing on a star.

"That's what Kate keeps saying too."

"You feel up to answering a few questions for me?"

He looked up. "About that day, you mean?"

I nodded. "If you're not up to it…"

"Is this gonna help you catch the guy?"

I looked around instinctively. "I'm not supposed to be looking for the guy, but since I know you can keep secrets, I'll trust this to you. I *am* looking for the guy, and I'm gonna find him. So, yeah, this is to help FD."

"Then I'm up to it. What do you need?"

"Tell me what happened that day."

Alex filled me in on the details and on how CPS had come by the day before. "I was home by myself and heard a knock on the door. I was about to open it when I saw the handle turn. I *knew* that wasn't right, so I hid under the bed like FD told me to if anything ever happened."

"Did you see the guy? Was there one or two?"

"I didn't see nobody. FD told me to get under the bed and cover up. Don't look. That's what I did."

"What happened next?"

"The guy came inside. I heard him walking around. And I heard talking…but only one voice."

"I don't understand."

"I mean, the guy was talking, but I don't know if he was talking to himself or to somebody else."

"Okay, then what?"

"It seemed like I was under there forever. It was hot, and the blanket was itching my face. Then I heard the door open again." Alex looked at me with big sad eyes. "Is FD gonna be okay?"

"I don't know yet, Alex. How about you tell me the rest of the story first."

"Okay, so after the door opened again, I heard FD's voice. He said, 'Hey, Ace. You here?' And then the other guy said 'Nobody here but us.'"

"Nobody here but us? You're sure that's what he said?"

"Positive. Then I heard FD. He didn't scream, but he kind of…I don't know…grunted, I guess. And he said… 'fuck.'"

Alex looked up at me. "Didn't mean to curse, Rat."

"That's all right. I've said worse." I rubbed his head. "Anything else you remember?"

He shook his head. "No…wait a minute. The guy was *singing*."

"Singing? You sure?"

Alex popped off the bench like he'd discovered something important. "I'm positive. I know the song. It's…"

"Something you listen to?"

"No. It's FD's…no, it's one of Kate's songs. She sings it when she's happy. I can find it if you want."

"You know any of the words, or the words he was singing?"

"I remember because it's the same part Kate sings. 'It's a Beautiful Morning.' It's an old song."

I smiled. "I know *exactly* the song you're talking about. Good job."

"Does that help?"

I rubbed his head again. "It sure does."

Alex laughed.

"What's funny?"

"FD always rubs my hair the same way you did."

Tears built in his eyes. He tried not looking at me but then he wrapped his arms around me and started bawling. "What's gonna happen to me if FD dies?"

I patted his back. "He won't die."

"I should have done something. All I did was hide under the bed like a *pussy.*"

"There was nothing you could have done."

"FD would have saved me."

"And from what I heard, you saved him." I knelt in front of him and held his face. I wiped his tears with a handkerchief and stared into his eyes. "If you hadn't called 9-1-1, he'd be dead. And if you had tried to help him, you'd be dead too. Trust me. I know what I'm talking about."

"Why did that guy do this to FD?"

I hugged him again. "I don't know, but when I catch him, I'll find out. I promise."

From behind us I heard a panicked voice. "Alex!"

He looked over. "Kate, right here."

She stormed over, a look in her eyes that was half panic and half rage. She grabbed Alex and yanked him to her side. For a moment I thought she was going to punch me.

"Who are you?"

I held out my hand. "Nicky Fusco."

The look in her eyes shifted to fear. "You're his friend from Wilmington?" Her eyes shifted left and right, but never once straight at me.

"We grew up together. Yeah."

"Why are you here?" She seemed tentative, cautious.

"To see Bugs."

She appeared to be shaking. She was definitely nervous. "What's the matter?" I asked.

Her eyes finally met mine, and they locked there. She leaned down to Alex and whispered. "Go inside to Detective Mazzetti. Tell him where I am. I'll be there in a few minutes." She waited for Alex to leave before going on. "I've seen your work. You scare me."

"I don't hurt innocent people."

Kate looked at me, scowling. "I can't trust a person who is capable of doing those things to anyone."

I stared at Kate. She reminded me a little of Angie, maybe tougher—at least on the outside. New York did that to people. But inside, I suspected that Angie had her beat. *Nobody* was tougher than Angie when it came to holding her ground. I nodded. "I won't argue with you."

I knew I should let it go, but I couldn't. Some people just didn't understand. "Some days God doesn't do His job. That's when I take over."

"And is this one of those days?" Her hands were resting on her hips, not unlike Angie did when she felt a little above herself.

"This is one of those days, Kate. Count on it." I thought of what Alex said about the song. "Alex said there is a song you always sing. Maybe just the chorus."

"I sing a lot of songs."

"He said this one was when you were happy."

She thought, then nodded. "Young Rascals. *It's a Beautiful Morning.* Why are you asking me about a song?"

"Alex said the guy who did this to Bugs was singing it."

"What a sick son of a bitch." She shook her head. "How come Alex didn't tell that to the cops?"

"I have a way of getting people to tell me things. Sometimes *without* torturing them."

She stared, concern in her expression. "Why don't you let the cops handle this? It's their job."

"Cops are good at some things—catching crooks, putting people in jail. But not at administering justice." I patted Kate on the back and headed for my car. "Call me Michael the Archangel."

The distance between us must have given her courage, or comfort. Before I reached the street I heard her yell, "Good luck, Michael."

Bugs was right; Kate was a good person. I hoped things worked out for them.

CHAPTER 37

RUN FOR YOUR LIFE

It had been two days since Detective Donovan was stabbed. No cops had busted down the killer's door, or anyone else's door, which meant that either Donovan was still out of it, or he didn't recognize the person who attacked him. The cops were running all over town looking for the vicious person who attacked Donovan, so…the killer decided to give them a clue. He'd decide what the clue would be once he had prospects in sight.

He decided to run. No car. Prospect Park wasn't far. He jogged down Ninth Street, past the old row houses, past the expressway, and all the way to the park. A small crowd was gathered at the Ninth Street entrance. The killer turned and went down to Fifteenth Street. He entered the park from there. No sense risking anything.

At first he didn't see anybody, and wondered if everyone had parked their fat asses on sofas, but as he ran he started spotting some joggers, and some walkers, too. He turned right, toward the lake. A pair of females were just ahead—running buddies, he guessed. Paired up so they'd be safe. He thought about shooting them to prove them wrong, but opted not to. At the next bend, an older couple were doing a *fast-walk*, hands swinging like robots from a sci-fi movie. They wore matching blue jogging suits and what appeared to be identical running shoes. Or maybe they were walking shoes. Who the hell knew? The killer didn't give them a second thought. They were too boring to kill.

It was almost dark. The joggers were thinning out—going home to shower, watch TV, talk to each other about how fit they were. The men, in particular, amused him. The ones in shape thought they were invulnerable,

able to handle themselves no matter what came up. But one pop from a gun and they'd fall just as hard as a couch potato. *Invulnerable my ass.*

He didn't see anyone as he passed the lake. He turned left, hugging the lake, running parallel with South Lake Drive. An older woman sat on the grass by herself. Two guys, who looked as if they should have stayed home, walked by panting, ready to call it quits. No doubt they were heading for the exit. The killer continued, smiling as he slowed to inspect a couple with a dog. They looked young—thirtyish—both with iPods plugged in. The woman was runner-thin, taut and tight. The way he liked them. With the proper mindset, she'd be good in bed.

Almost as good as Susan.

The guy was a hair on the chunky side. He *needed* the run. The killer wondered if he ran as an ultimatum—run or you get no sex. He took a final glance at her body and nodded to himself. Given those circumstances, he'd run, too.

The dog kept changing pace. Moving in front of the couple, then behind. The leash had him restricted, but even with that, he looked more bored than the killer felt. He was probably thinking he could be home watching TV or humping somebody's leg and wondering why they brought him out here—*he* didn't need to lose weight.

The killer wondered why he always called dogs of an unknown gender *he*. As he thought about it, he realized he did something similar with cats, but called them *she*.

Weird, he thought. *Do other people do that?*

"Try to keep up," the woman jogger said to her partner as they passed by.

The killer turned his head. The guy was sweating, his tongue hanging out as he struggled for a good breath, and that bossy bitch had the nerve to push him? Bossy Bitch didn't know it, but she had sealed her fate. Unfortunately Chunky was destined to share it. The killer let a minute or so pass, then he turned around and picked up his pace. He'd catch them before long. Bossy Bitch might have given him a run for his money, but only if she abandoned Chunky.

For a moment he worried they might leave the park, but then she turned on West Lake Drive. "Fate's Warning," by Iron Maiden came to mind, the lyrics popping into his head.

He wasn't sure he had the lyrics all right, but he recalled something about destiny, and staying alive, and bullets. That was enough for him.

The killer closed to within about fifty yards. He altered his pace, falling back a little, then inching up near, but never too close. No need to attract attention. Bossy Bitch stopped, reached down and undid the leash on the dog. The killer glanced at his watch—8:45. Leash laws ran till 9:00.

Shame on you, Bossy.

Before he realized it, he had closed to within about twenty yards. A quick check showed no one around. He pulled out the gun, kept it by his side. When he got within ten feet, he raised it and popped Chunky in the forehead. Bossy Bitch gasped. He shot her in the face, then fired a second time into the side of her head. The dog growled, moving toward the killer. He looked to be some kind of terrier. Ordinarily, he liked terriers.

Oh well, he thought, and shot the dog in the chest. "Sorry, friend. You should have stayed home."

He took out the little notepad he carried and penned a quick ditty. Afterwards he removed her top and bra, sharpened a small stick, stuck it next to her breast, and attached the poem. He did a quick glance around, saw no one, then headed for the Ninth Street exit. He'd be home in no time.

CHAPTER 38

SOME WOUNDS NEVER HEAL

I woke early and called Angie, but she didn't answer, which made breakfast miserable. I liked to enjoy breakfast, not worry about whether she would be waiting for me when I got home.

If I get home. This morning's meeting would go a long way in deciding the if.

I stopped a few blocks from Dominic's house, took the gun from under the wheel well and put on my cap, the one with the derringer rigged inside it. I didn't want any trouble, and had no intentions of causing any, but I couldn't control what might happen.

If Manny had told the truth, Dominic Mangini was the lone holdout of the Five Families when they granted me a reprieve for killing Tito. He was also the most vicious Mafia boss since Lucky Luciano. One story said he had a guy's eyes cut out while he was still alive and that even after the guy told Dominic what he wanted to know, he continued cutting. I shivered. Not many people frightened me. Dominic Mangini did. And there was no telling how he'd react to me being in New York.

I kept a slow pace, looking for traps or spotters. As I climbed the steps to his house my stomach turned a few times. I hadn't seen anybody but I didn't know if that was good or bad. Either no one was there, or I missed them. I dreaded the thought that I could be slipping.

The sidewalk leading to the house was brick—old from the looks of it, but well maintained. Brick steps led to the door. I knocked firmly. As I waited, shifting weight from one foot to another, I noticed a bullet mark in the door. It brought to mind one of the other stories about Dominic, how a rival family tried killing him one night and missed. Within a week everybody involved disappeared. The stories said he never fixed the door, kept it as a reminder never to be caught off guard. I saw now the story was true. That was good to know.

The door was answered by an older man who looked as if he ate pasta a little too often. He had a smile that went ear to ear. *No way is this Dominic.*

I held out my hand. "Nicky Fusco. I'm here to see Dominic Mangini."

He grabbed my hand with zest. It seemed as if that zest came naturally to him. "Nicky Fusco. Son of a bitch, I've heard tales about you." He still had hold of my hand. I was beginning to get worried, but then he let go. "I'm Zeppe Mangini, the nice brother." He laughed when he said it. The laugh came naturally too. Already I liked this guy.

Zeppe led me across a small marble foyer. He moved fast for a heavy man. I glanced around as we walked, keeping alert. I felt like I did those first few weeks in prison, when the showers were like a minefield and I never knew who might try to grab me for a back-ender.

I got my second kill that way.

French doors opened into a living room with hardwood floors and an Oriental rug. The house was impeccable; I expected no less.

An older man, about sixty, sat in a chair by the window. He looked like somebody's grandfather, except for his eyes—piercing eyes that burned holes all the way to my soul. The saying from *Julius Caesar* came to mind about Cassius' lean and hungry look. I suspected Dominic was more dangerous than Cassius.

I was halfway across the room before he stood. He was shorter than me. Thinner, too. The hair on the sides of his head were distinguished gray; the rest was bald. I got a lot of impressions right away but the predominant one was danger. This man would make a bad enemy.

I shook hands with him, making sure to give him my best smile. "It is an honor to meet you."

"Niccolo Fusco, I knew your father. *He* was a respected man."

I nodded, taking note of the slight. I decided not to do the same to him. "As you are respected, Signor Mangini."

"You already met my brother, Zeppe, and this" —he gestured to his left—"is my lawyer."

Being in Dominic's presence changed Zeppe. The plump, jolly man with the quick smile was gone, replaced with the look of a worried man. Not a good sign. He wasn't a threat himself, but the change in attitude told me lots. I extended my hand to the other man. I had felt his eyes on me ever since I entered. This man might have been many things. A lawyer wasn't one of them. He had the eyes of a fox and the posture of a tiger. I pegged him for Fabrizio, Dominic's feared enforcer I'd heard so much about. If he was Fabrizio, then Manny was right. This guy was good. I could sense it. He looked me up and down in a heartbeat, but didn't bother to offer a handshake. I'm sure he wanted his hands free.

"It is a pleasure, Signor Fusco."

He spoke good English but with the Italian cadence. Definitely Fabrizio.

"The pleasure is mine, Signore."

I turned back to Dominic. "I'm grateful you could see me, Signor Mangini. I should have called."

The one I pegged as Fabrizio moved closer. "I'm sorry, Signore, but I assume you don't have weapons on you?"

I kept my eyes glued to his. Neither one of us was fooling the other. "*Mi scusa.* Back of my waistband."

"*Grazie.*" He reached behind me and grabbed the gun. "It will be returned, of course." With that said, he continued to frisk me better than any cop would have.

I gave him my best fake smile. "Of course." All the while I thanked God he hadn't checked my hat. Maybe Fabrizio wasn't as good as everyone thought. One of the first things Johnny Muck taught me was to *never* underestimate an enemy. I removed my hat, like any respectable person, and held it in my hand, beside my leg.

I waited for Dominic to take his seat, and then I sat too. A guy who didn't look like a servant came out from the kitchen. He waited for Dominic to speak.

"See if our guest would like espresso."

It went without saying that Dominic did. The man looked at me, but not like a waiter. More like a guy who wanted to break my legs. He didn't speak either.

"I'll have a cup," I said, "assuming Signor Mangini is."

Dominic didn't have to look to know when the man was out of earshot. "What brings you to New York, Niccolo?"

I felt certain that Manny had told him, but I played it safe. "My best friend, Bugs Donovan, was stabbed. He's in critical condition."

Zeppe looked genuinely surprised. "No shit? Bugs? He's a good guy. He helped us—"

Dominic never took his eyes off me, but his hand moved slightly, enough to shut Zeppe up. I figured Zeppe would be in the East River if he wasn't Dominic's brother. Again, it told me what I needed—that Dominic already knew about Bugs.

"Isn't he a detective?" Dominic asked.

"He is," I said. "Homicide."

Dominic shook his head. "No one has respect anymore."

I knew he meant it as another slap at me. *Time to test the water.* "Not like the old days."

Dominic shot me a glare. I think he'd have shot me if he wasn't afraid of getting blood on the furniture.

The servant/waiter who wasn't a servant/waiter returned with espresso for all of us, then brought in a plate of biscotti.

Dominic broke a small piece from a biscotto and nibbled on it. "*Buon appetito.*"

I took a sip of my espresso. "*Perfetto. Grazie.*"

He looked at me. His eyes were as riveting as Pops' were. Maybe more.

"You've been to visit your friend?"

There was no sense lying to him. If he caught me in a lie, it would go far worse. "Last night."

"When will you be leaving?"

I had to hand it to Mangini, he didn't dally around. I thought about how to answer it and decided the truth was best. "Not until I get the guy who did this."

I glanced to my right as I spoke, checking on Fabrizio. He sat on the sofa, his right hand lying across the top of the cushions. One hand moved a little until he saw me look. I figured there was a gun hidden there. When I first came in he had opened his jacket, exposing his waistband to show me he was unarmed. I stared back to the sofa cushion where his arm lay. He seemed a little too tense. If Dominic did anything, I'd have to shoot Fabrizio first.

Dominic munched on his biscotto and took a sip of espresso, and all the while he stared at me. "I granted you the courtesy of a meeting even though I shouldn't have. The Families didn't come after you for a lot of reasons, but it does not change the fact that you killed a boss without sanctions. It was not your place."

"I understand that, and I offer no excuses. What I did was wrong, and many of us have suffered. I hope that the Council is more pleased with Manny Rosso than they were with Tito." The last part was a jab at Dominic. He couldn't deny that Manny was far better for them than Tito had been.

Dominic took another bite from the biscotto. He took his time, as if he had just sat down to a six-course meal. "If someone kills the president and the next one is better, they don't let the killer go."

"True, but if he hasn't been caught, perhaps they don't search as hard for him."

He took time to evaluate me, his stare intimidating. "It was my understanding that you would leave New York, never to return."

"The circumstances with Bugs forced me to return." No need to say that I came to get justice. That would be taken for granted.

A long silence followed. "I heard tales of why you killed all of those people. They say it was over a woman."

"Tito wanted me to kill a woman. I told him I would, but decided not to when I found out that she was innocent. He killed her himself and tried to kill me." I shook my head. "He shouldn't have done that. We would have left him alone."

"And the killings? You did them alone?"

"All of them."

"And now you are here to avenge your friend Detective Donovan? A noble cause."

I bowed my head. "Thank you, Signor Mangini. You have my word, I will be in and out quickly. I'm not looking for trouble."

"No one wants trouble," Dominic said. "But I cannot allow you to stay. You have broken the rules again. It seems as if you are in a habit of breaking rules."

Dominic stood. Fabrizio tensed, like a snake coiled to strike. I smiled and stood with Dominic, offering my hand. "I'm sorry to hear that, Signore, but I understand. Not everything in life is as easy as we'd like."

My response took him off guard. I could tell by the way he eyeballed me, as if expecting me to do something. But Dominic had control of his emotions; he recovered quickly.

"I'm glad you understand, Niccolo. It would have been…unfortunate, if we had to disagree."

"I'm not here for that," I said. "I hoped we could have done this differently, but I *will* ask a favor."

Dominic narrowed his eyes. "Yes?"

"I would like to stay until Bugs is stable, at least able to talk."

"And if I refuse?"

I shot a glance to Fabrizio, made sure the servant/waiter wasn't around, then stared into Dominic's eyes. "I hope you won't."

"But if I do?"

"I'll stay anyway."

Dominic flashed a smile that was not a smile. "Of course you will. But I knew that." His glare turned hard and he moved close, his whisper a threat in itself. "No one wants trouble. You should go home to your family."

I shifted my hat to my left hand, holding it as we chatted. "Thank you for your advice, Signore." I turned to Zeppe and thanked him, then I turned to Fabrizio, extending my hand. "My gun?"

I had my hand on the derringer inside my cap, praying I didn't need it but ready if I did. Fabrizio got a nod from Dominic and handed it to me. His other hand was behind his back, gripping his own gun of course. I tucked mine into the waistband behind me, put my cap on.

"Don't be a fool," Dominic said. It was a threat, not a plea. This man had no fear.

"You're thirty years late with that advice."

Dominic stared. The guy from the kitchen, the servant/waiter, appeared with a gun in his hand. So much for disguises. I kept my eyes on Dominic. He'd have to give the order for anything to happen.

"I didn't come here to kill you or you'd be dead already. I came to get the guy who stabbed Bugs. When that's done, I'm gone."

Mangini glared. "We have rules for a reason."

"I know all about your rules. And a hell of a lot of your people don't follow them. What I did was Tito's fault."

Dominic's face muscles tightened and his eyes narrowed even more. "It was not your decision."

"I know how you feel. But it's done with. I've moved on. I'm not even in this life anymore."

"And yet here you are, with a gun, in *my house*."

"I mean no disrespect, but I can't let the guy who did this to Bugs get away."

"Leave my house," Dominic said.

I nodded, staying alert. Dominic had already made up his mind. Fabrizio would be coming after me, and he'd probably have help. I headed for the door. No sense in threatening him. It would just make him come after me harder. When I got to the front door, I turned. "Signor Mangini, I know this is your home, but you're being unreasonable. I hope you'll reconsider. I only want the guy who did this to Bugs."

Dominic didn't answer. Neither did Fabrizio. Even Zeppe said nothing. I backed out the door. Halfway down the sidewalk, I heard Dominic's voice.

"I'm not an unreasonable man. You have twenty-four hours."

I nodded. He didn't need to say anything else. I hustled to my car, wishing I'd parked a lot closer. I needed to act fast. Dominic would put Fabrizio on this right away. I needed to switch hotels, get a rental car under a fake name, and watch myself whenever I went to the hospital. I never

thought it would be easy; to come to New York after I'd been gone so long
and track down a killer; now it had gotten a lot harder.

As Angie would say, I sure knew how to fuck things up.

CHAPTER 39

A MORNING AT THE PARK

Mazzetti got out of bed for the third—or was it sixth—time to piss. There had been a time, long ago, when he could last twelve hours without pissing. He'd wake up with a rod like he'd taken Viagra, but at least he got sleep. Now he was lucky if he could go two hours. And people wondered why he was grumpy in the morning.

In the middle of a particularly strong stream, the phone rang. He hated to stop. Actually he couldn't stop or he'd piss on the floor. On the toilet seat at best. So he let it ring until he finished. After the ninth or tenth ring he knew it was important.

Suppose it's about Donovan.

That thought forced him to rush through the living room to the kitchen. "Mazzetti."

"It's Sherri. We have more bodies."

"Are you shitting me?"

"Not this early. You want me to pick you up?"

"Where are they?"

"Prospect Park."

"In the park? What the hell…" Lou turned water on for coffee. "Yeah, pick me up. Give me twenty minutes."

"Make it thirty. I haven't showered."

Twenty-five minutes later Sherri pulled up in her red Honda Accord. Lou moved the newspaper off the seat, and tossed an empty coffee cup into a rolled-up breakfast bag from some deli.

"Nice car, Miller, but it needs cleaning."

"Needs cleaning? I've *been* in your car."

"I understand, but you're single. You've got to think about the image you're presenting. Suppose you pick someone up in this. How's that gonna look?"

"*If* I were to pick someone up—and that won't happen—but if I were to pick someone up in my car, I wouldn't worry about how clean it is."

"All I'm saying is that if a woman picked me up in a car this dirty…I'd have to give some thought to a second date."

Sherri laughed all the way to the next corner. "Okay. I'll keep that in mind."

***

Dave Shu was at the scene when Lou and Sherri arrived.

"Guess you actually have to work now that Kate's out for a few days," Lou told him.

Dave looked around then shot Lou the finger.

Mazzetti smiled, but it disappeared as he walked up on the first vic—the woman. Blood covered the side of her head. The male vic lay next to her with a forehead shot.

Lou turned when he heard Sherri gasp. Then he saw the dog.

"Who the fuck kills a dog?" he said.

Sherri knelt next to Dave. "You got anything?"

"Single shot to each of them. Close range. Looks like the guy was facing the shooter when he got it. The woman probably turned to run and caught it in the side of the head. I can't imagine why he shot the dog."

"Who found the bodies?" Lou asked.

Dave gestured to a lady standing off to the side with her arms wrapped around herself. "An officer who was here said she was jogging early this morning when she found them."

Lou looked around. "Where's the officer?"

"He's out questioning people, hoping to find a witness. And he said to tell you he called for additional help on the canvas."

"Good luck with that," Sherri said.

"They'll send them," Lou said. "Too many murders makes the big brass nervous. They don't want to scare tourists off."

"We need to find out where Benning was last night," Sherri said.

"We don't know if this is connected yet."

"It's a couple," Sherri said.

"Yeah, it's a couple, but nothing sexual. And they were shot in the head only." Lou lifted his hat and scratched his head. "And why did he switch to the park?"

"Nothing sexual?" Sherri looked at Lou. "She's naked from the waist up and a makeshift dagger is stuck next to her tit."

"Other than that and the note, and that they're a couple, and…" Lou laughed. "Damn, Miller, learn to lighten up, will you?"

"I can't lighten up when I see stuff like this." Sherri looked at the bodies again. "Nothing else, Dave? No rape, no messing with the genital areas?"

Dave shook his head. "Shot in the head, and, from what I can tell so far, nothing else. Looks like he shot them and took off. The bodies are where they dropped for sure. The guy doesn't look like he's been moved. The killer took the woman's top off, and her bra, to attach the note, but she's still in the general vicinity of where she fell."

Sherri leaned down and read the note aloud.

"Her ass was tight and round

She had a bushy mound

But the sweat deterred me

Really disturbed me

So I put them in the ground."

"This is a sick fuck," Lou said, and looked around. "The way I see it, he came up to them on the jogging trail and just popped them. Why? What the fuck did these kids do to him?"

"That's another thing, Mazzetti. The other murders had definite infidelity involved. You might be right about this one being different."

"I think he's fucking with us now," Lou said. "I don't suppose we have an ID?"

"No sexual overtones but it looks like the same caliber gun," Dave said. "I'll have specifics after I get them back. As to the ID, we got lucky. The guy had his license attached with Velcro to his sleeve." He handed Lou an evidence bag with the ID inside. "John Albans. Nothing on her, but they're wearing matching wedding rings."

Sherri looked closely. "Gold and diamonds. Definitely not a robbery."

"Keys were in his pocket. I bagged them, too."

Lou copied the address from the license while Sherri called Carol. "See what you can get me on a John Albans and his wife." Sherri read off the address, which was in Park Slope.

Lou got Morreau to authorize leaving a few uniforms at the park entrances so they could question people, though he didn't hold out much hope for it. If anything, they'd get lucky tonight. Joggers tended to run at the same times, so maybe one of the nighttime crowd saw something. Lou also put a couple of uniforms on questioning people from victims' neighborhood to see if anyone knew if they ran every night and at what time.

Sherri pulled out her cell. "We need to find out where Benning was."

"Call his lawyer," Lou said. "We can't talk to Benning."

"That's who I'm calling." Sherri looked up the number, and a few seconds later she was on the phone with his attorney. "We'd like to ask Mr. Benning a few questions. No, it's not about that. This is another case, and I think you'll want to be there for this."

She hung up and looked at Lou. "He said he'd be at the station at 2:30."

"Good," Lou said. "I can't wait to take another shot at him."

"Don't you think it's strange that his lawyer was ready for this? He didn't even have to check with Benning to see what time he'd be available."

"Almost as if he was expecting the call," Lou said.

"Exactly."

"Don't worry, Miller. We've got the right guy."

Sherri shook her head. "We better, because there's nobody else."

CHAPTER 40

DEALING WITH THE CONSEQUENCES

I drove away from Mangini's in a pissy mood. Things had not gone well; in fact, they'd gone worse than I expected. I checked the rearview mirror for the millionth time, something I'd be doing a lot from now on. Dominic had given me twenty-four hours, but Fabrizio would be following me sooner than that.

The first thing I did was get a rental car. I opted for a small agency run by a guy I knew from Queens. He could keep his mouth shut. Besides, he knew my reputation, and he wouldn't tell anyone unless Dominic had his balls in a vise. He stashed my car in his private garage, promising it would be safe. I headed to the hotel after that, parking a few blocks away and making damn sure I wasn't followed. Even so, I circled the block a few times on foot, checking everything that moved and especially the things that didn't.

I thought about checking out of the hotel, but went with my first idea and opted not to. If I passed the deadline Fabrizio would come looking for me. It would be better if he thought I was still there. Might buy me some time. I followed the same routine to get back to my car, grabbed my stuff from the room, then searched for a new place to stay. After a lot of driving I decided to stay in a dump in Staten Island, a place where nobody knew anybody. The manager of the place was so high he wouldn't know who he had as guests.

Once inside the room, I used the burner to call Lou. He answered after a few rings.

"Yeah, this is Mazzetti."

"It's Fusco. Anything on Bugs?"

"I don't know. I have two more bodies. Call Kate. You need her number?"

"I've got it. Thanks." I hung up and called her, but there was nothing new on Bugs. He was stable, but hadn't talked yet.

I thought about what Lou said—two more bodies—and wondered if they were connected. Never one to believe in coincidences, I figured they were. By the time I got to the hotel, I'd heard plenty of news about the joggers. It was all over the radio.

I went to the room, set the copies I'd made of the case files on the bed. What I really wanted to do was take a shower, eat a nice meal, and go to sleep. But I had to review these files. I couldn't afford to waste time after what happened today. With that in mind, I called Angie. I let it ring ten times, which was against my principles. No answer. Now I was worried.

I grabbed the notebook and made a list of what Alex told me.

The guy came into Frankie's apartment and waited. Just waited. He knew Bugs wasn't home and was confident enough to break into a cop's apartment. And he didn't bring a weapon. Or if he did, he decided to use a knife from the kitchen instead. Adjusting on the fly. This was no amateur.

The cops coming must have scared him off. Otherwise, Bugs would be dead. Or maybe he'd thought Bugs was dead. Either way, he had the presence of mind to take Bugs' gun.

Two days later he killed two joggers, who appeared to be random targets.

Why? If it were me why would I do it? Why kill the joggers?

Even as someone who had killed people, I couldn't think like that. And why kill the dog?

Alex had said the guy was singing in the apartment. "It's a Beautiful Morning."

Does that tell me anything?

I had a lot of questions, but nothing else. I opened up the folder containing the case files and looked at the notes:

No signs of rape with either victim.

No forced entry at hotel or the second victims' apartment.

No witnesses.

Both women worked at the same building.

Both were young professionals and in a relationship—one married, one engaged.

One lived alone, one with her husband.

One killed at home, one in hotel.

Didn't go to same hairdresser.

Not same nail salon.

Didn't get to work same way.

Didn't shop at same stores, even online.

According to their iTunes lists, they didn't even listen to the same music. One Country, one hip-hop.

They only had two things in common: they worked in the same building, and they both had a relationship with Chad Benning.

I had to admit that Benning looked good as the primary suspect, but I wanted to see what else the cops had.

Benning called Krenshaw's phone, or alleged phone, several times the week before the murder.

He was seen by the doorman at her apartment the night of the murder.

He was having an affair with Debbie Parnell and, apparently, with Sandy Krenshaw, though that hadn't been confirmed with any of her friends.

Had a key to Parnell's apartment.

His hair found at the scene.

Apartment cleaned excessively, as if to get rid of DNA.

No alibi for night of Krenshaw's murder. Later he claimed he was with Parnell that night.

Notes left at scenes.

Benning not only looked good, he looked *too* good. I approached this case using Sister Thomas' rules. She taught us to consider all options, eliminate the impossible, then choose from what remained. According to her method there were only two or three primary paths to solve any problem. Each path might have many branches, but using this method the first decision involved a maximum of three choices. Even when it appeared there were only two, she encouraged us to look for the third.

There is almost always a third choice, she said.

Since I was absolutely certain it was Benning, the first order of business was to disprove it. I learned that from killing. When you plan a killing you figure out how you're going to do it, and then you take every step of the process to see what's wrong with it. You presume that something will go wrong, then adjust. I used the same methods for Benning.

I saw this as black and white. Either Benning did it, or he didn't. Two choices. As I jotted down the pros and cons to each, Sister Thomas' voice haunted me about a third choice. I stopped and looked at the situation again. I had four dead bodies, all connected, plus an attack on Bugs and two joggers killed. All of it pointed to Benning. Two choices—he killed them, or he didn't.

Sister Thomas' voice nagged me until I saw it. Lurking in the gray between the black and white was another option. Someone could be framing him. There were still only two choices—he did or didn't—but this third "choice" would affect how I looked at the evidence.

With that in mind, I went back over the notes even though I felt as if I had forced that third option. I still saw it as two: he did or didn't.

The first thing that raised a question was why Krenshaw's disposable cell phone activity started only one week before the murder. And *why* for God's sake, would Benning leave that damned incriminating message on her phone, and then leave the phone where it could be found so quickly?

Which brought up another point—was the "Do Not Disturb" sign at the hotel turned the wrong way by accident…or was it part of the plan? It was Benning's voice on the phone message. He said it was business. *Was it?* If so, who set him up?

If I assumed the killer was Benning, and he was smart enough to leave no clues, how was it he was stupid enough to be seen by the doorman at Parnell's, who Benning knew could recognize him?

The affairs might have given him motive in a perfect world, but if he was such a Cassanova, why would he care about other women getting it on with one more person? One was married and one engaged, and he already knew that.

It doesn't add up.

The key to Parnell's apartment was nothing. If they had a relationship, she'd have given him a key. The hair they found—same thing; it could easily have been there from innocent visits. However, and this was the big thing, I didn't buy that *only* his hair was found. It looked more like a plant than a coincidence or an oversight.

I thought about the apartment being cleaned. Again, I asked myself *why*. It wasn't to get rid of his DNA, which could easily have been explained by the affair. But the excessive cleaning made it *look like* that was the reason.

And the bars alibi didn't fly. He had to know they'd check with patrons and bartenders.

I looked at the notes found at the scenes, and came to the conclusion that they were left to distract the detectives. Make them think the killer was crazy. Unless something popped up to show me differently, I'd go with that theory.

I thought about the sequence of events. After they arrested Benning, Frankie was attacked, and then the joggers killed. The attack on Bugs and the killing of the joggers were different, and yet, oddly the same. He used the same weapon as the first two killings, but the pattern didn't fit.

A few hours ago, when I started this, I had Benning pegged for the murders. Now I wasn't so sure. I didn't like it when cops made assumptions, which a lot of them tended to do. I picked up my notes and looked at Benning from the opposite angle—if he was guilty he *wouldn't* have left the phone where it could be found so easily; he *wouldn't* have been seen at the scene with Parnell; and he *wouldn't* have left his own hair at the scene? It didn't add up and I didn't like it. If Benning didn't do it, I was back to square one. And I only had one day. I looked at my watch. Twenty hours to be exact.

CHAPTER 41

A CONVENIENT ALIBI

Lou leaned back in his chair, feet on the desk, trying to catch a short nap before Benning and his lawyer arrived. He was getting too old to get up early and go the whole day without *some* kind of rest. Fortunately, all he needed was a ten- or twenty-minute snooze to recharge. *Unfortunately,* about five minutes into the nap his phone rang. He snatched it from the desk, cursing himself for not putting it on vibrate.

"Mazzetti."

"You sound agitated, Detective."

He looked at the caller ID. It read Unknown. "Who the hell is this?"

"It's Nicky Fusco. I wanted to see how Bugs is doing."

Lou pulled his feet off the desk and planted them on the floor. "You just woke me from much-needed sleep."

"Sorry. I tried Kate but couldn't reach her."

He sighed. "Last I checked he was the same. A little more stable maybe."

"That's good news."

"I didn't say he was going to a dance, Fusco. I said a *little* more stable."

"I heard you."

Lou looked around the office to make sure no one was near. "How about you?"

"I'm still reviewing things. You have anything on those bodies this morning?"

"We're bringing Benning in for an interview this afternoon."

"I don't think he did it."

"Hey, *detective*, how about you let us do the hard work."

"Fine, but I'm telling you, I don't think he did it."

"All the evidence says he did."

"I'm not saying you can't pin it on him. I'm saying I don't think he did it."

Mazzetti looked up when Miller walked in. "Okay, thanks, I gotta go."

"Who was that," Sherri asked.

"One of the unis at the park. They got nothing so far."

"We figured that much," Sherri said, and glanced at the clock. "Fifteen minutes till he gets here. How do you want to work this?"

"Not much we can do other than ask for an alibi. If he doesn't have one, we'll know where to look."

"And if he does?" she asked.

"Let's wait and see."

Carol announced Benning and his attorney, and Lou led them to the interrogation room. Chad started to speak but the attorney took control.

"What is this about, Detective?"

"I'm sure you've heard about Detective Donovan being attacked in his home." Lou stared at Benning as he talked, but the attorney answered.

"I did. That is a tragedy."

"Where were you when it happened, Mr. Benning?"

"I was—"

The attorney stopped him. "Mr. Benning was at work until four o'clock, and then he went home to pack for a trip. He was there until he went to bed."

"Is there anyone who can corroborate this?"

"No. He was alone."

Sherri smiled. "And how about last night?"

The attorney smiled. He reached into his briefcase and handed Lou a slip of paper. "He was at a hotel in Atlanta. Here is the receipt. He arrived at the airport this morning at 9:45. His boss occupied the seat next to him."

The news seemed to take the wind from Sherri. She shook her head and sat back in the chair.

Lou looked the receipt over and made a few notes. "If you had this great alibi, why did you come down here?"

"You didn't tell me what you wanted to see him about."

"Bullshit. You knew."

"We're trying to get clear on this," the attorney said. "Mr. Benning wants this over with so he can get back to work without being harassed. I'm not going to let you bully him."

"This doesn't change anything about the other murders," Lou said.

"I want you to drop those ridiculous charges," the lawyer said. "You know he didn't do it, and my client is tired of his name being dragged through the mud."

Lou stood. "You can go, Mr. Benning. I'm sorry we wasted your time."

After they left, Sherri grabbed Lou's arm. "I'll check with his boss on the alibi, but I'm starting to wonder—are we looking at the wrong guy? Is he innocent?"

"Maybe he didn't do the two in the park, but I like him for the others."

Carol popped in, handing a coffee to each of them. "You're gonna need these. We just got the ballistics report. Whoever did the joggers did it with the same gun as the others."

Sherri tapped her pen on the desk, her right leg jiggling at high speed. "This doesn't make sense. This killer—whoever he is—breaks into Donovan's apartment, waits for him to get home and tries to kill him. If it weren't for Alex calling 9-1-1 he probably would have." She looked at Lou and shook her head. "Then he goes out and randomly kills a few joggers?"

"And let's not forget, he stabbed Donovan with his own knife."

"I hate to say this," Sherri said, "but we can't be sure the person who stabbed Frankie is the killer."

Lou broke the pencil in half. "You're right. And as much as I don't want to say it, I don't think Chad Benning is good for Frankie. I can picture him doing the others, at least the women, but not Donovan. I don't think he's got the balls."

"Then who does?"

Lou stood and tossed the pieces of pencil into the trash. "That's what we have to figure out. Let's go."

CHAPTER 42

NO MORE SUSPECTS

"Where are we going, Mazzetti?"

"Back to the goddamn street when Morreau hears about this."

"He's already heard."

Lou looked back to see the lieutenant, staring at them with his really-pissed-off look. He motioned toward his office. Lou took the seat closest to the door in case he had to run for it. Sherri wasn't as smart.

Morreau started yelling before the door slammed. "How the fuck does this happen, Mazzetti? I have two seasoned cops and my best young detective on this case. Tell me how you fuck it up this bad."

"We thought it was him," Sherri said.

"Clamp it shut, Miller. I'm not blaming you for all of it, but you're sharing." Morreau kept his glare aimed at Mazzetti. "Still waiting."

"Until today, everything pointed to Benning," Lou said.

Sherri jumped up. "I think he's good for it, Lieu."

Morreau pointed his finger at her and moved closer, backing her into the chair. "You don't know *shit*, Detective. If you did, you'd have a *real* suspect in custody."

Sherri gritted her teeth. The muscles in her face tensed.

"I've got six bodies now, *and* a detective in critical condition. Do you know what time the chief called me this morning?"

Lou stood. "We'll get him. After what he did to Donovan nobody wants him more than we do."

"So what do I tell the chief?"

"Tell him to call me," Lou said, and walked toward the door.

Sherri followed. "Where are we going?"

"We're going through those files until we break somebody's alibi."

"Whose?"

"I don't know yet. But *somebody* is going down for this." As he passed Carol's desk he snapped at her. "Did we get the DNA on the hair from Parnell's place? Or Donovan's?"

"Not yet."

"Call them. Find out what the *hell* is holding it up."

Carol looked as if she might snap back at him; instead, she saluted. "Yes, sir, Captain Mazzetti. Right away, sir."

Lou stopped. Then he laughed. "Sorry, Carol."

"I know, sweetie. Just a reminder, is all."

"A reminder that I was being an ass?"

"You said it."

Lou grabbed the files and sat at the table. Sherri pulled up a chair and sat across from him. "I'm beginning to like Carol more than ever."

"Screw you, too," Lou said, and flipped through the notes. "Benning had no alibi for anything until the joggers."

"But since they are connected…"

"Yeah. How about Krenshaw's husband?"

"He was out of town, remember?"

"I do now. And Stewart. What about him?"

"He was home working on his computer when his fiancée was killed. I don't think we asked about the first murder. He wasn't connected."

"And we checked that alibi about him being online?"

"Carol did but I think she said it wasn't a guarantee."

"Carol."

"Yes, dear? I'm always listening."

"Don't I know it," Lou mumbled.

"*Always,*" she said.

"Can you get back to your source on the alibi for Stewart? See what he can tell us about that."

"I'm on it," Carol said. "I'll tell him we need it quick."

"Thanks."

***

Two hours later Carol got back to Lou. "My guy said he could have easily faked it if—and it's a big if—he knew what he was doing."

"Tell me about it," Lou said.

She read from her notes. "He said the program to fake activity is trivial. Any ten-year-old with some smarts could do it, and if the guy ran the program from a True Crypt volume, he could have easily hidden it by wiping the volume. There would be no evidence that the True Crypt volume even existed, let alone what was on it. There might be logs showing the traffic in Stewart's system, his local network device logs, etc., but he could have removed those too. So if he knew enough to make it to begin with, he probably would. And another thing: service providers don't keep this information for long, so chances are, it would be gone by now."

"So what you're telling me is if he did cover his tracks that way, we can't prove it."

"Bottom line, yes. We might be able to find evidence that the program existed, but we'd have to get his computer to find it."

"And for that we'd need a warrant." Sherri slammed her hand on the desk. "You know what makes this worse? We already checked that alibi and it basically proved him innocent. It would be tough to go back in now and say he could have done this or that."

"It's not all bad news," Carol said. "The DNA report came back. The hair at Parnell's apartment belongs to Chad Benning. And guess what—it matched hair at Frankie's apartment."

Lou jumped up. "What!" He reached his hand out. "Let me see that."

Carol handed him the report.

"Hair from two people was collected at Frankie's. They ruled both Frankie and Alex out. It belonged to another male besides Benning."

"Son of a bitch!" Sherri got up and paced. "How the hell did Benning's hair get at Frankie's place? And if he didn't do the other murders, why would he try to kill Donovan?"

"I don't know, but let's go see Mr. Stewart. I'd like to look at that computer of his."

On the way over, Lou called Benning's lawyer.

"I don't mean to bother you, but we're trying to clear this up so we can scratch Mr. Benning from our list."

"I'm glad to hear you've come to your senses, Detective."

"One question I forgot to ask. When we processed the scene at Detective Donovan's house, they found some of Mr. Benning's hair. Can you explain how it got there?"

A long pause followed. "I will get back to you on that."

Lou looked at Sherri. "I bet it won't take long either. He'll come up with some asshole excuse."

"Maybe these cases aren't connected, Lou. It could be a coincidence that someone attacked Frankie. Think about it. We've got nothing to tie his attack to the murders."

"Except Benning's hair."

"But he looks clean for the others now. And if he's clean for that, why in the *hell* would he go after Frankie?"

"Turn right at the next street," Lou said.

His phone rang; it was Benning's lawyer. "Mazzetti."

"Detective, I just spoke with Mr. Benning. He said he cannot explain his hair being at Detective Donovan's house. He was never there and other than his exposure to him during your investigation, has never met him."

"Okay, thanks for getting back to us so quickly."

"Benning's lawyer?" Sherri asked after he hung up.

"Yeah, and you're not going to believe it. He had no excuse or explanation."

"That doesn't sound like a lawyer."

"I know. This case keeps getting stranger."

CHAPTER 43

SISTER THOMAS' RULES

I glanced at my watch before taking off on a short jog. I had about 18 hours to go before Fabrizio would be stalking me. Running helped me think. Maybe it jarred my brain and let the pieces fall into the right spots. Whatever it did, it often worked and I never discounted things that worked. A mile or so into the run, my thoughts became more fluid, Sister Thomas' Rules opening up new avenues while they closed others. One was as important as the other. I figured by now there were thousands of theories about how to solve problems, but the one Sister Thomas taught never let me down. It worked, so I used it.

The evidence pointed to Chad Benning, but the logic didn't. Sister Thomas taught us to look beyond the obvious, dig deeper, think harder. Ask lots of questions. Being a killer helped me in this case. It allowed me to think like a killer thinks. A few cops thought like that, really put their heads into a case and *felt* what it was like to be a killer for a moment. But it was only that—a moment. They didn't have the sense of a killer. That was something different altogether.

I started at the beginning. Six dead bodies. I left out the attack on Bugs. According to the rules, dead bodies were either accidental, from natural causes, or murders. These were definitely murders. Were the victims random or targeted? It was highly unlikely they were random: Both of the first two women were cheating on their husband/fiancé, and both worked in the same building.

That left targeted victims—which brought up the question of *why* they were killed. It looked like jealousy, but I didn't want to focus on psychiatric bullshit. Anyone could make a murder look like jealousy.

I had to look for real motives and ignore all else, for now. It might come back to jealousy, but I couldn't assume that. In my opinion, motive was always behind a killing, unless the killer was crazy. But if there was motive, then the person wasn't crazy. Disturbed maybe, but not crazy.

The first two women were fooling around—motive. *But whose?*

The dead men were single—no motive.

Who had motive? Husband of Krenshaw. Fiancé of Parnell. Boyfriend of Parnell. No one we knew of for the joggers.

Krenshaw's husband has an airtight alibi.

Fiancé has weak alibi.

Chad Benning has no alibi for first two murders.

I had to look at this. The trick was not to look *at* evidence, but to look *beyond it,* or *through it,* to see why it was there.

I went in assuming the killer could easily have made a stupid mistake.

For Benning, we had the voicemail and the calls to Krenshaw. Admittedly, stupid.

The bar alibi and being seen by the doorman. Stupid again.

Cleaning Parnell's place beyond belief but leaving *one* hair. Stupid.

And where was the gun? It wasn't at his apartment, or work. They didn't find a storage facility. It wasn't in his car.

This guy supposedly killed six people without leaving a single clue that he didn't want to. *That* is *not* stupid. I knew as much. I'd done it myself. It was damn difficult to kill someone and leave no clues.

I wiped sweat from my forehead, wishing I'd brought a towel. I looked at my watch, guessed I had gone about two miles. *Few more and I'll quit.*

My reasoning so far had me back where I started—Chad Benning. Which meant I wasn't trying hard enough. Cops thought a lot about *connections* and *things in common* when they solved cases. They should learn to think like killers. Killers only think of one thing—how do I kill this person and get away with it? And they will do *anything* to achieve that.

So I returned to motive. Who had reason to kill Sandy Krenshaw? Her husband. I scratched him off. He was on a plane when it happened.

Who had reason to kill Debbie Parnell? Her fiancé, Bruce Stewart. I felt certain his alibi could be broken. But Stewart had no connection to Krenshaw.

If I were Stewart, how would I do it?

I'd stalk her building until I got a connection. If there wasn't one, I'd make one up. *But there* is *one connection—Chad Benning.* Chad was having affairs with both women, both of whom worked at his building. It would be easy to make him look guilty.

How?

I thought about the evidence. An incriminating piece was Krenshaw's cell phone, and the voice message on it.

Easy enough. Buy a burner. Fake calls to Chad. He did *say they were business calls. Some investor bothering him. Then I'd make sure to dump the phones where they could be found. And leave the "Do Not Disturb" sign on the hotel room turned the wrong way.*

My adrenaline was pumping. I kicked it up a notch, excited by the progress.

A woman about my age passed me by. She wasn't even sweating. I vowed to train harder when I got home.

I focused on how Stewart would do Parnell. He could easily sneak by the doorman, but a smart killer wouldn't count on that. Not a guy this careful. He wouldn't leave something like that to chance. I needed to check out the apartment. I had to figure out how he got in without being seen.

I finished my run, took the steps to my room in the hotel, and thought about Krenshaw and the joggers. Unless I found some other connection to Stewart, it meant he killed them to cover up killing Parnell. If that was right, my initial assumption was wrong. This guy was *stone-cold* crazy. All I had to do was prove it. I slid the key card in, opened the door, and looked at my watch. Eighteen hours.

Get your ass in gear, Fusco.

CHAPTER 44

ANOTHER INTERVIEW

ou and Sherri got out of the car and knocked on Bruce Stewart's door. Lou finished the last few drags of his cigarette while they waited.

"You're disgusting, Mazzetti. You *do* know that, right?"

He crushed the butt on the porch. "Because I smoke?"

"Because you disregard the rules."

"I'm grandfathered in. I was insulting people long before the laws."

The door opened. Stewart popped his head out. "Yes?"

Sherri flashed her badge. "Detective Miller. This is Mazzetti. We met at Ms. Parnell's apartment."

"Of course. I knew I recognized you, but couldn't place it." He moved out a little, stood with one foot on the porch and the door open. "What can I do for you, detectives? Has there been a break in the case?"

"We're still looking at the same man, but we have some additional questions."

He moved his other foot onto the porch and let the door shut. "How can I help you?"

"Maybe we should go in and sit?" Lou said.

Stewart smiled. "I would love to invite you in but the place is a mess." He smiled, then said, "Renovations."

Sherri nodded. "You want to come down to the station?"

"If we must. Let me get my things. I'll ride with you." He turned as he went back in. "You don't mind, do you? Me hitching a ride?"

"Not at all," Sherri said.

"I'll need a ride back," he said.

"We can do that."

"Great. I'll only be a minute." He disappeared inside, letting the door close and leaving them on the porch.

Lou looked at Sherri. "Renovations?"

"Odd sort, isn't he?"

"He didn't want us inside. That's for sure."

True to his word, Bruce returned a few minutes later. "I'm ready if you are, but I decided I'll follow you to the station."

"You're welcome to ride with us," Sherri said.

"No, thanks. I have errands to run afterward."

The whole way to the station, Lou fidgeted with a cigarette, and once Sherri parked, he had it lit before the door was all the way open.

"You go ahead," Lou said. "I'll be in when I finish."

Sherri waited for Stewart to park, and then she took him upstairs to the interview room. "Would you like something to drink? Coke, coffee, tea?"

"Tea would be wonderful, thank you. I take it with lemon, no sugar."

"Be right back," Sherri said.

Lou was in the room when Sherri returned with the tea. He sat in a chair next to Stewart, an unlit cigarette in his mouth rolling from side to side.

Stewart looked at Lou, then Sherri. "What can I help you with, detectives?"

"We're looking at Ms. Parnell's case again," Lou said. "That means we have to re-verify alibis, so how about you tell us again what you were doing when Ms. Parnell was killed."

"I understand. As I told Detective Donovan…by the way, how is he doing?"

Lou scooted his chair closer. "Just answer the question, Mr. Stewart. And please, don't give me that bullshit about browsing the Internet. Anyone can fake that."

Bruce sipped his tea, made a frown. "Tea in a paper cup isn't quite the same."

"Getting back to that night," Sherri said. "Where were you?"

He looked at Lou. "I wouldn't know about faking the browsing, Detective, but I was on the Internet. And I *do* have an alibi for the first murder." He put his finger to his chin. "What are they calling them…the 'couples murders'? I said that right, didn't I?"

"Where were you on the first murder?"

"At the opening of a new art gallery."

"Witnesses?"

Stewart put his index finger to his chin and cocked his head. "Ten, possibly a dozen people, both friends and acquaintances. We left around 10:00, then went to dinner."

"I'll need those names," Lou said.

"Of course," Stewart said, and sipped more tea. "Is that all?"

"A couple of other things," Sherri said. "We matched your DNA from Ms. Parnell's apartment to hair found at Detective Donovan's. How do you explain that?"

"First of all, I'm shocked that you could get DNA processed so quickly. But assuming that's correct, I have to ask how you *know* it's mine? I never volunteered my DNA. And I won't fall for your tricks of drinking coffee or Coke while I'm here and then leave my cup." He wiped the rim of his cup with a napkin. "In case you're wondering, I'm taking this with me." A smile followed his statement, a smirk really, kind of a fuck-you smile. "So while I don't doubt you have someone's DNA, you cannot prove it's mine. Not legally."

"And how did it end up at Detective Donovan's house?"

Stewart looked hurt, then agitated. "Detective, I volunteered to give you my DNA earlier, but Detective Donovan didn't take me up on the offer. Now I'm a little pissed at the insinuations. And as far as my DNA being in Detective Donovan's apartment, let's speculate. He was at my house the day he was attacked, and he drove me home from the station in his car. I remember his jacket being on the seat when I got in the car. If he laid it back on the seat after I left, I'm sure trace evidence transferred to the jacket." Another fuck-you smile followed.

Lou fought to control himself. He wanted to smack the smug look off Stewart's face. The son of a bitch planned it. He invited Frankie to his house for an alibi. And he attacked Chad Benning to get his hairs and skin. Then he used Frankie's own knife so there was nothing to trace or catch him with.

Stewart drained his cup and stood. "If there is nothing else…"

"We have more questions," Sherri said. "Take a seat."

"I don't think I will. I have wasted enough of my day. If you need anything else, I'll give you my attorney's name."

"Attorney?" Lou moved into his space. "Why do you need an attorney?"

Bruce laughed. "Perhaps I have watched too many TV shows, Detective. I find I'm not as trustful as I once was when it comes to New York's finest." He motioned for Mazzetti to move aside. "If you'll excuse me, I have groceries to purchase."

Sherri squeezed the back of the chair until her knuckles turned white. When Stewart left, she kicked the chair aside, then another one, knocking over the waste can. "That son of a bitch is guilty. I know it."

Lou nodded. "We said the same thing about Benning."

"Benning at least was believable. When we told Stewart that his DNA was at Donovan's house, he didn't flinch. He had an answer prepared." Sherri pounded her fist on the table. "Goddamn, I'm pissed. And did you see the look on his face? He was screwing with us."

"And doing a damn good job," Lou said. "I was about ready to pop him, and I'm not a violent guy."

Carol walked into the room, taking note of the chairs and the trashcan. "All I know is that if Lieutenant Morreau sees this shit, somebody's ass will be on a desk."

Sherri reached down to pick up a chair. "Lost my temper."

"I understand, and you're young so it's almost forgivable. I'm just saying…Morreau will drop you like a bad habit if he sees something like this."

Lou put the other chair back in place. "Listen to her, Miller. She's been here longer than this building."

"You know where you can stuff that, Mazzetti. Anyway, I see it didn't go so well with Stewart. Anything you need me to check on?"

"I'd love to get a warrant," Sherri said, "but it's not gonna happen."

"It would be nice to see what he's got inside his house." Lou pulled out his cell phone. "Be right back, Miller."

"Where you going?"

"To take a piss. Is that okay with you?"

Lou stepped out and dialed a number. It rang twice. "Hello."

"Fusco, this is Mazzetti."

CHAPTER 45

WATCHING

I was parked a block away from Stewart's house when I spotted Mazzetti and Miller pulling up. *What the hell are they doing here?* Maybe I didn't give them enough credit. If they had gotten this far with the investigation they were doing a good job. Last I talked with Mazzetti he was fixated on Benning.

Stewart came to the door but didn't let them in. Soon afterward he disappeared for a minute and then got in a car and followed them. I presumed he was going in for questioning, which left me with two choices: Follow them and wait, or have a look inside Stewart's house while he was being questioned. I opted for the peek. I promised Angie I'd stay out of trouble, but that wasn't to say I couldn't help the cops do their job.

I looked at my watch and frowned. Sixteen hours left. *You need to hurry, Fusco.*

It didn't take long to get inside. I could get in most houses in less than a minute. Another benefit of a prison education. The house was undergoing renovations, but a few things struck me about it. The place was a mess—but a *perfect* mess. The tape covering the woodwork had been applied *perfectly*, and the dropcloths fit the furniture like custom slipcovers. The lamps looked as if they were wrapped for shipping, and the sheet covering the TV fit so nicely it resembled an old drive-in theater screen. I found more of the same in the kitchen. Glasses perfectly aligned in the cabinets, the boxes and cans in the pantry arranged by size, left to right. The Tupperware labeled, matching tops and bottoms. And the glass top on the kitchen table didn't have a smudge on it. Bugs' notes said the killer was a clean freak. Stewart's house fit the bill.

I searched everywhere I could think of for the gun—taped to the toilet tank, in the access slot for the plumbing, taped to the bottom side of the box spring, closets, oven—nothing. I didn't overlook the obvious either—drawers and coat pockets. The backyard consisted of a large stone patio surrounded by a patch of perfect green grass, cut to the perfect length. The patio had a few chairs, two wooden benches, and half a dozen life-sized sculptures. One was a man walking a dog on a leash. Another was a waiter with a serving tray. The oddest was a woman lying on the ground holding a cat in her arms. She was naked.

I went back inside to finish searching. Next to his computer lay an iPod. I quickly searched for the song Alex said the guy was singing. I looked under artists—Young Rascals—then looked under songs for It's a Beautiful Morning. It wasn't there. I couldn't imagine a guy singing a song while he's waiting to kill someone not having it on his iPod, so I looked some more. Maybe he made a mistake and spelled it wrong. Maybe he was a moron. I searched for "beautiful" and for "morning" but it didn't come up even under a few alternate spellings just in case he'd made manual changes.

The missing song puzzled the hell out of me, but I figured Mazzetti couldn't keep him much longer, so I got out of the house, making my way to the station. I waited half a block away, hoping Stewart was still there. Five minutes into the wait, my phone rang. At first I thought it might be Mazzetti, but it was my regular cell. I looked at the caller ID; it showed Kate Burns. My heart raced.

"Everything okay, Kate?"

A whisper answered. "It's me, Rat. Alex."

"Is Bugs okay?"

"Yeah, he's the same. I was just checking to see if you knew anything yet."

"Knew anything?"

He lowered his voice even more. "Yeah, I know you're workin' this."

I damn near laughed. This kid was something else. "You're right. I *am* working it, but that has got to stay between me and you. Got that?"

"I got it."

"How's Bugs? Any better?"

"Nothin' yet. I keep talkin' to him but he doesn't hear. The doctors won't say anything. Even Kate won't say much."

There was a long pause, then a few sobs. "Hey, Rat. What am I gonna do if FD dies? I got nowhere else to go."

"You know any prayers?"

"A few."

"Say them every night. Every day."

Another pause. "You think that shit helps?"

"I wouldn't call it *shit* in case somebody's listening, but…yeah, I think it helps."

"*You* do it?"

I laughed. "I'm not laughing at you. I was just thinking that if you only knew how many times I prayed, you'd be surprised."

"For real? No shit?"

"No shit. So get busy. And don't worry about Bugs. If anything happens—and it won't—but if anything does, you can live with me."

"FD told me you'd say that."

"When did he say that?"

"One night when we talked. You know, about death and stuff. He said if anything ever happened I'd have a place with Kate or with you. It'd be my choice."

"He was right. Now get your ass busy praying."

"Thanks, Rat. I feel better."

I hung up wearing a smile.

My other phone rang. On the second ring I picked it up. "Hello."

"It's Mazzetti."

"Yeah?"

"Listen, I—"

"Whatever it is, just ask, Detective."

"I need a favor. We just had a guy in here for questioning. I know this isn't your place, but I'd appreciate it if you could follow him."

"This guy happen to be named Bruce Stewart? If it is, I'm already on him."

"How the fuck…"

"Leave the hard work to me, Detective."

"Yeah, sure. But before you join the force, let me fill you in. Benning has an alibi for the joggers. Rock solid. He was on a plane with his boss. And Stewart has an alibi for the first murders at the hotel. We haven't checked on it yet, but he seemed confident."

"Work on busting that alibi, Mazzetti. Stewart did it."

"You think?"

"I *know*," I said, and hung up.

Stewart walked out of the station and got in his car. He didn't look the least bit disturbed. I followed him to his house, parked down the block and waited. After an hour, I decided he might be staying put for a while. It seemed like a good time to check out Parnell's apartment. I would have loved to inspect the first murder scene, but the hotel was out of question. Debbie's apartment would have to do.

I parked down the block, taking in the surroundings as I walked toward her apartment. A bodega sat across the street and half a block down, and a decent amount of cars passed by. Not much pedestrian traffic, but it was a good mix—suits, joggers, moms, kids—the perfect opportunity to blend in. The doorman for Parnell's building seemed busy. More accurately, he kept himself busy gossiping and chatting up the women. Panning for tips. I couldn't blame him for it. Might mean a bottle of Brunello on Friday night instead of Chianti.

The case files said the doorman—Jack—swore that no one got in without him noticing. Furthermore, he swore that Stewart wasn't there that night. I didn't necessarily believe Jack, but following Sister Thomas' rules, I had to check it out. If that proved wrong, which I figured it would, then I had to work on proving Jack wrong.

With that in mind, I walked around the building, inspecting all the bottom floors and any window that had access. I was about to give up when something caught my eye. One window was noticeably cleaner than the others. It was so damn clean it looked as if they used it for a TV commercial. I went back and looked at the others to double-check myself, but there was no doubt this window was ultra clean. I risked being reported and checked it. It was locked. I checked the next one and found it open. I closed the window, stood back, and looked.

What the hell is going on?

People in Brooklyn didn't leave their windows open. I decided to really tempt fate, and knocked on the window. When no one came, I knocked harder. Still no sign of life. I thought I had it figured out, but I needed to verify it. First, I finished checking the other apartments. Then I headed back to see Jack the doorman.

I put a dealer's button I carried with me for good luck inside my wallet. It was a two-ounce piece of silver that, at quick glance, looked like a giant silver dollar. With the right attitude it might pass for a badge. I walked up to Jack, flashed the wallet open, then closed.

"Detective Mazzetti sent me. I have a few questions about the broken window out back."

The look on his face told me everything I needed. The lies that followed told me more.

"Broken window? We haven't had any broken windows."

I looked him in the eyes, held him. "No broken windows. You're sure?"

"I told the other officers everything. There were no broken windows. And nobody came in that night that wasn't approved."

I nodded. "That's what I needed to know. Thanks."

I walked down to the bodega and talked to the guy behind the counter. He turned out to be the owner's brother, and he was working the night Parnell was killed. I showed him a picture of Chad Benning from the file. I didn't have one of Stewart—an oversight on my part—but he didn't seem interested in remembering anything, let alone an ID from almost a week ago. Common sense told me to go back to Bruce Stewart's house and watch him, but I wanted to talk a little more to good old Jack. I waited for him to get off, and followed him home.

I gave Jack about half an hour to get settled in then went inside and knocked on his door. Fortunately Jack lived in an apartment without a doorman. He opened the door, a surprised look on his face.

"What do you want?"

"Just the truth, Jack."

"I told you earlier—"

I pushed my way inside, shoving him back against the wall. "Anybody home?"

"I live alone."

"Good."

"Good? Who are you? Let me see your badge."

"I don't have a badge. And I said it's good because if you live alone no one will hear me kill you." I quickly scanned the apartment. "I'm thinking of how your blood will look on that powder-blue carpet."

Jack half-laughed, the kind of laugh when you hope the person is kidding, but you're not sure, maybe even think he isn't.

I shut the door behind me. Pulled out the Beretta. "I don't fuck around with people who lie to me. And I have no time for bullshit. Tell the truth or say your prayers."

Jack told me the story of how the little kid came to him with the broken-window story and how he'd get in trouble.

"For Christ's sake, he gave me two hundred dollars to get it fixed." Jack looked at me, like…What the hell was I supposed to do?

"And you never wondered where the hell this kid got two-hundred dollars?"

He shrugged. "I guess not."

"I'm sure you didn't. You just called insurance and got them to do it."

"This will stay between us, won't it?"

"Maybe. Are the people in that apartment away?"

"For three weeks."

"Who knew?"

He took a moment. "I don't know. Probably half the building. They were socializers."

There was no sense asking him any more questions. I had what I needed. I stared at him long enough for him to know I was serious. "You know how in the old movies, the bad guy leaves and says 'Forget I was here'? Well, forget I was here."

"I will."

I walked out of his apartment and headed back to the car. I knew how the killer got in. *So this guy, whoever he is, planned this pretty far in advance. This was definitely not an act of passion.* And the guy was clever. Not only busted the window but had the foresight to get it fixed in advance. And was smart enough to get a kid to say he broke it. He knew the doorman would pocket the money, and the kid probably didn't know him. *Smart. Real smart.*

My body ached. I was tired. I desperately wanted a good night's sleep, but I had to watch Stewart. I called the guy I rented the car from, offered him a nice piece of change if he'd drive my car and park it a block or two from Stewart's house, knowing I might need it. And then I changed into my jogging clothes and parked my ass where I could see Stewart coming or going.

No way this fucker is killing someone else.

CHAPTER 46

DIGGING THROUGH TRASH

When the killer thought about Cantaloupe Girl he shivered. He knew he should let it go, forget about it, go on with his life, but she was sooooo special, with such a fine body. He could only imagine how ripe she would be, like that first bite of cantaloupe, the one just below the seeds. Sweet and juicy.

He popped a couple of cherry tomatoes in his mouth and poured a glass of water. If he decided to kill her, he would have to make sure it was perfect. Even more perfect than the others. The cops would be watching his every move. So, *if* he did it, should he use the detective's gun or the same one as all the others? Which would confuse them the most? After eating a few more tomatoes he decided to stew on it.

***

I knew there was only one way to find out about the killer. Watch him. It might take a while, but I learned patience long ago. It was one of Johnny Muck's most important rules—murder takes patience. The fact that Dominic Mangini would probably sic Fabrizio on me in a few hours complicated matters, but I decided to give *patience* a try. For now.

I parked down the block from Stewart's house, rolled down the windows so I didn't miss anything, and put both cell phones on the seat beside me, making sure they were on vibrate. I couldn't start the car or he might see the exhaust, and I couldn't afford a mistake. If anything went wrong it would be easy to get caught up in the moment, forget about my promises, so I kept reminding myself that I was here for observation only.

I promised Angie I wouldn't kill anyone, and, almost as bad, I promised God. With that in mind, I forced calmness through regulated breathing. Closed my eyes and pictured the path of the air—in through the nose, down the back, curl at the bottom of the stomach, then back out through the mouth. Slowly. *Very* slowly.

I had a good view of the house but from this far away I couldn't see much, other than whether he went in or out of the door. I raised the binoculars and zoomed in. Lights were on in the living room—the one under construction—and a light shone in the kitchen. Nothing upstairs. I ran the layout through in my mind, wondering what he was doing. I doubted he was painting. Maybe he was peeking out the windows. He *had* to suspect the cops were on to him.

I wanted to go inside, shove a gun down his throat, and make him talk. If the gun didn't work I had other ideas. I shook my head to clear it. Prison hardened me, sure, but I couldn't blame this on the system. Maybe it was genetics performing at its best. My father was a killer, ergo…*Ergo?* That bit of bullshit I could blame on Sister Thomas. I sure as shit didn't learn words like that in the neighborhood.

I sat up straight, thought I saw a window blind move. My pulse quickened, heart rate increased. I *could* make him talk. That would be no problem. I'd made men a lot tougher than Stewart talk. *Made them beg. And cry.*

***

Stewart cracked the blinds and looked out the window for the fifth time, wondering if the detectives followed him. The look on their faces had been priceless when he'd said he was taking the cup with him. They were counting on his DNA.

Lot of good that would do.

The gun was another matter. He couldn't be caught with that. It would be incriminating as hell. That thought settled his dilemma regarding

Cantaloupe Girl. He would *not* do her. Too risky. All he had to do was get rid of the gun and then he could hibernate. Home free. But he had to clean it first. He couldn't risk DNA on the gun. DNA in Donovan's apartment was something he could explain—DNA on the detective's gun was another thing entirely.

He grabbed a flashlight but didn't turn it on. He went to the basement, then made his way to the crawlspace. After hoisting himself up, he got on his back and slithered in fifteen or twenty feet, using the joists to pull himself along. The concrete was rough, scratching his back.

The things I have to go through to be perfect!

When Bruce figured he was in the proper position, he turned on the flashlight. The gun was right above him, tucked into the braces of the joists. *Could I be any better?* He got the gun, tucked it into his waistband alongside the flashlight and began inching back out. Moving this way was more difficult, with nothing to pull on.

Back in the kitchen, he initiated the cleaning process. A baby diaper worked well for things like this. He wiped the barrel, frame, and trigger. Paid special attention to the grip and the magazine. He didn't think he had touched the bullets, but just in case…He emptied the magazine and wiped each bullet clean.

He thought about dumping the gun empty, but that might not work as well. If a junkie or gangbanger got it and shot someone, they would be tied to Detective Donovan. That would work much better for him. After checking everything again he placed the gun in a Ziploc bag and sealed it. He tucked the gun behind the refrigerator, taped it to the coils, then settled in for the night with a bottle of beer. A small celebration was in order.

Needing to get rid of the gun bothered him. A feeling like he'd lost something came over him, almost like when he'd quit smoking and had thrown out that last pack of cigarettes. Still…now that he had a plan he could sleep.

Bruce got up at exactly 6:00 AM, as he always did, put on his coffee, and wished he was at his other house. He couldn't risk that right now, though. First he had to determine if the cops were trailing him. A morning jog would take care of that. No way could the old detective keep up. The woman looked as if she could, but he'd spot that black bitch anywhere. She was too sexy to miss.

Maybe I should do her. As he slipped his jogging pants on he mulled the idea over, wondering how she'd taste. *Like a chocolate bunny,* he thought, and laughed.

He rinsed his coffee cup, washed it, dried it, and put it away. Then he took the gun from behind the fridge and placed it into a small bag he carried—that matched his gray jogging suit. He peeked out the blinds, up and down the street. Waited a few minutes and peeked again.

Guess it's time to see if I'm being followed.

***

Somehow I heard the door open on Stewart's house. I don't know how, because I was damn tired, surviving the night on a few twenty-minute naps. I ducked, low enough so he couldn't see me, and waited thirty seconds before poking my head up. He was halfway down the block, jogging at a good pace. *Shit.* I'd have preferred to follow him in the car, but it was difficult to track a jogger that way.

Stewart turned left at the corner. Now I had a decision to make. *Do I trail him right away and risk being seen? Do I give him some space and risk losing him?*

One thing was sure, he didn't know me and that gave me flexibility. I opted to see how he was playing it. I started the car, slowing as I approached the corner where he turned. Fortunately it was a stop sign. I looked both ways, saw him watching from a position a few houses down. *So he* is *watching.*

Once I got through the intersection I gunned it, raced three blocks and then turned left, heading the same way Stewart did. When I hit the first block I looked left. He was just crossing the street, heading north. I kept going, hoping to get ahead of him, park, and then fall in behind him as a jogger from another direction. I zigzagged, staying three or more blocks from him until he turned onto Ninth Street. I figured he might stay there for a while. That was good.

I drove five more blocks, turned left and passed Ninth Street, finding a parking spot halfway down the block. The next move was risky but if it worked he wouldn't suspect a thing. I jogged back to Ninth Street. He was still a few blocks south of me, so I turned north and kept a slow pace. If he stayed on this street he'd pass me soon. If he turned, I was screwed.

I passed the industrial area and was coming up on a bunch of row houses, mostly old two- or three-story brick, with an occasional stone front. A lot of them had the front door raised four or five feet off the street. I kept going at the same pace, and soon passed St. Thomas' at Fourth Avenue, praying he was still with me.

I didn't have long to wait. He passed me at a decent clip and never looked once. I had him. When he got to Seventh Avenue he turned right, stopping a few blocks later to get a coffee at the Park Slope Deli. I was still a ways behind him. I slowed down more, then passed the deli without looking in. I kept going on Seventh for almost two blocks, ducking behind a delivery truck so I could watch without being seen. It didn't take long.

Stewart came out carrying a bag. He looked both ways down the street, then walked across and dumped the bag into a trashcan. Once again he checked to see if anyone was watching, then he took off down Twelfth Street heading toward Prospect Park. I thought about cutting him off, but something bugged me about him dropping that bag.

Why didn't he use the trashcan inside the deli? Why walk across the street to dump a bag?

I thought for a moment more, trying to decide what to do when it hit me.

Because the bag has something else in it!

That made up my mind. I had to risk losing Stewart if I wanted that bag. I waited a good five minutes, making sure he didn't double-back to check on a tail, then I walked to the trashcan. The bag sat right on top. I pretended to toss something in the can then pulled the bag out. It was heavy. Definitely not the last bite of a bagel in there. When I opened the bag I saw a gun. Using a napkin, I pulled it out by the grip, careful not to mess up any prints that might have been on there, but from what I'd seen of this guy, there wouldn't be any. I recognized it as Bugs' gun by the small nick on the handle.

Son of a bitch! You're dead, fucker.

I slipped the gun into the pocket of my hoodie and started a slow jog back to the car. I wondered why Stewart kept the gun so long, but I knew most people had problems getting rid of guns. For some strange reason they got attached to them. I got rid of mine after every job. If I used it, I disposed of it, and I made damn certain it wouldn't be found. Afterward, I'd buy a new one. Still, I had to give this guy credit, he'd gotten rid of it a lot sooner than most people would. It reinforced my impressions—he was smart. I had to be careful. I made a mental note to tell Mazzetti about the gun. I didn't know if there was anything he could do about it, but it would at least confirm what he was now thinking about Stewart.

The church bells rang as I passed St. Thomas'. *Eight o'clock.* That left me about six hours. Not nearly enough time. A bit of poetry the nuns had drummed into our heads came to mind.

Never send to know for whom the bell tolls. It tolls for thee.

How appropriate, I thought, and kicked it up a notch.

CHAPTER 47

CHECKING ALIBIS

Lou grabbed a fresh pack of smokes, his lighter, and a book of matches in case he ran out of butane. Sherri stood at the top of the steps, hands on hips.

"Mazzetti, Williamsburg is only ten minutes from here. We're not going on a damn trip."

"Never can tell how long we'll be, and I hate to be caught without cigarettes."

Carol handed Lou a note as he passed her desk. "Lieutenant Morreau said for you to see him before you go home."

"What's he want?"

"I don't know, but I'd bet it has something to do with the chief being here."

"When was he here?" Sherri asked.

"Left about thirty minutes ago," Carol said.

"Tell Morreau we'll be back," Lou said. "We've got to break Stewart's alibi."

Sherri got in the car and pulled out of the lot, heading toward Williamsburg. "Where was the gallery?"

"Off Metropolitan. Not far from the bridge."

"You have the list of names?"

"All ten of them," Lou said. "Which makes me think this is a waste of time. If the guy has ten names to use as alibis, we're screwed."

"Ten *is* a lot."

"I don't have ten friends, let alone ten who would lie for me."

Sherri laughed. "I don't think I've had ten friends in my whole life."

Lou nodded. "Hard to come by. You got me and Donovan, though."

"I got you."

"What's that supposed to mean?"

"Nothing."

"Bullshit."

"Frankie doesn't like me."

"Bullshit again."

"He *doesn't*. He as much as told me."

"Learn to listen, Miller. I have a feeling I know what Frankie said to you. What you have to understand is that he's scared."

"Scared? Of *what?*"

"Of losing Kate."

"Got nothing to do with me," Sherri said.

"Yeah, well listen, I know you haven't had the best life, but Frankie hasn't either. I'm the only one that's perfect."

That didn't even draw a small laugh; instead, she flipped off the driver of the car she'd been trying to pass. "Learn how to drive, asshole."

"You can ignore me, Miller, but ever since you've been back it seems to me as if you're cozying up to Frankie."

"Now who's full of shit? You're an asshole, Mazzetti."

"At least I've got company with the driver you flipped off."

Sherri slowed down as she turned onto Metropolitan. "You really think that?"

"Ask Carol."

"Why didn't somebody say something? I can't show my face now."

Lou put his hand on her shoulder. "I wouldn't worry about it. And don't *ever* think Frankie doesn't care for you. He fought like hell to get you back."

She turned and looked at Lou. "No shit?"

"Ask Morreau."

"Where's the gallery?"

"Turn left two blocks up."

She put her signal on. Slowed down. "Thanks, Mazzetti. I owe you."

"Tell Frankie when he gets better."

She pulled into a parking spot not far from the gallery. "I will."

***

Three of the people on the list worked at the gallery. The first name was John Davis. He turned out to be as plain as his name, but he vouched for Stewart. The next guy, Karl York, seemed right out of the seventies—long hair, headband, and funky shades. Sherri half expected to find him wearing bell-bottom pants and platform shoes. She showed him the badge.

"We've got a few questions about the night the gallery opened."

He stared at her. Just stared. Sherri wondered if he was partaking of other party favors from the seventies. "Were you here that night?"

"All night."

"Who was with you?"

He looked as if he had to think, then, "Everybody. The place was rockin'."

She sighed. "Okay, let's be more specific. Was Bruce Stewart here that night?"

"Stew? Oh yeah, he was here, all right."

She looked at Mazzetti, a wrinkle in her brow. "What does that mean? Was he messed up?"

"Stew? No way. But he was here."

"What time did you leave?"

"When it closed?"

This was like pulling teeth. "What time was that?"

He held out his hand. "I don't wear a watch, but after it closed we all went to eat."

"Who is we?"

"I don't know. Maybe eight of us. And no, I don't know what time we left." He held his arm out again. "No watch."

Sherri handed him a card. "Call us if you think of anything." *Like what your name is.*

She turned to Lou when they were out of earshot, but he beat her to the comment.

"Brain is fried. Seen lots of 'em in my day."

"I don't know if it's fried or boiled, but sure as shit, it's gone."

"Who's next on the list?"

"Abby Maines."

Abby Maines was all style—in *her* mind. A big floppy hat covered blonde hair streaked with orange, red, and deep purple. She wore the hat cocked heavily to one side, so heavy that it appeared to be falling off her head. Her glasses were *industrial*, held together on the sides with stylish colored bolts, interchangeable to match the wearer's outfit—or in Abby's case—her hair. She proved to be as vocal as she was colorful.

After hearing about the gallery opening and the *amazing* array of upcoming artists, she confirmed what the other two already said. That Bruce Stewart was at the opening and stayed until it closed. Afterward, they all, including Abby, went for dinner and drinks, not finishing until after 1:00 AM, perhaps later.

"And he was here all night?" Sherri asked.

"I can't vouch for every minute. I mean, we weren't glued to each other, but yes, I kept bumping into him throughout the evening. He was sponsoring several of the artists." She spread her hands. "And as you can see, it's not that big."

"Okay, thanks," Sherri said. Then to Lou, "This is bull. We're wasting our time."

"Doug Wilkins is next. He's an artist who lives down the street."

Doug told the same story as the others. "Bruce came early and stayed until they closed. Then he took us all to dinner. He paid, of course."

"Does he do that often? Take everyone out and pay?"

Doug laughed. "I guess you don't know Bruce. He does it all the time. At the last gallery opening he took about forty people to a club for the night. All on his tab."

"Must be nice," Sherri said. "Where did he get his money?"

Doug shook his head. "No idea."

"What else can you tell us about him?"

"Not much. He's a nice guy. Always supporting the artist community. Very involved."

"What about his personal life? Did you know his fiancée, Ms. Parnell?"

Doug lost his smile. "I met her once. Maybe twice."

"And?"

"She was nice. A beautiful woman."

"An ambitious woman," Sherri said.

"That, too."

Sherri moved in close to him. "Come on, Doug. You're holding out on me."

"No, I…"

"Doug, we can go to the station if you want, but I'd rather you tell us about it now."

Sherri let him mull over it, remaining silent while he decided. Finally Doug shrugged. "It's nothing really. Just that Bruce is a little…strange when it comes to his sexual preferences."

Sherri moved closer, flashing a sexy smile. "Can you be more specific?"

He backed up. "I'd prefer not."

Lou jotted something down in his notepad. "Likes guys."

"Hold on," Doug said. "That's not what I meant. I'm not…" he looked at Sherri with a scrunched up face. "You can't believe *I'm* gay."

She looked him up and down. "That's what I thought you meant."

"No way. No *goddamn* way."

A smile lit her face. "So tell me what these perversions of his were."

The guy looked around, then at Sherri. "He likes…threesomes."

"Two girls or two guys?"

"It didn't seem to matter." The guy shot another quick glance to see if anybody was around, then he whispered to Sherri. "One time, he invited me to share his fiancée."

"Did you take him up on it?"

"No way."

"As good as she looked? Come on, Doug. I know you wanted some of that."

"I don't care who the woman is, I'm not gettin' in bed with a naked guy."

"You know anyone who *did* take him up on the offer?"

Doug shook his head. "I don't want to get the guy in trouble. He was pretty messed up the night he asked me. She was too. Maybe it was a spur-of-the-moment thing."

"Okay, thanks," Sherri said and handed him her card.

On the way back to the car she looked at Mazzetti. "What do you think?"

"I think it's time for me to retire. And I think Stewart has too much money for his own good if he's got to get thrills by sharing his girlfriend."

"It could give us a motive," Sherri said.

"Not the way I see it. The only reason we might have had for him killing her was if he was jealous. If he's okay with sharing her, why kill her?"

"And it wasn't about money," Sherri said.

"Speaking of which, we need to find out where he got his money. The guy doesn't work."

"Morreau will have our asses if we piss off his lawyer."

Sherri got in the car and headed for the station. "I don't know what we've got, Mazzetti, but we *don't* have any suspects. Not Benning and now not Stewart."

"There was a case in Boston where they convicted a guy on circumstantial even though he had an alibi."

Sherri looked at him with a skewed eye. "How did that work?"

"The jury didn't like the guy, and didn't believe the alibi. Six years later they caught the real killer. The cops had interviewed him the first time around and let him go."

Sherri nodded. "That's my biggest fear. To have a suspect in custody and let him go. That would kill me."

"I'm back to Benning," Lou said.

"You want to tell me how he did it? He was out of town, *with his boss,* when the joggers were killed."

"I put a lot of thought into this, Miller. Think about it. The joggers were almost like a professional hit. One shot to the head. Nothing staged.

Nothing sexual. And the shooter did them in the park. This was *not* the same guy."

"I'm listening."

"Here's my theory," Lou said. "Benning does the others. He knows he needs an alibi, so he pays somebody to kill the joggers."

"You're saying the supposed hit man picked them out randomly?"

"It fits. The joggers have no ties to Benning, or anyone else. Think about it. He gives the gun to the hit man, tells him to pick a couple at random while he's out of town, and *bang*, instant alibi."

"I don't know, Mazzetti."

"It's perfect. It establishes an alibi for the joggers, and, by association, for all the murders."

"So now you're saying Stewart *didn't* do it."

"I don't know if we're crazy or just bad cops, but unless Stewart bought off ten or twelve witnesses, he didn't do it. And now I can't see a motive."

Sherri looked as if a family member died. "God help us, are we completely off base? I was sure he was our guy."

Mazzetti nodded. "I know. But I keep thinking how I knew it was Benning, too."

"So what do we do?"

Mazzetti put a smoke in his mouth, sucking on a dry cigarette. "You're not going to like it, but I think we need help."

"Shit, I'm not proud. If you think Morreau will give us help, get it. *Beg* for it."

Lou reached over and turned off the radio. "Pull over."

"What for?"

"Humor me. Pull over."

"I can drive and talk at the same time. What's so important?"

"I'm not talking about help from Morreau."

She sat up straight, shaking her head. "Don't even go there, Mazzetti. If you're even thinking about using that…killer, to help us, you're nuts."

"You have a better idea?"

"What can he do that we can't? He's not a damn cop."

"He can do *everything* we can't. He can get evidence we'd need a warrant for. He can follow him night and day. And if necessary, he can beat the fuck out of him to get a confession."

"A bullshit confession."

"I didn't say it would be one we could use, but right now we need to know if he's guilty or not. We *need to know* if we're on the right track." Lou rolled down the window and lit his smoke. "We *need* Fusco, and I'm calling him. If you're not in, ask for a transfer."

Sherri slammed on the brakes, stopping in the middle of the street. "You'd do that—to *me?*"

"It's not about you. It's about Donovan. Somebody stabbed our friend, our *partner,* and we need to find out who it was. I'd hire a hit man myself if I had no other choice."

Horns beeped behind her. She flipped them off then hit the gas hard. "From what I understand that is *exactly* what you're proposing."

"Think about it and let me know."

"What choice do I have? Go along or get a transfer? And what do I do when Morreau asks why?"

Lou gritted his teeth. "Tell him you've got the hots for Donovan and you can't control your urges."

Sherri drove the rest of the way in silence. Every block or so she turned to glare at Mazzetti. She pulled into the station lot, slammed the car into park, and sat there. Mazzetti didn't move to get out. After a moment, she said, "I'm in. I don't like it, but I'm in."

He opened the door. "I'll call him."

On the way into the station she grabbed Lou's arm. "What you said back there. That was wrong. You had no right."

Lou looked at her. "I didn't mean for it to come out like that."

She started for the station. "Don't call him from your phone. Nothing that can be traced."

Too late for that, Mazzetti thought.

CHAPTER 48

A SPECIAL ASSIGNMENT

Dominic Mangini sipped his espresso, then stabbed a piece of honeydew melon and let it loll around in his mouth. He loved the contrast of the sweet melon and the bitter espresso. Gone were the days when he took his morning fruit with a scoop of ice cream and then another dollop in his cappuccino. That habit disappeared with his first heart attack. He learned to appreciate this new, healthy way of eating, as long as it came with solitude.

Every morning should be started the same way: espresso, fruit, and then a cappuccino to savor while he read the papers. The Giornale di Sicilia, Sicily's daily newspaper, came first. That, he read for pleasure, and to keep abreast of events back home. The New York Times came with his second cup of cappuccino and signaled the start of the business day.

A knock on the front door was followed by the sound of Zeppe's footsteps across the hardwood floors. He got a cup from the counter, poured espresso, and took his seat by the window, basking in the sun. "Good morning, Dom."

Dominic's eyes never left the paper. "*Buon giorno*, Zeppe."

A few minutes later Dominic set the paper aside and finished his cappuccino. "Have you spoken to Fabrizio?"

"He's outside, waiting for you to finish."

Dominic wiped his mouth and set the napkin to the side. "*Avanti*, Fabrizio."

Fabrizio entered, gave a slight nod, then stood behind the chair between Zeppe and Dominic. "*Buon giorno, Signore*."

"Sit, Fabrizio. Tell me what you have learned about our friend."

"Last year the detective—Donovan—was in trouble in his hometown. It appears that Carlos Cortes was involved. Fusco helped him."

"How did this…help, arrive?"

"At least eight, perhaps ten of Carlos' men died. No one was ever caught, but information from Chicky says it was Fusco."

A smile lit Zeppe's face. "You see that, Dom? I told you he was all right."

Dominic shook his head slowly, but he smiled. "Fabrizio, I am glad that you learn from my brother's mistakes. He never knows when to be silent."

Zeppe took his cup to the sink. "You want espresso, Fabrizio?" Then to Dominic, "I say we let Nicky go."

Dominic looked to Fabrizio. "And you? What do you think? He is an enemy of our enemy. Should we keep him alive?"

"*Farò quello che vuoi, Signore.*"

"I know you will do what I *want*, Fabrizio. I asked what you thought."

"If the detective were my friend, I would have done the same thing as Signor Fusco."

Dominic nodded. "I thought you'd say that."

Zeppe said, "Hey, Dom, remember what happened to Tito and his men?"

Dominic took his plate and cup to the sink. "A man who is afraid to act based on fear has ceased to be a man."

"Yeah, well, you can have all the sayings you want about fear, but I remember what Nicky did to Tito. I ain't goin' to hell with a spike up my ass."

"You are getting too old for this business."

"I told you that ten years ago. Besides, Nicky did the right thing coming here to get your permission and all."

"He did that only because he knew I would find out."

"You don't know that. He's old school."

"If he were old school, he wouldn't have killed Tito."

Zeppe pushed in his chair and cleaned the table. "I gotta go, Dom. I'm picking the kids up."

Dominic waited for Zeppe to leave. He looked at his watch. "It is almost time."

"Si, Signore."

"Remember what I told you, Fabrizio."

"Si, Signore. He is a dangerous man."

"A *very* dangerous man."

Fabrizio got up, put his gun in the back of his waistband, adjusted his shirt to cover it, then headed out the door.

CHAPTER 49

SEEKING PERMISSION

By the time I got back to my car, sweat had soaked the back of my hoodie and my hair was drenched. I drained the last gulp of water and started the car. I didn't know whether to try to find Stewart or go back to his house and sit on it. I decided to call Angie instead.

The phone rang seven or eight times. "Come on, Angie. Pick up, goddamnit." A rotten feeling in my gut gnawed at me. Not much bothered me, but having Angie upset with me was one of them. I popped a few more Tums into my mouth, wishing I had some water to wash down the chalky flavor. She had no *goddamn* right to be upset with me about this. Bugs was my best friend. Besides, I told her I wouldn't do anything.

Even as I said it to myself, I knew how stupid it sounded. She knew me better than I knew myself. I came to New York to get even, avenge what someone did to Bugs. She knew it before I left. I tried convincing myself I wouldn't do anything but I brought a gun. Two guns. If I wasn't going to do anything why bring a gun? I was like an alcoholic who swears he won't drink—after this last bottle. Or the smoker who vows to quit—but buys one more carton. I had to get my shit together because if I didn't watch out I was going to lose my family, and that was the only thing that mattered.

I remembered what Sister Thomas told us in school, how we didn't have much time on this world, so we better make the most of it. If I planned on enjoying life with Angie and Rosa, and now Dante, I figured I better get busy, because God knows I wouldn't be with them in the afterlife. Angie would be up there with Mamma Rosa and Sister Thomas. Me? Unless God intended for me to be an avenging angel, I'd be with Pops and Doggs and Tony—burning in hell.

My phone rang. The caller ID said it was Rosa. *Thank God.*

"Rosa, is everything all right?"

"Where are you?" she whispered.

"I'm in New York. Where's your mother?"

"We're staying at Diana's house. You know, Mom's cousin up on Bancroft Parkway." She was still whispering.

"What's going on? Why isn't she answering the phone? And what the *hell* are you doing at Diana's?"

"Mom's pissed. I mean really pissed. I never saw her like this. And she's been crying every night." There was a pause. I thought I heard a door close, then, "Dad, what's going on?"

I didn't know what to say, or how to say it. I wasn't good at discussing feelings and emotions. "Just tell your mother I called. Tell her nothing's wrong. I'm with Uncle Mario, and I'll be home in a couple of days."

"How is Uncle Mario? Is he okay?"

"He's still in ICU. He hasn't talked yet."

"Tell him I'm praying for him. And Sister Thomas is too."

"That's good. Tell Sister Thomas I said thanks. And…"

"What?"

"Nothing."

"You were going to say something. What?"

"Tell your mother that I love her. And everything will be all right."

"I will. I love you too, Dad. Be careful."

"Thanks, Rosa. I love you."

I hung up. It broke my heart when Rosa said Angie had been crying at night. "You're a dumb fuck, Nicky Fusco. A *real* dumb fuck."

I got out of the car and walked back to St. Thomas'. I had no idea why, but at some of the worst times in my life, God had helped me. That was a puzzle I hadn't put together yet. *Why does He help* me, *when there are so many good people in the world?*

Traffic had picked up on Ninth Street, both cars and pedestrian. I continued my slow pace toward the church, wondering what I'd say once I got inside. Navigating through a small crowd, I almost turned back when I reached the short wrought-iron fence, but then I went on, entering the church under the Gothic arch.

I blessed myself but didn't use the holy water, not wanting to tempt the fates. The church was empty, although Sister Thomas taught us a church is never really empty.

God is always there, she used to say.

When I was young I didn't believe her. Now, I wasn't sure.

I opted for a seat in the back, and, for a few minutes, I sat and stared at the altar. I don't know what I was expecting, sure as hell God wasn't coming down to greet me. Three times, I got up to leave, but something made me stay. That something was the fear of losing Angie. After another minute or so, I got down on the kneeler and folded my hands.

I don't know what you want me to do, God. I know what Angie wants, and I know what I promised both of you. But this nut is killing good people, and he's going to kill again unless someone stops him.

I closed my eyes and waited. For what, I didn't know. After another minute passed, I went on.

I know it's not my job to stop him, that it goes against the law. The problem is, I don't know if these are your *laws, or if somebody made them up and said they were yours. But I don't think you'd want a guy like this hurting innocent people. People you care about. People who care about you.*

I know sometimes you get other people to do your work, like cops and soldiers. So the way I figure it is maybe you put me here to help you do some of the things they can't; the kind of things you might not want to get your hands dirty on. If that's the case…well, count on me getting it done.

I opened my eyes. I didn't have a direction yet, but I felt sure it would come to me. I stood and headed for the door, then went back and knelt again.

God, I have one more thing to ask. I know I ask a lot, but please…please don't take Angie away from me.

I blessed myself, stood, and walked out the door. As I walked back to the car, my thoughts became clear.

I climbed into the car, slammed it in gear, and hit the gas. I decided to go to Red Hook and wait on Stewart, but first I had to get something to eat. I had made up my mind about another thing; if Stewart didn't do something soon, I'd have to force his hand. One way or another that fucker was going down, because in less than six hours a dangerous Sicilian named Fabrizio would be all over my ass.

CHAPTER 50

BACK TO LIFE

Kate sat in the chair in the waiting room, Alex's head resting in her lap. She wiped the sweat from his brow, holding back tears. As sorry as she felt for Frankie, and for herself, she felt worse for Alex. First he lost his mother, a crackhead whore who made him grow up way too fast, and now he faced the possibility of losing the only person he loved in this world. She had no doubts he liked her a lot, maybe someday that would turn into love, but he already *loved* Frankie Donovan. For all his faults, and there were many, he was a saint when it came to kids.

She called the office. Dave picked up on the first ring. "Dr. Shu."

"Dave, it's Kate."

"Everything okay? How's Detective Donovan?"

"No change. We're sitting here waiting."

"Did you need something?"

"Just checking to see if you need me."

"This is the third time you've called. How about if you worry about Frankie, and let me worry about the dead people."

"You're right. I'll call when I get news on Frankie."

She hung up and stared at Alex, listened to his breathing. He was a *damn* good kid. *Don't let anything happen to Frankie, God. Alex needs him.*

A few minutes later, Alex's eyes popped open. "You still here, Kate?"

"I'm not going anywhere."

"Just like checking."

"I'll wake you if anything happens. Get some rest."

"Can't sleep."

"It is kind of noisy in here. Let's see if we can find a quiet place to rest."

"It's not that," Alex said. "I'm worried about FD. It's been a long time. What if he doesn't make it?"

Kate pulled a blanket over his shoulders, and tucked it into her lap. "He will," she whispered. "Close your eyes and try to sleep."

A few minutes later Alex dozed off. Kate leaned against the back of the chair and closed her eyes, praying she didn't wake to bad news. After a while she heard a familiar voice.

"Hush, girl. Don't you wake them."

Kate lifted her head. Keisha and her mom were standing a few feet away. Linda looked at Keisha as if she were ready to dish out a spanking.

"She didn't wake me," Kate said. "I've been dozing off and on, but can't really sleep."

Alex popped up. "Keisha!"

Keisha hugged him. "Is FD okay?"

"We don't know yet. He's doing better, but not much."

Linda took Kate's hand. "She drew some pictures for Frankie, and she's been dying to come down here, but I didn't think it was right."

Kate hugged her. "You're family, Linda. Frankie would love to see her. You know how much he adores your girl. The other day he—" Kate stopped, tears building in her eyes. She grabbed a tissue then broke down crying. "I'm sorry."

Linda took hold of Kate. "Let's step outside. Keisha will keep Alex company." She turned to Keisha. "Ms. Burns and I are going outside. Stay with Alex."

Halfway down the hall Kate stopped crying. "You know what's crazy? I do autopsies. I see the worst things in life without ever shedding a tear. But with Frankie…I can't stop crying. I held up pretty good until now."

Linda held the door for her as they went outside. "Maybe you needed someone to talk to. It's gotta be tough when all you got are a bunch of cops."

Kate squeezed her hand and then took a seat on a bench. "All they want is to get the guy who did it." The tears threatened to come again. "I don't give a shit about that. I just want Frankie to get better."

"I don't know what that boy is gonna do if something happens to Frankie. My Lord, it's not right that the good people have things go wrong."

Kate balled up the tissue and put it in her purse. "He *is* a good person."

"*Good?* That man is a saint. I don't know many people who would take in a ten-year-old boy, let alone one of a different color."

"I can't say this about many people, Linda, but I can honestly say that Frankie doesn't know color. He jokes and teases people about being different nationalities, but he never judges." Kate felt as if she was about to cry again. "He *is* a good man."

Linda hugged her. "I know. Even better, the kids know it. Kids can always tell."

The door opened and Alex ran out. He stumbled on a break in the sidewalk, but managed to keep his balance. "Kate, he's awake. Dad's awake!"

"What?"

Alex ran to Kate and threw his arms around her waist. "Come on. Hurry up!"

Kate took his hand and rushed into the hospital. "Who told you? What did they say?"

"A nurse came in and said he was awake and asking for us."

"Thank God," Kate said.

"I guess God does listen to prayers," Alex said.

"You've been praying?" Kate asked.

"Rat told me to. He said it helps."

I'll be damned. Kate turned the corner, stopping at the entrance to the ICU. She pressed the dispenser for the bacterial soap and scrubbed her hands. Alex reached up and did the same. She had to force herself to walk. She felt like running in and telling Frankie how much she loved him. She hadn't realized how strongly she felt about him until this happened. Now she knew she couldn't lose him. Not ever.

As they got close to his room, Alex busted into a run. She thought he might jump on the bed, he was so excited.

"Dad!"

Frankie smiled and his eyes lit up. "Dad? You never call me that."

"Now I do," Alex said, and hugged him.

"Careful, Ace. I'm hurting."

Frankie looked up at Kate. He blew her a kiss. "Hey, beautiful. Taking the day off?"

Kate cried. She leaned in and hugged him. "I love you, Frankie."

"All I had to do was get stabbed for you to say it."

Frankie squeezed Alex's hand. "You been hangin' out here?"

"All day."

He looked up. "How long…"

"Two days," Kate said. "We thought we lost you."

"You can't kill a Mick that easy." Frankie smiled and rubbed Alex's head. "Isn't that right, Irish?"

"Damn straight," Alex said. "Us Irish go down hard."

Kate laughed for the first time since the stabbing. "Irish, are you?"

"Black Irish," Alex said, then he laughed too.

The nurse came in. "We're going to have to limit his visiting time for now. He's still very weak."

Kate got serious. "Of course." She leaned in, kissed Frankie again. "We've got to go, but I'll be right outside in the waiting room."

"Thanks, Kate."

"Alex, you can stay with Frankie for a few minutes. I'm going to call Lou."

Alex waited for Kate to leave, and then he got close to Frankie and whispered, "Rat is here."

Frankie lost his smile. "Rat? Here, in Brooklyn?"

Alex nodded. "He came up the first night."

"How did he—"

"I called him."

Frankie looked at him, brow wrinkled. "*You* called him? How did—"

"You got his number on your phone, FD. What the hell? Some detective you are."

Frankie started to laugh, which turned into a cough. He reached to hold his side. "Goddamn, that hurt." The cough continued, Frankie's face twisting in pain.

Alex looked over. Blood soaked through the bandages. "Nurse, he's bleeding!"

She moved quickly to the bed. "His stitches burst. Okay, you've got to get out, young man." She pushed a button, an alarm went off, then people raced through the door.

God, don't let anything happen to FD. Please?

CHAPTER 51

GET RID OF THE EVIDENCE

I found a place to eat breakfast, and prayed the coffee was good. The run made me hungry, but I needed coffee to combat the lack of sleep. Besides, I figured I needed to stay away for at least an hour. Stewart might be watching, and though it was unlikely he'd recognize me with the hoodie, I didn't like taking chances.

After I got back to his neighborhood, I parked a block and a half in the opposite direction of where I was this morning, close to where the rental agency guy parked my car. I slipped out of the rental and slid behind the steering wheel of my SUV. If Stewart spotted me sitting in it, he wouldn't be suspicious when I tailed him with the rental. I didn't like being so far from the house, but it was safer, and I could use the binoculars if I had to.

I didn't like just sitting here and waiting, but belief in Sister Thomas' rules kept me going.

A little patience solves most problems. Undying patience solves them all.

I lay my head back and decided to test the theory. About half an hour later, a call came in on my burner. "Hello."

"Fusco?"

I recognized Mazzetti's voice. "It's me. Anything wrong?"

"No, nothing new. But listen, I have a…favor to ask."

"That must have been difficult, Detective."

"Tougher than you know."

"What is it?"

"You still on Stewart?"

"If you want to call it that, yes."

"He's not the guy," Lou said. "We just finished checking his alibi and he has half of Brooklyn swearing he was with them the night of the first murders."

"He's the guy."

"It's Benning," Mazzetti said. "I'm telling you. If you want to tail somebody, make it Benning."

I didn't want to piss him off, but I had to make him understand. "Mazzetti, I understand what you think, but maybe you should know that I found Bugs' gun."

"What? Where?"

"I was tailing Stewart and he dumped it in a trashcan."

"You got it, didn't you?"

"Of course I did, but it's not going to help you make a case. I'm telling you so you can spend some of the city's money on catching the real killer."

"All right, I'll figure something out. In the meantime—"

"Yeah, I know. I'm staying on Stewart."

I hung up and crouched low in the seat. It wasn't long before Stewart returned. He jogged around the block twice, checking the area. I sank lower in the seat, but I was far enough away that he wouldn't take note. At least I hoped he wouldn't. After his second pass he went into the house. I hoped he was in for the long haul. I needed sleep.

A tapping on the passenger window woke me from one of many short naps. Startled, I reached for my gun, but then saw the guy looked harmless. His face wore a mean look, but his eyes were weak. Couldn't kill a bug. I rolled the window down.

"Yeah?"

"What the fuck you doin' sittin' here?"

"I'm on a stakeout."

"Stakeout? You a cop? Let me see a badge."

"I'm undercover, asshole."

"Undercover my ass. Show me a badge or get the fuck off my block."

"Check with Detective Lou Mazzetti in homicide. He'll vouch for me."

The guy didn't listen. Started running his mouth again. I didn't want to, but I got out of the car. "If you fuck up my cover, I'll bust your ass for interfering with a police investigation. If you want to check me out, call Mazzetti. Now get the fuck out of here."

He puffed himself up real big, tried to make himself look mean, clenched his fists, but in the end he turned and walked back into his house. He'd bitch to his wife, brag to his kids and neighbors, but he wouldn't call Mazzetti. That would take all the fun out of it.

I looked to make sure Stewart wasn't out, then got back in the car and slouched in the seat. This was going to be a *very* long day.

***

Fabrizio parked three blocks from the hotel, got out of his car and walked north. He made sure to keep with the crowd of people. A lone man sticks out more. Signor Mangini warned him about this one, but there had been no need. From the moment he met Fusco, Fabrizio knew he was dangerous. It would be Fabrizio's first real test for Signor Mangini, and he couldn't afford to let him down.

By the time Fabrizio reached the hotel, only one person remained from the crowd. He split from the other man and entered the hotel, making sure to keep his head low and his cap pulled down to cover his eyes. Cameras were everywhere nowadays but there were ways to beat them if you were alert. He passed the lobby, found a house phone in a secluded spot and called the front desk.

"Nicky Fusco, please."

"Just one moment," the clerk said. A phone rang. After seven rings he came back on. "I'm sorry, sir, Mr. Fusco is not in. Would you care to leave a message?"

"No, thank you. I'll call later."

If he hasn't checked out, he is still here. Fabrizio hoped Nicky would leave, as Dominic asked, but Fabrizio knew he wouldn't go until he found the man who attacked his friend. It is the same thing Fabrizio would do. He stopped outside the hotel, and looked up and down the street.

Where would he go? If I were tracking Detective Donovan's attacker, where would I go? Fabrizio called one of Dominic's contacts at the paper. Fifteen minutes later he had the name of a suspect in the case, a man named Bruce Stewart. He lived in Red Hook, not far.

***

Stewart finished his second pass around the block, checking every car and looking for anything suspicious. No one seemed to be following him, though he took nothing for granted. He thought that one jogger, the one who had kept close behind him, might have been a plant, but then he disappeared back on Seventh Avenue, and Bruce hadn't seen him since. Perhaps he worried too much. The cops weren't *that* smart. Not as smart as he was. He was home free now. No way could they pin anything on him. All he had to do was get rid of the other gun. He hated to do that—it had been such a good gun—but sacrifices had to be made.

He opened the front door, checking to make sure all was as he left it. He turned the dials on the shower to the spots he'd marked, set the timer for three minutes, then lay on the bed and stretched. He wondered how much time he'd saved over the years by doing a few simple tests fifteen or twenty years ago. Find the perfect temperature of the water, measure how long it takes to get there, and mark the dials.

I wonder—why doesn't everyone do that?

When the timer went off he took his shower and wiped the tiles dry when he finished. He hated the little streaks the water left when it dried. They reminded him of the spots the dishwasher left on glasses.

Used to leave. He no longer used the dishwasher. Sometimes he stored dishes in there until he was ready to wash them, but they were washed by hand, scrubbed and dried to perfection.

He placed towels on the bed then lay on top of them, letting the fan blow across the beads of water, allowing his body to dry naturally. He remembered the time Susan saw him drying like this, naked on the bed. She took advantage of the situation that day and he hasn't looked back since. A smile spread across his face.

Susan. Sweet, sweet Susan.

It took a while to dry, but he had time. When he could no longer feel the fan's cold touch against damp skin, he got off the bed and dressed in black jeans and a gray shirt with a pocket. It was almost time to go. Before leaving he got a knife from his drawer, a standard kitchen knife much like the one that stabbed Detective Donovan. He didn't like being without a weapon, and since he was going to get rid of his last gun…

Bruce peeked through the blinds, waited, then looked again. If anyone was out there watching him, they were doing a damn good job. He put the knife in a small bag along with a bottled water, and walked to his car.

***

Luckily I wasn't napping when Stewart came out. He tried looking casual, nonchalant, but he was alert, and watching *everything.* I waited until he started the car and pulled out. Then I slouched in the seat, leaned my head against the door and closed my eyes. I'd give him fifteen seconds. If he didn't pass me by then, it meant he turned left at the corner.

I heard the car pass by without slowing down. I hoped that meant he ignored me. I *knew* he saw me. I checked the rearview mirror. He was looking back. I had a dilemma now. Hurry up and follow him—and risk being made if he doubled back—or wait and risk losing him. Stewart was the careful type, so I decided to stay put. A few minutes later he pulled around the corner, checking the street again. I quickly closed my eyes until he passed.

The son of a bitch was checking on me.

As soon as he turned, I got out of my car, ran to the rental, got in and fell in behind him, keeping a good distance. I also removed the hoodie so he couldn't recognize me from that. Most people were easy to tail, even cops, but this guy was suspicious. To me, that alone proved he was guilty as hell. Innocent people didn't check for tails. A shiver of fear ran through me. I had focused so much on Stewart that I forgot about my time running out. I looked at my watch. Two hours left. I adjusted the side mirrors to give me a better view of possible tails, glanced in the rearview, and looked around at the cars waiting to turn my way. It wasn't time *yet*, but Fabrizio was surely out there somewhere.

I know *he is. It's what I would do.*

ANOTHER HOUSE

Fabrizio assumed that the man named Stewart only had a few ways to go when he left the house; odds were good that he would pass in the vicinity of Columbus or Ninth Streets. He had never seen Stewart, and had no reason to follow him other than to find Niccolo Fusco and he was certain that Fusco would be tailing Stewart. He was not the kind of man to let the cops carry out his justice.

He was in no hurry. The time was not up yet, but it was nearing and he wanted to be in position. A half an hour passed before Fusco went by. Fabrizio almost missed him. He was driving a different car. Fabrizio smiled.

The hunt begins.

***

I followed Stewart from Red Hook into Brooklyn Heights. When he stopped at a café, I circled around and parked a block ahead of him. I could watch from there without being noticed. Stewart walked from his car to the café looking as if he had nothing to worry about. I wondered if this was a show or if he really thought he was home free. I checked behind me, then looked all around. On the way from Red Hook I thought I spotted a tail, but when I checked, he was gone. Maybe I was getting paranoid.

Stewart drank a couple of coffees, or lattes, or something, and pretended to read the paper, holding it up as a shield while he looked to each side. Then he went to the restroom. When he returned, he shifted his chair so he could look in other directions without being noticed. He was an amateur, but he wasn't bad. About forty minutes after going in, he cleaned his table and left. I was getting ready to follow when he walked past his car.

Where the hell is he going?

Halfway down the next block he walked up a few steps to a nice old house, pulled out a key and let himself in.

What the hell? Whose house is this?

I stayed in the car and turned my head so I could watch the door. Stewart was full of surprises.

***

Stewart convinced himself that no one had followed. If they had, they were damn good. He walked in the front door of the house.

"Anyone home?" he said, and laughed.

He walked across the sparkling marble foyer, through the sitting room and dining room with its polished hardwood floors, running his hand across the table as he passed. He looked at the dust on his fingers as he stepped into the kitchen, recently covered in Mexican terracotta tile. Bruce was not fond of carpet; it hid too much dirt. He liked surfaces where he could *see* the dirt. Who wanted dirt hiding in between fibers of God knows what, waiting to infect you with a new germ or virus? They were worse than computer viruses. He wondered if they could be connected, if somehow, viruses from the organic world had mutated and infected the digital electronics world. A crazy thought, but so was flying before the Wright brothers, and that was not so long ago.

Bruce stepped to the sink to wash the dust from his hands, grabbed a bottle of water from the refrigerator, and opened the door to look out back. The patio was the same and, by some miracle, his plants yet lived. A shovel leaned against the back wall of the house. Bruce used it to dig up a small patch of dirt near the back steps. He reached down and picked up a plastic bag. Inside was the gun.

Back in the house, he spread a newspaper on the table and cleaned the gun, taking the same care he did with the other: leaving no prints, no oils, or hair. Nothing that would have his DNA on it. When he finished he placed the gun in a plastic bag and zipped it shut.

He went to the sitting room, sat in his favorite chair, kicked his feet up to rest on the Ottoman, and stared at his favorite picture of Susan. She wore a midnight-blue gown cut low to expose her treasures. Her hair was tied back in a bun, accenting her strong cheekbones. A pearl necklace shone against her tanned skin. She was a beautiful woman.

And sexy. Yes, very sexy.

Bruce went to the closet and pulled a shoebox from the top shelf. He returned to the chair and looked through the photographs. Most of them were of Susan. In a few, she even wore clothes. He searched for the one he wanted, then stared for a long time. Susan was lying on the bed, her legs spread wide. A man's head was buried in her snatch. And the look on her face was…ecstasy. He remembered how sweet she tasted. How delicious. Bruce crumpled the picture. Squeezed it until his hand hurt. Unfortunately, the man's head in that picture was not his.

Slut.

Thinking of Susan made him think of the gun. He *had* to get rid of it. Had to get rid of everything. *Well, maybe not everything.* As he tidied up, he set the box on the table, undecided whether to take it with him. *So many memories in there.* Maybe he'd convert them to digital images and put them on the computer. He had time to mull that over later. For now he had to get rid of that damn gun.

He walked to the car and had the door open when he realized he'd forgotten the pictures. He started back to the house, and saw her— Cantaloupe Girl. She was right there on the sidewalk, walking toward him, sunlight dancing in her hair.

Why did she have to be here now?

He closed the door to the car and forced himself to walk toward the house.

Control. Keep control.

She was fifty feet away, her wiggling ass an invitation to heaven. Before he knew it, he passed the house.

Damn it, she's done it now.

***

I felt certain Stewart was leaving this time, then he stopped, as if he'd forgotten something, and headed back toward the house. Before I knew it he passed the house and appeared to be following a woman. I thought about taking the car, but decided trailing him on foot would be best. I grabbed my hat and hoodie, then walked to the other side of the street, keeping back half a block. I could switch the hat and hoodie so Stewart, at first glance, would see someone different behind him. After two blocks he hadn't looked back once. He was focused on something, and I knew what it was.

This fucker is going to kill that woman.

Thinking about Stewart not watching for a tail reminded me I wasn't, either. Fabrizio could be walking up behind me right now. I turned, checked the street on both sides. I didn't see anything, but I didn't expect to. I didn't know Fabrizio but he was no amateur. I turned the corner at the second block. It was a long block, a perfect spot to check for a tail. I ducked behind a parked car and waited for almost a minute. Then I moved around the car, keeping crouched, and crossed the street, popping up to see if anyone was behind me. With my first glance, I saw nothing, but then a guy ducked behind a delivery truck. I waited, but he didn't come out even after five minutes. I checked the time. I had about an hour left.

Hello, Fabrizio.

Now I had a decision to make. Did I continue to follow Stewart, and risk getting killed? Or did I ditch Fabrizio and lose Stewart? Maybe there was a way to do both. I dialed Mazzetti.

When he answered, I said, "It's Fusco."

He must have been around people, because there was a long pause where I heard him walking, then he whispered. "What do you want? You got anything?"

"I've been following him all morning. We're in Brooklyn Heights. Stewart has a house here."

"What?"

"Yeah. Why would a guy have a house in Red Hook and another one in Brooklyn Heights?"

"You're sure it's his?"

"I'm not sure, but he had a key and he was in there a long time."

"What's he doing?"

"That's the other thing. He came out, got distracted by a woman, and now he's following her. You need to get on this, Mazzetti. I think he might kill her."

"Stay on her. Don't let him out of your sight."

It was my turn to pause. "You need to do it. I can't."

"What the hell do you mean?"

"I mean I can't. I've got other things to do, so you better get people on this."

"I'm on my way to the hospital. Frankie's awake."

"Is he okay?"

"All I know is that he's awake. I need to ask him questions. If he can ID either Stewart or Benning, we can get a warrant."

"Tell him I said hi."

"If Stewart kills her it's on you, Fusco."

"Don't try that shit with me. Get somebody on her." I gave Mazzetti the address of Stewart's other house and the location where I last saw him and the woman.

"Hurry up, Detective. I don't think Stewart is a patient man."

CHAPTER 53

TRACKING THE TRACKER

I hung up on Mazzetti, cursing what I had to do. I hated abandoning that woman, but if I gave Fabrizio a free hand I'd be dead. I promised Angie I wouldn't hurt anybody, and implicit in that promise was that I'd not get myself killed. It had been almost ten minutes now and no one had emerged from behind the delivery truck. But I felt sure I had seen Fabrizio.

The best thing was to confront him. I walked toward the delivery truck. I had almost an hour left, so I had no fears about Fabrizio doing anything. He would stick to the orders down to the second. Even if I wasn't sure about him being that kind of guy, I knew Mangini was, and he would insist on his orders being followed. I wanted to see what happened when I confronted Fabrizio. It would tell me a lot about the kind of man he was. I half-jogged across the street and approached the truck slowly. My gun was within easy reach, just in case. I reached behind me, my hand on the grip as I came around the back of the truck. He was gone.

I shot a glance inside the truck, then around me in all directions.

Jesus Christ. Am I losing it? Was he here or not?

I didn't have time to wonder about it. I wanted to get back to the house Stewart had gone in to check it out. He would be gone for at least an hour, enough time to get in and look the place over. I made good use of my prison skills and got through the lock in less than a minute. It was hard to believe he didn't have a dead bolt, but a lot of people in the old houses didn't bother with them.

"Hello." I felt pretty certain no one was here, but it didn't hurt to check. Halfway through the downstairs I realized how immaculate the place was. I felt like I should take off my shoes or something. I picked up a shoebox sitting on a table, the only thing out of place in the whole house. The pictures inside were almost all of naked women. One woman, the one whose portrait hung on the wall, looked familiar, and she was in most of the photos. In one photo, the mirror reflection showed an older man holding the camera while another man screwed her, and two kids watched. I looked at the picture on the wall. It was the same man in the portrait.

What the fuck?

Then it hit me where I'd seen her face. *Holy shit. What kind of freak is this guy?*

I called Mazzetti again. It rang four times before someone answered, but it wasn't Mazzetti.

"Detective Miller," a woman's voice said.

"Where's Mazzetti?"

"Who is this?"

"Where's Mazzetti, and what are you doing with his phone?"

"Mister, it's none of your business why I have his phone."

I decided I wouldn't get anywhere with her playing this way. "I'm a friend of Detective Donovan. I'm calling to see how he is."

"Is this Fusco?"

"Does it matter?"

"It does, yes. You should leave Frankie alone. If you were *really* his friend you'd take your sorry ass home and forget you knew him."

"Lady, you don't know what you're talking about. But you have nothing to worry over, because I'm going home. Now do me a favor and tell Mazzetti to check Stewart's house in Red Hook. If you can get a warrant, I'm sure you'll find something."

"What?"

"Just check it," I said. "And you better have somebody find out about the house in Brooklyn Heights. Something isn't right here."

I left Stewart's house, knowing Fabrizio would be outside. I waited for several people to pass by on the street, then walked out the door and joined them. He wouldn't shoot me while I was with them. That would piss Dominic off. At the corner I turned and walked slowly down the street.

Halfway down the block I kicked it up to a fast pace, checking to see if anyone kept the same distance. At the next corner, I turned right and jogged toward Smith Street. I knew I wouldn't lose Fabrizio this way, but it might confuse him a little. I checked the Beretta, took the safety off.

When dealing with someone like Fabrizio every second counted. Every *part* of a second. If it came to a confrontation, I couldn't be messing around with the safety on a gun. Fabrizio would be pulling the trigger while I did.

***

From a store down the street, Fabrizio watched Nicky come out of the house. He joined the people on the street, staying close for safety. Fabrizio let him have space. On a street like this, at this time of day, he could follow with ease. At the next corner, Nicky started his run. Fabrizio broke into a jog and followed him all the way to Smith Street. The lunchtime crowd had the street jammed. Nicky fell in with a few businessmen, lagging a few steps behind them, acting as if he were part of the group. Fabrizio kept to the other side of the street, shifting a casual glance now and then in Nicky's direction. The men he pretended to be with entered a restaurant featuring Thai cuisine. Nicky followed them in. After five minutes, Fabrizio assumed Nicky was testing his patience. He decided to sit it out in a dry cleaners.

Ten minutes later, he caught sight of someone who looked like Fusco, but he wore a hat and a jacket. And he walked with a slight limp. *Is he that good?* Fabrizio might not have believed it was Fusco if not for the single-minded way he walked, even with the limp.

If he turns at the corner and looks back, I'll know.

The man he presumed to be Fusco did just that. He turned at the first corner and glanced back. *Signor Fusco é buono. Very good.*

Nicky would probably circle the block and come up behind Fabrizio, so he ran quickly, two blocks back, and positioned himself under the awning of a club. People were milling about and delivery men were coming and going. He blended in. Five minutes later Nicky came up the street. He moved slowly, keeping balanced. His hand stayed close to his gun, and he moved to a position where he would be approaching Fabrizio from a blind spot. At least from where Fabrizio had been.

Nicky's hand moved into the pocket of his jacket. He must have moved the gun there. Unless Fabrizio wanted a shootout on the street, he'd have to wait for a better time. That was all right. He was a patient man. As St. Augustine said, "Patience is the companion of wisdom."

Fabrizio liked this Niccolo Fusco. He might have even enjoyed working with him—if Signor Mangini didn't want him dead.

CHAPTER 54

A DINNER GUEST

Stewart followed Cantaloupe Girl for several blocks. She stopped at a small natural food center, well known for their good fruit. He waited a while then followed her inside. She was putting figs in her basket. Bruce loved the sweet taste of figs. He walked up beside her and noticed her phone peeking out of a pocket on the side of her purse. It wasn't strapped in like most women kept theirs. Cantaloupe Girl must be the trusting type. Bruce bumped against her lightly, taking the phone as he did.

"Have you ever tried baking the figs with gorgonzola cheese on top?" he asked.

She turned, startled. A hint of recognition came to her face, but it wasn't quite there.

"Remember? You taught me how to select a ripe cantaloupe."

Her face broke into a big smile. "Oh yes. I *do* remember. Did it work?"

Bruce put on his most harmless expression. "Haven't had a bad melon since. I owe you."

She wrinkled her brow. "What was it you said about the figs?"

"Figs and gorgonzola. You split the figs, put gorgonzola on top, then bake them until the cheese melts. Oh God, it is *heavenly.*"

"I'll have to try that," she said. "Thanks."

"You won't regret it. Promise."

He placed a few figs in his basket, walked down the aisle, grabbed some grapes and a mango, then wasted time while she finished shopping. He shouldn't be doing this. He should get rid of the gun and quit while he's ahead, but…he wouldn't. His mind was made up the moment he saw her again. No, she made up his mind. The nerve of her taunting him like that. Wiggling her ass like she had a right to. She might as well have given him a key to her house with a written invitation.

Damn her.

It was all right, though. He'd do this one last job, then quit. Her ass was so pretty and soooo tight. He couldn't wait to see it. Rub it. Squeeze it. Maybe even sniff it, to see if she was ripe—like she suggested he do with the cantaloupes. Yes, he *had* to do Cantaloupe Girl.

And this one I'll take my time with.

He checked out a couple of minutes after her, then followed her to her house. He gave her time to get inside, get settled, then he walked to the front door and buzzed her. *Jan Morris. Cute name.*

She answered quickly. "Yes?"

"Ms. Morris, this is Bruce…God, that was stupid. I'm the guy you just bumped into at the market. Figs and gorgonzola, remember?"

Her voice was hesitant. "What can I do for you?"

"You dropped your phone at the market. I tried catching you but you got inside before I could."

She paused, probably looking in her purse. "Dear God. I did. Thank you."

"No problem. I'll just set it on the front steps."

"No. For heaven's sake, someone will steal it. Wait there, please. I'll be right down."

Bruce juggled his bag of groceries from one arm to the other while he practiced his spiel. He was certain she would be thinking of questions on her way down.

She opened the door, but only partially, as if afraid to let him in. She blushed. "I can't thank you enough."

"It's the least I can do after your cantaloupe lesson." He handed her the phone.

She looked up at him. "How did you know where I lived?"

"I was in line behind you and saw you drop the phone. I tried catching up but was a little slow."

"But how did you know my name to buzz me?"

"That was easy. I called my phone from yours and saw it on caller ID."

She blushed again and laughed. "That was smart."

"I'm just glad you got it back. Listen, I hate to run but I am *dying* for a cup of coffee."

She grabbed his arm. "Don't even think about it. The least *I* can do is make you coffee. I just bought some Kona at the store. Come up and try it."

Once inside, Bruce was impressed with her clean apartment. It wasn't like his, but far better than most. He could train her to be good if…no, her fate was sealed. Cast in stone, so to speak. He looked the place over while she made coffee. A picture of her and who he assumed to be her husband was prominently displayed on top the end table. It made him think they hadn't been married long. After five years or so, those pictures usually went into a storage chest. *Or the garbage.*

"I don't ordinarily do the shopping but my fiancée is out of town. I'm stuck bacheloring it."

"Oh, poor you. Men are such babies."

Bruce laughed. "We *are* babies, aren't we?"

Jan served coffee, offered him a piece of cake, then sat at the table to join him. "You must live nearby."

"A few blocks west. Whenever my fiancée is out of town I stalk the grocery stores for lonely women."

She laughed. "I love this neighborhood. I can walk to get most anything I need."

"And we get the added benefit of staying in shape."

Bruce made small talk for a few minutes, finished his coffee, then rinsed the cup and placed it in the sink.

Jan walked toward the door. "Well, thanks again for bringing the phone by. I don't know what I'd have done without it."

Bruce looked at his watch. "You're right. I really must be going, but first I would *love* to see your pussy."

Jan gulped. "What?"

He smiled. "Just kidding."

She looked for something to protect herself with, but nothing was close. She raised her shoulders and took a firm stance. "I think you should leave."

"Ah, yes. The threat." Bruce cupped his chin with his hand. "What will it be—your husband will be home soon? He won't, not until two days from now."

He smiled when he saw the look on her face. "I listened to your voicemail."

She screamed and reached for the doorknob. When he stopped her, she ran down the hall, heading for the bedroom. Bruce grabbed a knife from the counter. He caught her before she got the bedroom door locked, and forced his way in.

"Don't make me hurt you. If you scream again, I'll do more than look at your pussy."

"I have AIDS."

Bruce laughed. "That's a good one. And if I were going to rape you it might cause me concern."

"You're…"

"No, I am *not* going to rape you. I just want to take a peek."

"And then you'll let me go?"

"Yes, you will then be set free."

He held the knife to her throat and forced her to the bed. "Take your clothes off."

She started to turn around. He pressed the knife harder. "No need to turn. Just take off your clothes."

Jan trembled, her whole body quivering. She removed her pants and stood still.

"All of your clothes."

"But you said—"

"All of them."

She took off her top, then her bra, and stood hunched over, arms wrapped around herself.

"Good. Now lie on the bed, face up."

"Why are you doing this? I didn't—"

"No talking." He clamped his hand over her mouth and sliced her leg with the knife, not deep, just a little. She tried screaming, but his hand muffled the sound.

"From now on, every time you make a sound, I will cut you more. And each one will be worse. Understand?"

She nodded.

"Good. I'll let go now, but if you scream…"

"I won't." She whispered it, almost too low for him to hear.

"Spread your legs."

She opened them.

"Wider."

She spread them as far as she could.

He leaned in close, real close, and then he licked her. She jumped.

"You said—"

Bruce cut her on the lower belly. A thin stream of blood ran down to her vagina.

"Now look what you've made me do. Guess I'll have to clean *that* mess up." He started licking again. Her body tensed. She froze. He heard the sobbing as he tasted her. She was sweet. *Very* sweet. But not as sweet as Susan. Not even close.

He stood, shoved her panties into her mouth, tied her hands behind her back with the bra, then sat next to her on the bed. Her big brown eyes begged him to let her go. He could see in her eyes that she knew it wouldn't happen, that she'd realized now what a mistake she had made in letting him in. She made moaning sounds and looked as if she wanted to talk. He removed the panties, but held the knife to her throat.

"Yes?"

"Please don't hurt me. I'm pregnant."

Bruce feigned shock. "Pregnant. Oh my, that does change things." He put his finger to his chin as if in thought, then said, "Is it a boy or girl?"

"I don't know. It's too early, but if it's a girl I'm going to name her Cindra."

"Cindra…a pretty name. Unfortunately, the world doesn't need any more sluts." He shoved the panties back in her mouth, then slid the knife across her throat, drawing a thin line of blood. He threw a quilt over her, leaving only her neck exposed, then he sawed at it, using all his strength until he sliced through the jugular. Blood spewed out, and her eyes went wide. She thrashed about, but he held onto her. It didn't take long. While she was still alive he shot her, once in the head, once in the vagina.

When it was over he cleaned up. His arm was a mess and required several scrubbings. More could be done at home. After that he cleaned the sink drain to get rid of hair, used bleach to rinse it out, then moved Jan to the tub. He sprayed her off with the shower, front and back, washed her down with bleach, then made sure to use more bleach on her pussy. It wouldn't do to have them find his saliva on her. Fortunately his grocery bag was full of bleach, so he used more for one final cleaning, including his gun, checked everything, then took a seat at the table.

He grabbed the cantaloupe she bought, sliced it in half, cleaned out the seeds—making sure to get every strand of pulp—then peeled it from the rind. From the drawer he got a tablespoon and cut the melon into delicious little bites. He swirled the first bite in his mouth, caressing it with his tongue, letting the juices fill his taste buds. Jan had been right. This one was perfect.

When he finished he put everything down the garbage disposal, went to the bedroom and spread the sheet and quilt out and doused them with cooking oil. He stuck a note to her forehead using a thumbtack, spread oil, and a few other flammables throughout the kitchen, walked to the door and checked that no one was in the hall, then he struck a match and left.

This should throw those cops for a loop. They couldn't imagine Bruce Stewart would be out killing someone right after questioning him. All he had to do now was get rid of the gun.

CHAPTER 55

LUCK OF THE IRISH

lex ran to the waiting room, turning the corner at high speed. "Kate, FD is bleeding."

She grabbed hold of Alex as he wrapped his arms around her. "What happened?"

"He was laughing and then he started coughing and then…then his stitches broke."

"Who was in there with you?"

"A nurse. She chased me out."

Kate turned to Linda. "Will you…"

Linda took Alex by the hand. "Don't worry, I'll watch him and Keisha. You go."

Fifteen minutes later, Kate returned.

"Everything okay, Kate?"

"He's okay. Thanks."

Alex ran to her. "Is FD all right?"

She hugged him. "He's okay, Alex. They had to stitch him up again, but he's doing fine. We can go back in a little later."

Kate was explaining to Linda all that had happened, when Lou and Sherri came in. Lou gave Kate a big hug.

"Hey, girl, you doing all right?"

"I'm fine. Frankie's stitches broke and they had to redo them. Scared poor Alex half to death."

Lou knelt beside Alex. "You been through a lot, tough guy. Keep hanging in there. That's what Frankie would want."

Almost an hour passed before the nurse came in and gave the okay to see him. Lou looked at Kate, but she waved him on. "You and Miller go on. I'll be here all night."

Lou started for the room, turning to Sherri. "You coming?"

"Be right there," she said, then to Kate added, "You got a minute?"

Kate looked at Linda. "I'll be right back." She walked outside the room with Sherri. "What is it?"

Sherri looked at the floor, at the ceiling, and finally, at Kate. "I know you don't like me, Dr. Burns, and I don't blame you. But I want you to know one thing. Frankie has *never* done anything to give you reason to be upset or jealous."

"I don't need to hear this," Kate said, and turned to walk away.

"Yes, you do. Frankie tried getting me off his team because of the way you feel."

"He—what?"

Miller nodded. "He told me to get a transfer. Said he wasn't going to ruin the best thing he ever had because of me."

"If he didn't…"

Sherri took a hard stance. "He didn't do *anything*. He just wanted to make sure that you weren't upset. If anybody's to blame, it's me. I might have acted inappropriately."

"Don't try clearing your conscience on my watch."

"Bullshit. All I'm saying is I had feelings for the guy, okay? We didn't do anything, and Donovan never even hinted at it. So if your jealous ass wants to blame somebody, blame me." Sherri turned and headed down the hall.

"Miller!"

Sherri stopped. Turned slowly. "What?"

"Don't transfer because of me. I won't have that hanging over my head."

"Don't say it to be nice, because I got to tell you, I want to stay with these guys."

"I'm not nice. Not when it comes to sharing Frankie Donovan."

Miller laughed, and then she walked back to Kate. She offered her a hand. "Fair enough, Dr. Burns. That's something I understand."

Kate smiled with her. "Okay."

***

Sherri grabbed Lou's arm as he headed toward Frankie's room. "Mazzetti, are we working this case or not?"

"Yeah, we're working it, but I have to see Frankie."

"Your killer friend called and mentioned something about a house of Stewart's in Brooklyn Heights. Do you think Parnell was referring to him in her email?"

Mazzetti looked at her, and, for a moment he just stared. Things were coming together in his head. "Damn, Miller. You might be right about that. Let me talk to Frankie and we'll get busy. Call Carol and light a fire under her ass about it."

He stepped lightly into the room and across the floor to Frankie's bed.

"You can't be quiet, Mazzetti, so don't try."

"Hey, Donovan. How's it going?"

"Not so good, if you must know. I feel like shit, and I've got to piss through a tube."

"Okay, heard enough. And don't expect me to clean anything."

"That's why I love you, Mazzetti. Full of compassion."

"Lovable Lou."

"Where's Miller?"

"You remember anything about that day?"

Frankie looked at him. "Where's Miller?"

"She just finished talking to Kate."

"Fuck me."

"Yeah, and you only *thought* being in the hospital was bad." Lou took out his notepad. "Tell me what you remember."

Sherri walked in just as Frankie was starting. "Hey, Donovan. How's it going?"

"He's doing fine," Lou said. "Do you mind, Miller? I'm conducting an investigation."

"You seen Nicky?" Frankie asked.

Lou sighed. "Yeah. He was here the night it happened."

"And you haven't seen him since?"

"He might have come by once."

Sherri shot Lou a look he thought only his wife could make. "He's got your *friend* working the case."

"What?"

"Miller, you're an ass," Lou said.

"Screw you," Sherri said. "Maybe Donovan will talk sense into that head of yours."

Lou looked to Frankie. "Pay her no mind. I had him do *one* thing for me."

"One thing?" She looked at Donovan. "He just called. He's at Stewart's house."

Frankie tried sitting up. "What?"

"He said we better go to Red Hook and check out Stewart's house. He wouldn't say why. He also said Stewart had a second house in Brooklyn Heights."

"What the hell is this about Stewart's house?" Frankie said. "Will somebody tell me what the fuck is going on?"

"Don't worry about it," Lou said. "Tell me what you saw the day you got stabbed."

"Nothing. The guy stabbed me as soon as I walked in. I almost blacked out. Maybe I did. I don't remember. All I could think about was Alex, hoping he was safe."

"You never saw anything? Not a glimpse of him?"

"When I was on the floor, I grabbed my gun and shot at him, but it was all a blur. Obviously I missed."

"You got any ideas who might have done it?"

Frankie shook his head. "I figured it was Benning. Are you telling me Benning is in the clear?"

"Far as we can tell," Sherri said.

"And you think Stewart did it?"

"I don't see how, but your pal from Wilmington said he caught Stewart tossing your gun. The problem is Stewart's got an alibi that we can't break, and Benning's got an even better one."

"I'm worried about Nicky," Frankie said. "He shouldn't be here. If…"

Lou nodded, patting Frankie's arm. "Yeah, I know. But Nicky said he was going home. I'm sure he will."

"Speaking of which," Sherri said. "We have to get busy."

"Tell Kate to come in, will you?"

Lou and Sherri waved as they left.

Lou's phone rang as they walked down the hall. Sherri handed it to him. "Forgot to give this back to you."

"Mazzetti."

"Lou, it's Carol. I have the information you needed on the house in Brooklyn Heights."

"Go ahead."

"House is owned by Leo and Susan Caruthers. They also own a house in the Catskills, and one in Newport, Rhode Island. Wealthy doesn't describe them."

"You find any connection to Stewart?"

"Maybe. Probably."

"Don't make me guess."

"Susan was Leo's third wife. A *much* younger wife. They had no children together, but he had a son with his second wife, a Paula Stewart. You want to guess what the child's name was?"

"If I were a betting man, I'd say Bruce."

"And you would hit the jackpot. Wilfred B. Stewart, to be precise."

"Okay, so that gives us nothing. He went to his parents' house."

"Not so fast, Mazzetti. The odd thing is that his parents died in the 9/11 tragedy."

"Cops look into it?"

"There was no reason to. Back when it happened they questioned Bruce, and he said they were lost during the Twin Towers' attack. End of story."

"Where did all the money go?" Mazzetti asked.

"Stewart received a small sum, and by that I mean more than a few million. The rest went to a foundation to support up-and-coming artists."

"Did he file an insurance claim?"

"No, but he had so much money he wouldn't need to."

"All right, get with Morreau, tell him I need people on—"

"I already checked, Lou. He said he'd give you two guys for Red Hook, but nothing for the Brooklyn Heights house."

"Who's he giving us?"

"Saperstein and Hill."

"We'll take it. Get them over to Red Hook and tell them to call me the minute Stewart comes home."

"You got it."

Lou turned to Sherri.

"I heard most of it," she said. "The rest you can fill me in on the way."

"Where are we going?"

"I assume we're going to Brooklyn Heights."

"I knew there was a reason I liked you, Miller."

CHAPTER 56

AN UNLIKELY LEAD

Frankie Donovan tried sitting up. He tried stretching. He tried everything, but he couldn't reach his phone. He finally resorted to pushing the button to call a nurse. When she came in he smiled. "Nurse, can you please hand me that phone?"

"You should rest, Mr. Donovan."

"I will after I make one call."

The door opened and Kate walked in carrying a small box.

"What's in there? A present?"

"It was delivered by special messenger. The guy was kind of mysterious about it too, so it better not be from a woman."

Kate handed the box to Frankie.

He couldn't manage opening it and had to ask Kate for help. He didn't know if it was a bomb, but he knew he'd rather it be that than from a woman.

Please don't be from Shawna.

Kate finished opening it and stared inside with a puzzled look on her face.

"What is it?"

"A phone."

"A phone?"

She handed it to him. Frankie looked it over. It was a burner, and it had a note taped to the back with a number written on it. Frankie looked to Kate. "I hate to ask, but…"

She shot him a glare. "I'm leaving."

Frankie dialed the number.

"Hello."

"Who's this?"

"Hang on."

"Bugs, you alone?"

Frankie paused, trying to recognize the voice. *Who calls me Bugs except the old gang?* Then it hit him. "Manny?"

"Yeah, it's me. How you doin'? You feeling better?"

"I'm doing great for a guy who's gotta piss through a tube. So what's the call about? I know you're not that interested in my health."

"Yeah, all that shit back to you. But listen, I thought I'd pass something along."

"I don't like talking to you, Manny."

"How about listening then? You good at listening, 'cause this you should listen to."

"I'm listening."

"Rumor on the street is that someone is looking for your friend."

"Nicky?"

"How many friends you got? It ain't like they're knocking on your door every night."

"If they're looking for Nicky," Frankie said. "I assume they don't want to take him to dinner."

"Not from what I heard."

"Thanks."

"No problem. I like the kid. Tell him so."

"You know who's looking?"

"I can't say, but you might want to write this number down. At least report him missing or something."

Frankie wrote the number. As soon as he hung up he dialed it. It was answered on the second ring.

"Pronto."

Frankie recognized the voice. "Mr. Mangini."

"Who is this?"

"Frankie Donovan."

Silence, then, "I heard you were sick."

"I'm getting better, thanks."

"What can I do for you?"

"You once told me you owed me one."

"If I remember, Detective, you refused that offer."

"I'm asking now."

More silence. "What?"

"Call off the dogs."

"I can't do that."

"You owe me."

"Favors are a strange thing, Detective. Once you refuse one, it is gone." He paused. "Ask me something else."

"I have nothing else to ask. This is what I want."

"I am truly sorry."

"You will be, Mangini. If anything happens to Fusco, you'll be more than sorry. It'll just be me and you. No fucking badge. No rules."

"I hope you get better soon, Detective."

The line went dead. Frankie shut his phone and punched the pillow. If he didn't do something, Nicky would probably be dead. What the hell could he do? Who could he call?

Kate came back in the room. "What was that all about?"

Frankie's nerves drove his impatience. "Nothing."

"Nothing? A mysterious delivery man brings you a phone with a number scribbled on a piece of paper…and it's nothing?"

"Where's Alex? He okay?"

"The phone?"

"Nothing, Kate. Okay?"

She looked ready to shout. She was definitely pissed. Nothing could hide that. But she held her temper, even put on a smile.

"Alex is doing fine. He was scared to death you were going to die and leave him." She leaned down and kissed Frankie on the cheek. "He loves you, you know. More than anything."

Frankie smiled. "I'm sorry." He kissed her back. "About the phone…"

"You don't have to tell me."

"I want to. It was about Nicky. Manny Rosso sent the phone to tell me someone was after Nicky."

"Why?" She seemed genuinely startled.

"Because he came back to New York. He's not allowed."

Her eyebrows raised. "In the whole city?"

Frankie laughed. The way she said it made it seem like the end of the world, as if someone couldn't live without going to New York. "Yeah, Kate. The whole city."

"Who…never mind. I don't want to know."

"No, you don't."

"What are you doing about it?"

"I know you don't like Nicky, but—"

"I met him."

"What?"

"He came here and I met him."

"What did you think?"

"He's not as bad as I thought. I wanted to not like him, but it is obvious the guy loves you. I couldn't bring myself to hate a person who loves Frankie Donovan so much."

Frankie coughed. "Don't make me laugh again. I'll bust another stitch."

Kate stared for a long time. "I hope that someday we'll be that close. As close as you and Nicky."

Frankie reached for her hand. "I think we will, Kate Burns. I *do* believe we will."

"I'll leave you alone now. Let me know when you're done. Alex is dying to come in, and Linda and Keisha are here. She's eager to see you. I think she drew some pictures for you."

"She's a doll baby, I'll tell you that. And thanks for the privacy. I need to get something done here."

Kate headed out. "I know."

Frankie raised his head toward the ceiling, thinking of what he could do. Who could he call? Who could help? It hit him like a brick. *Connie.*

Frankie dialed Lieutenant Morreau, who answered quickly.

"Lieu, it's Donovan."

"Good to hear from you. How are you?"

"I'm alive, Lieu. That's better than the alternative."

"Is Mazzetti there? What do you need?"

"I need Connie Gianelli's number. You got it?"

A long pause followed. "Connie Gianelli's number? All of a sudden, out of the fucking blue, you need her number?" Another pause. "You gonna tell me what the fuck is going on?"

"Connie and I got to be friends when I worked her case. I wanted to update her, that's all."

"Is that right? You figured you'd just call to update her on your status. Let me ask you, Donovan. Have you called your family? Your sisters, other friends, relatives? No, I'd bet a thousand dollars you haven't. So why Gianelli?"

"Lieu…"

"Okay. Here's the goddamn number. Don't let me be surprised by anything. I don't want to get a call from the chief asking me about some strange connection between you and Gianelli. They don't like her, remember? They chased her out of town."

"I know all about it. Give me the *goddamn* number."

Morreau gave him her number and hung up with a few final warnings. Frankie dialed fast. It took him twice to get it right. All he got was a voicemail.

"This is Connie. I'll get back to you."

"Gianelli, it's Bugs Donovan. Call me as soon as you get this. It's important." He almost hung up, then added, "Damned important."

Shit. No telling where she was or how long it would take her to get back to him. Nicky might not have that kind of time. He thought of who else might be able to help, but came up empty. Manny risked everything giving him what he did. No way he was getting any more from him. If Tony were alive, he'd be an option but…*Paulie.*

Frankie got into his phone's contact list and typed in "Suit," which is how he had Paulie listed. Paulie "the Suit" Perlano had been another of his best friends growing up. He'd fallen in with Tony Sannullo, who was part of Tito's crew in Brooklyn. If anybody would know something about Dominic, Paulie would. He was best friends with Dominic's old driver.

Frankie dialed the number, which was somewhere in Texas. God bless Paulie for surviving down there. Three rings and no answer.

"This is Paulie. Tell me what you want."

"Suit, it's me, Bugs. Call me, man. I mean quick. Nicky's in trouble."

CHAPTER 57

A BODY TO SPARE

Lou dialed Saperstein's cell.

"Speak, Mazzetti, but make it fast."

"You on your way to Red Hook?"

"As much as I don't want to be, yes, I'm on my way. And did I say thank you very *fucking* much for this peachy assignment?"

"Yeah, it's about time you put in some real work. Anyway, watch for this guy. He's no slacker and he probably suspects something."

"And if we see him?"

"Call me. That's it. Just call."

"Okay, Mazzetti. See you later."

Sherri waited until the phone line was dead. "I take it you don't have all the confidence in the world in Detective Saperstein."

"You are being overly kind, Miller. He's a goddamn asshole, loser, son of a bitch who should have been thrown off the force years ago."

"And we're going to Stewart's other house, the one he stole or inherited, or one way or another got from his father?"

"That's where we're headed."

Lou turned onto Flatbush toward Brooklyn Heights. He didn't get five blocks before the phone rang.

"Mazzetti."

"Lou, it's Carol."

"What have you got?"

"We have a fire in Cobble Hill that Morreau wants you on."

"A fire? I'm a detective, not a goddamn fireman."

"This one's got a body in the bathtub."

He punched the dash. "Give me the address."

Lou repeated the address to Sherri, and then said, "A fire in Cobble Hill, but with a body in the tub."

"They think it's our guy?"

"I guess they do or Morreau wouldn't be sending us."

"What about Stewart?"

"Let's hope he goes to Red Hook."

Two fire trucks and three uniforms were parked outside the building when Lou and Sherri arrived. The trucks had finished their job; the unis hadn't started. Lou identified himself and introduced Sherri.

"What have you got?"

"Don't know anything other than a body," one cop said. He was young, not more than a couple of years on the force.

The second officer, a more seasoned one, added relevance. "She's got a note with a poem pinned to her head, Detective. That's why we called you."

"Pinned to her head?" Sherri asked.

The officer looked at her. "Yes, ma'am. Not a nice scene. Even without the fire."

"How about you canvas for us?" Lou said. "I'm sure you know the drill—everything and anything on the vic and on who and what they saw today."

"You got it, Detective."

Lou and Sherri went to the apartment. An overweight fireman stood at the door, sweating. "I'm glad to see somebody besides me is out of shape," Lou said.

"I hear you, Mazzetti, but I can lose weight. You can't get younger."

"Thank God for small favors."

Lou patted him on the back. "This is my partner, Sherri Miller. How's it going, Sean?"

Sean reached his hand out to her. "Nice to meet you, Detective. You caught a bad one here. Lucky for us it was called in early." He tilted his head down the hall toward the bedroom. "Not so lucky for the lady."

Sherri entered the bathroom, backed up, and bumped into Lou. "God bless her."

Lou moved to the side. The fire hadn't done much in the bathroom, but the victim's throat was slit, and she was shot in the head, right next to where the note was pinned.

"Anybody touch anything?" Lou asked.

"We checked her to make sure she was dead. That's all," a fireman said.

Lou leaned close and read the note aloud.

"Chocolate pudding
Chocolate pie
I ate them both
And then she died."

Lou read the note a second time. "Do you think he means he ate her? What's the pudding and pie reference?"

"It means he performed oral sex on her—front and back," Sherri said.

Lou stared at her. "I'm not asking how you knew that, Miller."

"Good damn thing."

"You notice that this is different," Lou said. "She's black. The others were white. She's a single kill, not with a lover."

"And it looks as if he did her in a hurry," Sherri said. "This is the first fire."

"Maybe he didn't have time to clean up. Figured he'd get rid of his DNA another way."

"Lou, we should have Saperstein pick Stewart up if he sees him. He might still have her blood on him."

"Good idea." Lou called Saperstein and told him, then joined Sherri, who was talking to one of the firemen.

"How did you get here so quickly?"

"Somebody called it in. It was an unknown caller, so I suspect it was on a disposable, which means I suspect it was the guy who set the fire." The fireman wiped sweat from his forehead. "Lucky he did, too, or this whole place might have gone up."

Sherri nodded. "I don't think he wanted that. He just wanted to get rid of the evidence."

"Sick bastard."

"Tell me about it," Sherri said.

After checking the bedroom and kitchen, Sherri went back to the bathroom and searched the cabinet. She pulled out a couple of bottles of pills. "Hey, Lou, when Dave Shu gets here tell him to check and see if she was pregnant."

"Don't tell me that," Lou said.

She nodded. "I'm afraid so. I found a test kit, and she's got a drawer full of prenatal vitamins, recently bought. I can't think of any reason to have them around other than being pregnant."

"This son of a bitch."

Lou dialed Saperstein. "He get back yet?"

"No sign of him."

Where the fuck is he? "Okay, listen up. If he comes, nab him. Hold him on anything. Just don't let him in the house to clean up."

"You got it."

Lou turned to Sherri. "We need to get to Brooklyn Heights. He hasn't shown his face in Red Hook."

CHAPTER 58

GATTO E TOPO (CAT AND MOUSE)

I rounded the corner and shifted my eyes left to see if I could spot Fabrizio. At first I saw nothing, but with a second glance, I picked him up, blending in with a crowd under the awning of a club. I kept moving, as if I were advancing on his old position…but then I passed it by. He had to be wondering what I was doing. Questioning himself.

A local delivery truck finished unloading supplies at a restaurant, of which there were plenty on Smith Street, and he was getting ready to pull out. I stuck my head in his window.

"I got two C notes if you drop me off at my car. Maybe two miles from here."

The driver looked at the hundred-dollar bills and smiled. "I'll take you to Jersey for that."

"But who wants to go to Jersey?" I said, and climbed in. We both laughed as I closed the door. I laughed a little longer than he did, knowing Fabrizio would be watching and wouldn't be smiling. I wished I could see him now.

I made small talk with the driver as he maneuvered the traffic. He never asked any questions—why I needed to get to my car so urgently, or why it was worth two hundred, when a car service would be less than half that. It was another day in the life of a New Yorker. Wilmington was nice and safe, but I *did* miss New York.

***

Fabrizio watched Nicky pass the cleaners, and then he passed the restaurant.

Where the hell is he going?

When Nicky got into the delivery truck Fabrizio knew he'd been had. Fusco was good.

He picked me up, but how?

Fabrizio looked around, checking to see if anyone was watching. He was screwed, but he wasted no time. Nicky would go back for his car. He *had* to. Fabrizio ran in the other direction. His diligent physical training would come into play now. He had to get there before Fusco got his car and left. With traffic as it was, it was not an impossible thing. He regulated his breathing and pushed a little harder. Dominic Mangini did not tolerate mistakes. When a person worked for Signor Mangini mistakes were buried with the ones who made them.

***

I had the delivery guy drop me off at the rental car. I put the keys under the passenger seat, left the doors unlocked, and walked down the street, settling in about two blocks from the car. Fabrizio would look for me here first, and he'd ignore all common safeguards and take the shortest route. Which meant he'd come right past this bodega, the one I was staring at from a shoe store a hundred yards behind it. I didn't have long to wait. He must have set a record running there, which gave me more information to store about Fabrizio.

Don't try to outrun him.

As he neared the bodega he slowed, peeked around the corner toward my car, then grabbed a bottle of water from the store. He drank it inside. I smiled. Fabrizio would wait until I came to get the car, or until he realized I wasn't coming. By then it would be too late. I walked a few blocks in the other direction, called a car service and got a ride back to Red Hook to get my own car. It was time to get the hell out of New York. Tomorrow I'd call the rental guy and tell him where I left it. Fabrizio would be long gone by then.

As far as Stewart, I'd given Mazzetti enough information that he should be able to pin these murders on him, assuming he obtained a warrant, or got into Stewart's other house.

I had cleaned out the first hotel room, so I could check out by phone. The one in Staten Island was a stop on the way home. An electric feeling ran through me. I had tempted the fates and won. Again.

I'm coming home, Angie.

***

Fabrizio finished his second bottle of water and his second cup of coffee. Why Americans called this coffee was beyond his understanding, but he drank it so he wasn't forced to infuse himself with a high-energy drink to get his caffeine. He checked his watch. It had been two hours and still no sign of Fusco. Once again he had been fooled. Fusco was *not* coming back for his car. He left it there on purpose to keep Fabrizio busy while he made his escape.

Or did something else. But what?

Fabrizio made the call he dreaded. Unfortunately, it was answered on the first ring.

"Pronto."

"Signore, queste é Fabrizio."

"*É fatto?*"

"No, Signore, it is not done. I have lost him."

A long silence followed, one Fabrizio dare not break.

"*Bisogna farlo.*"

"*Si, Signore. Sarà fatto.*" *It* will *be done.*

Fabrizio thought about what Nicky might do. He still had not accomplished what he came for, so Fabrizio must start there. He walked to his car and drove to Red Hook. It was time to see what Signor Stewart, suspect number one, was up to. If Fabrizio stayed with Stewart he would find Fusco sooner or later.

Patience was the key.

***

I wanted to stop to see Bugs but for obvious reasons opted to head straight for the bridge. I had the sleazy hotel to stop at in Staten Island, then it was straight home to Angie and Rosa and Dante. I shouldn't have come up to begin with. Angie had been right.

As she always is.

Halfway across the Verrazano-Narrows Bridge, I realized I still had Bugs' gun.

Goddamn! Now I have to go back.

I was nearing the Staten Island side of the bridge when my phone rang—it was the burner. I had planned on dumping this phone in the Pine Barrens on the way back. Maybe I should have used the East River. I flipped it open.

"Hello."

"It's Mazzetti."

"What's wrong?"

"The son of a bitch got another one."

"What?"

"Stewart. Goddamnit, aren't you listening? We have a dead woman in Cobble Hill, and I'm sure Stewart did it."

"I'd like to help you but I'm on my way home."

"Did you get a good look at her?"

"At who?"

"The woman Stewart was following. You said he was tailing somebody."

"I was pretty far back. I don't know how much help it would be."

"Give me what you remember."

I thought about it, recreating the memory of her in my head. "Five foot three, black, great build, dark hair." I thought a little more. "That's all."

"That's enough. It's her. This one's on you. You should have stayed with him."

"Fuck you! It's your job. I have a family. I got—"

"Yeah, guess what, asshole. She was pregnant. She won't *ever* have a family."

The line went dead. I wanted to call him back. Scream. Go kick his fucking ass…but he was right. This one *was* on me. I shouldn't have left it to them.

You should have told me what you wanted me to do, God. Now, I'm *making the decisions.*

I drove zombielike until I hit the other side of the bridge, took the first exit, and turned around.

That motherfucker shouldn't have killed her on my watch.

CHAPTER 59

AN ULTIMATUM

Stewart walked casually from the scene. He had done his good citizen duty and reported the fire. That he set it made little difference. He lived by a different set of rules. In his world, one right canceled two wrongs. What preceded each made no difference. Bruce wore a wide smile. He was only moments away from complete freedom. Ditch the gun, change clothes and get rid of them, and he was clear. Three blocks away the first leg of that journey was accomplished when he put the gun in a large trash can, tucked inside a paper bag with God knows what else inside. Either someone would get the gun or they wouldn't. It didn't matter to him.

Next he walked to his car and drove to his house in Red Hook. As he went down the street he noticed an SUV with two men inside. Bruce slowed down. The car was running, windows rolled up.

And they're just sitting there. They might as well have their sirens on.

No question they were cops. The question was what were they doing there? *What could they want?* They couldn't have had anything on him from Cantaloupe Girl, and he couldn't imagine they had gotten any new evidence from the other scenes.

So why are they here?

He circled the block, slowing after he got out of their sight. It didn't matter *why* they were there. The fact was, they *were* here. And he had blood on his clothes. He couldn't afford to be taken in. There was only one thing to do, go to the other house. He turned right at the next street, then took the first left. Brooklyn Heights was only a few minutes away. Not a high price to pay for freedom.

***

Fabrizio sat low in the seat of his car, two blocks from Stewart's house. The idiot police on stakeout were busy playing cards, or something else, when Stewart drove by. They didn't even see him. But Fabrizio did, and, more importantly, he noticed Stewart saw *them*. Fabrizio had a good idea where Stewart would be going, so he turned and headed toward the Brooklyn Heights house, ahead of Stewart. If he guessed wrong, he'd pay the price, but he seldom guessed wrong. In all of his time in America, only Fusco had ever outwitted him. And Fusco would soon pay the price for that. The game was not over. Not yet.

***

With caution infusing his body, Bruce approached his Brooklyn Heights house at a crawl. He wasn't about to actually drive past it—not yet—but he figured he could spot any cops from a few blocks. They wouldn't get close. From half a block away he spotted the sexy black cop, the one he dreamed of doing while she was tied down. He pulled to the curb, a fortunate space waiting for him, and watched as she joined her partner. Bruce hated that old man; in fact, he made up his mind right then he would kill him if he had the chance.

He sank very low in the seat. Sniffed himself. He probably had Cantaloupe Girl's juices on him, maybe in his hair, or in his mouth. And he knew there were traces of blood. The gun was gone, but…he had to get rid of her DNA. Okay, that was easy enough. He could check into a hotel and shower several times, really scrub.

Yes, that's what I'll do.

He reached to turn the ignition, but stopped.

But what if they go inside the other house? I should have gotten rid of those pictures long ago.

Besides, he had to get his passport and his money. He could go to France. Isn't that where all sophisticated criminals went? At least ones like himself with dual citizenship.

So what to do? Clean up first.

That *was* the priority. He had to clean up. Bruce waited for the detectives to get settled in, then he started his car and headed for the hotel down the road. It was dark now, so they wouldn't see him, and it wouldn't take him long to get back to a virgin state, free of all DNA except his own. After that, all he needed to worry about was Red Hook. He laughed, and, as he drove to the hotel, he wondered if the detectives went home at night and did crosswords, or did they practice their ABCs.

Instead of a hotel, he went to the art gallery to scrub. He used the private bathroom next to his office to shower, then he changed clothes and wrapped his old ones in a plastic bag, which he disposed of a few blocks away in a dumpster. Afterward, he bought a cup of coffee from a bodega and returned to keep an eye on the detectives.

He parked three blocks from the house in Brooklyn Heights and found a place to rest, next to a stoop. He could wait, at least a little while. Come morning though, he was going in, no matter what he had to do. He was getting comfortable that things would work when he saw the detectives heading toward him. He pulled out the knife, held it by his side. He never did like that old man. The bitch either.

***

Mazzetti looked at his watch. "It's damn near two o'clock, Miller. I say we pick it up in the morning."

"I'm with you. All we've seen are a few stragglers shuffling back and forth. Not even a hint of Stewart."

"Let me call Saperstein first."

"You think he's still there?"

"He better be. I blackmailed him."

Sherri gave a half a chuckle, lacking the energy for a full laugh. "What do you have on him?"

"Pictures of him with small children."

"Don't even joke about shit like that. It makes me sick."

"Me, too. Which makes joking about it one of the only things to do. That, or killing the perverts. And I leave stuff like that to Donovan."

"We got anyone to cover for us?

"This is unauthorized, remember? If Morreau finds out we're doing this…"

"Call to see if Stewart ever checked in at Red Hook."

Lou dialed the phone and waited a long time.

"Saperstein."

"Where the fuck are you?"

"I'm in bed. It's late."

"I thought you were covering the house."

"I stayed till midnight. Malone said he would stay till two."

"Fuck you," Lou said, and hung up. He turned to Sherri. "They're long gone. Saperstein left two hours ago. Malone said he would stay until two, but I'd bet he left ten minutes after Saperstein."

"Shit."

Lou lit a smoke, staring out the window. "See that homeless guy pushing the grocery cart?"

"I see him."

"He's been here for a couple of hours now, walking back and forth, rummaging through garbage, picking up trash."

Sherri laughed. "That's what homeless people do, Mazzetti. You need to get out more."

Lou opened the door. "I'm gonna check on him."

Sherri got out with him. "Pretty soon it won't be worth going to sleep."

Lou headed toward the homeless guy. "Don't worry, Miller, we'll get an early start."

"I'll pick you up at six," Sherri said.

"Not *that* early."

Sherri glanced to the side and noticed a man crouched against the wall next to a dumpster. She nudged Lou, then, to the guy, said, "Hey you. What are you doing there?"

The man didn't answer. Didn't move.

"Is he alive?" Mazzetti asked.

Sherri moved to check on him. The man jumped up, grabbed her with one hand and pressed a knife to her throat with the other. He grabbed her gun and pointed it at Lou.

Lou froze. "Hold on, Stewart. You don't want to do anything stupid."

"Handcuff her."

"What?"

"Handcuff her," Stewart said.

"Listen, Stewart—"

"When you're done with her, clamp one on yourself."

"What do you think you're doing?"

"I'm handcuffing both of you, then putting you in the dumpster. I hope they find you before the truck picks it up."

Lou didn't believe for a minute that Stewart would let them go, but he had little choice. At least until he could get a clean shot. And he didn't know how he'd manage that. "Stewart, listen—"

"Old man, if you say one more fucking word, I will slit her throat like I did the last one."

"You don't want to do this," Sherri said. Her body shook, and her voice revealed her fear. She had to be thinking of last year when she got shot. Being with Mazzetti and Donovan had not been good for Sherri.

"Murder is one thing," Sherri said, "Killing a cop will get you the needle."

Stewart laughed. He pressed the knife into her neck, drawing blood. All the while he kept a firm grip on the gun pointed at Lou. "I'm not going to kill you, but when I get you cuffed, I *will* fuck you. If you're good, I'll do it twice."

CHAPTER 60

OLD HABITS DIE HARD

I watched Stewart from my SUV. A homeless man walked up my side of the street, pushing a cart. On the opposite side, Stewart had Lou and Miller held captive. He had a knife on Miller and a gun pointed at Mazzetti. Not a good situation. Not impossible, but not good. I opened the car door *very* slowly, thanking God I remembered to disable the interior light. I crept onto the sidewalk, crouching so I could stay low enough to not be seen. Halfway down the block my legs started cramping and I stopped to stretch. I couldn't afford the time, but I couldn't afford a mistake either.

I crept forward to the next car, then the one after, inching toward Mazzetti and Miller until I could get in a position to do…something. The homeless guy bothered me. He kept rumbling along, making noise. I worried that Stewart might panic and decide to do them in. Two cars later, my fears took fruition. I was only twenty feet away when I heard Stewart.

"Detective, I think I've decided to just kill you and get it over with. And your partner goes when I'm done with her. I kind of liked the last black I had."

Mazzetti tensed, started to make a move.

Don't do it, Mazzetti.

Stewart moved forward, pushing Sherri ahead of him. "Don't get brave, Detective. You're not young enough or quick enough to do anything before I kill her."

I flexed my muscles to prevent any creaking of bones, got on my knees and crawled to the front of the car. When I figured I'd moved close enough, I stood. I stepped silently toward the detectives, focusing on Stewart. I had a gun in my front waistband and one in the back. And the derringer in my cap.

Stewart had a gun pointed at Lou and a knife at Sherri's throat. I wasn't a prophet, but I knew someone would die tonight.

He tensed as I approached, his hand shaking.

"Who the fuck are you?"

"Nobody."

"Nobody? What the fuck is that supposed to mean?"

"Put the gun down and we can talk."

"Are you a cop? If I'm going to kill two cops I might as well kill three."

I smiled at him. I found out long ago that a smile can disarm a man quicker than a threat.

He seemed astonished. His brow wrinkled and his eyes went wide. "What the hell are you smiling about? I said I'm going to kill you."

"You're not killing anyone."

Miller trembled. Lou stayed calm. That was good. I needed him calm. Stewart shook as if he was going to explode. Exactly what I wanted. I watched his eyes, and his hands. I saw his eyes shift from Lou to me. It was going down now.

He moved the gun to fire at me. The instant he shifted off Lou, I drew a gun and fired. The first shot whizzed past Miller's cheek and hit him in the right eye. Sherri screamed and broke away just as the second shot entered his skull. Sherri lay on the ground, curled into a ball. She was reaching for her backup gun. I stepped on her arm.

"Hold up. I'm a friend."

Mazzetti knelt to check on Stewart while I helped Miller up.

"He's dead," I said.

Lou stood. "Deader than duck shit."

I looked at him. Almost laughed. "I don't think I've heard that expression before."

"Old goofy Mazzetti expression."

Miller hadn't stopped shaking, but she gathered enough composure to talk. "You must be Fusco."

I wiped my prints from the gun and handed it to Lou. "This is Bugs' gun."

Mazzetti stared. "Great. How am I going to explain Stewart getting shot with Frankie's gun? The lieutenant knows the killer had it."

"Tell him you struggled with the guy, took the gun, but he attacked with a knife and you shot him."

"Just like that?" Lou said.

"Just like that," I said.

"Forensics won't support that argument. Distance, range, all of that matters."

"You'll figure it out, Mazzetti."

"Maybe we will." Lou extended his hand. "I owe you one, Fusco."

I shook his hand. "I don't think you want to owe me one, Detective, but I appreciate the thought."

Miller stood with her head lowered, staring at the ground. "You okay?" I asked.

She glared at me. The kind of look when someone is grateful, but hates having to be. "Don't think *I* owe you anything."

"I never said you did."

"Yeah, well, you're right. I don't."

I looked around. "Mazzetti, I'd love to stay and discuss the problems of the universe, or the problems with your partner, but I have to go."

"We've got to stay here until reinforcements come. I'll tell Frankie you said hi."

"Do that. I'd appreciate it."

***

Fabrizio went to Nicky's car and left his cart beside a pickup truck at the curb. He removed the overcoat and wool gloves and placed them in the basket, and then he moved silently and hid. Fusco had given the detective his gun, but he might have another. It didn't matter. After tonight, he wouldn't need it.

CHAPTER 61

BLACKMAIL WORKS BOTH WAYS

Frankie reached for the phone when it rang. Stretching hurt his side more than coughing. He finally nabbed it with the tip of his finger and dragged it toward him. He flipped it open. "Donovan."

"Bugs. Christ's sake, how are you?"

Frankie lit up. "Paulie? I can't believe it's you."

"What's up? You said Nicky was in trouble."

"It's a long story, but the bottom line is Nicky is in town, and Dominic Mangini isn't happy. I think he's got his top man after him."

"Fuck me."

"What's that supposed to mean?" Frankie asked.

"It means I've seen the guy work. I know Nicky's good, but if this is Fabrizio, Nicky could be in trouble."

"Shit. I'm hoping you have something I could use to blackmail Mangini."

"Use? You mean besides a cannon?"

Frankie stayed silent.

After a moment, Paulie said, "The only guy I know who might be able to help you is Manny. He grew up with Dominic."

"You got anything I can use with Manny?"

"Shit, Bugs, I don't know. Maybe."

Frankie boiled inside. "This is Nicky, goddamnit. If you have something, give it up."

"I'll make a call," Paulie said. "Sit tight."

Five minutes later, Frankie's phone rang. It was Manny.

"I hear you got troubles, Bugs."

"Thanks for calling, Manny, and yeah, you know what kind of troubles I have."

"I'm only gonna help you because I like you, and because I owe Nicky a favor."

"I don't care why, just tell me what I need."

"Okay, here's what I got…"

Manny filled Frankie in on a few details from Dominic's past. Enough, Manny said, to earn a favor.

"You sure about this?"

"If you tell anybody where you got it, I'm dead. You hear me, Bugs? Dead. Not hurt. Not maimed. Dead."

"I got it. Don't worry."

"You shouldn't fuck with Mangini. He's not right. He likes hurting people."

"I don't believe that. I think he's got a lot of heart."

Frankie thought back to the lunch he had with Dominic, to the look in his eyes when he talked about giving up everything he ever loved. Frankie counted on his judgment being right on this one. Nicky's life depended on it.

"Thanks for the help, Manny. This goes to the grave with me."

"Yeah, okay. Good luck."

Frankie dialed the number for Mangini. He answered right away.

"Pronto."

"Mr. Mangini, I need to talk."

"Talk."

"You once said you owed me one. Where I come from owing a favor means it goes without saying it gets paid back." Frankie waited a few seconds. "No matter what it is."

"We have already had this discussion, Detective."

"We're having it again."

"If I do this for you," Dominic said, "You will owe me a favor."

"I can't do that."

"Then we have nothing to discuss." A pause. "I'm surprised. Your friend risked everything for you."

"That's because he's an honorable man. Something you wouldn't know about. Back where I come from we honor promises."

"Ask something else."

Frankie had hoped to not have to use Manny's information. Now he had no choice. "I know about Connie's father."

A long silence followed. Long enough to let Frankie know he hit a sore spot.

"He was a drug user. Who cares?"

"Let me put it differently, Mr. Mangini. I *know* who killed Tommy Nunzio. And I *know* what he left behind."

More silence followed. Frankie thought he heard whispered curses in Italian.

"I only owe you one favor. Are you sure this is what you want?"

"Call your dogs off, Mangini."

"It might be too late."

"If anything happens to Nicky, what Connie finds out will be the least of your worries."

"Blackmail is a dangerous thing, Detective."

"Blackmail works both ways. Call your man off."

"If I do this, you will owe *me* a favor. Understood?"

"Bullshit. Call him off."

"For the favor I will."

Frankie thought about all the things Mangini might have him do for this *favor*. "No way."

"It is sad. Your friend risked everything for you."

"Yeah, well I can't do that. But let me tell you something, it's going to be a bloodbath when I'm out of here."

"Think about what I said. But think quickly."

Frankie threw the phone across the room, almost hitting Kate as she walked in the door.

"You can just ask me to leave next time."

"Sorry."

She picked up the phone and handed it to him. "What's wrong?"

Frankie shook his head. "Nothing. Some asshole wants me to trade a favor."

"You want to explain that?"

Frankie sighed. For a moment he said nothing. "Nicky is in trouble with the mob. I can get him off, but I'd owe them."

"Don't do it." Kate seemed vehement about it.

"Don't? With all he's done for me?"

"You've saved his ass a few times if I remember correctly."

"Not enough."

Kate let him stew for a minute. "Frankie, there are laws we have to live by. All of us. You're a detective. You can't break those laws for someone just because they are a friend."

Frankie thought about what Kate said.

Laws to live by. Like the oath we took.

"You're right, Kate. Can you give me a minute? I've got to make a call."

Her head was still shaking when she walked out. "I hope it's the right one."

Frankie dialed the phone.

"Pronto."

"Okay, we're on."

"You will owe me a favor. Agreed?"

"Agreed."

"A wise decision, Detective Donovan."

***

I walked slowly to my car. It wasn't that far away but it seemed like a mile. It had been a long day and I had a long drive home. I couldn't wait to get back to Angie and the family.

About fifty feet from the car, I slowed down even more. The driver's side door wasn't closed all the way. I *know* I closed it when I got out. *Is someone inside?* The car wasn't weighed down so nobody was in there, but somebody definitely opened that door. I moved my hand slowly, got my gun from behind my back and held it close to my side. I had almost come to a stop, looking left and right. Someone was here. Watching.

Fabrizio. It has to be him.

I thought I lost him but he must have figured out where I'd go. I heard a footstep and whirled, ducking at the same time. Fabrizio grabbed my hand, twisting the gun away from me. At the same time, he shoved his gun in my face.

"Don't do it, Niccolo."

I stopped, stood up. I had a sick feeling in my gut, and my throat constricted. "There are two cops right down the street."

"I watched. You did well."

Everybody always used to say I wasn't afraid of anything. I wished they could feel my nerves right now. I was *terrified.* I didn't want to die, but worst of all, I didn't want to leave Angie and Rosa to fend for themselves and raise Dante alone. I had to stall until I could think of something. "Let's get it over with, Fabrizio. No sense wasting time."

"Not here."

"Afraid of a few cops? Guess what, I'm not going anywhere with you. I'm going to force you to do it here."

Fabrizio smiled. "*Sei pazzo.*"

"I may be crazy, but I'm no fool. If I go with you I just make it easier for you to kill me."

Fabrizio tucked my gun into his waistband. "It is a shame. I would have liked to work with you."

I needed a second, that's all. One second to get the derringer from my cap and shove it into his eye or his ear. But for that, I needed him off guard. He was quick. I decided to talk. Talking sometimes took people out of their game. "Tell Dominic it was something that had to be done. I meant no disrespect."

"Signor Mangini understands these things."

"You won't get away. The cops down the street already called the shooting in. Half a dozen cars will be here any minute."

"We'll see." Fabrizio lost his smile. "I am not an unreasonable man. If you would like to call your wife, do it now."

This was my chance. "I'm reaching for my phone. Is that okay?"

He stretched, frisked me with his left hand, then nodded.

I slowly pulled out my phone and started dialing. At the same time, I wiped my forehead and took off my cap. The gun was strapped inside it. I held the cap in my left hand with the phone, prepared to act at the first opportunity.

Fabrizio reached into his pocket and pulled out a phone. It must have been on vibrate. "Si."

He nodded a few times, but he never took his eyes off me. I moved slowly. Got hold of the derringer, cupped it in my hand. If his eyes shifted just once, he was gone.

After maybe ten or fifteen seconds, he put the phone away. "You must have an angel on your side, Signore."

I shot him a questioning look.

"Signor Mangini said you are welcome to stay as long as you follow the rules."

The lump in my throat vanished, as if it had never been there. My grip on the gun relaxed.

"What changed his mind?"

"You have a good friend in that Irish detective."

"Bugs?" I laughed. *Good old Bugs.*

I looked at Fabrizio. "Guess we're not enemies anymore."

He tucked the gun into his pants, then nodded to me. "Your gun, Signore."

I tried to feign confusion.

"You don't think I missed that gun, do you? The one in your hat?"

I put the derringer back inside the cap and laughed. Then I laughed some more. "Fabrizio, I like you. You need a ride?"

"*Sei pazzo,*" he said, and then he laughed too.

"Maybe we're both crazy, Fabrizio."

I opened the car door. "Hop in. I'll take you to get your car."

CHAPTER 62

RECOVERY

Lou and Sherri finished their paperwork and went to the hospital. They chatted with Kate for a while, then went to Frankie's room. After about fifteen minutes he woke from his first nap of the day, wiping tired eyes and wishing he had a pain pill in addition to his painkiller pump. Being stabbed was not a fun thing. Lou stood a few feet from the bed, Sherri beside him.

"Where's Kate? And Alex?"

"She went to get something to eat. Alex mentioned something about possibly being admitted after eating so much hospital cafeteria food."

"Little brat," Frankie said.

"He's adorable," Sherri said. "I'd take him in a heartbeat."

Frankie looked around. "Was Nicky here?"

Lou looked at his watch. "He should be here soon."

"And the case? If you two are here I'm assuming it's over."

"Primary suspect is dead," Sherri said.

"Stewart?"

Lou nodded. "Stewart. How your friend figured that out I don't know. But he did."

Frankie didn't want to ask who killed Stewart. He was afraid to know. "Smart guy, Nicky is. Street smart."

"Saved my ass," Sherri said. "Lou's, too."

Frankie tried sitting up, more interested now. "How?"

"Stewart was about to cut my throat. I thought I was gone. Then Fusco pops up from behind a car, and a minute later he capped him. I think I felt the bullet whiz by me. Got him in the eye and head. I still can't believe he took the shot with me right there. Didn't have more than an inch or two room for error."

Frankie started to laugh. It hurt. He held his stomach. "He'd have taken the shot with half that and still hit the guy."

"That's confidence," Lou said.

"So I guess you two are heroes," Frankie said.

"You, too. You're a martyr."

"What did Morreau say?"

"He suspects something fishy. Stewart was shot with your gun."

"My gun?"

"Stewart took it when he stabbed you."

"Then how—"

"Nicky took it back."

"Oh shit," Frankie said. "Morreau might take us all off homicide."

"Maybe he'll send me back to Narcotics where it's safe."

"You staying around, Miller?"

She looked at Frankie. "Guess I have to now. Somebody needs to take care of this grumpy old bastard."

Lou put a cigarette in his mouth, sucking on it dry. "In case you two haven't noticed, I'm the only one who hasn't been shot or stabbed."

"You look like you're going to keel over at any minute. Nobody is going to risk jail time to take you out a few days early."

"Yeah, keep telling yourself that. I'll be singing at your funeral."

The door opened and Nicky walked in.

"Hey, Bugs. How's it going today?"

"Do we need to deputize you?"

"I don't want any of that shit."

Frankie squeezed his hand. "Thanks for coming up." There was no need to say thanks for anything else.

Sherri lowered her head, then walked to Nicky's side and kissed his cheek. "I was an ass last night."

Lou made a noise that only old men who have been smoking for about sixty years can make.

Sherri raised her eyebrows. "Okay, I have been an ass since I met you. I just want to say thanks. You saved my life."

Nicky smiled. "That kiss made it even. But don't tell my wife. She hates it when all the beautiful women fawn over me."

Sherri laughed, the tension gone. "God, you sound just like Donovan."

Nicky turned to Lou. "You guys search his house in Red Hook yet?"

"They're tearing it apart as we speak."

"It was immaculate. Not a speck of dust, even with renovations."

Bugs slapped his hand on the bedrail. "Damn, I knew it. When I was at his house, it was dirty, but only superficially dirty. It's all coming back to me."

"What's coming back?" Lou asked.

"Stewart's house. There were no smudges on the chrome faucet or the sink. The mirror had no fingerprints, and the grout on the floor and walls was sparkling white. All the dirt in Stewart's house was superficial. Planted to make it look dirty."

Frankie shook his head. "It's like a slob who cleans up real quick before company comes. They can't hide the dirt—this guy couldn't hide the clean. I can't believe I didn't see it."

Nicky laughed. "A little dirt can't hide a pretty face."

Bugs slapped the rail again. "That's it, Nicky. And I even thought that on the way home, but couldn't place it at the time."

"Besides that," Nicky said, "Wait until you see the pictures at his Brooklyn Heights house. Stewart was a sick son of a bitch."

"How did he kill Krenshaw and her lover if he had so many witnesses to alibi him?" Frankie asked.

"I figure he bought them off," Lou said. "The guy had more money than he knew what to do with, and he wasn't shy about throwing it around."

"Not at all," Sherri said. "They told us he took them all out and paid everyone's way. Sometimes he would take a whole crowd to a club, all his treat."

Lou nodded. "People like that—leeches—they aren't ratting out their money horse. No way."

"Guess not," Frankie said. "Odd though. I can see it for something small, but when it's a murder investigation, I would expect a few of them to crack."

Frankie turned to Nicky. "When are you leaving?"

"Right now. I have to get back before Angie kills me."

Lou tapped Sherri on the arm. "We're going to finish up some paperwork. See you later, Frankie."

"Yeah, see ya', Irish," Sherri said. "You too, Fusco. Hope there's not a next time."

"There won't be."

Frankie waited for the door to close. He dropped his smile. "You shouldn't have done it, Nicky. We'd have gotten the guy."

"Sure you would. Mazzetti still thinks Benning did it."

Bugs laughed. "He's a good cop. Miller, too."

"I know. I need to practice my patience."

Bugs held his fist out, raised it in the air. "Friendship and honor."

Nicky laughed and did the same. "Just like old times, Bugs. We protect each other."

"And we always will."

Nicky seemed nervous. He fidgeted, something he seldom did. "Bugs, listen. I gotta go."

"Say hi to Angie and Rosa. And Dante. I almost forgot him."

Nicky's head drooped. "If she's still there."

"What are you talking about?"

"Nothing."

"What? You better tell me."

Nicky fidgeted more. Shifted his weight from one foot to the other, moved around, tapped on the bed rail. "She was pissed when I left. I haven't been able to reach her since."

"See what I mean? You shouldn't have come. Now get the hell out of here. Go home."

"You're right. I'm gone."

CHAPTER 63

POINT OF NO RETURN

As soon as the door closed, Frankie grabbed his phone. He tried to reach Angie but got no answer. He didn't leave a message; he didn't want Nicky to hear it. What to do…He remembered Rosa called him a few days ago. He looked for her number and dialed. She answered right away. Maybe all kids did.

"Uncle Mario!" She sounded excited.

"Rosa, how are you?"

"How am *I?* How are you doing? Dad said you were in the hospital. I wanted to come see you, but…"

"Never mind that, I'm doing okay. Listen, I was calling to talk to your mom. Is she around?"

A long pause followed. "She's not here."

"Where is she?"

"She…she's at her cousin's house."

"Do you have the number?"

"Uncle Mario, talk some sense into her. Please? She's really upset, and it's stupid."

"Give me the number."

Frankie called and asked for Angie. It took her a moment to get on the phone.

"What is it, Frankie?"

"Nicky is really upset, Angie. I've never seen him like this."

"*He's* upset? And I'm supposed to run home and coddle him?"

Frankie heard her breathing hard.

"I can't do it anymore. I can't. I've got two kids now. I won't sit around waiting for him to get out of prison again. And I can't bury him. I *won't* bury him."

"Angie, he didn't do anything wrong."

"Sure. Like he didn't do anything last year. I hear the talk."

"Angie, I swear. Read the paper tomorrow. It will have all the details."

She said nothing. "Call him," Frankie said. "His heart is breaking."

Angie cried. Frankie let her go on even though it tore him up to hear it. She cried for a long time. "*His* heart is breaking? Do you know what *mine* feels like? *Do you?*"

"I don't. But I've known Nicky all his life. And I can tell you, his heart *is* breaking. So please, do me a favor and call him. Give him a chance."

There was more silence. "I didn't even ask how you were. Are you okay?"

"Much better, thanks. I'll be a whole lot better if you call Nicky."

"Goodbye, Frankie," she said, and hung up.

***

Angie went outside and started walking. After circling the block three times, she called Sister Thomas. "I need to talk, Sister."

"Meet me at the bench in the park," Sister Thomas said.

"This might take a while. Maybe we should meet at my house."

"I'll meet you there."

Fifteen minutes later, Sister Thomas showed up. Angie had just pulled up in her car. They went inside and sat in the living room. "I won't waste time, Sister. I'm worried about Nicky. I'm afraid he might be getting into trouble, and he's…"

Sister Thomas took hold of Angie's hands and squeezed. "Angela, I've known all of you since you were babies. I know what each one of you is like—your personalities and idiosyncrasies."

"But you don't understand, Sister. How could you? Nicky—"

She gave Angela a glare. "How could I? I'll tell you. I know that Rosa is not Nicky's daughter. And I know that she's not Marty Ferris' daughter either. And if she is whose daughter I think she is, I know what must have happened for you to become pregnant."

Angela pulled back and looked away.

"And God forgive me for saying this," Sister Thomas said as she blessed herself with the sign of the cross, "I'm not sorry that Tony Sannullo is dead. All he did was ruin lives."

Tears formed in Angela's eyes.

"Nicky is a lot like his father. He needs help, and it's up to you to take care of him."

Angela stared at Sister Thomas, her eyebrows raised. "How do you know all of this?"

Sister Thomas looked up, while her hands fumbled with her rosary beads. "Because I failed a man just like Nicky. I should have been there for him. I should have been his strength. But I wasn't, and because of me he fell out of grace with God."

She mouthed a short prayer and then grabbed hold of Angela's cheek and turned her so they faced each other. "I pray every night for him, and I wish I could part a curtain and go back in time. But God doesn't allow such things. We get one chance. One decision."

She stared at Angela for a long time, then said, "Remember that, Angela. Don't make the mistake I did."

***

I took the expressway to the bridge and started the long ride home. It wasn't far—two and a half hours—but it was going to feel like twice that with all the worrying. Angie hadn't talked to me since I left Wilmington and I suspected she wouldn't be there when I got home. I was touching down on the Staten Island side of the bridge when my phone rang. It reminded me I had to get rid of the other phone.

"Hello."

"Nicky?"

The voice was soft, with no enthusiasm in it, but to me it sounded like an angel.

"Angie?"

"Where are you?"

"I just left the hospital. I'm on my way home."

"Is everything okay?"

She sounded upset, as if she expected to hear bad news. "Everything is fine. Bugs is getting better and they don't think he'll have any permanent damage."

"I meant with you. You're okay? Nothing's wrong?"

She was breaking my heart. I despised hurting her. "Angie, I'm great. And nothing is wrong. I should be there in three hours tops."

That seemed to perk her up. I heard a little more spark in her voice. "Rosa is making meatballs for you. And I thought we'd invite Sister Thomas for dinner. Is that okay?"

"Oh my God. I can't tell you how much I've dreamed of meatballs. I'll see you soon."

"Drive safe."

"You know I will." I almost hung up, but then, "Angie…I love you."

"I love you too. Just get your butt home."

"On my way. See ya' soon."

I was so damn excited I felt like doing a hundred all the way, but sure as shit I'd be picked up, so I kept it to the speed limit. Despite the boring drive I knew I was going to enjoy the ride. *And meatballs for dinner.* It didn't get any better than that.

As I thought about how good it would be to see Sister Thomas again, something gnawed at my insides. It brought to mind Sister Thomas' rules, and the logic I used to get to the bottom of this case. I tried chasing the thoughts away, but I couldn't stop them from swirling around in my head like a vortex.

Stewart had an alibi for Krenshaw's murder. Mazzetti and Miller didn't seem to have a problem writing it off as witnesses lying for him. *But that many?*

And why wasn't that song on Stewart's iPod? Nothing by the Young Rascals. And no "It's a Beautiful Morning" anywhere.

I called Kate. "Hey, I know this is a crazy question, but do you have "It's a Beautiful Morning," on a playlist?

"You bet I do. I *love* that song. Why, do you need me to send it to you?"

"No, just curious. Thanks."

I hung up. She must have thought I was crazy. If so, she wasn't the first. I had to check my gut, though. If the guy was singing the song, it *should* have been on his playlist.

Stewart was smart. He planned these murders and made them look as if Chad Benning had done them. He went to great lengths to do that—providing a disposable phone with calls to and from Chad to Krenshaw; selecting a woman Chad was supposedly having an affair with; the hair that was left at Parnell's house, and, Chad being seen by the doorman. But if Stewart was so smart, why did he provide Chad with the perfect alibi on the joggers? That bothered me. Why not kill the joggers another night when Chad had no alibi?

So, why *were* the joggers killed? It wasn't jealousy. The other murders were obvious, and they implicated Chad. What did killing the joggers accomplish? Nothing.

As I drove toward I-95, it hit me. Killing them *did* accomplish something.

It established an alibi for Benning. A perfect alibi.

Assuming Stewart did this—if he went to the trouble of making the connections between Debbie and Krenshaw and Benning—why would he kill the joggers while Benning was out of town, giving him a perfect alibi? How did that benefit Stewart?

Stewart had an alibi for Krenshaw, and Benning had one for the joggers. They both had weak ones for Parnell. And wasn't it a coincidence that Benning was having an affair with Stewart's fiancée? That brought to mind another problem. That's when it hit me. I dialed Bugs.

"Donovan."

He still sounded weak. "Bugs, did Stewart and Benning know each other?"

"Why?"

"Did they?"

There was a slight pause, then, "I don't think so, no." Pause again. "Why?"

"Thanks."

"Nicky, what's going on? Why do you want to know?"

If they didn't know each other, how did Stewart know what Benning looked like when he attacked him at the station? And how convenient that the attack provided a credible reason for both of their DNA to be at Bugs' house.

There was only one explanation.

They did it together.

I'd bet fifty dollars to a doughnut that Benning has 'It's a Beautiful Morning' on *his* iPod. *He* was the one who stabbed Bugs. They did all of the murders together, taking turns.

I got off the turnpike, took a turn under it, and got back on the ramp toward the bridge. Dinner would have to wait. Chad Benning was going down.

CHAPTER 64

TRAPS ARE MEANT TO WORK

I crossed the bridge on my way to Brooklyn. It wasn't the best time of day to be planning a murder but I had no time to fuck around. Angie had forgiven me and Rosa was cooking meatballs. I disregarded everything that Johnny Muck taught me about murder taking patience, and decided to do this guy quick. Lure him in and be done with it.

I had to be certain beyond doubt that Benning was guilty. My logic failed me once, and when killing a guy you didn't want to be wrong. I thought about where Sister Thomas' rules had gone wrong. She had taught us to break a problem down to its basic form—its simplest structure. In this case that should have been each murder by itself, but I lumped the first few together as one. Doing it that way, and applying the rules made me think Benning was innocent.

If I looked at it properly I would have never ruled Chad out for the hotel job. He was only ruled out because of stupidity. But I wasn't counting on them working it together and playing ahead to the fact that he would have an alibi in the future to clear him once they established a pattern. So Benning did the first job. Stewart did the second and the joggers. And Benning did Frankie.

Smart fuckers.

I thought about letting the cops handle it, but they were trapped. No way in hell could they convict this guy now. They already pinned it on Stewart and he was dead. With Benning's alibi for the joggers he was safe.

Unless I take care of it.

I still had the case files. I looked up Chad's cell and dialed it from the disposable.

"Yes?"

"Chad Benning?"

"Who's calling?"

"You don't need my name. All you need to know is I have pictures."

"Pictures?"

"Of you going into the hotel the night that couple was killed."

There was a pause, then he laughed. "I'm sure many people went in that night. Who is this? Is this a joke?"

"I was doing a job for a jealous husband, following another guy, and just happened to get you. After that, I 'happened' to get you a few more times. Like when you visited that detective's apartment the day he was stabbed."

"I'm hanging up."

"Fine, I'm selling these to the papers…unless you want to join the bidding."

"You're out of your mind."

"I may be out of my mind, but my camera was very much in focus both days."

I waited through a long pause.

"Where can we meet?"

"It has to be a public place. I'm not meeting you privately." I put as much fear into my voice as I could, hoping to reassure him, make him feel in command.

"There is a restaurant on—"

"No thanks. I'll pick the spot."

I suggested a café not far from him. The surrounding streets were busy, just like I wanted. Nobody pays attention to a person on a busy street. Get one stranger walking down a deserted street and everyone notices him, but that same man seen by fifty people will get the cops twenty different descriptions, the bad ones nullifying the ones that were spot on.

This was not the smartest operation I ever did; in fact, it probably ranked with the worst, but it was a rush job and I had to make it work. For one thing, the disposable I used to call him could eventually be traced to one that called Lou Mazzetti—if they looked into it. I was counting on Lou stifling that part of the investigation. If not, he'd have some explaining to do.

I had Benning meet me down in Park Slope not far from Sette's restaurant at Third and Seventh Avenue. I parked down by Second and Fifth Avenue, by the Laundromat, and walked to Seventh. I went down Third Street and stood with a couple of kids by a big maple tree next to a brownstone someone was renovating. This had to be quick and dirty. I had no time to mess with DNA and I couldn't afford to be in a situation where that would matter.

I called Benning to get an update. "Where are you?"

"Coming down Third Street now. I should be there in two minutes. No more."

"Okay listen, go past Seventh Avenue. Do *not* stop at Sette's. Keep the phone on, and stop when I say stop."

"I don't like these games."

"Neither do I. But I have to know I can trust you."

"I am crossing Sixth now."

"Good. Keep coming."

The kids left, chasing some girl down the street. There were half a dozen people outside, and another dozen or so on the corner or walking. He crossed Seventh. "About halfway down the block you will see some construction. Go past that fifty yards, then stop."

He followed directions well, coming to a stop about where I told him to. As soon as the car slowed, I ran for him. I came up in his blind spot toward the right rear of the car, ducked, then popped up on the passenger side at eye level, gun in hand. I opened the door and got in.

I started to say something, but his face stunned me.

He's the guy in the pictures!

I couldn't believe what I was seeing, but now that I sat a few feet away from Benning it was undeniable. "You're the kid in the picture."

"What the hell are you talking about?" he said.

I smiled. "The pictures at the house in Brooklyn Heights. In one of them, you and Stewart are watching a lady get screwed."

"I told that stupid fuck to get rid of them," he said, and shook his head. "Okay, let's get this over with. I'll give you $50,000 for the pictures."

"Not nearly enough," I said.

"How much?"

"Let's start with your life," I said, and pointed the gun at his head. "This is for Frankie Donovan." I fired twice. Both bullets hit his face.

I didn't bother checking; he was dead. No doubt. I ran down Third with the traffic. People would have to turn around to see my face, and few people were willing to do that, especially if they thought you did something wrong. I jogged all the way to the car, got in and headed for home. Now my job was done.

I drove the speed limit all the way, stopping in the Pine Barrens to get rid of the gun. I *always* got rid of guns I used. It was foolish not to. I got off the beaten path, dismantled it, cleaned it, then buried it. I stopped a few miles down the road and got rid of the hoodie and the disposable phone. No sense keeping anything that could in any way connect me to a murder. After that I got back on the turnpike and punched it. I was already way too late.

CHAPTER 65

TYING UP LOOSE ENDS

Frankie got moved to a regular room before the nurse's shift changed, and for that he was eternally grateful. It was bad enough being in a hospital, but intensive care made it worse. As the nurse wheeled him down the hall, he heard Keisha call his name.

"Hey, FD, how are you?"

He turned to her and smiled. "Hi, Little Princess. Did you bring me any presents?"

"You know I did."

She followed him into his new room, unable to sit still until the nurse got him settled. Keisha had an armful of pictures she had drawn and a pack of strawberry shortcake gum. Frankie looked through them one at a time, commenting on each one. There was a picture of her skipping rope, of Alex and her playing step ball, and of Frankie and her and Alex watching television and eating popcorn.

"I can't believe how great these are," Frankie said. "I mean these are unbelievable. You must have gotten that talent from your mom."

"Mom can't draw a stick," Keisha said. "It had to be from my dad."

Frankie laughed. "Come give me a hug."

She moved to the side of the bed and gave him a hug and a kiss.

"Thanks for coming Keisha, and thanks for the pictures."

"You really like them?"

"I *love* them. They're going into my special folder as soon as I get home."

Lou and Sherri came in, followed by Kate and Alex.

"Damn, the whole gang is here now," Frankie said.

"I'm just glad I can go back to work," Kate said. "Nothing against you, Frankie, but I was tired of hanging out here all day."

Alex sat on the edge of the bed. "You hear that, FD? Kate don't like spending time with me."

Frankie slapped the side of his head playfully. "Maybe she should have given grammar lessons while you waited. 'Kate don't like.' What the hell is that?"

Alex sighed. "Kate *doesn't* like."

Frankie smiled and rubbed his head. "Much better."

A phone rang. Lou flipped his open. "Mazzetti," he said, then walked out of the room into the hall.

"Did they say when you'd be getting out?" Sherri asked.

Frankie shook his head. "No word on that. You know how they work, Miller. They won't tell me until the day I'm getting discharged."

"I remember."

After a few minutes, Lou came back. "Hey, Miller. Let's go."

"Why? What's up?"

"We have to leave."

Frankie grew suspicious. "Who was on the phone?"

"Nobody. Go to sleep or something. Let us real detectives work."

"Mazzetti, who was on the phone?"

Lou looked at Sherri, then back at Frankie. "Morreau. We have a body."

Frankie could tell that something was up. "What's different about this body?"

Mazzetti sighed. "Chad Benning is dead."

Frankie tried sitting up. "Benning?"

"Shot twice in the head, right in the middle of Third Street down by Seventh Avenue."

"Did they get the guy who did it?"

"Nobody saw anything."

"Nothing?"

"We'll find out more when we get there, but from what Morreau said, there were dozens of people around, and all we got for ID is a jogger in a gray hoodie. They said he capped him and jogged away as if nothing happened."

"Goddamn," Frankie said. "Goddamn."

"Hey, we gotta go," Lou said. "I'll call."

"Keep me informed."

Lou waved as he and Sherri left.

Frankie got a sick feeling in his gut. An invisible assailant shot one of Frankie's original suspects in the head, twice, in broad daylight, in the middle of Third Street, and jogged away as if nothing happened. And nobody can ID him. Nicky's signature was all over it. He turned to Linda and Kate.

"Would you mind if I take a quick nap? I'm tired."

Kate shot him a look, but she said nothing. "Sure, Frankie. Call me when you get up."

After they left, Frankie dialed Nicky's phone. "Hey, Rat."

"I didn't expect to hear from you. Everything okay?"

"Great. They moved me to a regular room, and I've got more visitors than I can stand."

"So what's up?"

"Where are you? You home yet?"

"Almost."

"Almost, huh? Like where?"

"Just crossing the bridge. Why?"

"Which bridge, Nicky? Would that be the Delaware Memorial, the Commodore Barry, or the *fucking* Verrazano?"

"What the hell is up your ass? And why all the questions about bridges?"

"I just want to know where you are."

"If you have to know, the Delaware Memorial."

"Is that right?"

"Yeah, that's right."

"How about you do me a favor? Snap a picture with your phone of the river right now and send it to me."

"I don't do that shit when I'm driving."

"Bullshit. Snap the picture, then pull over when you get off the bridge and send it to me. I'm dying to see the river again. It's been a long time."

"How about you do *me* a favor, Bugs? Fuck yourself."

Frankie sat silent for a moment. "Why did you do it, Nicky?"

"I don't know what you're talking about."

"I'm talking about Benning. You could have told Lou or Sherri, or *me,* if you thought you had something."

"I'm late for dinner. Rosa is cooking and Sister Thomas is coming over. I gotta go."

"Okay. Yeah, you do that. Pretend everything is fine. Pretend you didn't just come up here and kill two people. Tell Sister Thomas I said hi. And tell Father Tom I said hi when you see him at confession."

The line went dead. Frankie threw the phone at the door. It shattered.

***

Frankie lay in bed, seething. He blamed himself as much as Nicky. If he'd been smart enough to recognize Stewart as the killer earlier, Nicky would have never had to come to New York. And Benning…*I hope he was really guilty.*

A nurse walked into Frankie's room. She handed him a phone. "Detective Mazzetti is on the line. He said he couldn't get through to your number. Call me when you're finished, and I'll come back," she said.

Frankie took the phone. "Thanks," he said, and then, "What's up, Lou?"

"We hit pay dirt."

"Tell me. I need good news."

"That house in Brooklyn Heights was a gold mine. Not only did it confirm Stewart to be the sick son of a bitch he was, but it tied him to Benning."

"How?"

"I know you're sitting, so I won't tell you to sit down. Stewart's mother was the second wife of Leo Caruthers, but Caruthers had a third wife. A young one. And guess who her son was?"

"Don't tell me it was Benning."

"Not only was it Benning, but we have pictures of Stewart and Benning together as teenagers, watching her get screwed by someone while old man Caruthers filmed it."

"Are you shitting me?"

"The goodies aren't over. We found Parnell's computer too. She was on to them. Remember that note we found in her email? 'What is he doing in BH?'"

"Yeah. What about it?" Frankie said.

"She did research on the house, and on the Leo Caruthers Foundation. Caruthers left all of his money to a foundation for artists, but the director of the foundation was Wilfred B. Caruthers, otherwise known as Bruce Stewart."

"Holy shit."

"Yeah. Parnell must have found out about Chad and Bruce. I'd bet all the money I don't have that they were siphoning millions from the foundation. Who knows maybe she wanted a piece of it. Maybe she was going to turn them in? In either case, they must have found out and decided to kill her."

Frankie thought for a moment. "Are you saying those sick bastards killed all those other people just to cover up killing her?"

"Don't write it in stone, but that's what it looks like so far."

"You know what, Lou. I'm glad I'm poor."

"Me too," Lou said. "See ya' later."

***

It was half an hour before Kate came back to Frankie's room. She had flowers in her arms.

"I didn't hear from you so…" she looked at the parts of the phone lying on the floor. "And now I see why."

"Sorry. I lost my temper."

"I can't believe it—an Irishman losing his temper."

"I'm not in the mood."

"Can't believe that either."

Frankie broke down and laughed. "Sorry."

"You're forgiven."

"Who are the flowers from?"

"It doesn't say."

"I see a card. What does it say?"

Kate's brow wrinkled. "I respect a man who struggles so much with right and wrong. And I respect loyalty. We are now even."

"Son of a bitch."

"What does that mean?"

"It means I get surprised by people all the time."

Kate lay her head on Frankie's lap and stared up at his face. Without a word being said, he leaned down and kissed her. "I love you, Kate Burns. I just don't know what took me so long to realize it."

She stroked his face. "You've always loved me. You just had to find a way to love yourself first."

CHAPTER 66

A QUIET NIGHT ALONE

It had been two hours since Bugs called. I was still pissed at him. The nerve of the son of a bitch, after what I did for him. As I started across the Delaware Memorial Bridge, Angie called. "Nicky, are you all right?"

"Hey, babe. Yeah, I'm fine. Damn traffic was a mess, though. Two accidents."

"Where are you?"

"Just crossing the bridge into Delaware. I won't be long."

"Okay, I'll see you soon."

"Tell Sister Thomas to get her game face on. We're playing Scrabble tonight."

She laughed, which made me feel good, and I thought I heard Sister Thomas in the background mentioning "punishment" or something to that effect. She was right. Between her and Rosa, I would be dead meat. It was hot and humid. My boss would probably be pissed, but despite it all, I couldn't keep the smile off my face.

Life is good.

It only took me about twenty more minutes to get home. Rosa was racing down the sidewalk to greet me before I got out of the car.

"Dad!"

She threw her arms around me and squeezed, then whispered in my ear. "Mom's suspicious, but she's glad you're home."

I smiled, then laughed. She might not have been my kid, but I loved her as if she was. "Thanks. I owe you one."

"You owe me a *lot* more than one."

"Okay. We'll settle up later."

"Let me take that," she said, and grabbed my bag.

Angie met me at the door. She never looked as beautiful as she did now: hair a mess, her green-and-white apron stained with red sauce, and no makeup. Just the way I loved her. There wasn't a person on earth I loved more than Angie. Not even myself.

Especially not myself.

"It's good to be back," I said.

She kissed me. A *damn* good kiss, then patted my butt. "You're late, Mr. Fusco. Wash your hands and open the wine."

"In that order?"

"Yes, in that order."

Sister Thomas was sitting in my chair, reading a magazine. "Sister, are you going to partake of the wine?"

"God doesn't object to wine, Niccolo. Pour me a glass."

"You know you're sitting in my chair, don't you?"

"Of course I do. But you wouldn't dare throw out an old woman like me."

We all laughed, and I gave her a big hug. "It's good to see you."

I looked around. "Where's Dante?"

"He's at my cousin Marie's house for the night," Angie said. "She begged to have him."

She started for the kitchen but Rosa stopped her. "I'll get everything, Mom. You sit."

"She's so grown up," Sister Thomas said. "You two are lucky to have such a wonderful daughter."

"You and Angie talk while I get the wine," I said.

Rosa elbowed me when I got into the kitchen. She was busy preparing a plate of crostini with olive oil, artichoke hearts, and caramelized onions. One of my favorites.

"You know, Dad, I'm thinking that for all of this mediating and matchmaking, this little girl deserves a new iPhone."

"I didn't know you had become a counselor."

"I'm the one who suggested Dante go to Marie's. I can give you advice too."

Rosa was getting too old too fast. "What kind of advice?"

"All I'm saying is that I saw Mom washing her sexy nightgown a few hours ago."

I damn near dropped the wine. "Rosa!" Then I looked around to make sure Angie or Sister Thomas weren't near.

"What? I'm not blind. I made an observation. I'm just saying, if you treat her right tonight…"

I could feel myself blushing ten shades of red. "Rosa…"

She stretched and kissed me on the cheek. "Love you, Dad."

I leaned toward Rosa. "Which nightgown?"

I thought she would fall over laughing. "The blue one with peach ties."

Oh my God.

I poured three glasses and was about to take them into the living room when Rosa set a fourth next to me. "I'll take one, please."

"You're a little blackmailer."

She took a sip of the wine and smiled. "I learned from the best."

I took the wine, and she followed with the tray of crostini and napkins. Sister Thomas took her first bite and smiled. "I know this recipe. It tastes just like Rosa Sannullo's."

Rosa blushed. "Thank you, Sister. Mom is the one who taught me everything about cooking, and she learned it all from Mamma Rosa."

Sister Thomas grabbed a second crostini. "This would have been enough to get you A's in my class."

"And she doesn't accept small bribes," I said.

Rosa called us to the table just as we finished our appetizers. It was a simple meal, but it was my favorite—spaghetti, meatballs, and garlic bread. Olives were served on the side.

Sister Thomas waited for Rosa to sit, then said, "Niccolo, why don't you say grace."

I blessed myself, repeating the prayers in Latin, as I always did despite Rosa's objections. At the end I added a special thanks. "God, thank you for giving me this wonderful family and such good friends. I pray you keep them safe and happy, Amen."

Sister Thomas smiled. "You forgot to thank Him for this *wonderful* food, Niccolo." She turned to Rosa. "If I tell Sister Julian about your cooking, she will insist on your being in her class next year."

Angie squeezed my hand and smiled. The words, I love you formed on her lips.

Goddamn, it's good to be home.

Sister Thomas left about two hours later. I poured what was left from the second bottle of wine and shared it with Angie. "So what are we going to do tonight? Want to watch a movie?"

"I'm tired, Nicky. I think I'm going to hit it early. You should come to bed too; you *must* be tired."

Rosa stood behind Angie. "You might as well, Dad. I'm spending the night at Sally's house." She winked at me and smiled.

"That settles it," Angie said. "We're both getting our rest tonight." She grabbed our wine glasses and took them to the kitchen.

I looked at Rosa, standing there with a shit-eating grin on her face. "I think I'll take the white iPhone," she said, and kissed my cheek. "Have fun."

The door closed and Angie called from the kitchen. "Did Rosa leave?"

"Yeah, just now. You need her?"

Angie walked out of the kitchen naked from the waist up. "Lock that door, Niccolo Fusco. Then get your ass upstairs."

"Yes, ma'am."

Making love for us had always been great. It was never a chore, or a duty, and we both seemed to want it at the same time. So while it was always great, having the house to ourselves was like being teenagers again— wild and uncontrolled. We played in the shower, teased as we dried each other off, and Angie teased a *lot* more when we got in bed.

We both moved slower. My lips lingered longer on different parts of her, but in the end…she was magnificent, as always. And it reinforced how much I stood to lose. When we finished making love, I lay next to her and softly kissed her lips.

"I love you, Angela Catrino."

She got a look in her eyes, and her response was another invitation wrapped in a kiss. "It is Angela Fusco now, not Catrino."

I laid my head on her shoulder and ran my fingertips up and down her side. "It will be Fusco forever."

She shivered, goose bumps running up her arms. "You *know* this night isn't over, Mr. Fusco."

"I sure hope not."

"We should do this weekly. Send the kids away and have the house to ourselves."

"We should do it *every* night," I said.

She laughed. "As if you *could*."

"I could."

"Liar."

We lay there for a moment. I felt her tense and wondered what had changed.

"Nicky, tell me what happened in New York."

Goddamn. I didn't want to go there. I tried to feign boredom. "Read about it in the papers tomorrow."

"Nicky…"

"Bugs' partners got the guy who did it. It was the same guy who killed those couples."

She grabbed me by the hair and raised my head. "And Detective Mazzetti got him? Not you?"

I stared her straight in the eyes. "Angie, look in the paper yourself. It will all be there tomorrow."

I didn't fool her with my lies, but she needed was something to believe in. Some thread to latch onto and to convince herself that I didn't kill anyone. I *had* to give her that. We needed each other, me probably more than her. I wasn't about to let something like killing a few scumbags get in the way.

She reached between my legs and grabbed me. "Aren't you ready yet?"

"For God's sake, you just interrogated me."

"Let's take another shower," she said. "I think I know how to fix that."

After the shower we made love again. I don't know how, but it was even better this time. But everything with Angie seemed to get better with time. A lot of guys complained about their wives, bitched about what they spent, or about their nagging, or never making love. I had no complaints. How could I? She was a saint. And all she asked was that I be a normal person. Not a killer. I felt like punching myself in the face. What the hell was wrong with me?

Look what you've got to lose, Fusco.

But then I thought about what Doggs used to say to us when we were kids—that God put everyone on earth for a reason.

"God doesn't have time to mess around with the little stuff," Doggs said, "So he put us here to do that for him. Make sure things run smooth, see that the people who like to gamble have a place to do it, and those who like whores know who to see."

Doggs was weird like that. He had a lot of strange ideas, but still…underneath it all, I had to wonder. Even Sister Thomas talked about avenging angels. Did God have them here on earth? Is that what I was destined for?

I got sick even *thinking* of killing an innocent person. An animal? Forget about it. But when faced with people like Stewart and Benning, my insides burned until something was done. I didn't know if that's what God had in mind for me, if He put me here to be one of His avenging angels…

But if you did, God, I won't let you down.

****

If you would like to be notified of future releases, click
here to sign up for my mailing list
http://eepurl.com/kS-IX

Thanks for taking the time to read the book. I hope you enjoyed it.

Authors live and die on recommendations and reviews, so if you liked the book, please tell someone about it. And if you have a spare moment, I'd love for you to post a review on Amazon or Goodreads, or Apple or B&N.

Frankie and Nicky will be back again next year in *Murder Is Invisible*. But be sure to sign the mailing list so you hear about all the special sales and new releases. *Old Wounds*, A Redemption Novel, is up next, followed by *The Good Words,* with Connie & Tip.

Thanks again for your time,
Giacomo

If you would like to be notified of future releases, click here to sign up for my mailing list

http://eepurl.com/kS-IX

If you want to email me about this book, please use: **gg@giacomog.com**

Acknowledgements

The tough part of writing a book is not the writing, it's all the stuff that comes after that. I'll take credit for the writing. For the tough parts I am honor bound to thank the following:

My great copy editor, Annette Lyon.

Natasha Brown for the fantastic book cover.

Jason Anderson from Polgarus Studio for the amazing layout and formatting.

And most importantly the beta readers who helped me get this book into shape: Missy, Otto, Chris, Nick, Rose, Carrie Shepherd, Elizabeth Hull, Wendy Justice, Marina Stevkovska, Rita Armstrong, Lee Carey, Mary Lee, Cary Lory, and Marc DiGiacomo. If I missed someone, please shoot me.

It takes a lot of technical help to write a book like this. I owe a debt of gratitude to my good friend, Skip Oliver, Retired Major in the Harris County Sheriff's Office. Whatever mistakes are in here, are mine alone.

I also want to give special thanks to my niece, Emiliana, for making me laugh on many nights when I needed a laugh, and to Braden and Bella for all the wonderful video chats.

Lastly, to my wife, Mikki.

Ti amo con tutto il mio cuore.

About the Author

I grew up in a large Italian family in the Northeast. No one had money, so for entertainment our family played board games and told stories. I loved the city—the noise, the people—but it was the family get togethers and the storytelling that stuck with me.

I still love storytelling, but now I write the stories instead of telling them.

My wife and I live in Texas, where we run an animal sanctuary with 45 loving "friends." One of them is a crazy wild boar named Dennis, who is my best buddy.

Sometimes I miss the early days, but not much. Now I enjoy the solitude and the noise of the animals.